Stchvk Casefiles #1

Bad Egg

&

Broken Record

Nathan Large

with

Laine Megan Lundquist

An **Empyrean Dreams** Novel

Interior Illustration by Z. Mann Zilla.

"Empyrean Dreams" setting created by Laine Megan Lundquist and Nathan Large. Please do not use this setting or its characters without permission of the creators. Your support of authors' rights is appreciated.

Disclaimer: This is a work of fiction. Any names or characters, businesses or places, events or incidents, are fictitious. Any resemblance to actual persons, living or dead, or actual events is purely coincidental.

Find us online at: http://www.empyreandreams.com

Published by Nathan Large and Laine Megan Lundquist through Amazon CreateSpace. Books may be purchased through Amazon.com.

ISBN-13: 978-0-9986609-8-1

Library of Congress Control Number: 2018903997

First Edition (via CreateSpace)

Our thanks to: Madeline Needles, Richard Ferris, Greg Levick, Benjamin Widmer, and Ian Chung. We appreciate your faith and support for more Empyrean Dreams.

Contents

Bad Egg

Chapter 1 - Show Trial

It was a lousy day for a trial. The sun was shining a brilliant white. We were ninety-two days into the warm season. It was perfect weather to stretch out on a shale beach unclothed, soaking in the radiation and the admiring gazes of potential mates. I wasn't entertaining any relationships just then, so I was open to the possibility. Except, I was stuck in a courtroom.

I'm not a bad specimen of a Vislin, if I do say so myself: a solid two meters of muscle; a tail that can crack tree trunks; sharp, clean claws; bright yellow eyes... all right, maybe my scales are a little on the yellow side. I've got other priorities than perfect grooming. And sure, my beak has a few badly healed cracks. I had a rough childhood and a career that didn't pay for extras like beak repairs.

Still, flaws add character. My bachelor status was probably more due to my attitude, not to mention the archaic, ragged leather armor I insisted on wearing even in court. On the beach, I could have shed both and maybe passed for a younger prospect.

Wearing formal armor – too hot outside and too cold in the temperature-controlled courtroom – on that fine summer day was clear evidence of civilization's insanity. Yet, there I was, shivering along with the other miserable citizens huddled in the sterile granite halls of justice. What in Kktkrkz' gargantuan gullet was I doing in this pantomime of her torturous afterlife? I wasn't the one on trial. I wasn't the wronged victim. I wasn't a member of either of their Packs... neither one was even Vislin. I wasn't prosecuting or defending or judging or even guarding the sanctity of the court. Why would I subject myself to such easily avoidable misery?

Nathan Large with Laine Megan Lundquist

Rrr, right: money. I had been promised a job.

I was supposed to exonerate the Taratumm slob on the block up front. He had Herd with money, even if he personally looked like trampled carrion. His bulk was slumped forward, leaning heavily for support on the railing that separated the trial block from the audience pit. His otherwise impressive crest was cracked and half the grey scales on the left side of his face were either chipped or gone entirely. His left eye was patched over with gauze. Prison wasn't providing him any cosmetic services. It was barely giving the bruiser enough care to avoid infection.

And no wonder, given the charges. Grust of Herd Torbur was accused of attempted murder, aggravated assault, destruction of property, public intoxication, and a list of secondary offenses. The state prosecutor, a Hrotata called Lagghitl, laid out the case in her opening statement. Her professionally groomed red fur fluffed dramatically in horror as she recounted the crimes of the accused.

Per the accounts of more than ten witnesses, Grust had exited a drinking establishment, challenged the male of a mated pair to a head-butting challenge, then went ahead with the act without his opponent's consent. That the target was a Hrotata, not another Taratumm, was as unfortunate as it was bizarre. The poor little sap went down like a puddle of limp fur, skull cracked.

When his Vislin bodyguards realized what had happened, they stopped laughing and started clawing. Only after getting bloodied did Grust go from piss drunk to pissed off. His frenzy left two Vislin with broken bones, cost a roast tuber vendor his cart, and made four shop owners down the street happy they had paid up their insurance.

It had taken another two Taratumm to slow down the dumb herbivore. They had to do it the old-fashioned way, stomping the sense back into his well-padded brain. Most of the damage on him was their work. It was tough to sympathize. For the sake of my paycheck, I did my best to try.

Besides the pointless violence of the rampage itself, its context was faintly scandalous. A Taratumm challenged a Hrotata over its female partner. That was perverse into dimensions that required a social psychologist to partner with a theoretical mathematician.

Bad Egg

First, Hrotata are matriarchal. Challenging a Hrotata male for his female is like asking your server to sell you the restaurant. He doesn't *own* it.

Second, there's the cross-species thing, *especially* where Hrotata are concerned. There's plenty of naughty stories about members of the Great Family fooling around across species lines. It's funny, dirty stuff because it's so unlikely. For one thing, the relevant parts just don't work the same. For another, our libidos don't run on the same timetables. And for a third, there's just no point. Sure, times have gotten pretty progressive, particularly after the Terrans were accepted into the Collective. There's zero doubt in my mind that Hrotata and Humans are all up in one another's nests. But a Taratumm getting excited about a Hrotata female? That's just impractical.

So, what frost had shut down old Grust's fruit pit of a brain? No, no, not just shut it down, twisted it like a Tesetsi's tortured genome. The prosecutor claimed that the fault was just plain old criminal tendencies topped off with a healthy dose of pickling liquid. Grust was a bad egg, a time bomb that finally went off in public. Empty eggs, this furry mother had a vicious mouth!

Grust couldn't blame any of his bad acts on frenzy. The "I wasn't in control" defense hasn't worked in centuries. That legal precedent was a good thing for the Vislin victims of Taratumm brutality over the years. The stompers had to learn: you keep yourself under control, either through personal discipline or by keeping a friend, Pack-mate, or handler close by, to talk you down or tie you down. Frenzy control was one of the things Herds were for. If you had none of those protections, then you stayed away from society, like the dangerous animal you were.

Listen to me sermonize. To those fine family folk, I wasn't much better. Pack-less. Unpredictable. Liable to frenzy in a packed courtroom.

Kkk, it was just uncomfortable in the crowd, not infuriating. But I *had* been in a few bad spots in the past. I'd done some stupid things, in or out of frenzy. It was just the luck of circumstances that kept me off that block up there… that, and the witnessed fact that the other guys bit first.

Nathan Large with Laine Megan Lundquist

You know who my helpful friend is? My heater, Rtrtr. A little package of ceramics, carborundum lenses, titanium silver mirrors, and fancy wiring, wrapped in fancier polymers and a very special hand-tooled leather holster. He sits on my thigh and reminds me that if I frenzy, I'll forget about him and the wonderful things he can do. He heats things: makes them very hot very fast, at a pretty good distance. Things made of meat explode when you do that. Other things also explode or melt or vaporize in pieces, depending on where Rtrtr points. He does his thing very well. The least I can do is stay lucid enough to let him argue on my behalf.

Rtrtr had to stay home that day. The courts frown on the introduction of firearms to their proceedings. You'd think that things would stay *more* civilized with more firepower easily at hand, but the matriarchs disagreed. Apparently, not everyone is as soothed as me by the companionship of potential flaming death.

Sss, Stchvk, I thought to myself, *think less about you and more about the client.* By that point, the prosecutor was done, having named her slate of witnesses to be summoned later. The defender, a more imposing Vislin female named Ktlrsh, stood to give her rebuttal. I got a good view of her thick aquamarine tail, which was enhanced as much as it was concealed by her rear armor plate.

Hey, legal proceedings are boring. You have to keep yourself attentive somehow.

"Mother Judge," she intoned, bobbing respectfully to the elderly Hrotata female that sat in office over the proceedings. "Grust of Herd Torbur first accepts blame for his lack of control. He accepts the charges of destruction of property and simple assault against those who suffered from his frenzy. He should have stopped much sooner. The costs of repair to property and persons will be repaid by him and his Herd, who apologize also for not being present to contain his outburst."

So far, this defender was doing a lousy job.

She continued, "However, as to the charges of attempted murder, aggravated assault, public intoxication, lewdness, and public disturbance, Grust of Herd Torbur denies guilt."

Bad Egg

She raised her voice to continue over the chitters and grunts of displeasure in the chamber: "The defense will argue that the defendant had not consumed excessive drink, to his knowledge. Instead, he was unknowingly administered psychoactive substances which impaired his judgment and led to his public actions."

The mother judge's frozen stare and rising white-tipped fur finally silenced the noise in her courtroom. No sane Family member would risk the anger of a Hrotata matriarch of such advanced age and rank. It was just as well. While watching the guards subdue and expel protesters was often the only entertainment value at court, this case was finally promising to get interesting.

Drugged? It was a solid defense, provided that there was some sort of proof. Hopefully, Herd Torbur and their lawyer were smart enough to demand blood tests right after Grust was dragged away into custody. The city constables probably could scrape a fair amount of the Taratumm's bodily fluids off of the street... and walls... and the roast tuber cart... but that evidence was only as good as the capability and fairness of the constabulary. Given the nasty nature of the accusations against Grust, it was entirely possible that any exonerating evidence could get lost.

Yes, lost. The law is dirty in Layafflr City, our fetid home. As prosperous a port as my nest town has become, its roots as an illicit settlement run deep. Smugglers, pirates, and slavers still manage to slip their business past dock customs, gaining access to and from the whole of the planet. Their money keeps a sizable chunk of local law enforcement comfortably 'employed', doing work other than reducing the actual crime rate. Our town's rough frontier past and nasty criminal present mix together to taint the morality of its institutions.

The Collective, the interstellar government, has been putting pressure on the Great Family to clean up our planet, particularly its largest port. The bureaucrats render our planet's official name as 'Spore'. The word was translated as such, into Terran and Zig and Mauraug equivalents, along with versions in other languages. But to the Hrotata, it is Rrawm Kshalll, "the furry egg"; to the Taratumm it is Mwasstchef, "fern pollen"; and to the Vislin, ChttKttp, "thorned seed". We each named it for something round, fertile, covered in protrusions, and perversely beautiful.

Nathan Large with Laine Megan Lundquist

Our world has mountains big enough to extend beyond the horizon when viewed from space. It has jungles the size of continents back on Hrotata Prime. It's the home world writ large. Of course, we settled here in droves, generations upon generations ago. Only recently, with the need to look good for the Family back home, were we slowly bending to the standards of the Collective.

That pressure translated into these elaborate, televised, increasingly frequent show trials. Grust was being made an example of as a public nuisance, the sort of low-life we were supposedly driving out in order to make Layafflr City a bastion of civilization. Except, he probably wasn't that bad. I didn't have to be on his Herd's payroll to give him a pass. He wasn't big enough, mean enough, or capable enough to be a thug. If he was any real threat, he would have caused more damage and looked more frightening doing it.

He sure as frost wasn't running any criminal gang. Taratumm are, as a rule, followers. Sure, they have leaders, but they're more like "the biggest" or "the oldest". To be fair, sometimes that means "the wisest" and "the best survivor", but you know what I mean. They're not big planners. Big eaters, big singers, big... *fine*. Back to the frosted trial.

The defense wrapped up their sketch of events, with promises to elaborate as the trial went on. Grust went to the bar to have some fun after work, his attorney said. He had a couple of drinks, sang some songs, then left to go home. Sometime between song K and departure T, some villain slipped him something funny.

According to her client, he then felt extremely aroused and jealous. He thought he was challenging a particularly small and weak Taratumm. He was confused by what he took as a cowardly refusal of his challenge, then further enraged by the honorless victim calling for help from Vislin. And after that, dear Mother, he only remembered waking up in medical restraints, half sedated.

It was a pretty rough skeleton of a defense. It was going to need a lot of meat before it could hope to walk around, let alone dance well enough to win a prize.

And that, patient listener, was where I came in. Sure, the defender had her own group of witnesses to attest to Grust's good character and odd behavior that night, but she was expecting *me* to fill in the details. I had to find the joker who allegedly shuffled the deck inside that big, hollow skull.

That's what I do. Like a lawyer, I make money off of trouble. I'd like to think that unlike a lawyer, I actually care who is responsible. I find lost reputations, lost merchandise, and sometimes lost pets. Occasionally, I end up adding extra services like videography, bodyguarding, and murder in self-defense.

Notice that I don't say "accidental killing". In a city like Layafflr, there aren't many jobs with my license. I've had to use Rtrtr to fatal effect, more than once. Amazingly, I've managed to avoid raising the crests on either the constables *or* the gangs. For better or worse, I've also avoided much notice by the honest gentry of my fair nest town.

Still, word of beak keeps me employed. Herd Torbur knew where to find me: just behind the sign that says "Stchvk, Investigations". My sign hangs on the opposite side of town from the courthouse, and not coincidentally, close to the street where Grust was out drinking. They needed a detective, and I was nearby, available, and qualified. They needed someone who wouldn't mind getting their claws bloody in the name of justice… and cash… and could produce results in two days.

Ttt, right, did I mention that I had two days? It was going to be a fast trial, one way or another. If Grust got convicted, I didn't get paid. No pressure.

Failure just meant going back to synthetic protein and home fermented beverages for a while. Sss, that was motivation enough.

Chapter 2 - Femme Furball

With a flourish of bureaucracy, the court's proceedings concluded for the day. All the preliminaries were laid down: charges, arguments, evidence, witnesses, and judges.

Great Family court proceedings always have at least three judges, one from each of its constituent sapient species. Usually, a Hrotata ends up senior-most judge. The little mammals are actually shorter-lived than either of us saurians but have more patience than Vislin and more ambition than Taratumm. Plus, they're clever manipulators. Whatever rivals they can't outlast, they can nudge out with politics.

Politics and law are considered fair game for competition, within and across species. The three species of the Great Family have always been competitive, which started as a struggle for survival: Vislin hunted and ate Hrotata and Taratumm. Hrotata stole and ate the eggs of Taratumm and Vislin. Taratumm trampled the nests of Vislin and Hrotata. Our civilization formed as an effort to curb the remaining animosity even after these barbaric practices ended. As a society, we've moved past bloodier, nastier means of resolving disputes. Mostly. It still isn't a good idea to let a dispute fester too long.

That rule applies as much for law enforcement as for politics. Technology and social research have pared trials down to just a few days. Evidence can be collected and evaluated quickly. No long waits for genetic identification, for example. The shorter trial periods also mean more efficient courts, less jail time for innocent defendants, and less stress on the surrounding society. Crimes don't hang around in the public sphere any longer than necessary. Like I said, no one in the Great Family is comfortable in a crowded courtroom.

This progress hasn't happened on a single trajectory. There was a phase of exaggerated politeness for one period of Great Family history, with a lot of long-winded protestations of civility and gentility. Back then, for example, trials actually dragged out longer than necessary.

That age collapsed under its own pretense. Then, the backlash resulted in a period of rebellious opposition and social upheaval. No wonder, in retrospect. Cultural arbiters can suck my cloaca.

Still, the defiance of convention started to get just as stupid as the rituals had been. People just try too hard, sometimes. Once revolution and counter-revolution died down, both sides saw how ridiculous they had been… no, I'm joking. There are still idiots pining for the days of both high and low culture. In reality, it was the apathetic middle that just stopped paying attention to either extreme.

Still, past follies serve as bad examples. Great Family society put serious work into building a mixed society that took everyone's needs into account. That included base, physical needs along with higher ideals.

In the interim between counter-revolution and the present day, some low-class rebels peeled off from Hrotata Prime and the early colony worlds. Among the unlicensed colonies built by those dissenters was our glorious Layafflr City. The settlement began as a thermocrete landing pad and a circle of plastic huts. It took centuries, but a prospering city unfolded from that sad little seed.

Now, we have all the trappings of urban civility. Even so, the jungles of ChttKttp aren't impressed by modern construction. As I emerged from the courthouse into the open air, I felt the static tingle of the repulsion field surrounding the grey stone building.

The charged fields are necessary if we want to keep buildings standing for more than a few decades. Otherwise, encroaching greenery will climb their walls, invade their cracks, pile onto their roofs, and eventually crush stone into rubble. Street cleaners scrape down the roads regularly to prevent vegetative invasions. Chemical suppressants were tried, but anything strong enough to cull our world's wildlife is strong enough to poison *us*, too.

City life is a constant battle. I like it that way. It reminds us never to take our prosperity for granted; every day is a fight to be won or else you give up ground.

In my life, that metaphor is less figurative. I was born a brawler. A con-flict-free career would make me chew my limbs off. If I had a little more toler-ance for authority, I might have been a soldier or constable.

I respect law enforcement… at least, I respect honest constables. They have a tough job, too. Tougher in some respects, since they have to show restraint and courtesy even in the face of the worst scale-rotted criminals. I can't do it. I have to call a villain a villain.

Frost, I don't even have the restraint needed to keep a Pack. You have to be loyal first to the Pack and second to yourself. That means defending one another even when a Pack-mate has done something obviously heinous.

That's what Herd Torbur was doing, circling around their disgraced member, Grust. They were offering me a year's wages for three days of work, just to pro-tect one of their own. The payment was contingent on success, but it was still a hefty chunk of credit. They didn't care if he was guilty or not, so long as they got him off the hook… by whatever means necessary. Personally, I can't manage that kind of intentional blindness.

Believe me, I've tried. My first – and last – Pack didn't even make it a diffi-cult choice… or a subtle one. They literally said, "Choose the law or us". Two of them are now permanent tenants of the City cages, one is dead from a fight with constables, and one is at large, somewhere in the universe. Hopefully, she's far away from Layafflr City and ChttKttp in general. I hate to think she holds a grudge and might visit again sometime.

Hey, don't start getting twitchy on me now. I'm not just talking to talk, es-pecially not about myself. You looked like you were getting lost earlier. All this background will be necessary if you're going to follow the rest of the story. A lot gets lost if you don't know the culture.

Sss, back to the narrative: I left the court building quietly. I needed to talk to a contact for Herd Torbur, but not in public. My job would be more difficult if word got out who I was working for. Their go-between and I had a meeting scheduled in my office. I was originally hired by phone, but I was pretty sure my contact was a female Hrotata, judging by her voice and her name: Shllokwa.

Bad Egg

I walked a couple of blocks down the street to a skimmer rental post. The little flying pods aren't comfortable, but they're cheap and fast.

I spared a few of my last remaining credits to unlock a skimmer. The cover slid back with a puff of hot, compressed air. There was also a musky stink: a mix of Hrotata oils, salt excretions from Taratumm and Vislin, the pheromones of all three species, plus a tracing of more alien effluvia from visiting foreign sapients. Public transport always manages to reek like its users. This one was unpleasant but at least not nauseatingly foul. They usually clean the things if a rider leaves anything bio-hazardous behind. Usually.

I climbed aboard, settling myself into the cushioned riding couch and adjusting the environmental controls. Despite the brightness of the sun, I kept the cover transparent. I liked to see where I was going, not trusting the system enough to darken the cover for shade. Last, I tapped in the address for my office.

Layafflr City is big enough that foot travel was out of the question. I'd be late for my meeting by half a day. I wasn't anywhere near enough financial security to own my own car, ground or air. Frost, at the time, I could barely afford to keep my own apartment lit, much less keep a car recharged and licensed. If my hypothetical car *broke down*, I'd be worse off than not having one at all.

The rent for my apartment usually takes up most of my occasional earnings. Even so, I live on the cheap edge of town, where the pest control sonics are less effective and the sprays less regular. I have to deal with the occasional native wildlife stealing my food, trying to nest in my wall, or, in the case of the bigger ones, challenging me for territory. Rtrtr is sufficient answer for the latter, but I hate leaving burn marks in my floor. At least my aim has been getting better.

As I rode, I watched the buildings change from the uniform, clean lines of the city center to the rougher, more random architecture of old Layafflr. One blessing of the surrounding jungle is that it spares our city the prefab dullness of suburban sprawl. Neighborhoods are each intentional expansions, fully planned and endorsed by the central government. This process has the usual effect of making each project a money sink of contractual corruption, but necessity demands that the construction barons at least make each new neighborhood a functional whole. Otherwise, the utilities won't integrate with the central grid, the static fields and sonics and whatnot won't work, and the defective outgrowth will get amputated by Nature itself.

This modular expansion meshes well with the family structure of Vislin and Taratumm heritage, since each neighborhood already has a ready population of groups available to move together. That's one way the matriarchs reward particularly successful offspring: give them leave to settle and start a new family. Sometimes, an extended will pick up and move as a whole, abandoning one decaying neighborhood for a fresh start further out. It's a little like the old days, when the Taratumm would eat everything green and move on, or a Vislin Pack would eat or chase off everything in their range and be forced to relocate.

Hrotata? Hrotata don't wreck their environment much. Mostly because they survive off anything other species leave unguarded.

Anyway, my nest is in one of the 'abandoned' zones, where the buildings are still habitable but a bit shabby. Unsuitable terrain – something to do with faults and caves and other geology – prevents the city from expanding further beyond us, to the north. Thus, ours is a 'historic' neighborhood, great for tourists and the entrepreneurs who prey on them, not to mention shady sorts who want less constabulary attention. I suppose I fall somewhere between the latter two types.

The area has character, at least. I could recline, watch the roof eaves scroll by, and still identify the neighborhoods from architecture alone. The builders of my district drew from a particular cultural and historical style that preferred a ribbed, fluted aesthetic for walls and roofing. The pattern was a stylized holdover from woven tree branches. Millennia later, we had faux branch huts three stories tall on a planet unimaginably far away, yet I still lived on the edge of a rainforest. I love a finely aged coincidence.

The particular fake hut I call home – or at least the 300 square meters of it I lease – is located at the cross of a T intersection. I was already stretching and preparing to sit up before the skimmer began deceleration. It descended along the far wall of the intersection. When the cover slid back, I hopped to the ground, relieved to be out of the artificial funk and back to the natural funk of my chosen hunting ground.

Bad Egg

Peppery, mulchy, occasionally fecal odors wafted from the forest in the background, overlaid with the stinks of urban rot: wet concrete, rusting metal, and the muted decay of food waste. None of the smells were potent enough individually to force anyone to really clean up the place. All together, they form a signature bouquet that says, "Welcome to the cheap end." Downtown, the wealthy spend a lot on labor and technology to keep the streets shiny, sterile, and scentless. Layaf-flr City is ostensibly civilized. Some parts are just more civil than others.

Crossing the street to my building's door, I tapped in the entry code. The door slid aside, getting stuck at the usual spot, two-thirds open. I didn't need to force it fully open to get in, so I hunched my shoulders and squeezed through. I made my way up the stairs to my second-story apartment, thinking how great it would be to peel out of my leathers and maybe wipe down my scales before the rep for Herd Torbur got there.

That was only the lesser part of my irritation when I opened my apartment door. My guest was already inside, waiting.

A Hrotata female, a bit under a meter long, was curled up on the lounge in my front room. She was either napping or trying to give the pretense of having slept. She lifted her head and craned her long neck to point her snout at me as I entered. By Hrotata standards, she was high-class: sleek, striped fur, ranging from dark brown to almost black; bright gold eyes; carefully groomed claws tipped with silver caps; all wrapped up in a red synthetic shift with woven designs in glittering metallic black thread.

She blinked drowsily, stretched, and muttered, "You took your time getting home."

"Home," I growled, "Supposedly a secure place of personal privacy?"

"Security and privacy are illusions, Stchvk, especially when your neighbors, your landlord, and your network provider are all willing to supplement their income."

"You're aware that I do this job because I don't like criminals...?" I began.

She interrupted my rant: "I'm aware. Herd Torbur wouldn't have hired you if you were anything less than honest and driven. But if you're naïve as well, you won't be of much use to us."

I was thrown off-balance again. "Wait, us? You're not Taratumm, ergo…"

She continued to hold the lead, "… I can't be Herd? You're really not impressing me with logic, detective. I'm honorary, an adoptive child. Shllokwa, if you hadn't guessed: employee and *member* of Herd Torbur. Taratumm understand the value of incorporating the strengths of other sapients into their Herds. It's a lesson Vislin have been slower to learn."

I let myself clack my beak derisively. "Or maybe we just like keeping one thing Hrotata can't squeeze themselves into… our Packs."

She sat up straighter on my lounge. "What Pack, investigator? While your… unattached nature… is an asset to us, most would consider you socially deficient."

"Sss, maybe I should find a nice furry matriarch to adopt me. That'd be *completely* normal." I rubbed my aching ear slits with the backs of my hands and hissed in irritation. "Look, you're not paying me in therapy sessions, and this conversation isn't getting Grust any closer to freedom. Let's just agree that you're sneaky and I'm brilliant but maladjusted and get to the point... before it gets late and you have to scurry home in the dark."

"Cute... but a very large aircar will show up *whenever* I call. You know, benefits of the job?" She wrinkled her nose and flipped her tail rapidly in what I recognized as a rude gesture.

Blessedly, she took my suggestion and got down to business: "You heard the public statements today. Most of what we know is out there already. The defense wasn't being clever; the little we have to go on comes from Grust himself."

While she talked, I worked my way around to my desk, a curved burl of pale, polished wood topped with a plate of rounded glass. Another oddly shaped chunk formed a surprisingly comfortable seat. On some worlds, these bits of natural art would fetch high prices. Here on Spore, they're backyard debris, picked up on my last nature walk. Sure, fine, I clean them up a bit, maybe carve and polish some, but don't go spreading it around. I like my vocation and avocations in that order.

Bad Egg

The natural beauty of my workspace was cluttered with bins of data beads, random souvenirs from past cases, and beverage canisters and snack wrappers that failed to make it to the waste bin. I slid my compad into the little clear area left and claw-tapped for a clean document. "Do you have a recording I can view?" I asked, all professional, myself.

"Not yet; everything official is in police custody, and we didn't want to risk making any recordings of the private counsel session. I can give you the relevant points: Grust went to the Trrptet Thunder Bar at eight in the evening, local time, as per his normal routine. He had two Herd-mates with him, Veruth and Ktuck, both male Taratumm. They work together in the Herd's manufacturing plant further south... you know the place?"

"Tsrrk-Tor Materials, yes, I'm familiar." The factory is a cornerstone in Layafflr's economic foundation. They take in raw metals and fabricate equipment for both housing and vehicle construction. My building undoubtedly has Tsrrk-Tor girders holding it up. The frame for the aircar I rode home was probably molded at the same plant.

"So, normal day at work, normal evening out with the other males. At worst, they might break some furniture, maybe get rough on the stomping floor. Some of our witnesses will attest that Grust was acting *completely* normal up until he started drinking that night."

"That's the part I'd like to hear about, from his perspective. When did things get *not* normal?" I took a note with an exaggerated claw gesture.

"He's little help there. He says he remembers a strong urge to go outside... a mating urge, like he'd smelled a female Taratumm in heat and heard her bellowing. Hallucinations, like the defense attorney said. Grust saw said female Taratumm, whom he described to us as 'the most beautiful mate ever', with no specifics. Literally, he could not describe her consistently; he was constructing a description based on his own aesthetic preferences. Said hallucinatory Taratumm female was in distress, restrained by a male... again, a male *Taratumm*, description also vague. Grust claims he felt very, very drunk, more than his actual consumption should cause. He reacted instinctively, both in making a challenge and in reacting to the injuries inflicted after his attack."

"So, the accused wasn't all there, but why? He could be lying about his drinking or about taking a drug. We have only the word of his Herd-mates that he didn't inflict his disability on himself. The prosecution could argue he got high on his own initiative. I'm assuming nobody *saw* anyone slip him anything?"

"No, no one so far. That's what we'd be paying *you* to find out."

"Right. So my first stop is the Thunder Bar, to see what I can turn up. Hence the sneaking around while you're in my neighborhood? The patrons – especially the culprit – won't talk to the constables or to Herd of the accused. Alone, *I* might get a lead. *If* they don't know I'm working for you."

"Very good! You might be worth hiring, after all!" Her show of approval took the form of an elaborate dance step. I winced as her claws dug into my lounge's upholstery.

"Right now, I'm cheap at free. No retainer, you said. The question is, are you going to pay for just a lead, or do I have to do the constables' work, too?"

"The terms are clear. If you turn up something, anything that gets Grust proven innocent, you get paid. You'll want to make sure there's enough evidence in his favor to ensure that verdict. A few drops of blood might not be enough of a trail to convince the court, so I'd recommend tracking your prey as far as you can, on your own."

We were both speaking in Hrotata Primary, but her use of Vislin idiom was solid. I could appreciate the subtle linguistic flattery.

I prompted, "Speaking of which, could you give me some more specifics? Addresses for Grust's drinking mates, name and address for the victim, constable reports, witness statements...?"

She clambered down from my lounge, crossed the room, and flowed up the front of my desk. I winced again at the claw-marks she was leaving in the formerly smooth wood surface. Perching across from me, she bent over my compad and reached forward to input data.

I barely managed to pull back my hand in time, before her furred shoulder brushed against it. Her eyes narrowed at my sudden movement.

Bad Egg

"What is your problem? Are you actually repelled by other sapients?" She sounded genuinely offended, but I wasn't sure it wasn't an act.

"No, I just have issues with touching Hrotata. For all I know, you spent all that time grooming, while you waited for me. I'd rather not have your spit clouding my senses, thanks."

If you're not familiar, Hrotata saliva contains a mild neurochemical that improves mood, reduces inhibitions, and generally makes the victim friendlier. They don't consider dosing other sapients a hostile act; in fact, I think they consider it a social duty or something. I don't like the feeling, and I don't like having my emotional balance artificially altered.

To my surprise, she gave me an ear-flick of amusement. "I'm not used to being turned down, not by any species. I *chose* to join Herd Torbur, but I made sure they extended the invitation first. Your resistance is admirable. Perhaps even valuable. It's still a little insulting."

"Kkk, maybe I haven't spent enough time around your charms. Want to go on a date? I'm going to a Thunder Bar tonight."

"No, I think you're right, we should keep it professional," she bantered back, all the while tapping on my compad. I watched her closely for any further violations of privacy, but she only opened an encrypted stream to a private server and downloaded a file to my system. Opening it, she showed me the witness list, including the names, addresses, and contact information for everyone interviewed about the case. That included the victim, the victim's mate, his bodyguards… pretty complete.

I scrolled through while she watched me, stretched out full-length on my desk. Again, the pose was probably alluring to Hrotata, maybe even erotic. I wasn't sure why she thought it would do anything for me.

It's not that I'm asexual. As you might be aware, Vislin don't have the same libido as mammalians or even mammal analogues like the Zig. Most sapients outside the Great Family can't even tell the Vislin genders apart. Most of the time, it doesn't really matter to us, either. There's not much sexual dimorphism; the idea of dismissing a female as less capable seems quite literally insane to us. Mating is the only time it matters, and once the eggs drop, that division is done again. There you go, the avians and the social insects of Vislin sexuality.

The funny part is, I *do* notice gender, but only within my own species. Maybe it's my unique observational talent and aesthetic sense. Maybe I'm a pervert. Whatever the reason, I *like* how other Vislin look, especially females. It might be hormonal, some kind of overactive mating urge. It's not like I have the credit to spare for psychiatric evaluation to find out. It's actually not much of a problem, as long as I don't say anything or act on my attractions. In a way, I could understand Grust's actions a bit better for it, particularly in his reaction to normally repressed urges surging to the fore.

The flip-side, though, is that I don't understand cross-species attraction, at all. Some Vislin and Taratumm purport to enjoy the looks of Hrotata and even understand their standards of beauty. Certainly, the fur-bearing sapients – Hrotata and Humans and Mauraug – seem to recognize one another's body morphics and language enough to translate the aesthetics. I just don't get it. If I wanted to be crude, I could call it an indiscriminate palate: I can't tell which foods look better than one another.

That's definitely far too much about me. Back to the narrative: I finished skimming the data provided and bobbed my head in confirmation.

"Good enough. Just to say it: I keep complete confidence. I'll ask your permission before sharing anything private. Terminate our agreement, and I'll delete every file… along with anything I've learned, shared or not."

Shllokwa writhed her way back down my desk. I wished she would have jumped down and spared the wood more scratches, but that probably wasn't sexy enough.

She retorted, "We would expect nothing less. Your word is nice, but don't forget who you're working for. If you *did* betray us, Herd Torbur could make your life very difficult. Maybe impossible."

I narrowed my eyes but stopped short of a full threat display. "I didn't forget that. Thanks for the reminder, though. I almost started thinking of this as a friendly chat."

Bad Egg

"Oooo, don't get offended now. I honestly don't know how you've survived, growing up in this city, a supposedly moral creature in a decidedly immoral land." She slinked away toward the door, her red shift rippling and sparkling in the last blue rays of the evening sun through my windows.

She turned back as she reached up to tap the door open: "Just do the job. Do it well, and Herd Torbur will pay well, and we'll all stay on friendly terms. I would look forward to working with you again, Stchvk."

The door slid open and she slid out. I waited a few seconds after the panel closed again, then walked over and changed the door code. It probably wouldn't keep her out if she was determined to enter again, but it improved my peace of mind. I needed to have a talk with my landlord. If she was, in fact, selling out her residents' door codes, I would be moving, not to mention reporting her to the constables.

Herd Torbur was not, actually, above the law. It just sometimes – frequently – avoided legal action. I wasn't terribly happy to be participating in their resistance against the law, but if Grust was in fact innocent, I could appreciate getting him exonerated. And if he was guilty, I wasn't going to "find" evidence otherwise.

If Herd Torbur wanted to play it that way, I'd drag them to the cold hells with me.

Chapter 3 - Tough Crowd

After Shllokwa left my apartment, my next priority was to clean up. That included myself, first. I stripped out of my leather armor and spent a few decads wiping it down with cleanser and oil. Then I applied a similar treatment to my scales. Salt, dust, and bacterial accretion can do nasty things to a Vislin's complexion. I'm not vain, but I hate being itchy.

That done, I pulled on a robe, gloves, and sandals and wiped down my lounge, my office floor, and my desk. I wasn't kidding about not wanting to rub up on Hrotata spit. That stuff is technically neurotoxic and sticks around in your system. It was inevitable that I had breathed in a little, but that was impossible to avoid. I got a bigger dose around the Hrotata in the courthouse, even with its industrial air filters. That little bit was *nothing* compared to direct contact. I still didn't like Shllokwa very much, though, which was proof that I hadn't absorbed much of her drool. If I let her give me a tongue bath, we'd be best pals for a few hours.

For good or ill, Hrotata drool isn't very specific stuff. I would be friendly and receptive to a Mauraug slave-master if one showed up right after a Hrotata licking. Maybe. Definitely would have been slower on the draw. Anything that gets between me and my heater is a bad thing.

Speaking of Rtrtr, it got a good wipe-down, too, inside and out. As I got dressed again, I secured it into its custom holster. Hopefully, I wouldn't need the weapon that night, but I never wanted to be without it. I could inflict bloody harm with tooth and claw, but a focusing lens pointed in their direction tends to intimidate more sapients.

Also for practical purposes, I bolted down a few chunks of synthetic protein. It was close enough in taste and texture to raw meat to satisfy my gullet and it would keep me sated for the rest of the evening. Technically, it was nutritious food. It tasted artificial, like chemistry pretending to be cuisine, and the composition was too regular to fool anyone's palate. Better synthetics existed, but of course, they were more expensive. I had to settle for the bargain version.

If I was going to a bar, I might need to drink to maintain my cover. If I was going to drink, I needed to eat first. I also didn't want to be starving if sudden activity became necessary. For one thing, a hungry Vislin is less rational and more instinctual.

It was bad enough that I was going to a Thunder Bar. They're a Taratumm cultural institution and *not* the preferred watering holes for Vislin. Not that Vislin were ever discouraged from visiting. Plenty of my kind made the occasional visit and some stopped in regularly. It just wasn't our kind of scene. Loud music, louder singing, stomping around, and mock challenges? In the bad old days, a Vislin hearing that racket would probably be dead soon afterward.

Worst of all, I had never been seen, personally, at that particular bar. It wasn't as if it was too far; only eight blocks from my apartment. Anyone from my neighborhood would be suspicious if I showed up there randomly.

I needed a cover story, in case anyone asked. Even if they didn't ask, I needed an approach so that secondary inquiries would get the wrong idea about my presence. I gave the problem some thought as I dressed.

I could just play dumb and pretend I was checking out the damage in the area... but that approach wouldn't open many mouths. I could say I was investigating on behalf of the Hrotata victim, Tharrliki. That lie might get me some information from witnesses interested in seeing Grust convicted, but it would still bias what I heard. I needed a role that would lead me to the "real culprit", the presumed miscreant who drugged Grust and sent him out horny and hostile. I supposed I also needed to avoid tipping off that criminal, or else *I* might get a funny cocktail and end up on the street molesting Hrotata.

I was still thinking over my plans as I stepped outside. I had some time to consider my strategy. Walking from my place to Trrptet Thunder Bar took a few decads. The route was familiar. The Thunder Bar might not be my usual destination, but a few of my favorite shops were along the way. Hopefully, I'd get to stop at a local butcher soon and spend some of my upcoming paycheck. I might even think about new armor. My favorite suit was comfortable but even I had to admit that the straps were corroding.

The block where Trrptet itself is situated has a few other nice features. There are a couple of pleasant ornamental parks nearby and the resident fried sausage vendor is a seasoned pro.

Well, the block *had* nice features, past tense. As I neared the area, I could see the path of Grust's rampage. The storefront across the intersection from Trrptet was sealed up with plastic sheeting. Chips of glass glittered here and there in the streetlights, where cleaners had not yet swept them away. Further in the same direction, a large disposal bin was stacked high with debris from the adjacent buildings: chunks of masonry, smashed electronics, and an entire steel awning.

I could envision the sequence of destruction, with Grust and possibly one or two other Taratumm crashing headlong into structures and ripping up architecture for makeshift weapons. Stompers on a rampage were *scary*, not only to Vislin but pretty much any other sapients, including themselves. Especially when anesthetized by drink – and possibly, other drugs – Grust would have been tough to take down without using deadly force.

The crowds were correspondingly smaller that night. It was a work night, so it wasn't going to be too busy anyway, but with fewer attractions intact, the neighborhood was suffering. Most of the folk I spotted out and about were an even mix of Taratumm and Vislin, working stiffs walking to or from work or relaxing afterward with a trip to a nearby social spot.

The occasional Hrotata passed by, as well: always males and often a bit scruffy, likely less favored offspring forced to struggle to prove their worthiness. They often received work assignments in 'rough' neighborhoods, tending a branch of a family business, establishing themselves in a trade, or even venturing out on their own with new, entrepreneurial ideas.

Anyone with real money or status was somewhere else that night. If they passed through my streets, it would be in an aircar. Shllokwa was definitely slumming at my apartment. A high-class Hrotata female stood out.

Bad Egg

The thought made me wonder: what *had* a mated Hrotata couple been do-ing in the area? The victim of Grust's attack, Tharrliki, and his mate, Yavirrt, were described as innocent bystanders targeted by a rampaging drunk. But why were they by-standing at all? Were they shopping for cheap souvenirs? Visiting the Thunder Bar for thrills? Or did they have some connection to their attack-er, some reason they would be standing outside his usual haunt... maybe some reason they were the focus of his rage? Was there more to their story than an accident of timing?

I had to stop chewing that bit of gristle when I realized I was only a block away from my destination. I was dismayed to see the park with my fried sausage vendor torn up and fenced off. The landscaped turf was scarred with deep ruts and the flower beds were trampled. I just hoped my greasy friend – and his cart – hadn't been hurt. Hopefully, he was set up in a new park somewhere less dan-gerous. The official list of casualties mentioned only the destruction of a roast tuber cart, so the odds were good.

I was definitely getting closer to the origin of the storm. I could already feel the bass vibrations from the Thunder Bar around the corner. Somewhere in front of that building, Grust had stumbled out and picked a fight with a guy one-eighth his mass.

So, what was my plan? I had been too busy observing the landscape to think about my method. Observation was a waste of time; the cause and scope of destruction wasn't in question. Even the defense agreed about what happened *after* Grust attacked Tharrliki. It was whatever led up to the attack that needed to be investigated. What approach would get me a lead on the real culprit, the supposed saboteur who slipped Grust a squirt of crazy juice?

Might I be a friend of the accused? Hardly believable. A clueless sightseer? No, I already considered and discarded that idea. Racist agitator exploiting the tragedy? *That* might work.

Hardcore species purists are a shrinking minority among the Great Family, but there are still too many out there. The majority of them are Vislin... no big surprise, I'm sure.

Nathan Large with Laine Megan Lundquist

Look, I may make jokes, but I understand the necessity, even the advantages, of cooperation between sapients. Nobody sane wants to go back to the days of predation and genocide. Still, there are agitators who straddle the edge of reason, making it sound plausible that Vislin would be better off on their own again. Some even claim that all three species are being held back by trying to find mutual solutions to every problem.

It's nonsense if you actually pay attention to the facts, but separatism is about emotions, not reality... about what "feels true". Sometimes, I get the feeling that hate and zealotry will endure until the last star burns out.

You know what I mean. The Collective has problems maintaining popular support. The various members hold centuries of mutual grudges on top of basic isolationism and xenophobia. The Great Family has *millennia* of animosity to overcome.

For the Vislin, who like to think of ourselves as superior, apex predators, clearly smarter and better-looking than any other life-form... Sss. There's no shortage of morons crying for secession. I share direct-line heredity with some of them.

Pretending to be one such moron would piss off Taratumm, giving them a reason to loudly protest Grust's innocence. It would also gratify any other species supremacist listening in, maybe ingratiating me enough to hear any rumors about "how the dumb grazer got doped". Right there was my first reasonable theory about a possible culprit. Disrupting a Thunder Bar and disgracing a member of a prominent Taratumm Herd would certainly be a coup for a Vislin separatist. Something that specifically triggered the Taratumm frenzy reaction would be po-etically appropriate. Killing a Hrotata bystander in the process would be extra organs in the kill.

Of course, dropping slurs in a Thunder Bar was also a good way to get my own skull fractured. If I took that route, I'd need to be ready for a quick escape... and maybe a few apologies later, once the case was done. It was a bit sad that I felt more believable as a hate-monger than a peacemaker. I'd manage. Doing Herd Torbur a favor would be better evidence of my goodwill and true beliefs than any public protestation of tolerance.

Bad Egg

So, I got ready to act like a major tail-biter. By the time I'd worked out my script, I was standing in front of Trrptet Thunder Bar. In fact, I'd been standing on the sidewalk for a couple of decads before I was ready… probably looking like a sapient planning trouble. I scanned the crowd to see if anyone was watching me. That didn't make me look even *more* suspicious. Not at all.

I didn't catch anyone staring back, at least. There were a few individuals that looked out of place. A trio of Vislin males were sitting just outside the park on the far side of the same intersection. I couldn't hear their conversation, but their body language suggested that they hoped to be provoked. Maybe they were looking for a chance for a legal hunt on another rampaging Taratumm. I tried to remember their appearances for later reference.

An elderly Taratumm female was stumping back the way I had just come. She kept stopping to stare at the damage, shaking her faded, armored head and grumbling. Probably remembering the days when the neighborhood was a prosperous new expansion, before the jobs moved away and the low-lifes (like me) moved in.

Nobody looked as if they recognized me. No one looked like they were returning to the scene of a crime, either. If I wanted any answers, I'd have to ask inside the bar. I straightened my helmet, prepped my schemes, and checked the catch on my holster for good measure. Only then did I walk up to the swinging door of Trrptet Thunder Bar and shoulder my way inside.

Seriously, I had to ram the door with my shoulder to get it open. It was heavy.

Opening the door doubled the volume from the music rumbling inside. As I stepped in, I recognized a popular song from a Taratumm artist. At least, I recognized the bass line. The vocals were provided by a decidedly amateur singer groaning into a hand microphone. It takes talent for a Taratumm to sing that badly. Usually, the worst of them is at least tolerable.

A herd of other Taratumm were seated in the pit around him, half-listening and chatting among themselves. A mixed group by age and gender, all dressed in work uniforms, they looked like employees of the same factory, maybe even the Tsrrk-Tor facility.

Nathan Large with Laine Megan Lundquist

On the upper level, where I entered, a handful of patrons sat either alone or in pairs, all drinking. Most of these were also Taratumm: a pair of greenish-grey males in engineers' jumpsuits, a lone steely female in private security armor, plus another two lone males: one grey-green, the other, older, tending toward chartreuse. The latter two wore simple strapped leather kilts, showing off their bulk for the appreciation of... somebody.

All of them seemed dedicated to silence and intoxication. Maybe they would join in if the entertainment picked up. I did my best to file away their features, but there's only so much you can pick out in poor lighting while trying not to make eye contact.

A sole Hrotata male also sat alone. I got an equally poor look at him: a sad sack who looked half-asleep already. He wore a business formal robe, badly, and stared into his drink like the other lonely souls.

A pair of Vislin, both females, one white with emerald patterning, bright even in the low lighting, the other with dyed amethyst scales, were sharing some sort of fried snack and tall, strong-looking drinks. Their armor was minimal, just some lacquered wood and silk for propriety's sake. They seemed far more interested in one another than anything else in the room... including me. That was fine. I wasn't there to make friends. Or find a mate. Sadly.

If anything, I was there to make enemies. I strutted over to the remaining occupant of the bar, the bartender herself, a Taratumm of interesting proportions. For one thing, she was short and slight for a stomper, maybe only a half-meter taller than me and twice my mass. Not young, though, as attested by a few missing scales. Her scales were also faded with age, but held a pattern of steel grey and sky blue that suggested an interesting mutation. She wore a heavy, dark indigo robe that complimented her natural coloring, cinched by a thick leather belt. Clever gaps and folds allowed her shoulder and elbow spines to poke through. I looked into her deep-set black eyes and thought, *What a fascinating sapient. Shame I have to stir her nest.*

"Hey, hard-head, you got anything worth eating in here? A steak? Or just leaves and bark?" I gave her my best naughty youngling stare.

Bad Egg

To her credit, she looked confused rather than upset. She rumbled, "Friend, in case you missed the enormous glowing sign... and you're deaf... this is a Thunder Bar. No meat. Taratumm culture. Maybe you want to be somewhere else?"

"Maybe you should check the menu. Some dumb beast trampled my favorite sausage cart, and I'm missing my evening snack. I'm pretty sure I smelled meat in here." I looked over the room with an exaggerated toss of my head, letting my beak drop open, tongue tasting the air.

"Well, we don't serve your kind here." She made the cliché sound like righteous defiance. Sss, I definitely needed to come back and beg her forgiveness later. Right then, though, I had to push the act.

"You don't serve us *anymore*, you mean?"

"What's your problem, dung-beak? Either settle down or walk out, or else I'll have the constables escort you out."

She was still trying to keep things quiet. I was aiming for the opposite.

I feigned disgusted rage and shouted over the soundtrack, "My *problem* is this place. A whole block is smashed up because you stompers come in, get drunk, get worked up, and then roll outside. Usually you just wake up sleepers and terrorize pedestrians, but once in a while somebody, like that nut-brain Grust, goes off. Then somebody gets hurt, maybe killed. Some shop owners lose windows; everyone loses customers. I don't expect *you* to be sorry. This is *your* business. But maybe some of your *smarter* customers will realize they're in the wrong place, too."

It wasn't bad for a speech prepped just decads before. While I ranted, I tried to draw in the crowd. The Hrotata gave me a bleary-eyed glance but little further reaction. The two Vislin stopped their conversation and turned to watch, but were only annoyed by my antics. One might say they were even offended. The Taratumm in the pit looked up briefly but either couldn't hear my insults or didn't care. They went back to their business as before. The ones that really took notice were the Taratumm couple and the loners. They were pissed off. I saw nostrils flare and heard toe-claws grind into the floor mats.

Still, no one got up. The bartender looked aggravated, but hardly enraged. Frost, she'd probably already heard worse, maybe earlier that same night. I was just one more angry Vislin to endure, a moment's indigestion in this part of the city's gut. As I hoped, though, my tirade prompted her to a rebuttal.

"You're stupid. I think you know you're stupid. Grust of Herd Torbur is probably brighter than you, tail biter. He's definitely less obnoxious, even when roaring drunk. He's never even come close to attacking anyone here, inside or out, before now. This so-called pit of trouble sees one, maybe two fights a moon, and nearly all of those end with the first kick. In fact, if I *do* have to boot you out the door, you'd be more provocation to violence than I usually see in a year. Go home, watch the trial on your screen, and cry when Grust is proven innocent."

Cry? I'd dance for joy if he were set free. But that outcome wasn't likely without some kind of proof. This female would be a great character witness for the defense – probably already was, I should check the witness list again – but she wasn't giving me anything useful.

I pushed again: "What, you buy that 'I was drugged' defense? I don't. And even if that story makes *him* sound blameless, how does it look for *you*, for this bar? Drugs just drop into drinks? Maybe the food? Maybe I don't want your cooking. I might go rip up an elderly pedestrian! I suppose somebody *not* from around here doped up your pal Grust? Is that your next excuse? Or did you see the so-called 'real criminal'?"

Her eyes narrowed and her nostrils finally did flare. "You know, it occurs to me that someone like *you* might have created trouble at my bar, exactly for the reasons you bring up. Seems like too much coincidence, now that I think about it. No, I didn't see who messed with Grust. For all I know, it could have been *you*. You *do* look familiar. Maybe I saw you in here a couple nights ago…?"

A very good theory, madam, if I do think so myself. As gratifying as it was to be reinforced by an independent thinker, being fingered as a potential suspect was not the outcome I had in mind. If brought to the constables' attention, I could explain myself out of trouble, but my alibi would blow the secrecy of my employment by Herd Torbur. Confession would be bad for many reasons.

Bad Egg

I was pretty sure that the bartender had nothing more to contribute. Even if she remembered a stray detail, she wasn't likely to share it with me after my rant. Nobody else was offering anything in defense of Grust. There likely weren't any separatists in the bar at the time, either. At best, I could hope the real racists would hear about my outburst and possibly approach me later. I could start with that gang in the park outside...

I backed away from the bar as the bartender shouted her accusations, making it look like I was backing down from the argument. I kept her in sight, maintaining an expression of disgust and fear.

Then, I heard a noise from across the room: tables and chairs shifting. When I looked in that direction, I discovered that the three lone Taratumm were rising from their seats, looking at me with unconcealed loathing. One of the males already had his shoulders hunched, leaning forward with head down, a definite threat display.

"Not a violent place, rrr?" I said, the sentiment appropriate both in and out of character. I expected to be shouted down and threatened. I had not expected to actually be attacked, at least not so quickly.

The bartender tared at the standing Taratumm. I caught her expression of surprise. She thought this behavior odd, as well.

"Hey, sit down," she bellowed, more upset at her patrons' behavior than at my harassment. "I have this joker handled."

The three Taratumm ignored her, pushing aside obstacles to move closer, picking up speed. The pair of males who were seated together were also starting to rise. Even the Hrotata who looked so dopey before was perking up. He stared at me with clear interest and a sneer of disgust. I couldn't see the pair of Vislin, not wanting to turn my head in their direction and lose sight of the oncoming Taratumm. I doubted I could expect any help from that quarter, anyway. I just hoped they weren't going to join in against me. Fortunately, the Taratumm in the pit remained oblivious and uninvolved.

I gauged my distance to the exit. It looked like I had plenty of time. I tried to look reasonably afraid but not panicked. I backed away slowly, casually, giving the bartender a sneer.

"Kkk, I thought so. Peaceful Taratumm, so superior. Maybe that's true…" I didn't get to finish my improvised parting shot. With no further warning, the foremost of the Taratumm, one of the lone males, charged forward at full speed.

He wasn't just angry… he was already at full frenzy. How was that even possible? They should have been bellowing and stomping, giving me at least nonverbal warnings before any of them hit the extreme rage of frenzy. Taratumm have an instinctual battle dance that telegraphs their eruptions. This guy went from grumpy to murderous in just a few seconds.

You can't blame me, then, for being surprised. Normally, I swear, I'm quick on my feet, quick with a claw, and quick on the draw. If I had known an attack was coming, he wouldn't have touched me.

As it was, I tried to leap backwards but got smashed to the side, clobbered mid-air by my attacker's forearm and shoulder. If I had frozen and stayed low, he might have trampled me into the floor mats. I was also fortunate not to be impaled on his shoulder spine. Some days, my armor isn't just formal wear.

I went sprawling into the nearest table, cracking my spine against the edge of its wooden surface. My tail whacked the adjacent chair. Both impacts stung fiercely. The air was knocked out of my lungs from the original slam. I staggered and struggled to get upright.

There wasn't much time for thought. My assailant was turning and getting ready for another charge. Worse, there were three more angry Taratumm behind him. They looked close to frenzy, themselves. How was that possible? How had I gotten myself in so much trouble, so fast? More to the point, how could I get out of it alive?

Chapter 4 - Graceful Exit

After I was attacked, things happened fast. I was kept busy just staying alive. I'll do my best to reconstruct exactly what happened. Sorry if I throw in some guesses and a little self-promotion in the process.

So, after the first stomper, the chartreuse, smashed me into the furnishings, I switched my wits from 'talk' to 'dodge'. I was ready for his second charge. He raced forward on a direct line. I hopped sideways, putting a table between us. The heavy wooden surface protected my body from his fists.

Unfortunately, his deflected charge placed him between me and the exit. I was sandwiched between one frenzying Taratumm and three more that looked ready to snap.

I assume that around that time, the bartender hit an alarm. That timing fits with when the constables arrived. It also explains why she didn't help me any sooner. At the time, I had to assume she condoned my mauling. She wasn't obviously jumping to my aid.

Frost, for all I knew, she was the one responsible for her patrons' bad tempers. She *was* the one serving the drinks, after all. Unlikely, I know, for reasons already explored. As it was, she *was* helping me by making sure that constables and medics were on their way to clean up the casualties afterward... myself potentially included.

The pair of female Vislin weren't helping me either. They chose that moment to stand up and scramble for the door. They were taking the smartest option. I really wished I could follow them out.

The lot in the pit were just starting to catch on to the problems upstairs. I could hear movement. I hoped they weren't coming to join their comrades in a group beat-down. My situation was already bad enough.

Nathan Large with Laine Megan Lundquist

It got worse. As Stomper Number One prepared to mash me between himself and the pit railing, Numbers Two and Three launched into full-rage frenzy as well. I could only spare each of them a moment of my attention. All three frenzying Taratumm were bellowing and stamping the floor, working themselves up to another charge. If all of them came at me at once, my odds of escape would drop below my lottery success rate.

I had to raise those odds to at least marginal. Any sympathy I might have had for my attackers – given my own provocations – was undercut by sympathy for myself. I reached down with a practiced motion and pulled Rtrtr from its holster at my hip.

Most rational sapients, when facing the wrong end of a weapon, will either freeze in fear or dive for cover. A frenzying Taratumm isn't exactly irrational, but their thoughts are mainly focused on removing threats, not avoiding them. Drawing a gun was an irrational move on *my* part. You get Taratumm to stop frenzying by convincing them that all threats are gone. I made myself a bigger threat.

For Vislin, removing the threat usually means removing ourselves, by running far away. I didn't have that option. My exit was blocked. Laying down and playing dead wouldn't work; I'd still be trampled to make *certain* I couldn't fight anymore.

I had to use lethal force, not threaten with it. I still did my best to cripple rather than kill. As the three frenzying Taratumm crashed forward, I darted to the far side of their converging paths and fired at the legs of the first attacker. A big chunk of his left leg was flash-cooked and burst across the floor in a spray of steam and charred meat. Without that support, he toppled to the side. I was heading to his right, so his flailing tumble missed me entirely... exactly as I intended.

I didn't get much time to appreciate my brilliant, skillful strategy. One opponent was down, but he was still a dangerous obstacle on the floor. I didn't want to shoot anyone else... but the two other attackers were still coming. I couldn't run backward toward the door; there was still scattered furniture between me and the exit. *Turning* and running might have made sense... except the pair of Taratumm upstairs had lifted chairs to throw. A hunk of wood whizzed past my shoulder. Their aim was terrible, but the projectiles were big enough that they might get lucky. Turning my back would make me an easy target.

I don't know if the damage to her bar finally stirred the bartender to action or if she just needed a few seconds to find her own weapon. Fortunately, she decided not to shoot *me*. She didn't exactly aim away from me, though. As the two frenzied Taratumm still standing turned and pounded after me, projectiles zipped through the air between us. In retrospect, I think the bartender was trying to lead her targets. She was just a terrible shot. At the time, though, I assumed she was aiming at me… and also a terrible shot.

I can't really criticize. *My* next shot was hurried and hit a table rather than the attacker I aimed for. The wood popped and spattered the nearby Taratumm with shrapnel. Fortunately for us both, the distraction slowed him down just enough for the bartender to catch. The unlucky target of our crossfire was pelted with her flechettes.

There wasn't much blood from the impacts. I guessed later that the bartender's weapon was throwing stingers: slivers of metal impregnated with a paralytic drug. It's a great weapon for discouraging rowdy customers and petty thieves: it inflicts lots of pain and disables movement with minimal risk of serious damage. By contrast, my Rtrtr is a vicious, hot-tempered brute.

Sadly, a big, angry Taratumm is only slowed, not stopped, by a stinger barrage. The wounded threat remained to my left, cutting off a possible escape route as he staggered forward. I *had* been planning to repeat my earlier trick and hop into the opening created by my heater shot. Finding that path blocked, I didn't have time left for new choreography.

The third frenzying Taratumm, uninjured, smashed its way through the décor and flailed a meaty fist in my direction. The impact caught me hard on the side of my neck. Lights flashed behind my eyes and my gut wrenched at the pain. Frost, it still hurts there now. At the time, the pain felt like the set-up to a killing blow. I couldn't even think.

Nathan Large with Laine Megan Lundquist

I felt the twinge of hormones I had kept suppressed earlier, the harbingers of my own frenzy. I suddenly wanted to turn tail and bolt as fast as possible for the nearest exit or hiding spot. What was left of my brain was screaming, "RUN!".

Frenzy was the last thing I needed. If I succumbed, I'd injure myself on the way out, leave myself vulnerable to multiple attackers, and get tangled up in the hurdles all around me. Basically, I'd do all the *wrong* things and get hurt worse. Good job, evolution.

I'm used to trouble and confident in my own reactions, so I can hold off frenzy longer than the average Vislin. That's not bragging; it's just a fact. As long as I felt in control of events, I could ignore the nagging voice of atavism. Still, no Vislin can ignore severe pain for long... not without strong drugs, at least. When your body is saying, "no more", even the best trained mind has trouble arguing it down.

I compromised by scrambling across the floor, bent low. Another hurled chair rocketed over my head. I was backing away into the only clear path but giving up my access to the door. Turned away from my attackers, I also couldn't aim for another shot with Rtrtr. I wasn't making myself an easy target, but I also wasn't doing the smart things that could get me out of danger.

The bartender continued to pour stingers into her original target, grinding him almost to a halt as the paralytic toxin accumulated. Her behavior suggested that she wasn't so much helping me as trying to reduce the damage to her business. Again, I can't complain. From her perspective, I started the whole mess.

My *real* salvation came from a less likely source: the party downstairs finally decided to join the party upstairs. The wage slaves from the pit started to move towards us after my second shot. Brawling alone hadn't triggered their notice, but blood and smoke caught their attention.

Thank the Ancestors, they weren't frenzied. Even better, they wanted to stop the fight. Half of them interposed themselves in front of the pair in the back. There was a lot of bellowing and shouting, followed by the thumping sounds of Taratumm grappling one another.

Bad Egg

The other half of the sane group came in my direction. Two of them pinned the two Taratumm who were injured and immobile, but still frenzying. The rest closed on my final attacker. They probably planned to grab me, as well.

Here's why we call it a 'mindless' frenzy: when the new Taratumm got closer to the Taratumm menacing me, they became his more immediate threat. It didn't matter that my opponent had just been fighting me, moments before. I was a smaller entity, moving away, and had not hurt him yet. I was the lesser danger. Maybe given a choice between neutral Taratumm and Vislin targets, a frenzied stomper would choose the biter, but right then, he was a lone male being assaulted by a hostile herd.

The gang beating turned into a bar brawl. I took my cue and sprang to the exit. Doing my best to absorb the impact with my less damaged shoulder, I slammed into the heavy swinging door and flopped out onto the street.

Once I was out of the racket in the Thunder Bar, I could hear a high-pitched screech in the distance. Constabulary alarms... getting closer. The part of me that was still sane thought, *of course they're coming, somebody almost got murdered here.* I needed to avoid getting caught up in the dragnet. I started running – at the best speed I could manage – across the street, toward cover.

At the same time, I didn't want to go too far. I was sure whatever just happened was connected to Grust's outburst. My antics should have only stirred up some anger, not multiple full-scale threat frenzies. Even if one unstable stomper thought I was personally antagonizing them, it would be rare for more than one Taratumm to react. There was something else going on. Something unnatural. I had a feeling whoever was responsible would also want to leave the scene, quickly.

At the time, I didn't consider one additional factor. The frenzies hadn't started when I was outright talking about eating Taratumm. The crazy didn't go off when my voice raised or when I started accusing the bartender. The trouble began when we were *both* talking about culprits, just after the bartender suggested me... or rather, the pretend racist me... as a suspect.

In other words, things got dangerous when our argument turned into an investigation. Later on, when I had time to look over the pieces, I wondered if the fracas was started as a distraction.

Nathan Large with Laine Megan Lundquist

In a way, I *was* to blame for triggering a reaction. Looking for the instigator and asking dangerous questions was what scared them into attacking. I had no idea *how* the attack was accomplished, but the pattern fit. From that perspective, it might have been useful to see who stayed behind after the show.

At the time, though, I wasn't really thinking, just trying to get away from danger. I bolted past the broken stores across the street and tore into the adjoining park. My headlong flight helped to burn out some of the stress hormones blocking my ability to form complex plans. Not that my deeply thought plans are any less stupid, on average.

I dove behind a stand of carefully sculpted underbrush at the edge of the park and collected my thoughts. The scree of the constabulary alarms was only a couple of blocks away, and I could see the flaring orange lights. It was too late to find a better hiding place. I realized that my only good options left were to sneak away and go home or hold still and see what happened.

No one had followed me out of the front door. The mob inside might still be slugging it out, for all I could tell. The pair of Vislin females were long gone. The young punks loitering in the park were gone as well. So much for the theory that they were waiting for an excuse to pounce on drunks.

I watched the door closely... then realized, belatedly, that the bar might have a back door. I hadn't checked. Good job, detective.

My oversight was forgiven by the appearance of two figures at the Thunder Bar's front door: two *big* figures, slightly battered but moving easily enough. Moving fast, in fact, for Taratumm. It looked like the pair of males who were drinking together originally: the chair-chuckers. They must have broken free from their opponents or convinced them they were calm enough to leave peacefully. Actually, I wasn't sure they had ever really *been* frenzied. That was suspicious. Maybe they were just opportunistically violent. They certainly weren't frenzying right then... but they *were* leaving in a hurry.

The oncoming constabulary transport was the most likely reason for their haste. They hit the intersection across from me and turned in my direction. The favorable spirits were sending prey my direction! All I had to do was stay still and avoid startling them.

Bad Egg

Where were they going? What were they saying? Were they my culprits? Even if not, they might have seen something I missed. They might know something I needed.

My primitive urges were actually being helpful for a change. I had no problem locking my muscles and stilling my breathing. These were natural responses when in the path of two charging Taratumm. I felt my skin crawl as my subcutaneous glands secreted chromatic compounds, recoloring my scales in a mottled pattern to match the underbrush and shadows. I successfully blended in and was overlooked.

My next problem came after the pair ran past me. I had to convince my brain that all threats were gone and it was time to hunt. Hunger made a good motivator: I thought hard about the wretched taste of synthetic protein and how nice it would be to haul home a slab of the real thing. No, I wasn't thinking of eating Taratumm. But, realistically, following those two stompers might be the key to getting paid. Money meant meat.

I just needed to tail them and not get scented. I let them get almost a block away before standing up. To be honest, it took about that long to overcome my fear. I had to move right away, fast but quiet.

I'm competent at tailing, but I was out of practice. A wide-open street also isn't the best venue for a stealthy chase. Not enough cover. Whenever too much open space intervened, I had to let the pair get out of sight before I felt safe to catch up. Afterward, I had to trust my ears and occasionally my instincts to guess which direction they had turned. I could sometimes hear them grunting to one another, but between the distance, the city noise, their caution and their lack of breath, the words were impossible to make out.

They seemed to be heading back downtown. Not locals, in that case. Given their dress, they could be anything from aircar mechanics to computer techs. Not quite upper class, but maybe not underclass slobs, either. Maybe they were contracted to a medical research firm and picked up some novel pharmaceuticals on the side? It was a long shot, but half of my job involves finding unexpected connections between crimes and culprits.

In this instance, the long shot did not pay off. The pair stopped at a public transit station to catch their breath. I managed to edge close enough to overhear the end of their conversation.

One of the two, the slightly greener one, was saying, "…that place. I know you grew up out there, but it's too rough for my taste."

The other one, less green but somewhat more bloodied, replied ruefully, "I know. Maybe it's one of those herd hysteria things? People get on edge and start expecting a fight. So, naturally, they're easier to set off. Anyway, you're right. At the least, we'll stay out of Trrptet for a few weeks and let it cool down. I'll miss seeing her, but it's not worth getting shot."

The first greasy stomper nodded and added, "Right. Get some sleep, tend to those scrapes… and let me know if any constables call. We'll make our statements together *if* they investigate. Otherwise, we still have to clock in on time tomorrow morning."

"Rrr, maybe getting shot would have been better," his friend joked, weakly. The other Taratumm slammed shoulders with him, a playful rebuke. They tapped foreheads in a gesture of friendly male bonding, then separated. One waited above ground for the local shuttle bus. The other descended below for the cross-town subterranean.

So, the pair were co-workers. Probably Herd mates. Maybe even brothers or other relatives. Their talk didn't sound like the plotting of co-conspirators. They likely had nothing to do with the outbreaks. They sounded like they had as little clue about the cause as I did. It was just as well, since pursuing them further without being spotted would be nearly impossible.

I decided to cut my losses and backed away, skulking out of sight down a side street. I really needed to get home and tend to my *own* scrapes. I wanted to wash again to get the stink of burnt flesh and wood smoke off of my scales. I'd have to change out my armor, as well, giving up my favorite old suit in favor of a newer, stiffer, more formal model I had in storage.

Bad Egg

It was bad enough that my description would be shared with the constables as the likely instigator of the evening's brawl. No need to make their job easier by looking and smelling the part.

I turned my beak toward my own part of the neighborhood, toward home.

So, what had I gained from the night's escapade... aside from setting back interspecies relations in Layafflr City by a generation? I could compare the night's clientele with the witness list and see if anyone matched up. That comparison would tell me who had opportunity, not just once, but both times Taratumm unexpectedly frenzied at that location. Obviously, the bartender was on that list, but I had my doubts about her as a suspect.

Another benefit: I was able to observe her, the venue, and some of its patrons. I gained some valuable information. Still, none of it was worth the pain and risk involved.

What I was missing were the two most important elements of the crime: means and motive. How had the culprit – and by then, I was fairly sure there *was* third party to blame – caused one, and then later three, Taratumm to hit frenzy without warning? Drugs could certainly do it, but how was the dope being administered? Or were my two escapee engineers on the right track, talking about herd mentality? Was it some kind of psychological effect? Conditioning based on a trigger stimulus? Maybe all the affected Taratumm had something in common. Or someone, a mutual acquaintance.

Each of the possible methods was necessarily tied to the *why* of the matter. If Herd Torbur was being targeted, the matter should have ended with Grust. Or maybe not. Maybe Grust *was* the true target and the other Taratumm were aimed at me, as a secondary victim. Maybe the second crime was done to obscure the reason for the first. Even if the two events were related... how? And what was the point?

Was someone trying to ruin Trrptet Thunder Bar? Two incidents might not do it, but a third uproar could certainly prompt the government to shut the place down in the interests of public safety... particularly if someone died as a result.

I still had plenty of leads to pursue. Not many possibilities were eliminated by what I had learned that night. If anything, I had more new lines of inquiry than before. Ideas were good, but I had limited time to pursue each possibility. I needed to think. With my head still ringing from my earlier clubbing, that moment wasn't the best time for deep contemplation.

I staggered back home, stripped off, and managed to scour myself passably clean before collapsing into my ragged nest. Fortunately, it was a warm night. I couldn't spare the energy to drag a cover over my naked scales.

If it were the cold season, I might have slept though my deadline. Waking up was already going to be painful enough without failure on top of my injuries.

Bad Egg

Chapter 5 - Quiet Morning

As predicted, I woke up miserable. My shoulder and neck ached so badly that I squeaked like a hatchling as I climbed out of my nest. A few scales flaked off, damaged so badly that the root had died. The skin underneath was bruised black. I had similar bruises and tears along my back and tail, but none quite as severe as my collar area. I had to sacrifice my last few hoarded pain pills just to get moving. Antibiotic, styptic salve ensured that my scrapes would heal cleanly.

Another foray into the urban jungle was not advisable in my condition. Unfortunately, I had already squandered a full day with little to show for it. I had only two days left before the court rendered its verdict on Grust of Herd Torbur. I decided to split my second day between self-pity and self-abuse.

For the first half, self-pity, I would stay home and study up on the case. Hopefully, my brain wasn't too badly damaged. I needed to find something that would stick a couple of pieces together and show a pattern. I didn't have much time, so I needed a direction that would pay off quickly.

In my favor, there wasn't any further need to go to court. Much of the day there would be occupied by routine statements from witnesses establishing their various versions of events. If I really needed to know more than I could glean from Shllokwa's pretrial notes, I could tune in the televised proceedings on my compad. If anything unexpected happened in court, I was sure Shllokwa would get my attention.

At some point, though, I couldn't afford to continue sitting on my comfortable stump, nursing my wounds. I'd have to venture out and *do* something. Investigators only solve crimes while sitting at home, nibbling cakes and sipping broth, in intellectual fiction. If this case could be cracked by compad, Grust would already be free.

The second part of my day, self-abuse, would involve stalking the streets, tracking down leads.

The problem was: what *should* I pursue? How could I best serve the case? Starting another bar fight was off the list. When my drugs wore off, I'd be an easy mark for a Hrotata pup.

I could do some interviewing, maybe even scare up some new witnesses to stretch out the trial. At best, though, the defense could only drag out proceedings to the end of the third day, and *that* far only if new witnesses had something relevant to say. A delay was only useful if I expected to find something worthwhile during that time.

Nothing said that interviews wouldn't turn into physical confrontations, either. If I stumbled onto the criminal responsible for Grust's very bad night, I might rouse them to action against me. Possibly, I already had. Hopefully, the second time around, I'd know who I was looking for and they wouldn't have pawns available to throw at me.

My research revealed one oversight right away. Neither side, defense or prosecution, listed the bartender as a witness. On my first read-through of the witness list, I had overlooked that omission myself. After visiting the Thunder Bar, I was more attuned to the players.

Did I think the bartender was my culprit? Not really, but I knew better than to let gut instinct alone guide my hunt. Even if she wasn't involved, she might still know something useful. And at worst, she was favorable to Grust.

I popped off a message to Shllokwa to relay to the defense counsel, Ktlrsh: *Put the Trrptet bartender on the stand.* I didn't elaborate about how I gained my insight. Shllokwa would find that out soon enough.

Immediately afterward, I reconsidered my 'insight'. Surely both sides had considered the bartender, at least as a present witness. Yet if that was the case, why exclude her? Maybe they thought she would contribute little. Maybe she seemed too risky either way. The prosecution might think she would bolster the defense's position, by favoring a regular customer if nothing else. The defense might consider her knowledge about the accused's drinking habits a problem. She might tell stories of past fights and make their victim sound like a brawler. If she really saw nothing, her testimony could be considered evidence against any drink tampering.

The other witnesses on the list were less likely to be personally connected to Grust, with the exception of his Herd-mates.

Leafing further through the witness list, I found something else interesting: a lone Hrotata was present inside the Thunder Bar on the night of the assault. Just like last night. The witness list gave only a name – Krrutoki – and contact information. That data was still enough to turn up a profile through the networks, including a picture. I couldn't be precisely sure, but he looked familiar. He *could* have been the same one I saw, watching me fight outnumbered.

The prosecution had Krrutoki scheduled to testify. As a Hrotata, they probably assumed he could give an impartial retelling of events at the Thunder Bar. Maybe he *was* just an innocent bystander. Twice? Maybe he was a voyeur who liked to watch the dumb saurians mix it up for his entertainment. I vaguely remembered him perking up when I got clobbered.

Were my suspicions worth mentioning to the defense? Krrutoki was already a problem for them, being a witness for the prosecution. There wasn't much they could do about him, until I gave them a specific reason to protest. If I wanted to explain my concerns, I'd have to explain where those thoughts came from… again, not so proud of my prior night's work.

Still, the coincidence was worth a note to myself: another potential connection to trace. I was doing great at finding overlooked elements in this case. I was failing at turning them into usable proof. I supposed anything was valuable that might create reasonable doubt. I wouldn't manufacture false leads, but I didn't mind sowing confusion to keep the legal system honest.

I went back and reviewed the defense's account of events. Nothing new popped up. The order and timing after Grust stood up to leave matched what I already heard presented in court. What were missing were the key events preceding Grust's departure: the unrecorded events that caused his odd behavior. I started a new notebook and listed my ideas again.

Drugs were still the top candidate. Hallucinogens, or maybe a really potent aphrodisiac?

Mental conditioning? Conditioning required that the programmer had access to Grust for some extended period prior to the event. The bar was the most likely point of contact. That assumption was also the only way I could reconcile the second incident at the same locale. Then again, there could be separate causes for the two eruptions.

I could come up with all sorts of other complicated conspiracies to explain the events as known. Genetic manipulation? Parasitic infestation? Before I wandered into a twisted mental maze, I needed to consider simpler explanations. How about... money?

Grust might have been hired to threaten the victim and took the deal too far. One or more of my assailants at the Thunder Bar also could have been paid to start a fight, to eliminate an investigator or create cover for the responsible party. It wasn't impossible for a Taratumm to frenzy at will, just unlikely. "Violently unstable stomper for hire," wasn't a job you could advertise publicly, but there were always private sellers and buyers of "accidents".

Frost and a malfunctioning heatsuit! I couldn't even consider means without tangling it up with motive. *Why* would someone mess with Grust, or Herd Torbur, or Trrptet Thunder Bar, or whoever this crime was meant to harm?

Wait. I was still assuming that the intended victim was my client. The victim might be *the victim*: the Hrotata still in intensive care. What if he was the target all along? That still left the second incident to explain... but *I* was the target in that case. The Taratumm were just the weapons: Grust in the first assault, other random bystanders in the second.

I looked up what I had on the victim, Tharrliki. According to his mate, Yavirrt, Tharrliki had no connection to Grust prior to the challenge. Their Clan, Takerrl, had some remote links to Herd Torbur, but no notable business dealings together. Clan Takerrl was moderately prosperous, though a newcomer to ChttKttp, having made their money among the newer Great Family colony worlds.

Bad Egg

Tharrliki was first-generation local, both to the planet and to Layafflr City; his matron was an immigrant. His mate, Yavirrt, was an 'acquisition' favored by the Clan matriarchy, a female with closer ties to the City's political establishment. Nothing exactly suspicious there, just the usual entrenchment of wealth into power. I made a note to myself to research the mate's background, but that seemed a less promising trail. I returned to focus on Tharrliki.

The victim's proximity to Trrptet also appeared to be a matter of chance. The couple, along with their Vislin bodyguards, were shopping on the adjacent street. One of the wrecked storefronts apparently belonged to a moderately successful silversmith, whom the couple was patronizing.

Per Yavirrt's statement, after browsing the shiny trinkets at the shop, the couple decided to sample the local atmosphere, strolling toward the ornamental park. They bought some candied insects… meandered through the hedges… boring… boring… and were preparing to leave when Grust approached.

The mate, Yavirrt, said they thought Grust was just drunk or maybe sick. They felt sorry for what they assumed was a Herd-less, luckless sot, reduced to beggary for train fare home. Unlike a properly cautious resident of the area, they let him get close enough to talk without ordering their bodyguards to block the way. Even after Grust voiced his challenge, they were more confused than alarmed.

Though it wasn't in the testimony, I suspected that the well-off Hrotata couple were amused. Maybe they had a laugh at the poor, dumb, pickled Taratumm. Maybe not. That scenario could be my prejudices talking... but then, why did they misread the situation so badly? What happened was weird, true, but they should still have anticipated the possibility of theft or assault.

Civilization doesn't preclude occasional savagery. Modern medicine doesn't always spot mental illness. Plenty of unpredictable, dangerous animals can leap out at you through gaps in the urban façade. In a place like Layafflr City, rapid growth and economic divides spread those gaps plenty wide. I know this from first-claw experience. Pile up inequality alongside organized crime, greed, and the daily sins of those striving for dominance, and… let's just say there's plenty of work for the constables.

Precious little of that workload comes to your noble narrating investigator, mind you. Usually, crime victims are dead or poor. Survivors are just happy to stay alive and avoid provoking their tormentors further. It takes a rare conjunction of variables to produce clients with credit to spare, something to gain from spending it on my services, and the courage to seek help... along with a problem not already solved by constable detectives.

Although, corruption among the constabulary forces is the main reason I can eke out a living doing what I do. If the wronged party can't outbid the bribes of their enemies, they can perhaps spend that budget on me and buy a chance at justice.

Other cases that came to me were like this one: weird. Cases where the constables couldn't or wouldn't look deep enough to find the real causes of a crime. "Grust of Herd Torbur is a violent degenerate" was a much easier explanation than, say, the experimentation of a mad social scientist in a slum neighborhood.

Yes, I wrote down that hypothesis, too. Stranger events had already come to pass in Collective history.

Where was I? Right, the flash point itself, the moment of violence. Grust issued a slurred, formal challenge in a language neither Hrotata spoke. When he got no satisfactory response, he bent double at the waist and smacked his bony, crested head into Tharrliki's forehead.

The medical examiner's report noted a fractured skull, intra-cranial bleeding, some neural damage, and spraining between the neck vertebrae. Tharrliki was knocked out into a coma that took him three days to wake from. He was still having trouble speaking as of the report date.

Yavirrt's account didn't have much more to add after Tharrliki was attacked. Grust struck, Tharrliki fell, Yavirrt dove to protect her mate, and her Vislin guards slashed at Grust to drive him back. One of the guards sounded a general alarm. The protectors took some whacks for their trouble. I could empathize with them: Taratumm hit hard.

Bad Egg

From there, Grust was driven away, pursued by bystanders struggling to bring him under control. The female's perspective from then on was focused on protecting and escorting her mate to safety and eventual medical care.

Tharrliki, of course, would not be able to witness on his own behalf. In all likelihood, the two sides of the trial probably agreed that they didn't *need* Tharrliki's account to make either of their cases. He wasn't likely to add anything to his mate's testimony. According to her, neither of them knew why he was attacked.

The guards weren't being put on the stand, either. They each submitted sworn statements which – no surprise – conformed to their employer's version with perfect precision. Kkk, they'd swear an Artificial Intelligence attacked Tharrliki, if Clan Takerrl paid their Pack enough and said Pack ordered the guards to corroborate the official story. I know my own species all too well. They'd even perjure themselves on the stand – publicly, blatantly and gladly – if Pack demanded.

Where did the reports leave me? The remaining witnesses broke down into three groups: those who had been in the Thunder Bar earlier, those who were out in the street later, and those who were character witnesses for and against Grust. I looked more closely at the latter category. The defense's notes indicated that the two negative character witnesses were Taratumm with grudges against Herd Torbur. They should be easily discredited as hostile.

Reaffirming my suspicions about an outside agency, Grust had no prior criminal record, no previous assaults, and therefore, no prior victims. That didn't mean he was a paragon of virtue. He could have had minor charges dropped or expunged, particularly given Herd Torbur's influence. At the least, though, he couldn't be considered habitually unstable or violent. The main assets the prosecution had on their side were the flagrant and public nature of the crime, plus a lack of any credible competing explanation.

I couldn't do much to debunk the known facts. The testimonies were largely in agreement. What I needed was a strong alternate theory, if not comprehensive proof of causation. My explanation had to be stronger than the current defense, namely "drugs".

Nathan Large with Laine Megan Lundquist

Right then, my biggest question was: *Why that particular form of assault?* Why challenge and attack anyone for a mate Grust had never met, much less a Hrotata? Grust's account was very specific about being aroused, albeit toward a hallucinatory Taratumm female. Tharrliki's mate agreed that Grust seemed very intent on her and very aggressive toward her partner. That fixation could be a side effect of something chemical, I supposed, but it might also be the intentional purpose of the influence itself.

'Aphrodisiac' was rising on my list of possible causes. Maybe the bartender had the ruts for Grust and tried to get him to reciprocate... then somehow mis-targeted his arousal? Other patrons could have been triggered to come to her defense in the same way when I became a problem. Protecting the matriarch? Looking back later, this theory was stupid, but at the time, it gathered up more facts than any of my other knotty nets.

The main problem with the aphrodisiac scenario was that *I* didn't believe it. Besides the extent to which it stretched logic, that explanation didn't match with my impressions of the bartender. Not that I thought she was innocent, necessarily, but she *did* exert herself in my defense... sort of. Plus, I hadn't gotten any sense that she was grieving personally for Grust's plight. She defended him, but in a general way, like any other patron. So, she was either a villain *and* a great actor or else innocent... in this case.

All this deduction was great, but I was deducting myself out of ideas. So far, the one gap that really gaped was the specificity of the victim. There had been several more threatening targets for Grust to attack, either in the bar or on the street. If he was looking for love, there were female Taratumm right in the bar. There were better reasons to attack a couple of well-off Hrotata slumming in his neighborhood... theft, resentment... but if he was going to act out, why not choose targets without guards? Or why not take down their guards first? The consensus of testimony said that Grust left the bar, walked half a block over, and went on a direct approach to Tharrliki. What was the attraction?

I came to a decision. I needed to find out more about the injured party. The case notes, corroborated by several news reports, said that Yavirrt and the rest of Clan Takerrl were maintaining a vigil at Tharrliki's hospital bed. That hospital was where I needed to be. I might learn something from the Clan, given the right approach. Maybe there was some link even Tharrliki's family didn't know. They might be willing to explore the matter with me. I had some ideas about how to gain their cooperation... better ideas than the ones I tried earlier.

My traumatized, screaming flesh gave me added incentive to be cautious. I stood up with some difficulty and risked a second dose of pain pills. I was getting low on those. I might have considered picking up another bottle, except that I was going to have to wager my remaining savings on transportation. There was no way I could walk to the hospital and back, not in my condition. The day's gamble had to pay off or else I'd be broke and still no closer to cracking the case... and no closer to money or medicine.

While looking up the hospital and checking my credit balance on my compad, I tuned in the court proceedings in a separate window. The summary text said that Yavirrt had already testified, followed by Grust's Herd-mates, Ktuck and Veruth, and most of the patrons of the Thunder Bar.

I left that feed running while I prepared to venture out, holstering Rtrtr and applying a bandage to my shoulder. My stiff, slightly too small, second-hand suit of formal armor was actually helpful in that it limited my range of motion. I'd have some problems moving quickly – or breathing deeply – but it might reduce the agony from my torn shoulder.

The next witness caught my attention: an expert witness for the prosecution, the constabulary's forensic scientist reporting on evidence collected from the scene and from Grust. I watched with a sinking stomach as they ticked off the simple questions:

Was there any evidence of psychoactive chemicals in the defendant's body? No.

Any evidence of said chemicals or residues in the containers seized from Trrptet Thunder Bar? No.

Anything found on the furnishings, in the garbage bins, or anywhere on the premises? No.

The Thunder Bar was apparently the cleanest recreational facility within kilometers. It contained not a trace of anything more mind-altering than good old alcohol, vinegar, and the usual trace intoxicants found in exotic liquors both local and imported.

The defense's "drugs made him do it" argument was pretty well sunk. It was still a possibility, sure. It wasn't impossible to introduce a chemical that did its dirty work, then metabolized into something untraceable. It also wasn't impossible to bribe a constable to lose, alter, or misread evidence. But either explanation suggested a level of expert manipulation well beyond anything the court would believe… without reason.

I needed to get out there and find that reason. Maybe that reason would lead me back to the cause of Grust's strange behavior.

The way things stood at that moment, Grust was going to rot in the cages, and I was going to starve to death. Both tragedies taken together outweighed my desire to stay home and sleep off my aches.

I have to admit, either one separately might not have been enough.

Chapter 6 - Visiting Hours

To be honest, I wasn't entirely sure what I was doing. Like Grust, I couldn't blame the drugs for my confusion. The pain pills *were* making my thoughts a little fuzzy, but that impairment was minor, especially compared to the potential distraction of the pain they were blocking. Besides, neither my suffering nor its treatment was the problem. The problem was that I had very little plan about how to proceed.

Once I got to the right place, I could probably get someone talking. But what, exactly, was the right place? My research hadn't turned up the room number for the Hrotata victim, Tharrliki. No surprise there. Medical privacy was carefully guarded, particularly when the patient was the victim of a globally televised assault case. I was fortunate that the media managed to scent out the right hospital. That name came as no surprise: any of Layafflr City's affluent afflicted would choose Vaktrri Medical.

Once I found the room… who would I find there? If there was more than one member of Clan Takerrl present, who was my preferred target? How should I approach that target? What was my backup plan, if my initial tactic failed?

All this planning presumed I wouldn't get barred from entry, thrown out after entry, or arrested… A side benefit of being narcotized was that I wasn't as worried about everything that could go wrong.

Aside from that neural glazing, I had confidence in my own abilities. I could probably bluff or sneak my way into the hospital. I could bypass any security that didn't involve a biometric or voice ident. If I rubbed one of the Hrotata relatives the wrong way, I could talk their fur back down. Despite prior evidence, I'm actually quite good at my job.

Yet, even if I successfully navigated to the right person at the right place, what would I learn? Was all my effort going to pay anything? What, exactly, was I looking for?

I didn't know. That question was the point. My trip was another fishing expedition. Ideally, it wouldn't end with *me* hooked and scaled. If I was lucky, my visit might turn up a connection between the various, seemingly random pieces of this case. I was hoping for a bite somewhere among the less trawled reaches of the affair. Had enough fish metaphors yet?

My preferred catch was the victim's mate, Yavirrt. At a minimum, she had a front seat perspective on the assault itself, plus some of the preceding and following events. I might pry something useful out of her memory. She also knew the most about Tharrliki's personal background, his associations, and maybe his enemies. If an attack was aimed at Tharrliki – like the second attack was aimed at me – then figuring out the why might include the who and how.

The first steps in my plan were hard enough. It required an act of will to step out of my apartment, descend the stairs, and exit to the street. From there, I had a couple blocks' walk to the nearest skimmer depot.

The exertion helped by stretching my stiff, abused muscles. By the time I got to the depot, I almost had my full range of motion back. The relief was short-lived. On the ride to the hospital, I would tighten back up and have to stretch all over again. It figured.

Still, the aircar was necessary to prevent me from collapsing from exhaustion, which would happen if I tried to walk the whole way. I also needed to travel fast and alone, out of sight. After the previous night's escapade, there was a good chance that constables would be watching for someone matching my description. No reason to make their search any easier by popping up on mass public transit.

It was probably too soon for them to identify and track me by my credit expenditures… I hoped. I'd find out soon enough if I was wrong; my aircar would be diverted to the nearest constable station for collection.

Again, I was confident that I could argue my way out of charges for provocation and assault, but that would waste time, blow my cover on the case, and possibly require a court appearance to get everything cleared up. I didn't have any time to spare at the moment.

Constabulary sloth was on my side. I had a quiet, uninterrupted ride to Vaktrri Medical.

The sculpted stone exterior of the ten-story monolith was a façade over a durable frame of Tsrrk-Tor steel and plastic, along with some fancier meta-materials. The hospital had ductless homeostasis, meaning that it regulated its own temperature and ventilation without requiring contact with the external air. It was near the city core and required minimal sonics and charged fields to keep its surface clear. Inside, the height of medical technology – or at least, the height of what could be imported to ChttKttp – maintained the health of the city's better insured citizens.

I had been inside before, but only on business. *My* health plan was the minimum protection provided to the registered citizens of Layafflr City. That meant my needs were administered through my local hospital, which was as proportionally shabby as the neighborhood it served.

I could have stopped at the emergency room near home for injections that would relieve my pain, stimulate the healing of my torn tissues, and even ensure the proper regrowth of my lost scales. The billing could be deferred until I had enough credit to seize.

The problem was, I didn't have all day to wait for diagnosis... and I couldn't risk the inevitable questions about how I received those injuries. I was pretty obviously an assault case. The med-techs would identify the assailant as Taratumm in short order. Even my cleansing wouldn't remove every trace of genetic material. The size and type of the injuries pointed to a heavy blunt object about the size of a stomper's fist. They couldn't legally hold me at the hospital, but they'd have the constables asking uncomfortable questions much faster.

I recognized the irony of entering a hospital, wounded, for reasons other than my own care. I caught that irony and forced it to work for me.

When I sprawled out of the aircar at the doors of Vaktrri, I was a wounded patient coming in for attention. I waved off the attentions of a pair of Vislin and

Taratumm attendants who each offered a supporting arm. I gave them my best act as a grumpy, insistently self-sufficient old loner.

They backed off, as intended. They weren't going to go out of their way to help a rude, snappish patient who could walk under his own power.

My next challenge was to find Tharrliki's room, without being tagged as unauthorized. I wasn't cleared for another patient's information and I certainly wasn't cleared to enter an inpatient ward, much less another patient's room.

In this case, I didn't feel bad about violating rules meant to protect the patient's safety and privacy. I wasn't doing him any harm. Frost, I might be helping him avoid an as-yet-unspecified threat. Self-justifications firmly in claw, I stalked the lower halls of the medical center, looking for an unguarded compad or terminal.

There are a few tricks you learn in the course of a career in investigations. At the hospital, I made use of a tidbit I scavenged from a more senior colleague while helping him on a fraud case. I'm not concerned about sharing this with you. Even if you warned the medical establishment for some reason, sapient nature would ensure the perpetuation of this particular security hole.

Basically, any big institution that uses shared electronic records will create multiple accounts. Inevitably, a few accounts are created as dummies, for testing or from duplication while making the real employee accounts. If you know the software used for that record system, you might know what default values are used to create its dummy accounts. Not all of the extra accounts are useful, mind you: most such accounts have minimal security clearance. But if you stumble onto a testing account, or a dummy for an administrator account, you can sometimes work backwards into useful access.

Finding those unguarded accounts is a matter of background knowledge plus access plus time. I had the knowledge, provided Vaktrri hadn't changed its data tech providers in the last couple of years. It pays to swap war stories with my compatriots in electronic snooping.

Still, those default codes were only useful if I was inside the hospital itself. A remote login would require me to defeat an extra layer of security just to make each attempt. I wasn't savvy enough to accomplish that kind of hack. But once I was inside, I just needed to find an entry terminal that wasn't being watched.

I was spared the trouble of creating a distraction. Favorable winds blew one up for me. Paramedics wheeled a pair of injured Vislin, struggling and hissing, into the emergency room. When attendants turned away to help restrain the maddened patients, I scrambled with my best possible speed to borrow a terminal.

I had to try three different default codes before gaining access, but my first search for Tharrliki was immediately successful. I only had time to locate his room number before someone looked up and spotted me tapping at the keys.

"Hey, that's a private system. What are you doing?" shouted a uniformed Hrotata female. She had the manner of a matriarch used to being obeyed. I guessed she was a head nurse or some such authority.

"Ttt, sorry. Left my compad at the hotel. Wanted to check the scores," I shouted in my best off-worlder accent. Between my overly formal armor and the implication that I was a clueless immigrant, she seemed to accept that I was merely ignorant and not conniving.

"Use the public terminals in the lobby," she chided, gesturing with her free hand. Her other hand held a coil of intravenous tubing. I hated to take advantage of her preoccupation, but couldn't waste the opportunity.

"Sorry, sorry," I groveled, acknowledging my grievous misstep. A couple more claw-taps logged me out of the system, drawing a stern glare from the matron. Still, when I backed away from the terminal, she had more pressing issues to deal with and returned to her work.

I would have liked to read Tharrliki's records more thoroughly, but I had to be satisfied with the necessary minimum. My target was in Room 1018, top floor, private room. Next, I had to get to a lift and onto to a private floor without being challenged.

Who can travel within a hospital unopposed? Medical staff, of course, but I wasn't going to be able to pass as a doctor or attendant, not even by stealing a lab coat. Patients... but for that ruse, I'd need an admissions tag. You know, the little radio tracking chip that links to your records and reminds the hospital who you are? I'd have to take the third option: pose as an approved visitor.

A little sleight of hand gained me an unformatted guest tag from the nurses' station. Hopefully, I'd get to the tenth floor before anyone noticed that my borrowed pass held no registered name. I looped the cord of the guest tag over my head and became a legitimate visitor, at least to the casual observer.

The chip inside, swiped over the lift panel, earned me access to the tenth floor. That scan would never have worked if I was trying to get to a patient under constable guard. Tharrliki's floor must have minimal security.

And why would Tharrliki be under protection? As far as the official accounts read, he was an unlucky bystander, a victim of happenstance. There was no reason to think he might be attacked again.

I had to wonder if that were true. Could Tharrliki still be in danger? Might someone else come after him, in the hospital? If Grust was aimed at Tharrliki, how was he set off? How was he aimed? Or was he part of the plot? The "drunk and frenzying" excuse could be misdirection to cover something more sinister...

That line of thought made little sense. It didn't help an assassin to use a cover story that would still get him convicted. If Grust had hoped to escape blame using the "drugged" defense, that obviously wasn't well planned. There was no lesser charge for assault under the influence, *unless* someone else caused the influence.

It remained more likely that Grust was an unwitting pawn. And it was still possible that Tharrliki was a deliberate target. So, I had to be wary: an enemy could seek to target Tharrliki again. For all I knew, approaching the Hrotata could make me a target... or an unintentional assailant.

These thoughts occupied my ride up. Nine floors later, the lift doors opened onto a pleasant if tediously beige corridor.

Unlike the temperate lobby, the atmospherically sealed patient floor was slightly chilly and smelled unnervingly neutral. The environment might be conducive to physical health, but it would eventually erode patients' mental health. If there's anything the sapients of the Great Family truly have in common, it's our love of strong and varied sensation... and warmth.

There was no reason to waste my time surveying the bland scenery. I loped purposefully into the hall, aimed toward Tharrliki's room. Left turn out of the lift, left turn again to block 15-20, then three rooms down…

I stopped two doors short of my goal. I wasn't caught by staff, though.

Instead, a Hrotata stepped out of the wing's guest lounge. She was a red-gold female with darker auburn streaks, head down as she slid a miniature compad into her leather shoulder bag. She wore a simple pale blue jumpsuit that could have either been budget cheap or fashionably expensive, depending on the actual fabric. Silver rings with sapphires dangled from her ear-flaps. I didn't recognize her until she looked up. The shape and pattern of her face matched a memory from Herd Torbur's case notes: Yavirrt, Tharrliki's mate. She must have come back to her mate's bedside immediately after testifying in court that morning.

Perfect! She was one of the best witnesses I could hope to interview, better than questioning Tharrliki himself. I just had to convince her to talk to me. I'd finally get the chance to test the brilliant approach I'd been cooking up all day. Hopefully, it would play better than my act at Trrptet Thunder Bar.

"Madame Yavirrt," I began, rushing forward to catch her before she could move far from the lounge, "may I have a word? My name is Stchvk."

She looked bewildered. It was evident that she hadn't had much sleep. Her topaz eyes took a moment to focus on me, lids too heavy to open fully even if she perceived me as a threat.

"Who…?" she began.

"Stchvk Investigations. I'm looking into the attack on your mate," I continued, intentionally crowding her both physically and verbally. I wanted her off-balance, before any preconceptions set in. I hated using her distressed condition to my advantage but couldn't afford to be considerate.

"Mmm? I've already talked to the detective and our Clan representative, not to mention, I just testified publicly. What else is there? Who...?" she tried to ask again.

"I'm representing Herd Torbur," I admitted, pausing to let her jump into my trap.

As expected, her expression hardened and she showed teeth as her lip lifted in a snarl. "I have nothing to say to them. Direct all inquiries to our Clan..."

I cut her off with a low bow of abasement, curling my claws under and saying, "I beg your indulgence. I am not here to defend Grust nor ask your Clan's forgiveness. I am actually not a publicly declared asset. My purpose is to determine if Grust will remain Herd or should be banished from Torbur."

As I intended, she stilled to listen as I started and then looked troubled as I finished my explanation. Banishment was a terrible punishment, even if Grust killed Tharrliki. It essentially meant that the Herd wished to end all association with its former member. Banishment was an implicit acknowledgment not of incidental guilt, but of deep flaws that made the individual unsuitable for family membership.

You have to do some really heinous, anti-social things to get banished. Among other things, formal banishment means very little likelihood of reproduction, probable poverty, minimal social support, and permanent stigma. It's very rare for a banished member of any Great Family group to be accepted again into any new group, with the exception of some renegade families.

The latter aren't a great alternative. Most of their members are already considered unfit by one group and usually have only that abandonment in common. At best, members get some social interaction but are still branded undesirable in public. At worst, members likely are involved in some criminal enterprise, willingly or not. After all, these are sapients with no other options and little else to lose, particularly their reputations.

A Vislin like me, left effectively Pack-less by the imprisonment or flight of his Pack-mates, is considered less unsavory than a member of a renegade family. At least, I left my Pack willingly. My Pack-mates disqualified themselves from ever banishing *me*, by being notorious criminals. I looked noble, by comparison.

That is, I'd look that way if I ever mentioned the circumstances of my abandonment in public. I keep my sordid past a strict secret. Until now, for some reason. You should feel privileged.

Anyway, out of our three species, banishment is hardest on a Taratumm. Isolated, they tend to develop mental problems that typically culminate in suicide or self-destructive behavior amounting to the same thing. That is, presuming they weren't already on a bad path to begin with.

Most Herds, finding a member guilty of a crime, will at least stand by them, continuing to plead their innocence or at least trying to explain the "temporary indiscretion". In severe cases, the Herd might admit guilt but then require the wayward member to seek help, in the form of psychiatric care, expiation, or whatever treatment is necessary to avert future problems.

In theory, family is a great force for social correction. In reality, most Herds just ignore whatever misdeeds don't tarnish their reputation too badly or hurt those within the same Herd. Not coincidentally, betraying members of your own Herd is the number one way to get banished. As I've said, that's great for enforcing loyalty but really lousy for an objective legal system.

For Herd Torbur to consider banishing Grust, he would have to be suspected of something particularly nasty and incurable or not worth the trouble to cure.

They weren't, of course. I was lying outright. But the suggestion that a worse fate than imprisonment might await her lover's attacker gave Yavirrt reason to stop, think, and talk to me. I hoped she would either be vindictive enough to share lurid details of the attack and ensure Grust's damnation… or else compassionate enough to offer moderating evidence to prevent Grust's doom.

It seemed to be the latter. She looked stunned and took a step backwards.

I prompted, "If I could just have a word, in private, I have only a few questions that would help the Herd make their decision."

She nodded and stepped further back into the lounge, "I understand. I'll answer what I can. What he did… it was terrible. Inexcusable. But I hate to think he couldn't be helped."

"That's what I need to find out. I've already reviewed your testimony, both to the constables and to the court," I lied again. "What I'm looking for is something further, most likely something you didn't know was important."

She continued to look perplexed. "Like what? I'm certain I mentioned everything I could remember."

I sat down on one of the low couches which worked as compromise seating for the three morphologies of Great Family sapients. She took my cue and sat as well, although she perched on the edge of a couch on the opposite side of the room.

"First," I ticked off, "Grust might have been influenced by others. Or perhaps others knew what he intended and failed to restrain him. Did anyone exit the Thunder Bar not long before or shortly after Grust?"

She twitched her tail in negation. "No, his Herd mates didn't come out until after the… attack. I said so."

"All right, I wasn't sure the detective had been that thorough. Still, someone could have stayed inside after speaking with him. Can I borrow your compad? I'd like to go through some of the witnesses and see if you recognize anyone. There were a few bystanders that weren't called by the court, after all."

She hesitated but eventually gave in. I may not be a social scientist, but I'm a student of the mind by necessity. By involving her personally in my questioning, by asking her for small favors, I was encouraging her to think of me favorably. We were on the same side, despite my employment by the other side.

I kept the compad angled toward her as I logged in to my remote storage and brought up the files from Herd Torbur. The fact that I had access to their case notes helped to validate my cover story. I flipped through the obvious roster, first showing her all the Taratumm that were at the scene of the crime.

Bad Egg

She recognized Grust's Herd mates, Veruth and Ktuck, both from their belated efforts to stop Grust and from their appearances in court. The other Taratumm were mysteries to her. I described the bartender, making up a name, 'Kmeth', to make it sound as if I had researched her background, as well. Yavirrt had no familiarity with her. The bartender never stepped outside, after all.

I went through the small number of Vislin who were present, with the same results. Other than her own Clan-assigned bodyguards, Yavirrt never saw any of the Vislin before or during the assault, only long afterward, in court.

I was actually impressed with Clan Takerrl's integrity. They could have briefed Yavirrt thoroughly about the case before her court appearance, ensuring that her testimony caused maximum damage to Grust's defense. Certainly, her Clan could afford *almost* as thorough an investigation as Herd Torbur.

Granted, they already might have done so… in which case Madame Yavirrt was a brilliant actor. She would have to be expertly faking both extreme fatigue and extensive ignorance of the case. I doubted I could be fooled so completely otherwise.

I suppose that's boastful. I might sound like I'm promoting myself as a smooth-talking master of urban espionage, with all sorts of tools to dig data out of unlikely cracks. That picture is only partially true. I do have some useful skills, gleaned through simple necessity, hard experience, a few generous tutors, a decent childhood education, and some self-study. But a portion of my success comes from luck. I *have* botched a number of cases. In *this* case, I was doing things quick and dirty, sacrificing stealth and secrecy in favor of speed.

For example, I imagine you picked up on my trail at the hospital. Maybe the throwaway login I used to find Tharrliki flagged some search for suspicious activity. Maybe Yavirrt talked to someone afterward who raised the alarm. Frost, maybe the constables' report on my mess at the Thunder Bar tipped you off.

Whatever it was, I couldn't worry about being noticed as long as no one caught me until *after* I exonerated Grust and earned my payday. If I did my job well, Herd Torbur might even defend me against any criminal charges racked up along the way. I hated that thought, but not so much as to refuse their help.

One of the lucky leaps that kept me ahead of you came when I finished the list of witnesses with Yavirrt. The last entries were about the Hrotata present. Yavirrt recognized the shopkeeper she met before but verified that she hadn't seen him again after leaving his store. She didn't recall the various passers-by who fled Grust's rampage later.

But, rrr, did she bristle when I showed her a picture of Krrutoki: the gawker who watched me getting bludgeoned the prior night. Per the investigation reports, he was also present at Trrptet Thunder Bar the night Grust blew a fuse.

He was also a familiar face to Yavirrt. She explained, "I know Krrutoki. He lives in that neighborhood... where I used to live until Mother was elected district Councilor. We grew up together. I didn't realize he was there that night. I suppose it makes sense. He likes that area. I just didn't know he'd be interested in the Thunder Bar."

My nostrils were quivering with a rising scent. "You know him from childhood? That detail definitely was *not* in any of the official reports. Krrutoki didn't mention it."

"I didn't realize he was a witness. I'm surprised he didn't say he knew me. Or maybe I'm not surprised. He might still be angry."

I restrained the urge to shake the already traumatized Hrotata female. "Angry? About what?"

She shook herself out of reverie and unconsciously licked her paw to start grooming. More Hrotata spit. I avoided pointing out her stress reaction and tried to keep her focused on the questions.

After a moment's pause to slick down her cheek fur, she answered: "Angry about Tharrliki. About Clan Takerrl. Krrutoki thought we might be mated. He courted me. My birth Clan had other ideas and introduced me to Tharrliki. We're a good match for many reasons; we really complement each other well. It is true that my mother's daughter becoming a matron of a rising Clan like his benefits us all. I am blessed that I also found love."

Bad Egg

She continued, the words spilling out: "Krrutoki pressed the issue. He wanted me to reject Tharrliki's proposal and return to him. I was young and indecisive. Our Clans put pressure on Krrutoki to leave me alone. Clan Takerrl, especially, warned him off. Tharrliki and I were mated. I moved into Clan Takerrl's housing and lost touch with Krrutoki. I thought it was best. I had hoped he would find someone else, move on, and forget me."

"But he didn't," I ventured, risking interruption to test a theory.

"No," she admitted, "but he seemed to have given up trying to win me back. We talked again about a cycle ago. Little things, casual things, like our work routine and dining preferences. I heard from him last about six days ago. He was telling me about a new silversmith's shop that opened in our old neighborhood."

"How did he sound then?" I prompted.

She caught my meaning and began to look sharper, more alert. Her tone when she answered was defensive. "Exactly the same: pleasant, calm, and open, like he just wanted to be friends again. Let me be clear: Krrutoki has never since brought up his suit, never threatened me or Tharrliki, and is not associated with your Grust in any way."

I lowered my head in agreeable submission. "I understand. It seems unlikely to me as well. You understand, though, that I must investigate every possibility. Are you certain Krrutoki has no prior connection to Grust?"

"Yes," she spat back, reflexively, but then reconsidered. "Actually, I don't know for certain. I suppose they could know one another, if they frequented the same bar. It might be worth talking to Krrutoki in case he does know Grust as an acquaintance. Perhaps he knows something of interest."

She sighed, deflated again. "If I know him, Krrutoki will try to defend even a Taratumm if he considers him a friend. He might be upset he couldn't stop the stomper." Her use of the Vislin epithet for Taratumm was an odd slip for a Hrotata, probably reflecting her anger at her mate's attacker.

"Well, I can't think of any other questions right now. I really appreciate your time, Madame." I spoke quickly, ready to hurry away. I was anxious to leave; I had been fortunate to have that much time undetected at the hospital.

I was also particularly anxious to talk to Krrutoki himself, given new revelations. Despite Yavirrt's defense, I was growing increasingly convinced that a certain lovesick Hrotata had a key role in Grust's actions... not to mention the bruises on my poor body.

For that matter, my pain pills were wearing off. I rose to my feet with considerable effort. A twinge made me stagger forward, gasping. Yavirrt rose hastily and steadied me. Her wet paw contacted my scales.

I had a few seconds to realize that we were soon going to be slightly better friends. Or at least, *I* would be more *her* friend than I was before. I had to get going before I started feeling bad about exploiting her.

"Thank you again, Madame Yavirrt. My injuries are a hazard of my job, I'm afraid. Some people get offended when you ask certain questions and demonstrate their displeasure with over-enthusiastic ejections." I tried to sound wryly humorous. To my own ears, I sounded pathetic and nervous.

"You're welcome... Stchvk. If you do talk to Krrutoki, please don't mention that I told you about our history. I'd like to keep him as a friend." Her words were diplomatic, but her gaze held a sharpened edge that made me wary. She was starting to suspect something.

"Of course. Very discreet. Well, good day," I concluded, turning and striding from the room. I must have looked like I had something to run away from. Again, haste left an obvious trail behind me.

Don't think I'm putting down your investigative skills. I'm sure finding me took some work, especially in this city, on *this* planet. I could have made it much harder if I was trying, that's all.

At the time, though, I had a Hrotata to catch fast and grill on high heat.

Figuratively speaking, of course.

Chapter 7 - Unfair Fight

The effects of the Hrotata neurotoxin actually came in handy, buffering the increasing discomfort from my aching neck. My second round of pain pills had almost worn off. I could feel a dull throb starting from deep inside my neck, spreading into my shoulder. I started to worry that something was seriously broken in there. Leaving the hospital felt like an increasingly bad idea.

That's where sapience comes in: following through on a bad idea because, maybe at some higher level, it's part of a bigger good idea. The good idea, in this case, was cracking a case, getting paid, and *then* relaxing in a hospital bed afterward. I know, funny to say in retrospect.

I took the lift down from the tenth floor of Vaktrri Medical to the lobby, then discarded the unregistered guest tag I had borrowed. I didn't know if an alarm would signal if I tried to leave with the microchipped tag, but there was no reason to chance it.

I did my best to look like a patient being discharged rather than a patient needing admission for treatment. My one-handed, homemade bandage job wouldn't pass close inspection as professional work, but it sufficed to get me out the door unnoticed.

I went out the front door. No sense exiting through the emergency room and chancing a second meeting with staff who could recognize me. From the entrance, it was only a few steps to an aircar depot. The skimmers were kept close for sapients exactly like me: patients with limited mobility.

As I keyed in my credit code to authorize release of one of the floating pods, disaster struck.

Insufficient balance. Frost, of course it was insufficient. I had already paid for two aircar rides in the last two days, from an account that was barely sufficient to keep me in synthetic protein for a week.

Nathan Large with Laine Megan Lundquist

To be fair, I really wouldn't starve, no matter how broke I got. There are public feeding stations in Layafflr City. Otherwise, the huddled masses would start dying in the streets… or rioting in them, more likely. The Great Family has enough sense to make sure basic survival needs are met. Starving Vislin are dangerous neighbors, after all. Most families take care of their own and the government does its best to pick up what slack remains.

However, surviving isn't living, and it's still very difficult to lift off from the bottom of a financial gravity well. Mobility is a problem, for one thing: not just economic mobility but the literal problem of getting from one place to another. Public transit has a cost. That cost hasn't been socialized in Layafflr City, at least not yet.

There are also some areas you have to have clearance to enter, which means registration fees, background checks, and other credit sinks. For instance, I couldn't actually have registered as a patient at Vaktrri Medical. I wasn't cleared for its access. If I were more socially or economically valuable, I could obtain that clearance in the span of a few tail twitches.

I wasn't. I still am not. I'm not sure I *want* to be, if you catch my meaning. Still, it could be nice. Right then, I would have settled for enough credit for an aircar ride, plus maybe another bottle of pain pills. Since that wasn't happening – and I wasn't going to steal any of the above – I had to find another route to visit Krrutoki.

I slumped further down the street to a public info terminal. At least their major functions were free: weather reports, public media, shopping services, and directory assistance. I looked up Krrutoki of Clan… Chevrruk. I made sure I was matching up the right Hrotata of that name by confirming the address. It was in my neighborhood, as it turned out. I committed the address to memory. Now, I had a destination. I just needed a way to get back there.

I *could* afford a tram or train, but that route would be slow, cramped, and exposed. If I let it get past dark, Krrutoki would likely return to his favorite haunt, the Thunder Bar. I suspected my appearance there would be unwelcome.

I was wasting time. There *was* one other avenue I hadn't explored. No, not aircar hijacking. Asking for help.

Bad Egg

Continuing with the directory search, I looked up Shllokwa of Herd Torbur. 'Counselor' was her official title on the Herd's business site. *There's* a word with many meanings.

Her business number was listed as well. I initiated a call. A minuscule fee was charged to my credit balance, a tiny cost in comparison to transport fare.

If I'd been foresighted enough to bring my compad along, I could have accessed Shllokwa's private number and placed the call from the miniaturized computer. The problem there was that the device contained some sensitive information I'd rather not worry about protecting. Plus, the compad itself was an important tool in my work, an expensive one, and thus literally irreplaceable. Besides the possibility of theft, the likelihood of damage was high while I was working a case... at least as high as the likelihood of damage to myself. One of these days, I'll get myself a nice, shock-proof, lockable compad case... around the same time I buy a full larder, a new set of armor, a personal aircar, and a penthouse apartment, in that order.

So, I used the public systems: easy to overhear, easy to tap, easy to trace. You're welcome. At least the conversation wasn't too suspicious out of context.

It started with the standard answer: "You have reached the offices of Mistress Shllokwa of Herd Torbur. My name is Esstvarr. How may we assist you?" This greeting was delivered by the image of a chubby, young, tan-on-brown male Hrotata.

I played it calm and professional, my manners helped by Yavirrt's lingering saliva. "Stchvk. Urgent news to report to your Mistress regarding Herd business. *Extremely immediate.*"

The Hrotata kept a bland expression but typed something into his keypad with admirable speed. The result must have been encouraging, because he didn't challenge me... much. "Mistress Shllokwa is currently meeting with elders. May I relay any important messages?"

"No, sorry, and she'll want to hear this on a secure line. She can call me back right here, if she really can't get free this second, but it's time sensitive and private. Sorry, but she likely will punish you if you fail to inform her soon." I refrained from speculation about the personal relationship between "Mistress" Shllokwa and her youthful secretary. Judging from her behavior with me, her punishments might take some interesting forms.

"I… understand. Please hold," Esstvarr responded. He might have been placating me, except that his answer was punctuated with a bristling twitch. I was handing him a dilemma, but I wasn't sorry. He was getting paid – likely very well – to make such judgments correctly.

The video feed switched to a pastoral scene from Hrotata Prime, something neutral and relaxing for any Great Family species. I only had to watch the video pacifier for a couple of hectads before the picture swapped back to Shllokwa, seated at the same desk Esstvarr had vacated.

"What is it?" she snapped without preamble. Her disapproval stung my narcotized feelings. I wanted her to be pleased with me. Too bad the Hrotata couldn't just dose themselves with their own neurotoxins, I thought, they'd be more amiable.

"I have a solid lead. I can go into detail if you want, if you think it's safe. I think I know who set up Grust, and why… I just need to check them out to determine *how*. Problem is, I'm stuck downtown, they're back near my office, and I'm broke as an empty eggshell. Any chance of an advance on the promise of success? A retainer? Low-interest loan? Please?"

She sneered at the camera pickup. I couldn't see from that angle, but I was sure her tail tip was flicking in aggravation. "This is *not* the proper method of contact. No, don't give any specifics. Even if I encode your call on this side, you're still at a public terminal. Unless you truly are seconds away from a breakthrough, my opinion of your professional ability will plummet, fatally. I can advance you enough for a couple of aircar fares. If your next call to me doesn't give amazing and specific revelations – in complete privacy – expect to be billed double for repayment. Anything else to waste my time?"

"No, Mistress," I answered respectfully. She finally realized that my wheedling, courteous approach wasn't just pathetic beggary or a bad attempt at comedy. Her fur lowered and she stared at my image on her screen with a slightly wider eye.

Bad Egg

"You're drugged," she cleverly deduced. "Who have you been consorting with?"

I stuck out my tongue, pleased to have shocked her, even if her suspicions were exaggerated. "Sorry, Mistress, can't say. Not a secure line." To keep her from going away angry, I backpedaled, visibly curling my claws under. "It's just narcotics for pain. I took a couple of punches while asking questions."

She looked impressed despite her suspicions. "I see. The wrong questions... or the right ones? Never mind, the funds are transferred to your account. See that you use them well."

"Of course, Mistress." I was starting to come out of the Hrotata-induced daze but continued my act for maximum tail-nuzzling effect. I could use the credit for later, when I returned to my usual surly self.

Shllokwa cut the connection. I used a few more seconds of public comm access to verify my credit balance. It had more than doubled after Herd Torbur's contribution, however stinting. Enough crouching; it was time to spring.

I returned to the aircar stand and wasted no time selecting and settling into my transport. Again, I had the luxury of a few quiet decads to collect my thoughts and prepare for my ambush meeting with Krrutoki.

If he wasn't home, I might take the opportunity to break into his quarters and see what I could find. I wasn't sure whether he lived alone in a public apartment, in a private building owned by his Clan, or in a shared dormitory. Given what I already knew of him – an unmated male fixated on an unattainable female – he wouldn't have a partner or family members sharing his space. There could be roommates, though: other bachelors splitting a room or apartment.

If Krrutoki *was* home, we'd have a very frank, pointed conversation. I planned to confront him with what I knew. If he ran or attacked me, I'd be certain I had found the guilty sapient. Then, it would become a matter for the constables to sort out. Given my previous call, Herd Torbur would prevent him from wriggling out of arrest. I was fairly certain I could defend myself in a fight, provided he wasn't better armed or shot me without warning.

Nathan Large with Laine Megan Lundquist

The worst outcome would be if he just ignored me or protested baffled innocence. I wouldn't let up on him – I couldn't play nice with so little time left – but I'd have to work much harder if he played cool and let nothing slip. I could be in for a slow night of stalking, if I had to tail him throughout his social rounds. Actually, the worst result would be Krrutoki barricading himself at home all day and night, into the next day, letting the trial run out while I waited.

I was going to have to be a provocative bastard once again. Good thing I've had practice. It was almost tempting to start a fight, myself, just to get him tangled up in the legal system… but I didn't want to get stuck in a cage, myself.

No, I needed him to react to my presence and my accusations. I wanted to see the guilt register on his greasy little face. The only thing I could effectively threaten him with was the truth.

Too bad I didn't have much truth to throw at him. Then again, I didn't have to *admit* the limits of my knowledge. If anything, pretending to know more than I really did could work just as well. I allowed myself a predatory flex of claws and beak. Might as well enjoy the hunt.

When the aircar pulled up at the specified destination, my crest rose still higher. I was in luck: mass housing. The target building was just one of a half-dozen identical stacks of plasticized concrete spanning one side of an equally nondescript lane. Even if Clan Chevrruk owned the whole block, Krrutoki's apartment was nothing special. I didn't have to worry about armed security or even protective neighbors. My arrival was likely being recorded from two or three angles, but surveillance was hard to avoid anywhere.

My primary obstacle was the locked outer door, a sandwich of clear plastic and steel built securely into the wall. It opened by sliding along a fixed track. I didn't have the tools to force it open. There was no lock to pick, only an identity scanner. Lacking the necessary code or retinal or genetic configuration to identify myself as a resident, I would have to be admitted from within. An intercom panel offered the only means of access.

When in doubt, I default to improvisation. I punched the number for Krrutoki's apartment and waited a few seconds. No answer.

Bad Egg

I tried the same sequence again, but this time, spoke aloud: "Hey, you in there. I know you recognize me. We're going to have a conversation one way or another. Either you let me in and we talk privately inside… or else I start talking REALLY LOUD out here, by myself. I hope you're home, or else your neighbors are going to hear some really interesting thoughts."

My clever gambit paid off. The intercom spoke back, with a voice obscured by fur and phlegm. "I don't know who you are or what you're talking about. Go away now or I'll call security."

Kkk, this prey was terrible at deflecting suspicion. I laughed – just like that, "Kkk" – and called back, "Krrutoki of Clan Chevrruk, I'm here to talk about your visits to Trrptet Thunder Bar…."

My introduction was cut off by a buzzer from the door and a yowling curse: "Filth in your nest! Come in, then."

This visit was shaping up to a really memorable discussion. I might get to run through my entire vocabulary of vulgarities. Frost, I might learn one or two new ones.

I hurried to seize the offered entry, sliding the rightmost door along its track and slipping into the building's lobby. Playing it safe, I skipped the lifts and took two flights of stairs up to Krrutoki's floor. From there, I only had to pass two doors on the left and I was at the right number. That proximity was just as well. After all that exertion, I was feeling nauseated and a pulsing flame was working its way up the side of my face. I'm fortunate I didn't suffer a stroke or embolism, now that I think about it. I had much more suffering to look forward to.

I scratched at the plate on Krrutoki's door. He yelled from somewhere inside, "It's open!"

I couldn't blame him. In the same circumstances, I wouldn't have opened the door myself if I could avoid it. I obliged the yolk-sucking little vermin and toggled the latch, pushing his door open carefully in case he was hiding behind the barrel of a plasma thrower.

Nathan Large with Laine Megan Lundquist

Nothing came flying at me except more vitriol. Krrutoki did have a weapon: an ornamental wooden staff usually carried by Taratumm elders during... some kind of ceremony, I forget the name. It was the kind of thing you can pick up at antique stores as tacky ethnic home décor. He was holding the massive staff in two hands... Kkk...

Sorry, sorry, I'm getting silly now. I'm nervous, you know? Dumb jokes are funnier when you're afraid for your life. Not as funny for you? Vvv, your loss.

Anyway, he waved the substitute phallus in a sad attempt to look menacing. I was concerned when I thought I might be incinerated. Actually seeing him, I was amused. I could take three of Krrutoki, even injured as I was.

Like I thought at the Thunder Bar, he seemed small for an adult male Hrotata and maybe a bit thin. His eyes were sunken but still bright, not sick but probably stressed. His light brown fur had thin stripes of black in a rippling pattern, easy to miss in the dark. He was still wearing the same business outfit I saw him in before, although it looked better laundered that second time.

I stepped confidently into the apartment. It was bigger than mine, no surprise. Even a struggling bachelor Hrotata in a middle-class Clan rates better housing than I can afford. The furniture wasn't as nice as mine, though. It was all prefab, budget, assemble-by-the-numbers junk, covered with souvenirs of equally boring vacations. Some miniature projectors showed still images and videos of other Hrotata. Family recordings, most likely.

I counted no fewer than five likenesses of Yavirrt in my initial survey. Krrutoki definitely had a problem letting go.

After taking a leisurely look around – confirming that there were no roommates or other confederates waiting to jump me – I closed the door.

"What's this about? I didn't have anything to do with those Taratumm attacking you. I'm sorry I didn't help, but neither did the Vislin who were there. If you hurt me, my Clan will ruin you." He chattered almost too fast to follow, his native language's accent muddying the Great Family's mutually pronounceable patois.

Bad Egg

I waved to Rtrtr, at my hip. "If I wanted to hurt you, I would have already. If I didn't already *know* you set those Taratumm on me, I'd be certain of it after that pathetic protest. I know how you did it... what I want to know is why. You didn't like how I was talking to that stomper at the bar? You were bored and wanted another floor show? Or was it because I was getting too close to figuring out how you ruined that filth-eating imbecile... Grust?"

His lip quivered between a defiant snarl and panicked tightness. His eyes ricocheted around the room, watching me, the exits, maybe other available weapons. I didn't need to be a student of Hrotata behavior to recognize guilt and fear.

He snarled, "I told you, mother-eater, I was just there for a drink. You made your own trouble. Obviously, you can't help your paranoia. Go get psychiatric help. Leave me alone."

I abruptly changed direction to ease him back from the brink. This furball wasn't any sort of mastermind. Definitely an amateur, way out of his burrow.

With my best intimation of confidence, I told him, "You have me all wrong. I only threatened to get your attention. I'm hoping we could work together. See, I hate living around Taratumm. I hate having their noisy pit in our neighborhood. If you're manipulating them, humiliating them, like I think you are, we might be able to do business. I know you were there when Grust frenzied. Having him proposition that high-class matron... brilliant."

Wrong approach, again. Krrutoki's expression stayed wary but became tinged with disgust. Nostrils flaring, he spat back, "Yes, I was there. But it wasn't my fault. You sicken me. You're full of excremental fantasies and the constables will deal with you."

I tried Plan C: sinister. "The constables? If I have to, I'll talk to them instead. The stompers are already shamed... but I could explain how the Hrotata 'masters' exploit the violent nature of their thick-skulled slaves, using them as weapons..."

Pause a moment here. Even given my stated goal to provoke Krrutoki, this taunt was laying it on a little thick. I'm not really that kind of bigot. As I talked, though, I was getting more and more angry, disgusted, and yes, paranoid.

Driving these emotions from underneath, as it always is, was fear. At the time, I interpreted my own rising fear as worry about the case. I *had* to crack this furry egg. I was in too deep to stop. If I didn't make my threats believable, I would lose the lead, lose the case, lose my business… I could lose everything.

I won't take up more time detailing the rest of my rant. You probably don't want to hear that kind of foulness. Suffice it to say I outdid myself, laying out a grandiose plan of interspecies war and apartheid, with Krrutoki as the instrumental genius… or the martyred patsy, as he so chose. He stood aghast, both of us feeling the grip of unreasoning terror and hatred.

Finally, he had had enough. He screamed, "GET OUT!"

Between words, between thoughts, I obeyed.

I had no choice. My mind agreed with him completely. I was too afraid to think. I needed to GET OUT, that very moment. If I didn't leave, something unimaginably horrible would happen to me, probably involving horrendous pain.

I sought out the nearest exit. The door was closed. The window was closer, not to mention a faster route out. My hyper-focused mind pointed my body in the necessary direction and kept it moving forward.

My panic was like frenzy, but frenzy at a new level. This feeling was to frenzy what orgasm is to a caress. There was *nothing else* in my mind, no little voices suggesting alternate ideas or guiding me away from hazards… nothing. Just fear and the most clear and immediate response to relieve that fear.

When I was outside, it would stop. That thought wasn't a promise, it was certain knowledge. Just get outside, and the dark, wrenching torment would let go of my mind.

The worst thing about that experience wasn't the horrible feeling itself. The worst part wasn't even when I went through the window and fell two stories to the street below.

I was lacerated, both by the glass and by the reinforcing wire meant to hold it in place. I hit the pavement below with an impact that wrenched my upper ankles and tail. I narrowly missed cracking my beak on the ground as I fell forward. I *did* lose two claws catching myself as I landed.

No, the worst part came afterward, when my mind eventually began to clear. The worst part was the memory of what I had felt, lurking just around the corner of my psyche. It was the knowledge that the nightmare could *come back* again, at any time, just as awful and just as unavoidable. I've dealt with criminals I considered monstrous. They were adorable hatchlings compared to this horror.

I would have run further, except for my sprained ankles. Every step was making the damage worse, so after two blocks I was basically crawling. The pain kept trying to renew my frenzy, but by that point, I was burned out. There weren't any more hormones left for my glands to pump. I collapsed at the edge of an alley between two businesses. I remember one was a diner; the awful smell was distinctive.

There was also an awful sound. It took me a couple of hectads to recognize it: the screech of a constabulary alarm. No surprise, in retrospect. I probably tripped an alarm going through the window, or else a neighbor noticed my elegant dive into the street. A cruiser raced by and stopped half a block away from me.

I was still far enough gone to fumble for my heater… I was afraid Krrutoki would catch me and hurt me more. Praise Kktkrkz' crushing jaws that I was too weak to draw the weapon. The constables would have used their paralytic darts first, just to be safe. As it was, the two of them, both Vislin, approached me cautiously with their guns aimed.

I lay still and let them disarm me. My mind was finally pulling itself together, despite the agonies shouting at it from every direction. I heard the constables call for medical support and I clicked in agreement.

Let them take me into custody, into care. I could finally rest, recover, and then recount what I had learned. Herd Torbur would take care of the details.

You see, I finally knew what caused Grust to become so strangely aroused. I knew what directed that arousal toward an unlikely target. I knew what made those other Taratumm rise in anger against me. The same source had just projected its terror into my mind, sending me running in sympathetic flight.

Nathan Large with Laine Megan Lundquist

We were all puppets of Krrutoki's psyche. The rotten sack of entrails was psychic. He might not even realize it. He might only be able to affect others when experiencing extreme emotions. But he most definitely was the cause of all the recent troubles surrounding himself.

Whether or not Krrutoki was a bad egg, Grust was not. Being reeking drunk probably made him more vulnerable, but intoxication was no crime. His proposal to Yavirrt and challenge to Tharrliki were all Krrutoki's wishes being acted out by proxy. Everything else that happened afterward was also Krrutoki's fault.

I'd have to leave it up to the authorities to determine if his mind bending was intentional or not. Did Krrutoki lure Tharrliki into proximity near the Thunder Bar in order to attack him? Or did he only want Yavirrt close… then became jealous at seeing her with a new mate… then overwhelmed a nearby, receptive mind with his projection of that frustration?

The specifics weren't my problem anymore. I was out of the game, benched with injuries. I got my medical care, in the secure clinic of the nearest constable station. I was left there overnight. I slept in a medicated haze, while other sapients worried over my recent actions and my fate.

When I woke up, I was stripped bare except for a neck support collar and casts wrapped around my upper legs. Nothing remained of the multiple cuts I sustained going through the window. The benefits of advanced medicine are grand, for those who can afford them or get the government to pay for them. There was still deep, throbbing pain in my neck and tail base, but it had receded from 'fatal' to 'unpleasant'. My ankles, though, hurt even through the drugs.

I sat up in the bed and looked around the room. Not far away was a folded prison jumpsuit, the gleaming red of freshly spilled mammalian blood. I don't know if those things are meant to be humiliating or just easy to spot. It was less embarrassing than going around nude, so I struggled to pull on the provided uniform.

You know how the story goes from there. I expected, eventually, to be led from the clinic, either to an interview room, a less comfortable holding cell, or else a judge's bench. I was prepared to ask for counsel – hopefully Herd Torbur would take my call – and then explain my whole insane but factually supported story.

Instead, you, and you, and that cute spotted female that hasn't come back yet, you all showed up. I got a dose of happy gas sprayed in my face and woke up here. Considering how long I've been talking, happily and honestly, without the urge to shut up and ask for my lawyer, I'm still under the influence of *something*.

Drugs? Grust didn't have that excuse. I suspect I don't, either.

You also just listened to that entire insane story   I didn't see any skepticism on your faces or hear any objections, so I suspect I got it right. I'm really, *really*, hoping my information gets back to Herd Torbur in time.

I also hope you caught Krrutoki, unless he's smarter than he looked and started running at the same time I did. He's dangerous to everyone around him, left unsupervised.

I suppose it's too much to ask that the truth be made public. This kind of back room discussion suggests something more private, maybe secret… possibly top secret. I hope you're not the kind of audience that makes sure I have another accident after this interview, involving memory-destroying brain damage if not my early demise.

If not, do you have enough conscience to prevent an innocent sapient from being disgraced and imprisoned for most of his life? If I'm right, and I'm talking to the psychic constables or whatever you call yourselves, then you could nudge a few minds the right direction. Even if you can't let the truth about Krrutoki get out, could you manage something believable that lets the dumb brute go free?

At the least, could you let his Herd know Grust is innocent, and that I found the proof? Presuming you let me leave here, with or without my memories, I'd really like to retain my reputation. I solved this case all on my own. I practically led you to the troublemaker. I hope that makes me valuable.

If you're really feeling generous, any chance I could still get paid?

Broken Record

Chapter 1 - Wish I Weren't Here

I was coming to the end of a spectacular warm season. The beaches were clean and perfectly warm, the skies were clear, and I was more fit and rested than I had been in years. It was a shame that I had to return home to Layafflr City. Still, a rented waterfront nest is expensive. Since my latest client was no longer footing my bills, I couldn't stick around.

I had only two major regrets from that last job. The more important problem was that I hadn't met any potential mates on my working vacation, not even a play-partner. I think I'm a pretty impressive Vislin male, physically speaking: good scales, clean beak, nearly all my claws, plenty of youthful muscle still hanging in there.

I might not be the best bet for stability – self-employed in a dangerous field, still Pack-less after several years, and considered a rogue element by my local constabulary – but old Stchvk ought to be good enough for a warm season romance. I was out among the resorts, wealthy enough (while the pay lasted), well-dressed (when I was renting formal armor on an expense account), confident...

Sss, those coastal females know a poser when they see one.

The other problem was that I hadn't actually *finished* the job. I was looking into a theft. The client never actually said what was stolen. He only described its container: a suitcase. I was supposed to track down the whatever-it-was and tell him who took it.

Broken Record

The client was Jevvettr, a Hrotata hotel magnate, hence the swanky beachfront property. I got to pretend to be a well-heeled guest while I examined the building, Jevvettr's penthouse suite (from which the whatever disappeared), the surrounding neighborhood, and whatever other lead I thought worthwhile. I wasn't trying to stretch out my free stay. The trail was too thin to make much progress, but *just* thick enough to keep me searching and my patron paying.

I did narrow the field of culprits, but never pointed my claw at any single suspect. After two weeks, Jevvettr got tired of waiting and cut me loose.

On my maglev ride home, the names of the suspects were already getting fuzzy. I hadn't been too personally invested in the case, anyway. Stealing a whatever wasn't the same as murder or even cheating on a mate. It was a crime, sure, but a rich furball like Jevvettr could buy a new whatever. Frost, he hadn't even been too upset about losing the thing. It was more like he was funding my search as a formality, maybe as a show to convince his insurer that he hadn't just broken or lost it. Or stolen it himself. Whatever it was.

But if I was hired just to help with insurance fraud, the whatever must have been worth quite a few credits. In addition to the cost of my suite, my host allowed me a free meal each day – after all, I had to eat in the restaurant to impress the other high rollers – and an allowance for clothing. The total cost in expenses far exceeded my usual retainer. Jevvettr was spared my final fee, since I hadn't closed the case.

I wished I could care more. Maybe all the luxury dulled my usual instincts. Usually, I get pretty uptight about lawbreaking, even little nonviolent stuff. Somebody got away with theft. Why wasn't I angry about that? I typically also have more professional pride. The job wouldn't go in the 'failure' column – for one thing, I was alive and not even wounded – but it wasn't a success, either.

Rrr, I'd have to call it a much-deserved vacation. Apparently, my moral meter considered me off the clock. I could get extra uptight about the next murder, assault or whatever case I was hired to solve after returning home.

Come to think of it, I hadn't closed my previous case, either, had I...?

Nathan Large with Laine Megan Lundquist

I drifted off in the midst of self-recriminations. By the time I roused from sleep, the maglev was minutes away from Layafflr City. Home again, to the aggressive flora and equally aggressive fauna – especially the sapient kind – of my chosen territory.

I disembarked at Kchzzkt Station, the main maglev depot for Layafflr City. Since my home-slash-office is located in outer Layafflr, where the maglev lines don't penetrate, I was obliged to take an aircar the last few kilometers. I might have walked it, but my ankles were acting up from an old injury. For some reason, my flank ached, too; I must have slept awkwardly. I decided that I didn't need my usual desperate thrift. I still had some credits banked from Jevvettr's retainer.

Not that I had much luggage to haul. One small case held everything I needed to take on vacation: my best armor, a cheap grooming kit, my only slightly less cheap compad, and my best friend, Rtrtr the heat projector.

Sapients on most worlds might be horrified that I brought a weapon on public transport, much less a weapon without proper registration. Frost that; I'm a Vislin on a Great Family world. A Vislin's right to personal armament is enshrined in the treaty creating the Family. Besides, we carry deadly weapons on our faces and hands.

Moreover, this world is *ChttKttp*, and only the poor, stupid, young or powerful travel here unarmed. I'm a decently intelligent adult. I'm not wealthy or important enough to have guards. As I mentioned, I don't have a Pack for protection. I *am* pretty poor, but I was better off when I bought Rtrtr.

Sss, I was better off financially. I suppose I had other advantages of a Pack back then. No one would mess with me when Pack Vzrrk was around. But when they *weren't* around, I needed a weapon. We weren't known well enough to intimidate anyone with just our Pack name... not like Pack Tktkrrf or Herd Torbur. *Those* are names to back away from, apologizing profusely. Nope, Vzrrk was small-time, vicious but unestablished.

We *wanted* respect, of course, even if that meant notoriety and infamy rather than reverence. We were criminals: thieves, smugglers, hackers, and confidence tricksters. Pack Vzrrk really wanted to be a mercenary outfit, but none of us were trained enough – or threatening enough – to manage real combat. Maybe Tklth, I suppose, but she balanced physical competence with mental instability.

Instead, we mostly handled undercover stuff: breaking and entering, transportation, illegal credit transfers, rigged lotteries, and so forth. Jobs with a low probability of violent contact.

I'd like to think we were smart. Most of what we did took finesse and cleverness. I'm a natural sneak and good at finding ways in and out of secure facilities, talents that come in handy in my current profession. Tklth was a great driver and a good urban scout, the best for flying a getaway aircar. Rsspkz was our tongue, good at persuading marks out of their keys or credit codes. There were two others in the Pack: Fzpktk and Vztrrp, our engineer-slash-saboteurs, familiar with high and low technology, respectively.

As I rode the public aircar, I wondered why I was reminiscing so hard about the old gang. Sure, I was passing some of our Pack's old hangouts, but our actual territory was several kilometers further south. A little more industrial, a little further from the wild border forest surrounding Layafflr. Just returning home shouldn't have me rewinding my whole sordid past. I had flown past the same region dozens of times. It never triggered so many memories before.

I was pretty sure I wasn't dying, so my life wasn't dumping memory before termination. Maybe my thoughts had something to do with my recent travel. I hadn't had a vacation like that in a long time. I rarely ever left Layafflr City, to tell the truth. It was possible that the change of scenery was enough to draw out the years I'd prefer to forget.

Frost, the *nature* of the crime – a sneak theft of a valuable but probably unsellable bauble – smelled like something Pack Vzrrk would pull. Even back then, I could have schemed a handful of ways to manage the same heist. With my deviancy now fully matured, I imagined a couple dozen more possibilities. Which method the *actual* thief used remained a mystery. If I had worked that out, I might have snared the culprit.

On reflection, I was working with a handicap. Jevvettr never trusted me enough to give me full access to his security systems, just their output: audiovisual recordings and access records. Without key information about how the system worked and how it could be circumvented, I was hunting without scent. I never saw the penthouse suite without a guard present, and that guard blocked any in-depth exploration. I couldn't interrogate the automated systems, take apart the locks, pry up the carpet or even open the windows. Jevvettr apparently expected me to solve his case using only surface scrutiny, social investigation and pure logic.

Kkk, that happens… in detective fiction. Real investigation means taking things apart. Sometimes those things are evidence. Sometimes those things are people. I don't mean evisceration, although that happens from time to time. I mean getting inside heads, checking stories, making people uncomfortable, and pushing hard to see what shakes loose. Since my gangster days, I'd learned the lessons they teach constabulary detectives: how to interrogate witnesses and suspects, how to rattle them both, and how to avoid provoking them to violence *or* having to apologize for your uncivil behavior.

Those skills are useful, but they're only half the P.I. package. I'm better than a constabulary detective because I can do things they can't and won't do. I can enter buildings without a search warrant… ideally, when the resident isn't home. I can short-circuit an alarm system and make it spit out its records or identify me as a friend. Thanks to my checkered past, I could have hijacked the aircar I was riding and traveled for free.

With that thought, I was home. Just seeing the place again was bringing up more memories. At least they were recent, petty thoughts, not the decaying dung-piles of my distant past.

I dismounted the aircar at my building's front door. The 'car lifted away to rejoin its own kind at the neighborhood docking station. I stood still a moment, looking around.

Not much had changed during my absence. The same garbage still cluttered the corners and alleys, refreshed daily despite the best efforts of automated clean-ers. The same green overgrowth still threatened to strangle the nearby buildings. The fact that it *hadn't* was a credit to the automated brush cutters. None of my neighbors were visible, coming or going, so I couldn't tell if anyone old was missing or anyone new had arrived. My neighborhood wasn't exactly a place where you wanted to loiter outdoors, anyway.

I decided to take my own advice and get inside. Doing so seemed like a shame. The weather was nice, for a change, and I hated to leave the direct sunlight. I couldn't help comparing the climate to the coastal beaches'.

It's actually cooler out there, on average, with the ocean breeze. The sun just seems bigger, brighter, and warmer. You can bathe in sunshine, covered fully in light during any daytime hour. In the City, you only get indirect light, except at certain hours of midday, when the sun is highest and slips between the buildings. It might be hotter at home, between the latitude and the pollution and the insulation, but it feels artificial even when you're actually outside. Sss, I supposed I wasn't missing much by retreating into my nest.

The weight of urban life settled on my shoulders as I climbed the stairs to my apartment. I hoped I wasn't going to end up feeling more drained than rejuvenated by my time away. I'd have to focus on the vacation as a bright memory – maybe a future reward and an incentive to work harder – to avoid being dragged down by the contrast. Ttt, maybe I should consider moving, opening up a practice on the coast? Stchvk, beach detective. I liked the sound of it… even if I couldn't afford the first month's rent on a packing crate down there.

Speaking of packing crates, I opened the door to my "spacious" nest-slash-office-slash-crate. I stepped through and was just about to drop my travel case when I spotted an anomaly. My keen detective senses picked up a big brown envelope sitting on my bare grey plasticrete floor. Somebody must have shoved the old-fashioned thing under my old-fashioned door. How quaint. Also, how suspicious.

Anyone who wants to message me can easily find the public listing for my compad. I usually answer voice calls and read most of my text mail, particularly if a correspondent offers money coming *to* me rather than demanding money *from* me.

If people want to talk business without calling, they can stop by in person. My hours are listed on my business profile. Sometimes I even update those hours to reflect my actual presence. My place is even reasonably secure… at least, more secure than a physical letter. There are security cameras downstairs, but dropping off a letter will get you recorded just the same as a conversational visit.

I could think of some alternate explanations. Maybe the mysterious author hid their identity by sending a courier. Maybe the visitor didn't know I was out of town – I didn't advertise *that* fact – didn't have my number… and then decided to go buy an envelope and paper and leave me a note rather than stop by at another time. Or, maybe they had the stationary already on hand. Or maybe a Ningyo dropped it off through folded space. Lots of things were possible, many of them stupid.

I was being stupid, theorizing before I had any information. I doubted that the envelope was dangerous. Nobody I knew hated me enough to go shopping for biological weapons or deadly nanotech. A cursory lift and pat-down convinced me that no spring-loaded monofilament blades would shoot out when I opened the letter.

It was just a brown paper envelope with a yellow sheet of paper inside. On the paper was a brief message, signed at the bottom. The danger was in the message itself. I read:

> *Stchvk - I know we parted on bad terms, but I hope some attachment remains. After Rsspkz went to prison, I tried to stay out of trouble. I found a good mate, trained for a real job, even started thinking about laying eggs. Seems like trouble follows me. My mate is dead. The constables don't know who did it, but they're starting to suspect me. I don't know who to ask for help. If I'm seen talking to you, they'll connect us to the old Pack, and I won't get a fair hearing, for certain. I might never find out who really killed Vzktkk. Worse, I might go to prison. You know he's waiting for me there. Please help. You're all I have left: the closest I still have to Pack. I'll be in the lounge bar at Tk Kzztkrt every rest-day, working. Come in for a drink and we can talk without raising suspicion. I'm sure we'll recognize one another. I remember you well. I hope you have some good memories of me, still. - Pkstzk*

Kktkrkz' oversized ovipositor, of course I remembered Pkstzk! If she hadn't been Rsspkz' intended mate, I would have courted her myself. She knew it, too. She was playing on that old attraction to beg for help.

Broken Record

She had avoided prison time the same way I did: by ditching my Pack when disaster struck. I didn't blame her. She wasn't even Pack or part of our operations, not directly. She never actually participated in any of our criminal activities. She was Rsspkz' mate, but otherwise she just hung around, looked good, and spent his money. She knew what was happening and was an accessory, legally speaking, but her claws were clean otherwise.

Maybe she wasn't playing any angle. It was possible she finally found an honest mate and ran into bad luck again. Maybe she did think of me fondly, and her pretty words weren't just calculated flirtation. Frost, I wished I could believe all that. I hated having to be cynical about every sapient I met.

Unfortunately, cynicism was too often justified. I had to allow for all possibilities, virtue and villainy included. While I didn't want to be played for a sucker, I also didn't want to push away a genuinely innocent client. I could at least hope she was a *paying* client. I needed another one of those, soon.

But *should* I take the job, paid or not? Pkstzk was right about one thing: the two of us seen together would *not* help her criminal case. Chill and scale rot, *my* public standing might be in trouble if we were connected to one another and thereby, to Pack Vzrrk. Even if I kept dodging criminal charges for my past actions, my detective license could be pulled if enough suspicion piled up. Pkstzk overlooked *that* concern with a typical lack of empathy.

Whether I owed her anything from our past… that was another big question. I suppose I owed Rsspkz something for him staying quiet about his Pack-mates. He'd never opened his beak to name names, that I knew of. At least, the constables never linked me to any of Pack Vzzrk's past crimes.

Then again, Rsspkz might *want* Pkstzk to go down for her crimes and betrayals. He might still blame her for abandoning him. He might want her in prison, like she feared. I could repay him best – not to mention protect myself – by staying away from his ex-mate.

World-blighting frost! For all I knew, Rsspkz might have arranged a hit on Pkstzk's new mate! What better way to punish her than to kill his replacement and frame his ex-mate?

Empty eggs! Rot in the shell! I should run far away from the whole case, but I couldn't. I had to find out more, precisely because it was so close to my own skin. At the least, I needed to know enough to protect myself.

Solving a frosted murder case would just be extra entrails on top of the rotting corpse. *Maybe* I might even get paid. Or maybe I'd earn a little mating play with Pkstzk…?

NO! Stupid gonads. Freeze and crack off. I take you to the beach and you go completely insane.

Chapter 2 - Kicking Old Habits

I tossed Pkstzk's letter onto my couch and carried my travel case into the office. After unpacking my compad and grooming kit, I decided not to take any chances and removed Rtrtr as well.

Stalking back into the front room, I moved the offending envelope onto the floor and blasted it with Rtrtr's lowest setting. Destroy the evidence. Burn the writer, by proxy. The cremation left a charred mark on the plasticrete, but the property damage was worth it. I felt a little better for indulging my anger.

I would need my best emotional management strategies to deal with Pkstzk and her troubles. Even if she stayed well-behaved – and that was never guaranteed – I would still have to manage nosy constables. The investigation of this new crime might stray into old, deep waters. My past self, a more nervous, trigger-happy self, still lurked within, waiting for an excuse to attack... or run away. Swimming backward against time made it easier for younger me to influence older me.

There were a couple of days yet before the next rest-day, Pkstzk's requested meeting date. Lots of time to relax. I was glad I didn't have to scramble uptown right away to meet Pkstzk. I'd be able to calm my agitated mind first.... assuming I didn't upset myself further in the meantime.

Despite that need for detachment, I felt like I should do some research. I ought to check the history on Pkstzk and her mate. I could review public records about the murder. Maybe I'd even see what I could find about the old Pack.

I already knew that one Pack-mate, Fzpktk, was dead, killed by constables while resisting arrest. Rsspkz was in prison for life, along with Vztrrp. The three of them were identified on a bad job where sapients died. I wasn't sure which of them, if any, had actually killed anyone, but as far as the law was concerned, they were all guilty of murder. I wasn't there when it happened. I was emphatically and provably *somewhere else.*

Another Pack member, Tklth, managed to escape the dragnet and made it off-planet. Her trail was cold. While I grabbed a drink and a snack, I confirmed the absence of information about her. Her name turned up nothing on the news media. She wasn't listed in any Collective death notices. The only warrant for her arrest was the original one, years old.

I sent a query through the constabulary just in case, claiming that I was doing research for a client. The bureaucrats would most likely give me a form response after a day or two, after skimming the same public files. I already knew that search would come back empty.

If I was lucky, my inquiry might spark some interest and prompt someone to dig deeper. My request *could* backfire if someone linked Tklth and Pkstzk, but that was unlikely. The two females despised and avoided one another, and like I said, Pkstzk never worked jobs with Pack Vzrrk.

I went through the same searches for Pkstzk, Rsspkz, and Vztrrp, along with a few other hangers-on who weren't part of the Pack but still associated with us: Rsspkz' siblings Zfzptk (off-planet, asteroid miner) and Ktchvch (diner cook), and Vztrrp's childhood friend Ssptkt. That last search turned up an interesting story: in the last year, Ssptkt had picked a fight with a Taratumm Herd and was paralyzed from the neck down. I found nothing relevant to my concerns, though.

Nobody had a clear connection back to Rsspkz. Nobody was an obvious candidate for him to use to stalk or threaten or kill Pkstzk or her mate. I also didn't see any indirect links between any of the old Pack-mates.

That list included me. Back then, I didn't have any associations *outside* of my Pack, other than my parents and their Pack. My parents moved away and passed away off-planet after I reached maturity.

Vislin don't generally maintain lifelong genetic family relationships like mammalians tend to. I suspect that the modicum of affection Vislin offspring receive as adults – or any contact between Vislin siblings – is a cultural imposition from the Hrotata and Taratumm. Pre-Great Family, Vislin were more like our prehistoric forbears, kicking young out of the nest to form their own Packs as soon as they could hunt alone.

Broken Record

Pack association is the strongest relationship in Vislin culture and society, far more important than any genetic ties. I reminded myself of this obvious fact to prepare my mental defenses. Even mates are secondary to Pack-bonds, although a good Pack rarely forces the two allegiances into conflict. Ideally, one mates within the Pack and avoids the whole issue.

Scientific research is still trying to untangle all the ways Vislin Pack members bond: chemically, mentally, and maybe psychically. Those bonds helped us survive in the past: a Pack can make survival decisions faster and better than any of its component members, alone. Obviously, a coordinated Pack hunts better. Pack-mates know when one of their own is in trouble and will do whatever is necessary to assist. The Pack-bond can overrule frenzy in ideal circumstances.

Even in modern times, the Pack-bond is still a significant asset. Those frenzy control effects can't be discounted, especially when there are fewer and fewer places where you can acceptably vent your anxieties. A call from a Pack member is sometimes sufficient to calm down a Vislin on the edge.

Packs that work together produce superior results to mixed work groups. That truth applies to intellectual work as much as physical labor, which explains some of the historic technical and military advantages enjoyed by Vislin.

What all this biopsychology meant was trouble. I only escaped my old Pack's downfall through a combination of chance and idiosyncrasy. I was fortunate to be absent for their last job, the one that went bad and cost most of the Pack their lives or freedom. I was also lucky to be absent when the constables came to round the others up.

Otherwise, in either case, I might have been caught up against my better judgment. With Pack-mates present and in trouble – no matter that it was trouble of their own making – I'd have felt obligated to help them fight or escape. Or, possibly not. My Pack-bond was suspiciously weak, then and now.

After the arrests, if I was 'normal', I might have attempted a jailbreak rescue. Or, more likely given my restraint and pragmatic streak, I still should have been in the courthouse standing by to help their case. Some Pack-mates would threaten witnesses, destroy evidence, even assassinate court personnel if they thought that would help… presuming they weren't jailed or killed first. Even years later, I should have tried to assist Rsspkz and Vztrrp in prison, taking their calls and sneaking them contraband. I certainly would have identified, proudly, as their Pack-mate, earning me constant constabulary observation.

I am not 'normal', thank the sun's warmth. For some reason, I don't have much loyalty for my former Pack. The fact that I can have a "former Pack" is anomalous, in that they're not all deceased. Running away from one's Pack is supposed to create mental distress in Vislin, not relieve it.

When things went bad, I *was* relieved. I was having second thoughts about the Pack's activities for years but didn't see any way out. Mine was the sole voice that encouraged them away from dangerous, violent jobs and found opportunities for stealthy, zero-casualty crimes. I wasn't any paragon of virtue, but I did what I could to minimize bloodshed.

Maybe I should give myself credit for discovering a personal code of ethics. My moral conflicts might be the counteractive force that weakened my Pack-bonds. It's certainly a more comforting theory than just thinking I'm defective, unable to bond properly or capable of discarding bonds for my own convenience.

Where I *found* a 'personal code of ethics', only the Egg-Thief knows. My parents didn't teach me much, except how to function socially, keep myself fed, and stay in school. Civics was taught in my nursery, but only as a set of dry ideals, not a practical lifestyle. My Pack wouldn't know an 'ethic' if it burrowed under their scales. I didn't have a friend, mate, or neighbor to teach me right from wrong or be disappointed about my moral failings. I just somehow came to realize that what my Pack was doing was wrong.

The realization took a while, too. When I first joined up, crime seemed exciting. We were pulling tricks on society, taking what it couldn't protect, proving ourselves quick, clever hunters in a world gone soft. We loved our rough, frontier planet and our grim, gritty home town, Layafflr City.

Pack Vzrrk was part of a tradition of lawlessness stretching back to our colonizing ancestors. We had dreams of scaling the walls of society and taking our rightful places among the high kleptocracy, once we amassed enough wealth to prove ourselves worthy. Our victims were pathetic, weak fools who couldn't defend their possessions. They didn't deserve to keep anything we could steal.

In short, I now make a career out of finding and capturing the type of idiot I used to be. That's how I understand them so well. It often comes as a revelation to criminals – especially thieves – that anyone else could be as clever and tough as they believe themselves to be. I suppose you could argue that I'm so talented precisely because of my criminal past. I'm not one of the soft marks of society, unlike the clients I assist, who can't defend themselves. But *I* think that I'm smarter and more skilled, defending the law, than I ever was back when I *thought* myself better than everyone else.

I managed to make a clean break from my foolish youth. I stayed out of reach and out of contact from my Pack until they were safely in prison, in space, or in the grave. Any urgings I felt to come to their aid were quashed by my better sense. Maybe I rationalized, at the time, that I could do more for the Pack by staying free and anonymous than I could by sticking close and getting spattered with their same stink.

Yet even afterward, I could deny our bond without much effort. *Someday,* I'd help them out. *Someday,* it would be feasible to step out of the shadows and risk contact. I kept pushing that *someday* further and further into the future. Until that someday came, I could stay away from temptation and out of trouble.

Apparently, that someday was coming up, in just two days. Pkstzk wasn't Pack, exactly, so I probably wouldn't feel the same urgings toward her. I might feel a different urge, though. I had to be ready for those feelings, as well.

I also couldn't forget that she was once deeply linked to the old Pack. Helping her might mean contact with my past Pack-mates. Even without any direct contact, my motivations and perceptions could be influenced by our mutual past.

I still *felt* some Pack-bond. I wasn't completely insane, no matter what my neighbors or clients thought. I could just push that bond aside better than most. I had to hope that if I stayed introspective and made sure my decisions were rational, I could avoid doing something loyally stupid.

Speaking of bonds, I eventually remembered to look up the murder victim, Pkstzk's dead second mate. I found both their public mating certificate and the record of his death.

The stiff was named Vzktkk. From the little I could find, he sounded pretty dead even when he was alive. Accountant... what a terrible job for a Vislin. Office worker. Low income, likely working his way up. Liked to play space fighter sims. When that's the highlight of your obituary, you did something wrong in life.

Not like me. I'm sure my death notice will be spectacular, a tribute to my wonderfully varied existence, capped off with an explosive ending. Kkk, not boring like poor Vzktkk.

I suspected this guy's herbivorous lifestyle was what attracted Pkstzk. He was safe, a refuge after the wild ride with Rsspkz. He wasn't too bad looking, either, judging from the pictures on record. Probably would have been a great provider for her and their young. His loss was a shame; Pkstzk deserved stability.

Knowing Pkstzk, though, she probably would start chewing her claws off from boredom. Back with the old Pack, she enjoyed the craziness, at least until things turned bad and bloody. It was the messy ending that scared her off. We had that in common as well.

Frost, to be honest, most of my current life is pretty boring. It just gets punctuated with moments of deadly hazard and occasional frenzy. Plus, I wasn't as good looking as Vzktkk. I was even poorer than an office drudge. And the guy *had* gone out with a blast.

The official cause of death was stated as murder, but the public obituary didn't go into any details. A news article on the crime only added that Vzktkk was found dead, shot once through the head with a laser. A bystander spotted his body on a side street in central Layafflr City, somewhere in Isstravil, a middle-class neighborhood. There were no witnesses and no evidence on the scene. The murder was thought to be a mugging, an accident, or maybe a random act of pointless violence. These things happened. Constabulary investigating.

The article was dated from the last week. Not much time had passed between the death and Pkstzk's visit, maybe between one and six days, depending on how long she waited before seeking me out.

Broken Record

I didn't find much else. Even the news article didn't name the street or address where Vzktkk's body was found. They omitted the time of discovery and time of death. I noticed, also, that nothing implied Vzktkk died where he was found... the shooting might have happened elsewhere. These omissions suggested that the facts were being kept out of circulation by constabulary request.

On some worlds, such requests wouldn't matter to the media, but the press on ChttKttp was conditioned to stay on the constabulary's good side. The government could wield the law as a bludgeon against troublesome publications, if it chose. Keeping the constables happy also meant easier access to information... when they chose to provide any.

I wasn't bound by such friendly arrangements. I'd get the details personally. The first step was to see Pkstzk, to hear what she had to say and figure out what she knew.

That was the logical choice, right? I wasn't just being influenced by my own desire to see her again? I was fairly sure *both* motivations, professional and personal, were involved. I'd just keep it professional and not get more personally involved. That resolution always works (it never works).

I had two days to fill. What was I going to do with myself in the meantime, if I wasn't out scrounging for leads? Sit around my nest, hunting around the networks? Play space fighter sims? Go tempting fate and take a walk around my neighborhood? There weren't many options, if I was trying to hold onto my saved credits. Even taking a public aircar to take a walk in a safer uptown park cost a bit. Actual recreation would take a chunk out of my finances.

Just thinking about leisure was wearing me out. Between my post-vacation depression, travel lag, and the thought of enforced downtime, I was getting tired.

I stripped off and curled up in my nest for a nap. I'd just sleep for a couple of cycles, to refresh myself before dinner and decision time.

I woke up the next morning, confused and then irritated.

Sss, that was one day down.

Chapter 3 - Window Shopping

I staggered through my usual morning routine with my usual lack of grace. Dust and polish the scales. Heat up artificial broth and choke it down. Check messages. Brush beak. Strap on armor. The whole time, I kept checking myself for signs of illness. These abrupt, long naps weren't normal for me. Should I see a doctor?

I felt fatigued, but that was normal in the morning. Eyes usual color, scales no yellower than last I checked, claw beds and beak clean, no unexpected aches. For me, that's peak health. I decided to explain my sleep schedule anomalies as post-vacation adjustment. Self-diagnosis was cheaper than a medical scan and less likely to turn up nasty surprises.

Avoiding the problem, I settled in to work on more immediate troubles. Pkstzk. I'd see her tomorrow. What could I do today? It was tempting to visit a constabulary office, but after some thought, I ruled out the idea. I could get access to unclassified records using my private investigator badge. The problem was, those records would be flagged and someone would start asking questions about my case.

Layafflr City, officially, has a 'cooperative relationship' between P.I.s and constabulary detectives. Private investigators can take risks and pursue leads the constables legally can't. If our investigations pan out, the constables often overlook any illegal searches, break-ins, or other nonviolent offenses committed in the course of detection. Lesser crimes to prevent greater threats.

If a P.I. screws up, though, we're still liable criminally and financially for any damages. The constables can take credit for our successes and avoid blame for our mistakes; a perfect setup. Suckers like me accept this arrangement because, one, we still get paid if the client is satisfied, and two, some of us actually want to see justice done.

Broken Record

In return for being the disposable protective sheath of law enforcement, a licensed private investigator receives a few privileges with the constabulary, beyond a provisionally blind eye. We can read official criminal reports, up to a point. Anything considered confidential may still be blocked or redacted. Ironically, the details most likely to be omitted are usually the secrets necessary to solve a case. In practice, any P.I. worth their badge can deduce the missing info from context. It just means a little extra brain- and/or legwork.

Technically, a P.I. can call for constabulary presence, including an arrest, provided they have sufficient cause. Again, in practice, the speed of response tends to vary with the quality of an investigator's past work and the number and rank of their friends among the city's authorities.

I've been fortunate not to make many enemies, but I don't have many friends in power, either. An influential Pack would help there… go figure. Lacking that asset, I could have tried cozying up to the big crests in town, parlaying my past successes into private work and a high reputation. I have the talent. Maybe I even have the charisma.

Problem is, I don't want that much attention. Getting too friendly with someone important means that their handlers will start doing background checks. I know what they'll find in my past. Better to remain a relatively unknown, struggling jobber than risk being outed as a criminal.

Worse than being retroactively arrested, I'd be blacklisted and lose my license. After that, I'd be lucky to get work cleaning sonic wildlife repellers at the city borders. Did you know, some of the smarter wildlife will endure the pain long enough to defecate on the emitters?

The other privileges of a licensed investigator mostly have to do with access: entry to crime scenes, permission to interrogate witnesses and suspects, and some opportunity to view evidence. We can't actually *collect* evidence, not legally, nor are statements or confessions made to us legally admissible. Any P.I. who botches a case by mishandling evidence or otherwise overstepping their rights can be prosecuted for obstruction of justice. He or she deserves it, too. There have been times I wanted more latitude to pursue a case, but if my zeal means a thief or murderer goes free on a technicality, all my work is wasted.

Nathan Large with Laine Megan Lundquist

I'm not the type to shoot a suspect and cry "self-defense" later. I know a few of that sort. They think of themselves more as hunters than detectives. They stalk their prey until it gets spooked and runs... or fights back. I consider them murderers with excuses, not much better than the crooks they 'investigate'.

What options did all this leave for me to pursue? Legwork, and lots of it. First, I could canvas the area where Pkstzk's mate, Vzktkk, was found. The residents had already been questioned by the constabulary, so my investigation might seem redundant to them. I'd have to deal with people asking why I couldn't just read their previous statements.

My answer: I was looking for something the constables missed. After all, if they could catch the shooter based purely on their original investigation, he'd already be in prison, right?

Just seeing the neighborhood itself would be useful, to give context to other information. Plus, I could really use the exercise. I'd get a nice long walk. If things got exciting, I might get to climb (into a window) or run (for my life). There's optimism for you. Even my worst cases improve my physical fitness... barring the ones that leave lasting damage.

What I *didn't* need right then was combat practice. I'd rather not waste time mending broken bones or lacerated scales. I strapped on Rtrtr's holster and threw a rain jacket over the heater and my battered everyday armor. Was it expected to rain? Layafflr City had about a fifty-fifty chance of rain on any given day, so the odds were high. I probably wouldn't look strange as long as the skies weren't clear.

As I stepped out of my apartment, I went through a checklist of potential targets, after the crime scene itself. Anyone who seemed reluctant to answer my questions about Vzktkk would be worth further scrutiny. I could talk to people who knew the deceased: friends, family, work associates, etc. If this wasn't an accidental shooting or random robbery, I might hear ideas about who might *want* Vzktkk dead. If nothing else, his acquaintances might know if he seemed nervous before he died, possibly afraid for his life. Had he done anything that seemed strange, outside of his usual routine?

Broken Record

For that matter, I was assuming the place where he was found dead was along his usual travel route. That might or might not be true. I needed more background on Vzktkk just to determine his baseline, before I started mining for deviations.

The target site was deep downtown, toward the central, wealthier districts of Layafflr City. I decided to conserve my energy and rent an aircar. Twice in three days... posh.

The smell of the not-recently-sanitized 'car reminded me that I could always spend more. The windows could have used a wipe down, too. I could see only about half of the landscape as the city sped by on every side.

Apparently, I used up all my quality thinking time on the way out the door. My aircar ride passed without any new insights. I needed new input before I could plan any further ahead.

The 'car deposited me at a quiet corner on the outskirts of Isstravil. Traffic got tight further in; otherwise I would have opted for a destination closer to my target. Aircars had lower priority than private vehicles and mass public transit outranked the little one-seaters. I'm no city planner; I'm sure the scheme makes sense at some level. It's just inconvenient when you live outside the mass transit grid and you're limited to the least-favorable option.

So, I had to walk a few blocks. I spent the time getting acquainted with Isstravil's architecture and amenities. It was an expensive neighborhood, though not yet priced out of reach for middle-class workers. Teachers, engineers, business managers, the people who did most of the intellectual work of Layafflr tended to like this area. Some were just one promotion away from the cleaner, trendier city center. Most were one demotion away from my neighborhood, on the overgrown rim.

The shopping in Isstravil wasn't bad. If I could spare the transit cost, I might go there more often for groceries. I thought briefly about looking for an armorer, to replace or repair my old leathers.

Then, I chastised myself for spending my little bit of savings already. How about holding something for food? Not to mention, the cost of a drink when I went to see Pkstzk? Sss, there were just so many possible ways to drop credits.

I walked a grid search, narrowing down the potential paths Vzktkk might have traversed. The news report mentioned a "side street": neither a thoroughfare nor an alley. I also assumed the spot wouldn't be on a residential road; otherwise, the killer risked more witnesses.

After a couple of hours, I found the street I was looking for. Discarded security tape and imaging markers told me analysts had documented a murder scene somewhere nearby. The debris lingered in the gutters of Kzk Tsstkt, a side street just off the 25th Ring Road.

There were no helpful signs to indicate the exact location of Vzktkk's body when it was discovered. I also didn't find any clues to mark where he'd died. Any scorch marks from a laser were already scrubbed away. Looking at the site, though, I couldn't imagine that the body was dragged there. The street was too exposed; anyone looking to hide a body would choose one of the side alleys instead. Unless they were trying to make sure the body was found? I decided to start on the assumption that Vzktkk fell where he was shot, until evidence suggested otherwise.

I picked a likely spot and turned in a circle, taking in the surroundings. A snack shop was at the corner I just turned down. Next door, a compad showroom offered hardware sales, repairs, and comm contracts. If either store was open at the time of the murder, the employees would have heard a shot. Laser weapons could be absolutely silent when fired, but the pop of superheated blood and flesh was usually audible.

There were some side alleys within sight: one near the compad store, one further down on the opposite side. Such hidey-holes are the classic choice of muggers, so I checked them out. Both alleys were shallow, barely three meters long, each giving access to a side door and trash bins. High steel fences cut my side off from the roads opposite. A shooter would have to climb those fences or else go down to the corners to leave the street... and I didn't see any obvious claw marks on the metal or on the adjoining alley walls or ground.

Broken Record

I saw apartments on the upper levels, all up and down that stretch of road. I could try the residents and see what they knew. That presumed they were present at the time of the shooting, had something to share, *and* were still at home and willing to talk. The odds of hitting all four points were low but better than null.

I noticed a closed storefront on the opposite side of the street from the open businesses. The sign indicated that the building once housed an importer/exporter of "Exotic Pets." No wonder it went bust.

Exports are a terrible idea. The fauna of Spore are tricky to domesticate and about half are toxic to the majority of carbon-based sapients. Even keeping one as a curiosity would be dangerous *and* expensive.

By a similar token, anything you wanted to import would have to be kept strictly indoors or risk being poisoned or eaten by the local wildlife. Plus, you'd spend a fortune importing food, if a foreign animal couldn't eat the local cuisine. Stupid, but sometimes there's a market for stupid if someone considers it fashionable.

The closed store struck me as a likely spot for a shooter. Its sealed windows and door made it look like a hunter's blind. All you needed was a few centimeters' gap to sight and fire a laser. If the glass was clear enough, you could even fire through it without much loss of beam coherence.

I walked over to the pet store and examined it more closely. The window shutters looked tight: reinforced plastic with no gaps. The door was only locked, not shuttered, and it did have glass panes high up, forming a design on the upper lintel. It looked like one of the panels was cleaner than the others. Was that the origin point? It would be an awkward shooting position even if the shooter was as tall as a Taratumm… maybe someone standing on a chair?

The possibility actually made some sense. A high shot was advantageous for several reasons. A firing angle above eye level would hide the laser from the target before it was too late. Onlookers wouldn't see the light easily, either. If that window was the origin, the constables might have overlooked it, especially if they were still focused on the idea of a "random criminal act".

Nathan Large with Laine Megan Lundquist

Why was *I* focused on a "non-random" angle, myself? From the beginning, I had defaulted to thinking of the murder as a planned act. Was I inclined to see every death as intentional, every crime as part of a deeper, more sinister scheme? I knew better than that. Most crimes, across time and space, are based on simple opportunity, not extensive plotting. Here and now, in Layafflr City, is no different.

I'm not paranoid, in general terms. However, regarding this *specific* crime, I was definitely looking for a plot. Because of the case's connection to my old Pack, through Pkstzk, I couldn't help poking around for some hidden thread tying it back to them. If Vzktkk's death was just a mugging gone bad... great, nothing further to worry about. But if the death of the second mate of my former Pack-mate's former mate held some significance, I needed to know.

I was either going to thank Pkstzk for warning me about this case or scream at her for getting me involved, depending on how it turned out.

Just for the sake of trying, I checked the door of the closed shop and confirmed that it was locked. If the constables checked it out already, they locked up afterwards. More likely, it went untouched since Vzktkk's death. Kkk, I have such a high opinion of my official counterparts.

Was there another way in? I surveyed the building and noticed that the apartment above the store was dark and had a 'for sale' sign in one window. The store and apartment were probably connected inside. Trying the next door over in the same building, I found it also locked. I could call the owner and ask for access, I supposed.

Or, I could save time and unlock either door by myself. The apartment door's mechanical bolt lock was simpler than the store's, which required a magnetic swipe card. I'd have to go home for better tools to override that type of security. But an physical bolt and tumblers? Those were easy.

My only problem was finding a few minutes unobserved to pick the lock. There was still too much foot traffic in the area. I was certain I had already been seen examining the building. If I set off an alarm or was noticed breaking in, the constables would have no problem linking me to the illegal entry. Since the place was closed and empty, I wouldn't be charged with much, but my arrest would lead to those uncomfortable questions I was trying to avoid.

Broken Record

When you can't avoid attention, one solution is to draw *more* attention. Specifically, make yourself so obvious and obnoxious that people have to react or else ignore you.

I started pounding on the apartment door, shouting, "Open up! I know you're in there, you hollowed shell! You're five cycles behind! You either hand me credits today or I'm starting eviction right *now!*" I continued with more hammering and a stream of well-seasoned curses.

As I hoped, people started giving the block a wide berth. Some looked more closely for a moment, but as my simulated fury grew, they moved on. Thank the Ancestors that no lawyers – professional or amateur – decided to intervene on the tenant's behalf. Like I suspected, nobody in that kind of neighborhood wanted to get personally involved in a rent dispute.

Once my cover was established, I went to work. Muttering threats the whole time, I worked the lock as fast as I could. I did my best to look like a disgruntled building owner forced to break into his own property. If anyone thought about it more carefully, they would have asked why the owner didn't have his own key, but nobody confronted me right then.

Finally, the lock gave up. I hurried into the inner hallway and shut the outer door behind me. To my relief, the entryway did have a second door opening onto the side of the pet store. A staircase curved up and away to the upstairs apartment. It had looked like a combined unit from the outside. I was glad to be right.

The inner door to the pet store also had a magnetic card lock. I skipped the niceties and melted that off with my heater. Hopefully, the damage wouldn't cause problems with any future criminal proceedings. Once the door and frame had cooled, I pulled open the door and stepped into the store's showroom.

It stank worse than I expected. The smell of dung from various species still hung heavy in the air. Old rotted meat – an all-too-familiar reek – mingled with some kind of decaying vegetation, probably a neglected bag of herbivore feed. Over top of these stinks were odors from two different eras: the medieval aromas of fur, feathers, and straw and the modern scents of ozone and oil.

Nathan Large with Laine Megan Lundquist

The place was abandoned with little preparation and left untouched for cycles, maybe years afterward. No wonder it couldn't find a buyer

After my offended nostrils stopped spasming, I made my way to the front of the room. Enough light came in through the windowed door frame to illuminate the front half of the store.

It was a big showroom, flanked by wide plastic and metal shelves that once held animal cages. Pegboards along the upper half of the walls still had metal hangers attached, with price tags for treats, leashes, and the other miscellany of pet ownership. I could just make out a door in the back, which probably led to a storeroom or office space.

At the front was a cashier's stand, with sockets for direct network connection. This place *was* old. Wireless networking in Layafflr City is getting close to Collective standards, but at one point, that infrastructure wasn't established. Some old-timers still prefer to use the direct, physical links.

The cashier's stand was just tall enough that someone could stand atop it and get a line through the lintel window to the street. I looked closely, hoping to see foot- or hand-prints in the dust. There *was* no dust on the counter. There was plenty of debris on the floor and dust on the side tables. The counter had been wiped clean. That anomaly told me I was on the right track, even if the shooter was careful not to leave any other evidence.

The crud on the floor didn't show any footprints, either. The shooter could have either swept the debris around or just been careful where he or she stepped. I wondered about pad prints. Pulling out my compad, I did a high-magnification sweep of the counter.

I found a few lines of body oil along the edge, but nothing patterned enough for identification. I swabbed up as much oil as I could get. It would be too much to hope for genetic material – and I didn't have the funds or friends necessary for a full bio workup anyway – but I could at least identify the species from their secretions. Give me credit for being an *amateur* biochemist.

Broken Record

Given a shooter standing on the tall, flimsy counter, I could reasonably rule out Taratumm. Probably not Hrotata, either, as they would have to stretch uncomfortably to shoot even from that height.

It was best to be certain, though. I couldn't just assume Vislin. There were other sapients of the right height in the City, including not a few Humans and maybe one or two Zig deviant enough to contract for assassination…

…which was still a stupid thought. Why would someone pay to kill a nobody like Vzktkk? It didn't look like that kind of professional job, anyway.

I froze and shifted my attention as a sound intruded into my thoughts. A scratching noise was coming from the back of the store. I realized I had heard it earlier, more quietly, and dismissed it as the usual background noise from neighboring tenants or traffic. As the scratching got louder, I could tell it was definitely inside the same building. It was getting closer, too.

Something bumped against the room's back door. The door moved. It wasn't locked, as I had supposed… not even closed tightly.

I pulled out Rtrtr again. The heater was still slightly warm from its recent use. I called out, "Hey, someone in there? Come out quietly, I'm armed."

In response, I heard a low hiss. Living but not sapient, then. Probably not even intelligent. Had something living been left behind with the pet store's stock? If so, how had it survived?

As if to answer my question, the door banged open and a snarling, drooling mass of black-scaled muscle shot out. The creature bolted toward me, fanged mouth gaping. I barely had time to fire before it reached me.

Fortunately, I did fire and took out most of that dangerous mouth in my first shot. Perhaps the beast intended to leap for my throat, but its attack was impeded by injury and shock. Its body skidded forward on momentum and collided with my legs. Its few remaining teeth bounced off my leather greaves, its jaws lacking any strength to puncture.

Nathan Large with Laine Megan Lundquist

I kicked the flailing body aside and put a second shot into its hindquarters, backpedaling toward the side door at the same time. If any beast could still chase me after those injuries, I wanted a barrier between us.

Two heater shots seemed to have taken the fight out of it. The quadrupedal reptilian, about a third of my size, dropped to its flank on the floor, heaving and whining in pain. Besides my blasts to its head and rear leg, it had other visible injuries: bites around its front shoulders and belly, plus scales stripped away in several places, as if from claw wounds. Its midsection was hollow, emaciated from hunger rather than naturally lean.

All the wounds made it hard to identify at first. After a while, I realized that it was a rktpk, a sometimes-prey sometimes-pet animal from the home world, Hrotata Prime. Totally ordinary there, at least in the countryside, but 'exotic' on an outer colony world.

Rktpk could be aggressive toward larger animals, but only if trained... or very hungry. They were usually a little round around the belly. This one was starving. It actually ought to be dead. What had it been eating before? I dreaded checking the back rooms, but I had no choice.

I decided that the kinder option was to end the animal's suffering. I euthanized the rktpk with a final heater blast to its head.

Afterward, I stalked back to the open rear door. With growing anger, I recognized that a creature that big was never going to be left behind by accident. Someone had, at the least, deliberately left the poor beast locked inside. Maybe they intended to come back but were unavoidably delayed. Maybe they died first. If they just forgot or didn't care... that was another crusade for another time, but I'd make sure the question stayed on my list.

There was another possibility, one that started to look more likely as I searched the back of the store. I found bags of kibble in a back storeroom, long since chewed apart and emptied. Nearby were bones from leftover meat, eaten and gnawed for the marrow. There were also two carcasses of what I suspected were other rktpk, mostly eaten but more recently slain. This carrion was the source of the rotten meat smell. After the food ran out, the animals probably turned on one another.

Broken Record

Someone was feeding the captive animals, then stopped. Why would you leave three animals alone in an empty building, hungry and isolated? If you couldn't sell them, why not release them to the wild? Spore wasn't an ideal world for Hrotata Prime wildlife, but they might manage.

Maybe they intended exactly what just happened. You might keep starving animals locked in a building if you wanted them to attack anyone who came inside. If you were setting a trap, you put them behind a closed but unlocked door.

Was the trap for me, personally? Or was it intended for anyone who entered the building? Maybe if all three rktpk were still alive, I might have been overwhelmed. That possibility suggested that I arrived later than the miscreant intended. Maybe they expected the constables to check the place out first. Was that the point of Vzktkk's death? To set up malevolence against the authorities? Then again, it was possible the miscreant misjudged how much food would be needed to keep three animals satisfied up to the right date.

None of the possibilities were pleasant. I really hoped that the animal abuse *was* related to Vzktkk's shooting, so that I could punish both culprits at once. It was too bad the legal punishment wouldn't involve locking them in this foul place without food. It was too bad I wasn't cruel enough to impose that kind of justice, myself. I was still sorely tempted.

Chapter 4 - Neighborhood Watch

I left the pet store still fuming but lacking a target. I wanted to ask questions around the neighborhood, but my anger might interfere with a friendly, casual approach. Worse than my foul mood was the lingering stench of rotting and burnt meat. Nobody was going to welcome a furious, reeking Vislin into their home or business.

Then again… they might want to answer his questions quickly and persuade him to leave faster. I could work the outrage angle. People tend to sympathize more with dead animals than they do with dead sapients, anyway. I could either work with what I had or waste time cleaning up and calming down.

I decided to start across the street with the two neighboring businesses. They didn't have an ideal view of the street where Vzktkk was shot, but they might know a lot about the neighborhood, especially the pet store.

I was perversely hungry, even after dealing with that putrescent hell. Old predatory instincts: I killed something, therefore it was time to eat. My appetite made the snack store a desirable first stop. Besides, if I stank as badly as I suspected, a food shop would have extra incentive to get rid of me faster.

A digital chime announced my entrance to the little shop. Like the pet store, the establishment was a throwback to early colonial times. It had the same hard-wired register stand, for one thing. It also had open shelves holding a variety of dry edible items, aging away in the sun. No coolers, no sealed bins, no hydrators, none of the amenities of a modern grocery or convenience store. There *was* a refrigerator in the back, behind the counter, which probably held fresh foods. I also saw a compressed-gas pump for carbonated or nitrogenized beverages. A faded menu card above the dispenser offered various brews. Everything was to-go, judging by the lack of tables or chairs in the room. Displays occupied all the available space.

Broken Record

Most of the available goods were protein-based. Dried insects appealed to Hrotata clients, though there were plenty of Vislin who appreciated the texture. Six kinds of jerked meat, plus processed cubes and sticks with a variety of spices, took up one entire wall. Dried seaweed, fruits, and sugared grain squares were on the opposite side – segregated for the herbivores, I supposed – while bins of dried nuts filled the middle area. Candies, puffed grains, and roasted grubs, plus a few oddities I couldn't identify, filled the odd spaces in-between.

The attendant was a middle-aged male Hrotata with dark fur just beginning to lighten at the roots. He popped up from behind the counter at the sound of my arrival. He ran a sleeved paw across his eyes, giving away his drowsiness. Quiet day in a quiet neighborhood. I almost felt bad disturbing his peace. I wondered if he slept through my racket across the street. Maybe he slept through Vzktkk's murder, too.

"Good day! How may I help you..." he began, on script, before his eyes informed his brain about what he was greeting.

I nodded, trying to look less threatening. My bloodstained rain slicker and well-worn armor probably set me apart from his usual customers. His nose caught up shortly afterward, warning him that I was recently in contact with burnt meat and blood. I wondered what conclusion he would reach after totaling up his senses.

"I just came from across the street," I started, conveying pure business. "The pet trader?"

The Hrotata looked puzzled for a moment. I waited for him to work it out.

"Um... the closed store?" he finally guessed. "Are you renovating it?"

I blinked and cocked my head. "No, I was investigating it. Did you know there were still live animals inside?"

His eyes widened in alarm, sensing real trouble. "No, no, of course not. I didn't know anyone was still using the place. Were... were they all right?" He knew better. The question was pure formality.

I answered with the derision he deserved. "No, they were *not* all right. Some starved to death. The survivor was so hungry it attacked me. That's animal abuse, at the least. You sure you didn't know... didn't hear *anything*?"

He raised one paw, swearing on an imaginary holy book. "No, I didn't know. I never heard, never saw... then again, I never paid it much attention. I just work here, odd days."

"You're not the owner? You think she... or he... might know something? Ignored some sign of trouble?"

"I'm sure Mistress Iyallette would have reported any worrisome sounds or activity to the authorities, right away." His loyalty was touching, but unhelpful. I gained a name, at least. I pressed for more.

"Could I get her contact number, please? I'd like to follow up on this matter. Actually, have you seen *anyone* else near that building recently, going in or coming out or just checking it?"

See, I had a plan. It just takes time to get around to the point, sometimes.

The clerk gabbled on as he called up a comm code on his business terminal. "No, not myself... there was that Vislin killed nearby, recently... do you think he might have been involved? Maybe he saw something..."

I did my best to seem surprised. "Actually, I think I heard about that. Hadn't considered it. Now that I know the state of that building, it might be relevant. Thanks. I don't suppose you know anything else about that murder... or the victim?"

"Not really. I was working at the time, but I didn't notice anything wrong until people started to gather outside. They were looking at the body."

I fixed him with a skeptical stare. "You were here, but you didn't hear anything when he got shot."

"It was a *laser*," he stressed, defensively. "They don't make much noise."

Broken Record

Well, he was half right. The beam doesn't make any noise, but your boiling, popping flesh does. Your screams make a bit of noise, too, if the shot isn't immediately fatal.

To be fair, the media reports indicated that Vzktkk died from a head shot. If he was far enough away from the snack shop – like at the opposite end of the street – the clerk might *not* have heard much, even if he was awake at the time.

I had to keep playing ignorant, though. "I see. Well, I'll have to read up on that case, then, and see where it leads me. Ttt, mind telling me what time it happened?"

"Around nine and a half? We close at ten on work days. He might have been shot a decad before that. Nobody I talked to said they saw the actual attack. Nobody's been arrested yet, either."

I shook my head, indicating a general disappointment with law enforcement. "Without a witness or a lead… well, I've got to report to the constables, myself. Maybe if my mess is connected, it might help with their case. Thanks for your help. Ttt, hey, if you or your Mistress…"

"Iyallette," he supplied brightly. I took the reminder to copy her comm code into my 'pad.

"Right, Iyallette. If either of you remembers or hears something, could you give me a call? What they did to those animals…" I finished with a beak grind that would give any Hrotata atavistic shudders.

He obliged with a wide-eyed flinch. "Right. What's your contact?"

I supplied him with my actual name and number, but a false cover story: I was working for an interested real estate buyer, appraising abandoned properties. The clerk didn't ask about my non-traditional outfit. Too bad, since I was all ready to regale him with stories about even worse cases where I had to pull out the biohazard suit. Of course, I'd wear working armor for protection and a weapon to chase off squatters… even in a "nice neighborhood".

As I walked back outside, I reflected on just how nice the neighborhood *wasn't*. There was a slow decay at work. Property owners were banking on historical charm to draw in middle-class residents, but the aging buildings hid a variety of flaws. Besides rust and dry-rot, there were old attitudes and old habits lurking beneath the skin. Like those cash registers, for example. Like abandoned properties hiding unknown cruelties. Like an old-timey snack shop just waiting to be shut down for health violations.

Hungry as I was, I wasn't buying something there and risking toxic mold. It was *probably* safe, if they rotated stock regularly, but I didn't have much faith in that clerk's diligence.

After I left, realized I never got his name. I could find it later, I supposed, or contact his Mistress if I wanted to discuss anything officially. That was the problem with playing out an act: I couldn't be as thorough as I ought to be. If I started pushing like a murder detective should, the clerk could become nervous, suspicious and even forgetful.

Frosted trade-offs. I'd have to play the same game next door, at the compad store. I wondered if the tech boutique would share the same aura of decline as the other businesses.

It actually did not. The façade was historic, but once you got through the door, the interior was all modern. Slick white plastic panels divided by chrome supports covered the walls, likely concealing rougher brick beneath. The floor was a spongy polymer you could stand on all day without fatigue. Brushed steel tables held a variety of compads and accessories, all current to the present year, some even up to the best Collective standards. Several models were capable of housing a Terran A.I., a feature they proudly advertised.

I wondered if the store saw enough Terran clientele to make that boast relevant or if it was just a sales tactic. Didn't really matter, unless it was somehow relevant to my case.

My entry hadn't set off any alarms, at least none I could hear. There was already a clerk at the ready, though: an attentive Vislin female who greeted me as I entered. She waited for me to browse the wares before approaching.

Broken Record

She was cute, if not as sleek as I liked. Big eyes, heavy tail. Dressed in simple pale red polymer plates, pseudo-armor to keep up appearances but still look non-threatening.

When I finally made eye contact again, she asked, "Is there anything I can help you find, sir?"

I resisted my instinct to make an easy joke. I really wanted to say, *your nest.* Or, *a job that pays enough to afford this tech.* Instead, I stuck with my pissed-off, beat-up investigator role. Normally, that one isn't a hard act to maintain, but I wasn't quite as angry as I had been before. I'd lost some of my rage.

"I'm actually not shopping. Just wanted to get a better idea what's here. I was across the street earlier, at the pet store..." I let the statement hang, letting her jump to whatever conclusion she preferred.

There was no way she couldn't see and smell the gore on me. If the Hrotata had, a Vislin surely would. She was more blithe than the furball, though.

She answered, "The pet trader? Long closed, I thought."

"It was, but not empty. I was checking out the building. Turns out someone left live animals inside. Some of them hadn't quite starved to death yet."

"Vvv, so that was the noise," she replied, still intriguingly nonplussed. "I thought I heard an energy discharge. It's a little different than the usual noise around here... I still thought I might be imagining things, though. You know, after the shooting."

Was *she* baiting *me?* I couldn't resist.

"Shooting? Ttt, right, the guy who got burned a week ago. I read about that. Neighbor of yours?" I could play things warm and relaxed, too.

"No, a total stranger. First murder we've had around here in years... since I moved into the neighborhood, anyway. Did you just make it two?"

Her eyes bounced around my body in a way I'd normally appreciate. I realized that she was looking for my weapon. Rtrtr, I mean.

I clacked and rolled my eyes. "Depends on how sensitive you are to animal rights. It was self-defense, anyway. There was one surviving rktpk, nearly dead of starvation. I can't blame it for going after me. I'm a big chunk of meat."

She looked unamused. "Kkk, to a hungry rktpk, you probably look tasty. Too bad you couldn't catch it alive. Sounds like a terrible shame."

I got serious, finally. "It was. It was tortured, that one and at least two others. Who knows what other animals they had already eaten to survive. That's why I'm over here. I assume you didn't have any knowledge about their presence? Didn't hear any other noises?"

"Not like that," she answered, somber as well. "Nothing animal. I saw lights in the building a couple times over the last cycle, so somebody was inside. There could have been visitors during the day, too, but I didn't see anyone actually enter or leave. Sorry."

"In case it's relevant… what times? How recently?" I produced my own compad to take notes. The sight of the outdated model made her click, either from disgust or pity.

"Ttt… four nights ago, the last time? I think. I was shutting down. I usually don't stay open past dusk. Then maybe a half-cycle earlier, before that. Nothing the night of the shooting, if you're thinking what I'm thinking."

"I had wondered if they might be connected. Judging from the state of the store, I assume the constables *hadn't* thought to ask about it?"

She tilted her head to look me over again before answering. "No, they didn't. They asked about the victim, about what I saw and heard – nothing, by the way – and about whether there was any previous trouble in the area. There hasn't been, not anything like that. A fight or two, sure, but always indoors, between acquaintances. Crimes of passion, you know? Nothing random or for money."

"No robberies, stick-ups or break-ins?" I asked.

"Well, shoplifting. That's just a fact of life in my business. I usually recover the product, though. A good compad can call for help if it's accessed by an un-authorized user."

Broken Record

"But accessories don't have that protection," I prompted.

"Exactly." She fixed me again with a full stare. "You said you were checking out the closed building across the street. Checking it out for who?"

Challenge time! I had to decide: double down on my lie or see if I could get more out of telling the truth. My interest in impressing a cute, smart, well employed female had nothing to do with that choice. Absolutely nothing at all.

Frost, I can't even fool myself. I decided not to bother trying with her.

"For the family of the deceased, actually. I'm investigating the murder. Sorry I didn't say before... though you didn't ask until now." Warm, Stchvk. Practically sunny.

"Chchch... I suppose you thought being clever would get more out of me than just flashing your badge and being officious?"

She stopped and held an uncomfortable silence until I opened my beak to reply, then interrupted to answer herself: "You're probably right."

As I laughed quietly in appreciation, she continued: "Not that I'm hiding anything, from the constables or from you. I just don't like being treated like a suspect right away. Was the animal abuse thing for real?"

"Absolutely true. I'd offer to show you, but I suspect you don't want an eye-ful... or to leave your store unattended."

"I'll take your word for it. It's not exactly busy over here, but you never know, and you're right about not needing to see it myself. I can see enough on you. Smell it, too, now that I know that stink isn't just your natural scent."

"Thanks. You know, it wasn't too long ago that the smell of a fresh kill was considered arousing."

"Sorry, but whatever's spattered on you is a few days past fresh. Plus, I think we used to prefer meat raw back then, not charred."

"Fair enough. My odor aside, I've found something the constables missed. Any thoughts about a connection? Anything you didn't think of previously?"

"No... sorry, no. Unless the victim was a trapper or an animal rights activist... seriously. I'm sure you'll spot any connections like that yourself. I wasn't around when he died. Did you check next door? I think Hrusslitl was working that night."

Well, there was the name I missed. Hrusslitl the Hrotata. Easy to remember.

"I did. He didn't have much to add. What's your name, by the way?"

"Tskksk. You?"

"Stchvk. Investigator for hire."

"Shouldn't that line have a sound effect? A few notes of theme music?"

"I can't afford it yet. Maybe if I crack this case I can buy a sharp twang."

"Good luck, then, Stchvk. Want to leave your number? You know, in case I remember anything later?"

"Usually, when I do that, nobody ever calls." I wondered if I sounded witty or just whiny.

"Well, I've got no excuse. I'm always near a comm." Her gesture took in the ranks of compads mounted all over the store. She stopped, looking thoughtful. "Wait a second. I may or may not be an idiot."

I realized she wasn't talking about our obvious flirting. She walked around the room, looking alternately at the compads and then out the front windows. At a few of the front tables, she stopped and poked at the screen of the foremost compads. I eventually realized what she was doing.

"Were any of these on at the time? Eight days ago, about nine and two decads?" I asked.

"Exactly what I'm checking... although having the exact time makes it easier. At night, I usually put all the 'pads on shutdown mode except one, which runs the Kpst Six security suite. No reason not to use the stock I already have, rather than installing a separate dedicated security system. Plus, I can rotate through host systems, making the surveillance harder to find and hack."

Broken Record

I was just barely following her explanation. It all sounded reasonable, although the specific technology was beyond my knowledge.

She finally stopped at one station, scrolling through files on the compad. "This was the host system that night. Let's see... I have internal and external cameras, but the video doesn't show anything. I already gave the security output to the constables *and* looked at it myself. Both the shooter and the victim had to have entered and left the street from the same end, up toward 26th. That's my blind spot. Audio isn't very helpful, either; just an ambiguous noise around the time you suggested. From the acoustics, it could be a laser impact... or a trash can falling over."

Now, *this* talk was my kind of flirting. I was tempted to offer her a job, if she wasn't already doing better in business than I was. Maybe *she* would hire *me?*

Tskksk continued: "*But* that's just from the remote cameras, which are concerned with *my* security. This particular compad was also grabbing everything else its pickups could reach. That includes its internal microphone and camera, which are even more useless than the outside cameras... *but* it also collects wide-spectrum EM. That's mostly to monitor the network bands for intrusion, but I also get public comms, unsecured private calls, and with a little filtering, a magnetospheric traffic report."

My expression must have been transparently boggled, because she elaborated: "The sensor picks up electromagnetic noise. It's only illegal to *decode* private calls, but you can record whatever signals you want. I collect everything just in case. You never know who might discover a new way to hijack a compad or skim data."

"So... you'd pick up the laser firing?" I ventured.

"Ttt, yes, now that I know what I'm looking for, it's right there. You'd never be able to isolate it near, say, a major power line. You couldn't separate one shot from a firefight. But, by itself in this dead zone, the discharge stands out. Exact time: nine plus one-point-three decads, forty-nine hectads."

"Well, the precision is nice, but I'm not sure it gains me much..."

She interrupted to scold me: "That's not what's interesting. You just asked. What else we have is comm activity around that time. I've got one distinct signal, originating nearby, at one decad before nine. Then, the same signature again, immediately after the shooting. If it's the killer's compad…"

"Then it looks like they're calling in to report," I finished for her. "That's a stretch, though. I didn't see anything so far to indicate that this was a contract killing."

"Then maybe it was the victim's system. Maybe it's unrelated, sure. But the data is there. If it's matched up with a suspect's compad, that's evidence. I can't believe I didn't think of it before."

"I wouldn't have thought of it at all," I admitted, inadvertently flattering Tskksk. Her head bobbed slightly.

I continued, "The constable detective didn't think of it either. You should take some credit."

"I should call them," she realized, bounding over to her work station to pick up her personal compad.

"Yes, do. But could you make a copy of that data in case I come up with a lead?"

She tilted her chin up in amusement. "I'd do that anyway, but thanks for asking. Despite your professional rivalry, I've never had constables demand *every* copy of evidence."

"You've also never dealt with a murder investigation… though this victim seems like a pretty minor player. Trust me, if he was anyone important, they might confiscate every device in this store."

She took my warning as seriously as I meant it. "You're right. I've been lucky, only dealing with theft, and that indirectly. This neighborhood is – was – pretty safe. I imagine you've seen worse."

"Of course. This *is* Layafflr City, after all. And you're right, yours is one of the nicer areas." I didn't add that it was sliding downhill, in my estimation. No need to make the nice female unhappy about her home. She was probably one of the pillars still holding up the community.

"Well, I hope it turns out your case isn't connected to anything local. Even considering the pet store."

"I agree, although I've got to check out any possible lead. Thanks for your help. Anything else I should know?"

She looked up, her compad still in hand. "No… nothing I can think of. I'll call if I think of something, of course."

Frost. I was hoping she'd say, *I close up at nine.* But she hadn't blown me off, either.

"All right. Have a good afternoon, Tskksk. Hope your next visitor actually buys something."

"I hope they smell better, too."

Kkk, I was definitely calling her later, about the case or otherwise. *Especially* if the meeting with Pkstzk went badly. Dealing with my past reminded me how much I needed newer, better friends. A possible partner was almost too good to imagine.

Chapter 5 - Real Estate Agent

As I left the compad boutique, I realized I hadn't asked whether Tskksk knew the former owner of the abandoned pet store. On a positive note, the omission gave me an excuse to call her. And even if Tskksk didn't know, I might also ask "Madame Iyallette", the owner of the snack shop next door. If I guessed right, Iyallette was an ancient, patch-bald Hrotata female, stuck in the past by preference or dementia.

I still had neighborhood residences to canvas, although I didn't hold out hope for revelations there. Before knocking on doors, I surveyed the connecting streets once more. The pavements themselves didn't provide any evidence, but I wanted to see the whole region anyway. I still needed to know why the victim, Vzktkk, was walking in that area in the first place. What attractions did this part of Isstravil hold?

It seemed unlikely Vzktkk came there to shop. Aside from the closed pet importer, the compad store, and the snack shop, the only other commercial features I spotted were an automated electrical recharge station for vehicles, a similarly unattended public comm booth, and yet another closed storefront with a "For Sale" sign half-covering the name of a legal firm.

It was possible Vzktkk was only passing through, walking to a destination outside of the immediate neighborhood. For example, I had passed two restaurants on my walk from the aircar station. I might have to widen my search range to make sense of Vzktkk's route.

If the victim was just randomly passing through, there was no specific reason to expect him here… yet the shooter knew his or her quarry would be walking on this particular street. If Vzktkk habitually walked the same route, the locals might recognize him as a regular pedestrian.

Broken Record

I suspected that the victim was coming or going from a destination within the neighborhood. And if the killer knew to expect him… that meant…

Actually, what *did* it mean? Why *was* Vzktkk present, in this place, at that time? Was he lured by an invitation? Did he know someone in the neighborhood? Was he somehow connected to the absent owner of the decaying pet store? Was he chasing someone who lured him to the target site? Was he pursued and herded by a third party?

Lots of questions. Likely, most of them were irrelevant. As I walked the street, I knocked on doors and pressed buzzers. Most of my attempts met with no response. I wasn't surprised; the residents were probably out working hard. Good for them.

I did rouse a few locals at home: dependents, unemployed, elderly retired, a couple of sick homebodies and one Taratumm home on vacation.

As I suspected, the natives weren't much help. Everyone had heard about the murder, but nobody actually witnessed it or knew the victim. Nobody saw anyone suspicious or obviously armed in the area. I doubted any of them were hiding actual knowledge. Anything useful they might have seen was obscured by inattention, not complicity or cowardice. If you aren't expecting trouble, you don't spot its signs.

My inquiries did turn up a few useful scraps. The pet store had been closed since anyone could remember, at least twenty years ago, per the oldest continuous resident. That timing meant the owner hadn't just closed up without cleaning out excess inventory, like an rktpk or three. Someone entered – legally or not – and restocked the store with animals and feed. Like Tskksk, one other local remembered seeing the lights on inside the closed storefront, sometime in the last week. Someone was inside, using the building, recently.

One older female Vislin, a retiree named Ktvvsp, hinted at a possible reason for Vzktkk's visit to this particular corner of Isstravil. She relayed rumors that one of the buildings – she pointed vaguely down the street – had a notoriously high tenant turnover rate. While the residence wasn't advertised as a hotel or temporary housing, no one seemed to live there very long. Plus, no one living there was well-known in the neighborhood, and new faces almost always went to that door.

Her description brought several thoughts to my jaded mind. The more innocent options were a private hostel or safe house. It could be a legitimate but unadvertised business. It might be a safe house operated by law enforcement (local or planetary) or even the Great Family government. Or, it could be a flophouse for shadier characters needing a hideout.

Further down the morality scale, the building could be a criminal gang's meeting-house, a lair for conspiracy, a drug den, or a brothel. Any of those uses would bring in a variety of short-term visitors, enjoying the obscure and respectable façade provided by a working-class neighborhood.

And yes, all those suspicions might be wrong. The building might just be a terrible place to live, with tenants fleeing as fast as they could manage. Still, Ktvvsp's suspicion was enough to tag the site as one of Vzktkk's likely destinations.

My lovely old busybody was also familiar with all of the neighborhood's long-term residents. She vouched for Madame Iyallette's spotless reputation and the ambitionless innocence of her employee. She provided contact numbers for some of her neighbors and even seconded my opinion of technophile Tskksk's attractive competence. Of equal interest, she confirmed that Tskksk was unmated and not even seeing anyone, sad and surprising as that fact was.

But even the most productive font of local information could add little about the actual case. Ktvvsp had, in fact, been interviewed by the constables, who learned nothing from her. As with Tskksk, the little more I gleaned came from asking the questions the constables hadn't known to ask... or the ones they knew were irrelevant.

The interview with Ktvvsp took a full hour, including time to share a cup of broth and fresh marrow cakes. How can you refuse that? Pounding on doors before and afterward burned up another two hours. Between that search and my visits to the local shops, almost half the day was gone. The social snack stretched me past lunchtime, but I was going to need a solid meal eventually.

Broken Record

The advantage of lingering so long was that the workers gradually began to return home. I did my best to flag down whomever I could as the transports dropped off commuters.

My efforts met with even less success than my daytime rounds. A few individuals stopped to talk but added nothing to what I already knew. The others either ignored me outright or pled an urgent need to get home. No one struck me as hiding any dark secrets or repressed confessions. More likely, their reluctance to help had something to do with the lingering traces of rktpk blood on my armor.

At least, I had something to work with. I could research the owner of the pet store's building, as well as the ownership of the mysterious transient house. Eventually, Tskksk would transfer her surveillance data to my account. Possibly, one of my follow-up calls would lay further eggs.

I really wished I could cross-check my leads with the constabulary. In particular, they might have background on the transient house. If nothing else, I could rule it out faster if it was a known safehouse or private business. Theoretically, the constables would profit by the exchange, gaining any unique knowledge I held.

It wasn't exactly their fault that I couldn't share what I knew or ask for their help. It was my fault, particularly my desire to stay out of trouble. My youthful transgressions wouldn't be overlooked if I brought them up to explain my interest in a current case. The law held no provisions to trade past sins against present services.

If I were a better actor, I might play off my involvement as a random hire by the victim's mate. I never met the lady before, honest, constable.

The problem was, a good detective would pick up on the familiarity between Pkstzk and me, right away. An average detective would eventually notice the coincidental connections between us. Even a mediocre detective couldn't miss our association if the murder directly involved Pack Vzrrk. A terrible detective would be no help at all.

Nathan Large with Laine Megan Lundquist

It would be easier to build a cover story after I knew more about the crime itself, particularly after I learned what Pkstzk knew. If her first mate, my Pack-mate Rsspkz, *was* involved, then I couldn't officially investigate the case at all.. One of the hazards of P.I. work is getting summoned to court as a witness. Besides the conflict of interest, I wasn't sure I could accuse my former Pack leader in public.

Sure, I'd love to have a half-dozen bailiffs and a judge present when the accused recognized me! He surely wouldn't destroy my entire future in retaliation!

I might not be helping my old Pack-mates anymore, but I hadn't harmed them, either. For reasons of self-defense, I never testified as to their crimes. What would that accomplish? The two who weren't dead or fled were in jail for life already. Admitting to our other violations wouldn't lengthen that sentence.

I could only assume that my silence was the reason Rsspkz never named me as an accessory to his crimes. I wasn't a traitor, so he wouldn't betray me. Funny that *I* benefited from *his* Pack loyalty.

I was hoping this murder would be a nice, boring, armed robbery gone bad. What I had learned already in Isstravil argued against that possibility. Still, I could hope that Vzktkk was involved in some dirty business unrelated to *my* dirty business.

Maybe Pkstzk could add the glue I needed to make my scattered clues stick together. We'd assemble the mystery together, shake our heads, laugh or cry as appropriate, and move on with our lives. Maybe together?

I was way ahead of myself, as usual, about both the case and the potential relationship. I supposed it was bad form to ask a widow about her availability.

It was also too bad I couldn't sort out that old crush before chasing a new one. I intended to talk to Tskksk that night or early the next day, before my meeting with Pkstzk. I wanted as much background info as possible before confronting my 'client'.

In the meantime, a dust bath and armor wipe-down were in order, followed by a meal at whatever cost I could stomach. After that, I'd be ready for some heavy comm work.

Broken Record

I wrapped up my business in Isstravil and hiked back several blocks to the public transport stop. Sharing the big box with only a couple of late-shift workers, I was left alone with my thoughts during the ride.

The transport dumped me, once again, several blocks from my actual destination. Nobody got off with me. It had been too much to hope that I'd discover a neighbor who worked anywhere near Isstravil. Most of the time, it was too much to hope that I had a neighbor who worked, anywhere. My building is practically a shelter for the unemployed.

I'm kidding, of course. Layafflr allows only one cycle of public assistance before you get assigned to "civic maintenance". Most sapients would rather apply for a job cleaning toilets, rather than scrape dung off of the sonic emitters at the city border. Sometimes, the wildlife applies new dung while you're scraping off the old stuff.

I wasn't that far from dung scraping, myself. I could *walk* to the city borders from my apartment, for one thing. I would also need another paying job, fairly soon. Too bad I was spending all my business hours on *personal* business.

Right then, my personal business involved some personal grooming and dinner. I walked up to my apartment, shed my stained jacket and armor, and powdered and scraped my scales until I smelled only the scented dust. After I finished, I popped a frozen meal into the oven and toweled off while it reheated.

I almost mistook the ping of my compad for the ring of the oven timer. Once I figured out the difference, I checked my messages: the data from Tskksk had arrived.

I didn't expect her to follow up so fast. Her speed probably had more to do with diligence – or boredom – than any attempt to impress me. I considered calling back right away, just in case she was interested in my good opinion.

Kkk, better to play it warm and wait. Even if she had found some free time, it was still within business hours. After closing time, I'd have her full attention.

I may have mentioned, previously, that I'm something of a deviant. No, not just about the Pack loyalty issues. I'm also a pervert.

Nathan Large with Laine Megan Lundquist

Vislin, in contrast to our Hrotata cohorts, don't differ much between genders, physically. *We* can tell the difference, but most other sapients can't. And most of the time, the differences really don't matter. There's not much, besides egg-laying, to base any discrimination upon.

We're also not as frequently driven by sexual urges as mammalians. When the time is right and the opportunity presents, Vislin still experience a strong reproductive drive, but you won't see, for example, an advertisement with a scantily-clad Vislin female hinting that buying a product will improve your chances of mating with her. No such product exists, sad to say.

Vislin mate-seeking is more about forming a close association with someone, as a well-respected acquaintance or even friend, such that reproducing with you seems like a very good idea. That equation doesn't rule out jealousy, but Vislin jealousy is less about fighting over an object of desire and more about competing for a valuable resource.

By contrast, my perpetual notice of and desire for association with females – totally normal among Hrotata or, say, Humans – would be considered indecent among Vislin. I can generally keep my reactions under control, but sometimes I can't help being distracted by an attractive female. Small as the differences might be, I can spot them, especially in those females where the distinctions are… pronounced.

There are compensations for being so askew. I can understand the motivations of other sapients more easily where romantic behavior is involved. In my line of work, those motivations are usually the darker kind. I can even spot some underlying threads beneath the surface of Vislin behaviors, needs we don't often admit to ourselves. Of less professional value, I have more fun, especially when I can interact with said attractive females.

Tskksk wasn't my usual preference: a bit short, heavy in less ideal areas, and eyes more wide-set than I liked. She did have an adorably sharp tongue and a bright energy that I liked. Her enthusiasm was particularly admirable, given the setting of her shop and the difficulties her business must encounter.

Broken Record

She was a sharp contrast to Pkstzk, who was tall, muscular, and outwardly confident but privately needing constant reassurance of her value. Pkstzk was… at least she used to be… fearless, wild, and unprincipled. My attraction to her came partly from her looks and partly from my youthful impression of her carefree glamour. She was also the Pack leader's prize and therefore desirable. Was it just my personal oddity that magnified that value into physical attraction, or did I genuinely like Pkstzk for herself?

Thinking about Pkstzk reminded me that I had some work to do before our meeting. It was still a little early for business calls. While I bolted down my processed imitation offal dinner with one hand, I made some notes on my compad with the other.

I sketched out the crime scene: the main street, the cross streets at either end, the buildings, and the hypothetical murder site. This exercise didn't generate any new insights.

Next, I organized my list of names, contact numbers, addresses, and interview notes, and added a few more observations I hadn't recorded at the time. Once that task was done and my eating hand cleaned, I searched the network for more information.

I found public listings for the snack shop (proprietor: Iyallette), the compad store (with links to a virtual storefront, savvy business owner), and several apartment buildings nearby. The pet importer had no network presence, nor was its upstairs apartment visible. It had no current resident listed at its address, no sale or rental information, and no listing for an owner.

In fact, the whole building was suspiciously invisible. Considering the building's long vacancy, it was odd that the building's original owner never tried to find a buyer or new tenant… or else kept such transactions completely private. It gave the impression of deliberately avoiding the public record.

Such dormancy should have raised alarms during a murder investigation next door. I was starting to wonder if the constable detective in charge was overworked, dangerously incompetent… or being diverted away from certain leads.

To be fair, the explanation could be less harsh. Honest oversights could happen when an investigator ran with the strongest explanation or suspect and missed the opportunity to pick up key details. That kind of mistake is what creates cold cases. Spotting the gaps can sometimes solve those cases later, depending on whether overlooked evidence is still available.

Such oversights also keep P.I.s like myself employed, so I can't complain when my official counterparts drop a few crumbs. I also can't criticize them for haste. Hesitating on an investigation, *not* picking a direction and running it down at full speed, is sometimes just as much of a mistake as caution. Give a suspect time, and they'll eliminate more and more evidence.

This store, though… it hadn't been hiding very well. *I* spotted the signs of recent occupancy, even from the street. The neighbors noticed activity, too. And though those rktpk were locked inside the store, they weren't caged in the back. The inner door was closed, but not tightly, so they could have exited into the front room at any time. After that, anyone looking through the door lintel window could have spotted them. And even before then, anyone listening closely should have heard them screeching in hunger.

Something wasn't adding up about the place. I couldn't decide which way it was tilted. Was I exaggerating the importance of the pet store due to my own experiences there? Or were its oddities directly relevant to Vzktkk's death?

Frustrated, I switched tasks and tried to identify the transient house my elderly informant indicated. Per the pointing of her crooked claw, the target was probably one of three buildings on the far side of the street, past the shops.

One building was listed as an apartment with units for rent. I ruled out that candidate with only a little digging. Matching names to the addresses of each unit, I identified residents with tenures following a normal curve: a few tenants of a year or less, one at twenty-two years, and the majority living there for somewhere between five and ten years.

The next property in line was also classified as residential, but not specifically an apartment complex. Its owner was a private company owned by Herds Boprad and Rosht, respectable Taratumm families mostly involved in freight, tourism, and other forms of transport. The building could be a private hotel for guests, I supposed, but the location wasn't ideal. More likely it was used as condominium housing for Herd members, friends, and business associates staying temporarily on ChttKttp.

Frost, if the second building was the source of that old Vislin's concerns, then its connection to the murder victim was unclear at best. Unless Vzktkk had business with the owners – and Pkstzk might or might not be able to answer that – then he probably wasn't going to their building. He might have a second-degree connection to one of the tenants there, but finding that link would take even deeper digging.

The last of the three candidate buildings showed mixed use. A real estate firm owned the property, leasing out sections to various tenants. The top floor was vacant, with an advertising agency listed as the prior tenant. The next floor down was rented as residence to a private individual named Kssptch. The name's morphology was Vislin, but I couldn't find a listing for any "Kssptch" to verify that against. A very private individual, it seemed. Below that floor was a block of art studios, each either vacant or rented to a named artist or working group. I was intrigued to find a wood-crafter among them… I might be able to indulge my hobby if I had to stop there in person. The lower two floors were also businesses: a law firm and a financial advisor.

Strange that I hadn't seen either business advertised at street level. Then again, some offices were kept unofficial, rather than opened as public storefronts. The owners might have reasons to keep their locations private, such as avoiding records theft or angry clients.

So, let's see. Vzktkk could have been: arranging his retirement, suing or being sued, learning pottery or painting, looking for an office for a new business, visiting somebody named Kssptch, or just saying hello to someone working on any of these floors. Maybe he had interests with Herds Boprad and Rosht next door or with one of their guests. Or maybe he was visiting any of a hundred residents in a particular apartment building… or the ones all around nearby… or another on another block… or possibly, *none* of this information was relevant.

I was gathering a lot of data without context. I was filling time and fully aware of that fact. My research killed a couple of hours, at least. It was almost time to start making calls.

I decided to start with Madame Iyallette. Given that her employee was minding the shop, I probably wouldn't be interrupting her there, though I might disrupt her dinner. I dialed the number the drowsy shop-minder gave me and waited through three signals before the line picked up.

"Iyallette... who is this?" came a decidedly female voice, heavy, as if forced through a thick throat. Her production sounded wet, even for a Hrotata speaking in their own tongue, not coincidentally the default business language of Hrotata Prime and its colony worlds.

"My name is Stchvk. I'm investigating a business in your neighborhood: the pet import/export shop. Did your employee... Hrusslitl... mention me?"

"No, I haven't spoken with him today. I assume you questioned him at my store?" For a ponderously slow speaker, she was very direct, getting to business without any evidence of bluster or confusion.

"Yes, Mistress," I continued politely. "He couldn't identify the owner of that property, but thought you might be able to recall more. It appears that the building has been continuously owned – and closed – for nearly two decades, yet I found evidence of more recent occupation. In fact, the last sale goes back far enough that there are no public records. It looks like your own business might have been a contemporary..." I let the thought hang, reluctant to say anything further which might be taken as an insult, either to the elderly matron herself or to her aging shop.

If she took offense, she didn't bother to express any. "I do recall when it was last open. All sorts of animal noises... and smells. I met some of the employees, but I can't recall but a couple of names anymore. I don't think I met any owner, either of the business or of the building. Pardon, but may I ask you: what is your interest?"

Broken Record

I did my best to match her approach: "Originally, I was checking out the property as part of a larger survey of Isstravil's real estate. The building looked ideal for my employer's needs. I discovered, though, that there were live animals inside... the last survivor attacked me. A rktpk on the edge of starvation tried to eat me. I had to put it down."

I put an edge of disgust into my voice as I continued: "There were originally more animals quartered there, but they were dead and eaten. After that incident, I asked around the neighborhood, trying to find out who was responsible for such abuse. When I file my report, I'll want to direct the constabulary to the building owner."

She remained quiet for a few moments after I finished, then responded: "I see. Well, I share your interest in reporting such cruelty. I'm sorry I cannot help you more directly, but I will inquire amongst my former neighbors to see what they might recall. Let me give you those employees' names, as well. They will have aged and moved on, of course, but the living might remember something more."

"Yes, please, and thank you," I agreed, "But are you certain you don't know anything more about that building? Any signs indicating space available or whom to contact to rent? Any other tenants, perhaps in the apartment above?"

"No... no, I'm sorry," Iyallette replied after some thought. "I confess I didn't pay it much attention, other than as a nuisance. I only own the provisions store. Once, I managed that site and several others, but I stopped spending much time there once I transferred management duties to subordinates."

Sss, absentee owner. That might be the case with the pet store, too. I realized I was probably screeching at vanished prey, but I had to try one more question.

"I see. One more thing: are you familiar with the recent murder on your street? Have you been contacted by law enforcement investigating that crime?"

Iyallette's answer came more quickly this time: "I am, and I have, but that call went much like this one. I had little to add to their knowledge. I don't see any connection between that event and your interests, Mister Stchvk."

"Nor do I, and there may be no connection, but it overlaps with my survey, nonetheless. Two cases of violent criminal activity in what appears to be an otherwise peaceful neighborhood? If coincidence, it suggests a general downturn in Isstravil's quality of life. If not, then it might be a relief to trace both troubles back to a single source."

"Yes, I understand your point." The hesitation in her reply suggested declining patience. "I won't take the time to regale you, but I'm sure you know that nowhere in this City is free of 'violent criminal activity'. Isstravil is more peaceful than some districts, but hardly quiet. I wish you success on your investigation, but I can't do your work, sorting out what might be relevant from what is merely gossip. I suggest you sharpen your questions and direct them to more appropriate sources. Now, do you want those names?"

She made her point, and it was fair. She wasn't going to share stories over broth and cakes. She was a busy matron... or at least a formerly busy matron trying to enjoy semi-retirement. I took down the employee names she could recall and thanked her for her time.

I filed these drips of new information and immediately went to call Tskksk. Her compad line went directly to voice recording. I thought I had waited long enough, but maybe she needed some time to finish closing her store.

I wanted her guidance to sort through the data dump she sent from her security program. Technically, I knew what I had: a raw recording of a wide swathe of the EM spectrum, sorted by frequency and intensity and somewhat localized as to direction of origin. A few translation programs pre-sorted the signals into components, chunked by frequency range, duration, continuity, etc. However, a viewer still needed to know what to look for in order to recognize what he was seeing. I couldn't tell a laser blast from a solar flare, even after recoding.

If I couldn't reach Tskksk, I could download a program that would label sections of the signal by likely source, providing limited identification. Besides being less enjoyable, that route would cost more in time and credits, and would lack any personal perspective or insight. Tskksk struck me as someone who paid attention to the details – a trait I admired – and would be familiar with the general background noise of her neighborhood. Either way, she would be fastest to spot any relevant highlights.

Broken Record

To keep myself busy while I waited to call again, I tried some of the contact numbers I collected throughout the day. These were mostly neighbors of the residents I already spoke with, offered in the hopes that someone else would know more.

Those hopes proved groundless. Of the numbers that picked up, most claimed ignorance due to absence, sleep, or thick walls between themselves and the murder. A few didn't want to talk, saying they'd already made a statement to the constables. One call was at least interesting, with the contact (a Taratumm male) trying to pump me for more information about the dead sapient. He had little to contribute in return.

Nobody had lived in the neighborhood long enough to know about the pet store or its owner. Nobody saw anything else suspicious in the area. Nobody knew anyone else to contact, otherwise.

After nine such fruitless calls, I tried Tskksk again. Still direct to recording. Nine decads, almost an hour after closing, and her personal line was still off? Was I being over-eager? Paranoid, maybe. She might just need time to unwind before dealing with business again. Still, why shut off your notification entirely? I didn't do that, often, and I frequently had callers to avoid.

Still, I couldn't wait until too late. Tskksk probably slept early. The last thing I wanted was to irritate her by calling during rest hours. Speaking of which, I was feeling tired all of the sudden. The day's work felt like it was taking a collective toll. I mistyped a couple of characters in my notes and had to set the compad down. My eyes were heavy and my movements slow.

Maybe I could just take a short nap, an hour or so, then get up and try calling again? I staggered over to my nest, still undressed from bathing, and started to kneel down. Then I remembered that my meal container was still sitting on my desk. It wasn't the first time I'd left trash lying around the place, but it bothered me that I forgot the mess so completely.

For that matter, it bothered me that I was again so deeply fatigued with little warning. I struggled to snap back awake, wondering whether my reluctance to seek medical help was dangerous folly.

How long would I sleep, this time? The last time I intended to nap, I lost the entire evening into the next morning.

The sleep itself felt normal and I hadn't felt sluggish when I woke, but falling asleep so deeply, without intention or drugs, was irregular for me. Usually it took me a few decads to get comfortable and slip under.

My efforts to stay awake were rewarded by a few moments of clear thought. I got up and threw away my dinner leavings and locked my compad in a hand-made cabinet, the closest thing I owned to secure storage. I cleaned my beak in the bathroom. During that process, I wondered how I had shifted so fully from drowsing to alertness. That, in itself, was strange.

As I considered the anomaly, my mind began to wander again. My reprieve from fatigue was only temporary. I decided I'd give it one more night, but if I started to daze out the next day, I'd have to see a doctor.

Tomorrow... I'd see Pkstzk. The thought sent me to bed with the hope of pleasant dreams.

Chapter 6 - Downtown Girl

True to pattern, I woke up the next morning feeling completely normal: stiff, irritable, and slightly nauseous, but no longer drowsy. While I filled a bottle from the tap, I tried once more to diagnose my symptoms.

I couldn't think of anything I might have done on my vacation – taken, eaten, been exposed to – that might bring on such lethargy. I wasn't feverish. I kept getting morning aches in my lower legs and side, but those faded soon after waking. I had no loose or discolored scales, and my eyes were clear. I was pretty sure I hadn't been bitten, licked, or otherwise touched by any strange wildlife... or any strange sapients, for that matter.

The real anomaly was how little I could remember about my beach-side vacation. Per my calendar, I was gone for three weeks. I certainly remembered enjoying the time. I knew I had roamed the warm sands and admired the other sunbathers, but few names, faces, or bodies came to mind. I remembered dining well, but I wasn't sure precisely what I had eaten.

I could guess, and the guesses seemed right, but a troublesome haze hung between probability and certainty.

My most solid memories were about the past case itself. The initial meeting with my employer, Jevvettr, was vivid. The names of my prime suspects came easily to mind. Those suspects' opportunities for theft, their roles in the building where the theft occurred, and even their personal backgrounds were still familiar.

Why was the job so memorable but the background detail wasn't? I may be a dedicated professional, but it was still odd that I retained so much job-related data yet couldn't recall any pretty faces or pleasant conversations.

I wasn't having any such problems with my personal history. For example, I could bring Pkstzk's image to mind, just fine. I wondered how much her appearance had changed between past and present. Hold on... *that* might be an answerable question.

I was already searching through social media sites before I realized I had changed subjects. First, I'm probing my memory for soft spots, and next, I'm stalking an old crush online? Why was I avoiding the problem?

The most obvious answer: because it *was* a big problem. It was too big to solve quickly. I had more urgent troubles to resolve before worrying about my health. Digging into my disorders – mental, physical or both – was more than I could deal with right then. As long as I could manage in the short term, I'd have to prioritize my health below my reputation and freedom. I could lose either or both, if this case unearthed the unsavory history of Pack Vzrrk.

Well, while I was already looking, *why not* see how time had treated Pkstzk? She did have an account on the planet's most popular social site, but her profile was neglected: bare-bones personal info, few updates, no controversial opinions, and pictures several years out of date. Her most recent image looked much the same as I remembered, though more drab: no scale paint, fewer spikes on her armor, and much cheaper jewelry.

By comparison, you won't find *any* picture of me on *any* site, unless you count an accidental capture in the background of a news story. A good private detective maintains a minimal public presence, a requirement that matches well with my personal need for secrecy. I had to advertise on business sites, but ads didn't require any pictures or biographical data... in fact, *not* posting my grimacing beak was probably better for business.

While I poked at my 'pad, I plodded through my morning routine. Nothing new came of my other research. I didn't have any new messages waiting... at least none I wanted to read.

I tried Tskksk's number again, with the same result as before: straight to messages. I left a new voice recording, mentioning my concerns for her safety and apologizing if I was overdoing the calls.

I wondered if I should stop by her shop in Isstravil, just to make sure she was safe. It was possible she was avoiding me. That would be strange, but I was paranoid enough to wonder if I'd put her in danger. Vzktkk's killer could have noticed me asking questions and threatened anyone I visited.

No, I didn't think Tskksk was avoiding me out of distaste. I was almost certain I hadn't said anything wrong. She also didn't seem like the type to develop sudden misgivings after being friendly before.

Either way, her compad was *off*. A user might forget to turn their 'pad back on after shutdown, but I hardly ever turned mine off. Surely, she'd have a model with better battery life. Hers should be less likely to fail and crash, also. I could think of several explanations why someone's personal compad might suddenly die, but few of them were innocent. Since her personal number was also her business number, it was less likely she broke her own system tinkering with the unit's hardware or installing questionable software. She seemed too savvy for that kind of risk.

I was hitting knot after knot of inexplicable improbability... the sort of tangles that make me want to gnaw them apart. Something valuable might be wrapped within.

Tskksk was unavailable. So were my vacation memories. So were the records on the pet importer, along with several details about neighboring buildings and residents in Isstravil. Individually, any one of these information gaps could be random, meaningless, or trivially explainable. Likely, none of them were related, to one another or to my case. But all together, they were making my jaw ache.

The same could be said for the concentrate bar I gnawed for breakfast. At least it tasted better than nothing at all. That's what a few credits will buy you: "better than nothing".

To combat my agitation, I decided to allow myself a break. If Tskksk called back, great. If I thought of a clue I had missed – regarding the case or my own mental health – also good. If not, I wasn't going to keep grinding my beak. Hopefully, my meeting that night would highlight the right path. Until then, I needed to relax.

Nathan Large with Laine Megan Lundquist

I set aside a budget for the day, enough for some travel and a snack. Since there was no rush, I walked to the public transport stop and took a leisurely flight to one of my favorite spots: a public park a few miles away.

While there was plenty of nature all around Layafflr City, the parks featured much more controlled, friendly flora and fauna. The same sonic technology that kept pests out of the city kept desirably attractive animals captive within the parks. The plants were neatly organized and conveniently labeled. If it wasn't for the greenery's tendency to wander out of its designated beds, the park would resemble a garden more than a landscape.

Even with all the artificial maintenance, I liked the soil underfoot and the fliers squeaking overhead. I walked the designated path around the park's perimeter three times, picking up a hot sausage from a familiar vendor on the second lap. The taste and texture brought back happy memories. In fact, it was an almost perfectly picturesque afternoon.

Ever have one of those experiences you question because it seems *too* perfect? I shook off the feeling, but for a few hectads, I was suspicious of how well my relaxation was going.

It was something about the sausage. It tasted *exactly* like I remembered, for one thing. Sausages don't usually do that. There was something else, though... some other memory linked to the sausage. Kkk, sausage link.

Trying to unravel that nagging thought bled poison into the rest of my happy afternoon. I forced myself to stop worrying at the feeling, to preserve what pleasure I could.

I felt good, and I looked good. Anticipating the meeting with Pkstzk later that evening, I was dressed in my best armor. That meant the outfit I wore least often, such that it was less faded and scratched than my working gear. It also had a hard leather cap that my usual armor lacked, a piece both stylish and functional. I might not be able to justify actual formalwear, but I could at least avoid looking broke.

Of course, dried blood and tissue were still stuck to my other armor. That fact strongly influenced my choice. I might have to pay for professional cleaning if I couldn't remove the gore myself. At least I knew people who could handle that sort of mess without asking uncomfortable questions... apart from "cash or credit?".

Sss, I really needed an actual vacation. Not a working vacation, a complete break. Separately, I needed a big, well-paying case. Mutually opposing needs. I supposed a big enough case could keep my mind thoroughly engrossed *and* pay well. Money would then reduce most of my problems, particularly by paying for a vacation.

There, a solution. All I needed was a major crime and a wealthy victim who somehow wasn't already being adequately assisted by law enforcement.

Anyone? No? I gave my compad a look of mock anticipation as I pulled it out of its carrying pouch. In return, it taunted me with a blank screen. Sitting on a park bench, I went through a few news articles, just to see if the city in general had quieted down.

It was actually a slow news day. No murders and no accidents, only a minor political scandal... the biggest headline was the visit of an interstellar celebrity and the problems their security was causing for local traffic.

For the sake of further avoidance, I pulled up Tskksk's EM recordings and played with them like a puzzle, sliding the time window back and forth, shading various frequency bands in and out, and looking for interesting patterns. I highlighted the two radio signals Tskksk already identified as compad calls. According to her expertise, the calls were both placed from the same 'pad, somewhere very near her store, possibly bracketing Vzktkk's time of death.

Looking backward in time, I didn't find any matching signals from earlier the same day, nor any others later that night. There were other compad calls, but I couldn't tell if their differences came from different personal frequencies (and thus, different compads), or if the calls might have come from the same compad at different locations.

Similarly, I could tag the laser discharge between the two calls but found no similar pattern anywhere else in the recording. At least, I was getting better using the program and reading its output. Unfortunately, I had no reference for analyzing the recording further. I couldn't make it answer my other questions: What type of laser was it? What size, frequency, or manufacturer? What sort of compad placed those calls? Could we identify the compad's owner or match it to a sample? Had any vehicles passed nearby, before, during, or after the attack?

Once Tskksk sent the recording to a crime lab, they would dig into all these questions and more, with better tools to get answers. I wished them luck. However, I needed to keep up as best I could, using any advantages I could steal. Pkstzk needed answers before the constables came knocking at her door again.

You might have gathered that I'm fluent in criminal forensics. It's an expertise born of necessity, on both sides of the law. As a youth, I worked hard to minimize the traces I and my Pack-mates left when "working". Later, I translated that vocational training into more legal (though less profitable) employment.

Most of my talents operate on the low-tech side, though. I might not be as thorough and precise as a professional criminal analysis team, but I'm much cheaper and sometimes faster. Expert software negates that speed advantage, but identifying a clue isn't the same as knowing its relevance. Until the Great Family embraces A.I., a good P.I. is still the most effective investigator in town.

Speaking of which, I was feeling overloaded with data without context. Seeking relevance was literally my next step. For multiple reasons, I was eagerly anticipating my conversation with Pkstzk.

I looked up from my compad to find dusk already stretching the shadows. Reverie, research and review had kept me busy for a long time. My appetite must have declined, too, since I wasn't distracted by hunger. Even a vendor cart sausage wasn't usually *that* filling.

I got my wish, though: I had passed the time. It was time to find transport to Kzztkrt Tk, the restaurant where Pkstzk worked.

The public transport schedule would make me late. Instead, I went over my self-imposed budget and rented a personal aircar. At least, I wouldn't show up at the restaurant on foot. I couldn't remember how fancy a place Kzztkrt Tk was, but hopefully, my armor would pass the dress code. I was just going to the lounge, so I didn't have to worry about reserving a table in advance.

Broken Record

On the flight over, I busied myself researching the restaurant. It held an enviable location between the city's shuttle port and government center, easily able to capture traffic between the two. At the same time, Kzztkrt Tk was outside of the primary transit routes and closer to the port than the seats of power. That suggested cheaper real estate, if not a certain intentional exclusivity. The restaurant claimed to be "fine dining", meaning that an actual meal there would blow the rest of my savings. Its reviews didn't uphold that status, though. Few critics agreed that it belonged in the upper ranks of Layafflr's culinary scene.

It had no dress code listed. Nothing else on its public site seemed relevant. For instance, nothing would tell me why Pkstzk was working there, nor whether she was happy at her job. I imagined it was just a job, neither desirable nor terrible. I wondered if she was tending bar – she used to enjoy drinking, at least – or waiting tables.

I was about to find out. The aircar drifted down, waiting for a open spot on the curb before releasing me.

I stepped out onto a cleaner, better-lit street than any I had seen since my return to the City. A glowing projection sign made Kzztkrt Tk unmissable. Just in case, though, the building was wrapped in three wide bands of different colored metals: blue, green, and yellow. Garish underlighting recolored the buff sandstone beneath in the same three hues.

Along the same row, three other restaurants announced themselves in varying style. The eateries were spaced between a live theater, an upscale Thunder Bar, a casino, and six little boutique stores. The latter were all closed for the evening, but the entertainment venues were packed.

I hadn't been to that neighborhood in far too long. For one thing, I hadn't been able to afford such pleasures in years. I also hadn't traveled there for any cases. Sadly, the kinds of cases I usually work don't involve such affluent surroundings. Otherwise, they might pay more.

Well, all that changed tonight... sort of. I was there on a case, but it wasn't the paying kind. And I still couldn't afford the area. It was probably too much to expect that Pkstzk would cover my tab. I should actually offer to buy her a drink.

If she was working as a hostess, I wouldn't even draw attention by inviting her to sit and drink with me. She'd get to sip something expensively priced yet secretly cheap and non-intoxicating, while she entertained a 'customer'.

I mentally swallowed the expense, again. Her drink, plus my own, would have to suffice for dinner. Squaring my shoulders and putting on my best "I belong here" expression, I walked up to Kzztkrt Tk.

The door guard, a stereotypical Taratumm brute, rolled a yellow eyeball over me as I neared. I must have passed scrutiny, because he opened the door before I walked into it. I didn't merit a greeting, though; he just watched as I walked inside. I thanked him anyway.

The restaurant's interior was more subdued than its exterior. The colors were darker, the floor was tiled with tasteful hardwood squares, and the lights were low. The smells of fresh meat and crisped skin were already making me drool. It was going to be a cruel, hard evening full of temptations.

The sounds of conversation drifted from the main floor, but the lounge where I entered was almost empty.

The bartender was definitely not Pkstzk. Instead, a grizzled, older Hrotata male stood on a raised platform behind the Vislin-height bar. The white streaks in his fur contrasted with their black background. His face was almost entirely grey and looked pushed-in, possibly from a broken nose. Despite his age, he looked solidly built, with feminine muscle mass and a broad jaw.

Like most restaurants in Layafflr City, Kzztkrt Tk served all three Great Family species, but its name and décor favored Vislin. The owner was probably Vislin. As such, one might expect entirely Vislin wait-staff, cooks, and bartender, but nothing required such.

I decided to satisfy my curiosity. Ignoring the host standing guard between the lounge and the restaurant entrance, I crossed directly to the bar and took an empty seat.

"Chchch, greytip, what's on tap?" I asked, like someone who didn't mind being noticed.

Broken Record

The bartender rolled his head around to look at me and answered without otherwise moving, "Locally, I have Thrap Green, Zchkt, and Old Shell. Imports are Terran Tkfsh Ht 90, Prime's Best, and Ktkzk Cht Pkz."

I was surprised, both by the small number of options and the wide range within them. A local fermented fruit juice, a faddish Terran grain 'beer', *and* a Vislin Cht Pkz? They really were trying to appeal to all customers. I ordered a glass of the Ktkzk Cht Pkz, a re-imagined version of a traditional Vislin brew, still made from the sugary secretions of insects, but with the shell pieces strained out and the psychoactive toxins denatured… mostly. Its texture was also greatly improved by nitrogenation.

As the bartender poured, I tried to engage him in further conversation: "No screens in here, I see. Customers must talk rather than watch the games."

The Hrotata gave me another lazy glance and half a smile. "Anyone who wants that noise can go to the bar down the street. Talk all you want, but you might find me a boring companion. It's usually better to bring your own partner here… no slight meant to your social life."

I was starting to like this curmudgeon. I decided to do my best *not* to irritate him. "None taken. I'm on my own tonight. The Pack's all busy, you know how it goes."

"Generally so." The bartender put down my bubbling, milky drink, garnished with an impaled beetle. "That's seven and a quarter."

I handed him ten in scrip and managed to squeeze out the words, "Keep the change." I would have liked to keep it, myself, but I wanted to stay friendly with my new acquaintance.

He nodded in appreciation, a little nod for a little tip. "Anything else you need?" he asked, also looking like he'd rather not say the words.

I resisted about five different sarcastic replies, plus the temptation to just ask where I could find Pkstzk. Instead, I kept making small talk: "This will be fine, thank you. Do you serve any small plates in the lounge?"

"No, food is only in the restaurant. Waiting on a table?"

"No, still a little early for me. Just the drink then, I suppose. Ttt, actually, do you have any recommendations for a show? Anything you hear is good?"

The bartender looked pained by the topic, but answered, "The place down the street is showing *Fifty Days Alone*, but I hear it's terrible. Other than that warning, sorry, can't help you." He panned up and down the bar, pointedly searching for some other, nonexistent customer as an excuse to escape.

I had pity on his curdled soul and let him go. "Thanks, anyway."

So, where was Pkstzk? I realized she might need some time to notice my presence. If the roles were reversed, *I* would have checked the lounge every few minutes looking for *her*. I bent my beak to my drink and turned a slow circle in my seat, surveying the room as surreptitiously as I could.

There she was, peeking out of the dining area. Our eyes met, and I managed to avoid staring. I turned back to the bar and carefully put down my drink. Just her face was enough to jostle my nerves. What was I going to do when her entire body came near?

I'd have my answer before much longer. I heard the dividing door open and footsteps clack across the tile floor. Warm, warm, I was totally warm. I looked up and saw Pkstzk walking up to the bar.

She paid me no attention, but instead addressed the bartender: "Vulletine, two Tkfsh Ht, then I'm on break for five."

The Hrotata poured two glasses of foaming brown brew and laid them out on a tray. He made no further comment as he slid the tray across for her reach.

I recognized a setup when I heard one. I managed to look up at just the right moment to catch Pkstzk's 'accidental' glance in my direction. I gave her my best appraising look, which wasn't difficult, and she returned the compliment, which I hoped was just as effortless. She walked away with the loaded tray and a gratuitous saunter. I watched her retreating tail with genuine interest.

Time hadn't been too harsh with her. Like me, her scales suffered a little yellowing and flaking, but no Vislin avoided that consequence... at least not without dying young. She was either avoiding restorative treatments and cover-ups or more likely couldn't afford either, which I could respect either way. She was still strong and healthy, and judging by her expression, aware of her assets. A workplace like that could grind down some sapients, but she didn't look fatigued or sullen. She wore a simple cloth uniform, brown tunic and skirt, with a pouched cinching belt. She'd look good in anything or nothing... particularly nothing.

Once she disappeared again into the restaurant, I turned back to the bartender, Vulletine, and wasted no time starting Act Two of our performance.

"The night has improved," I crowed with a pleased click. "Any chance I could have her favorite drink waiting for the lady when she gets free?"

"Water?" the Hrotata shot back with weaponized sarcasm. "That's what she usually has. You'd have to guess what she'd like when someone else is paying."

"I see. Well, let's take the safe bet and line up another of what I'm having."

"It's your credit, lonely. I should let you know, to be fair, that your chances are poor. She lost her mate just recently... dead... so she might want company, but nothing else. I'm telling you for *her* benefit, not yours. You try and take advantage of her, your next drink here will have an unpleasant mixer."

In contrast to his previous phlegm, the grizzled bartender was suddenly, intensely involved. Why was he so protective of Pkstzk? Simple courtesy between long-time coworkers? Some effect of her enchanting personality? He was pretty talkative regardless of the reason. He could have ignored us and let Pkstzk turn me down herself. My respect for the elder grew, even if I didn't fully understand his motivations.

I curled my claws under, hands on the bar, in a display of peaceful intent. "Slow down, greytip, I just wanted to meet her. You know it doesn't work like that for Vislin... I'm sure she'll be clear about what she wants and doesn't want."

If the Hrotata Goddess of Truth was listening, I'm sure she was retching. Pkstzk and I were already manufacturing a "first meeting" for public benefit. As it was, that public consisted of one old Hrotata bartender. I was already lying to him about what I was doing there, then defending myself with a known cultural truth... which *wasn't* actually true in my case... but was truer in *this* case, despite appearances, because Pkstzk and I already, secretly, knew each other. Just sorting out the logic makes *me* feel a little queasy.

Vulletine looked skeptical, but rolled his back and neck, dismissing all Vislin nonsense. "Just a fair warning. However it 'works', you mind your behavior."

I was spared the need for further protestation by Pkstzk's return. She tapped back up to the bar and set down the empty tray.

The bartender accepted it and told her: "The fellow there has a Cht Pkz lined up for you... you want the drink?"

Pkstzk gave me another calculated look, then answered, "Sure." To me, she added, "Thanks..."

"Stchvk," I supplied on cue. "I'm out alone tonight, in an area I don't know well. Trade me some time for the drink? I promise I won't waste your break."

Vulletine watched us with one eye, looking nonplussed. Maybe I *was* playing a little stiff, but I also didn't want to overdo the come-on and make Pkstzk's acceptance seem less likely.

"I'll hold you to that," she agreed, taking the filled glass from the bartender. "Join me at a table... clear up some bar space?"

I made a show of looking down the nearly-empty bar, but didn't raise any objections. "Wonderful."

I followed her, glass in hand, to a round wooden table near the entry doors, a good five meters from the bar. Nobody else sat at any adjacent tables. If we kept our voices down, no one should be in earshot. I assumed no one was *trying* to listen in on us. Thinking otherwise really would be paranoid.

We sat down together and assumed postures of cautious interest. Pkstzk stayed quiet at first. I waited until I decided I would have to say something first. While I was thinking how to start, she beat me to the shot: "Stchvk... thank you for coming."

"Rrr, you're welcome?" I managed, stupidly. Getting my balance, I shifted to bravado: "Why wouldn't I? You tell me you're in trouble, of course I'll come help."

"I wasn't sure about that. You stayed distant... and I respected that... but I didn't know *why* you kept away. Were you angry? Afraid? Threatened? Just didn't care?" She kept her voice calm and her expression flat, to make our conversation look like a polite social meeting. Unfortunately, I was missing the cues that would mark her words as accusations or expressions of sympathy. I leaned toward the latter out of hope.

I was practiced in the same neutral manner and gave it back with ease. "Some fear. Some practical reasons. If I was caught and joined the Pack in jail, I couldn't do them or myself any good. I still don't see how I can help any of them... but you, you stayed clear, too. I figured we were both better off, separate, silent, and safe."

"Practical? That's the Stchvk I remember. Always looking at the balance sheet. Taking the safe bets. I wasn't into 'safe' back then, but I guess yours was the winning play." Her façade slipped, and I heard traces of both resentment and respect.

Funny, being thought of as a stodgy old accountant. To the wider society, I was a barely tolerated rogue. In Pack Vzrrk, I was a conservative.

"Compared to prison, yes, you could say that. I haven't felt like a winner, though. It's lonely. From where I'm sitting, you've done better than me... a job, a regular paycheck, a mate... sorry, but that was true until recently. I haven't built even that much."

She hissed. "Let me make you feel better, then. You're *free*. Freedom may not seem like much, if you're poor, but a job like this *is* a prison sentence. It's the best I can do. And I only did this well because Vzktkk made me look good.

"I needed him, Stchvk, but not the way I needed Rsspkz... I needed Vzktkk to survive, to keep me out of trouble. I needed Rsspkz to feel alive. I've felt dead inside for nine years. Seeing you... well, it's bad circumstances, but it reminds me how I used to feel back then."

Nathan Large with Laine Megan Lundquist

I did *not* like where the conversation was heading. Sure, if I understood her correctly, it was nice to feel needed, especially if she needed *me* like she had needed her first mate.

But her nostalgia for the old days was not a sentiment I shared. Between past and present, I was much happier in the present... or was I? I'd *choose* now over then, having experienced both, but I suppose I did have a grand time back before things went bad. Pkstzk still remembered the happy times, but she hadn't found anything better since, to contrast against her thrilling, self-indulgent, destructive past. What a tragedy.

"I appreciate the thought... but Pkstzk, our good times used to come at the expense of others' misery. That's a big part of why I stayed away. I can honor Pack-bond without wanting to repeat our past mistakes. Helping them means more than just getting them free or being an accomplice. It means doing the right things, setting an example, and being available to help them... the right way. That calculation is why I can be here to help you, now. It sounds like Vzktkk did that for you. He helped you build something solid... something real. It might not be exciting, but it won't crumble like the Pack did."

I was surprised at my own speech, but then again, I'd been rehearsing it informally for years. Pkstzk was surprised, too; her mask cracked entirely and she fixed me with a hostile glare. Her voice remained calm, if a bit colder: "I don't know about 'right' or 'wrong'. It seems like misery comes no matter what we do. You're not happy. I'm not happy. Rsspkz sure isn't happy, and Vzktkk... well, only the priests would claim he's happy. Sorry if I'm not worrying about other sapients' happiness. I don't share your faith in any reward for virtue."

I let slip an exasperated hiss. "Look, I'm not here to offer explanations. I don't claim any moral superiority. I just know what works for me. I'm in a position to help you. That's why you came to me, right? I had hoped it *was* more than desperation..."

She interrupted, full of contrition: "Vvv, Stchvk, I'm sorry. I didn't mean to accuse you of anything. I'm just miserable. I do need you..." She left the pause open to interpretation, then continued, "I have to know what happened to Vzktkk, for my own sanity. He was all I had. Someone took him from me. I want them punished. Even if you *weren't* a licensed detective, you're still the cleverest sapient I ever knew... I know you can figure it out. The constables... even if they solve the murder, they won't do more than put the killer in prison. I want to make sure they suffer."

She really *hadn't* changed inside, and that wasn't a compliment. A streak of bitter, vengeful selfishness showed through, a flaw I'd glossed over in my memories. She thought she deserved everything. If she was denied, blood was due.

I put up a hand and took my turn being cold: "*If* I find the sapient responsible, before the constables do, I'll turn them over for trial. I'm an independent detective, not a bounty hunter. If someone threatens me... or you... I'll do what's necessary to remove the threat, but that's it. Are we clear on that much, first?"

She left claw dents on the tabletop, but eventually fluffed her crest in agreement. "Fine. I hoped you would be more... flexible... but I have to accept that. I suppose it's too much to ask that you give me a name, first, before calling in the law?"

"Since you ask, no. But I won't let a killer go free, either, no matter what they threaten or how much they offer, so you get that in trade. A P.I. with 'flexible' standards might sell out their client if the criminals offer more... I won't. And for old times' sake, you don't even have to pay me. Not even expenses. As long as you'll let me investigate properly, consider me hired... and on your side, no matter what."

Her expression softened. Pkstzk reached out and laid her hand over mine. I noticed neither of us had touched our drinks... a bit of a slip, if we were playing at newly-met romance.

She answered, "All right, hero. I'll accept your terms. And thank you, for that much. I just have to hope you find enough to sign the nest-defecator's death warrant."

"I can't disagree. To be honest, I've been working the case already, ever since I got your note. Vzktkk's death definitely looks premeditated."

I caught her surprised. "All week? Do you have any suspects?"

"I've only been back in town for two days, actually. You stopped by while I was away on assignment. No suspects, yet, but I gained some information about where and how it happened... more than you probably have time to hear. Aren't your five decads over already?"

She looked at the clock behind the bar and cursed theatrically. "You're right. I should have realized we'd need more time. Wait..." She reached into a pouch on her belt and pulled out a keycard. "This is for a room at Taburket's, near the shuttle port. I rented it in case we needed somewhere else to meet without raising suspicion."

A pricey hotel room in the center of the city *would* keep us away from the eyes of our neighbors... although, meeting at a prearranged room might seem odd for a "first date". The anomaly would draw attention if anyone was already watching Pkstzk closely. The proposition certainly seemed presumptuous to *me*.

Not that I was complaining, though. We might not be ethically compatible, but between my libido and my long isolation, I could overlook that dilemma for a few nights.

With my luck, she really did intend the room for conversation, not copulation.

I accepted the keycard, putting on a show of pleased, stunned gratitude at my good fortune. Quietly, I asked, "What time?"

"I'm off at twelve, so maybe one?"

A late night, then? I hoped I was up for it. Concerns about my recent bouts of narcolepsy bubbled up, but I kept them to myself. If I had to, I'd pick up some stimulants on the way. Sure, stimulants, contraceptives... and maybe a snack, just so I didn't look too obvious.

"See you there," I agreed.

We both got up. We briefly clasped hands and then she hurried back into the dining room. I hoped she wouldn't get into trouble for the long break. She left her drink at the table with me, obliging me to toss back my Cht Pkz and take both glasses to the bar.

Broken Record

Vulletine was scrupulously looking away as I approached. I set the glasses down and held out another ten-credit scrip to pay for the second, untouched drink. He looked at the plastic chit, took it, and went back to his thoughts without comment.

Only when I clicked quietly, to deliver my parting line, did he speak: "Don't even start. She likes you. You got something in common. Great. Have fun. Just don't bother me with the details. 'Doesn't work like that'..." He shook his head mockingly. He didn't sound so much dismissive as disappointed. I had to wonder, again, what stake he had in Pkstzk's welfare.

One mystery at a time. At that moment, I had the key to a beautiful female's hotel room. Almost as exciting, I would finally get the chance to put together a few pieces of this frosted case.

Chapter 7 - Getting a Room

I slipped out of the restaurant, only a little shakier for the drink. The intoxicant wasn't anything I couldn't handle, but I could probably blame it for a lapse of judgment. I flagged down a free-roaming aircar, spending twice what I should have for a ride. Right then, I wanted to get to the hotel, freshen up, and wait comfortably for Pkstzk. A nap wouldn't be a bad idea, either.

Would it be in poor taste to call Tskksk while I waited for Pkstzk? Not if my interest in both females was purely professional... which it could be... but wasn't. Terrible problem to have, really. As moral dilemmas went, it didn't even make my top ten.

Just to quiet my conscience, I tried calling from inside the 'car. No answer, again, but at least this time her number pinged before going to voice recording. She finally had the 'pad turned on, but still wasn't answering.

Well, maybe she had a social engagement, too. That turnabout would be more than fair. Frost, she could have Pack obligations, for all I knew about her. Just because she had sole ownership of a business didn't mean she might not co-habit with five or ten other sapients or take turns tending nursery for someone's young. Between my own isolation and the company of widows, I was forgetting how much Pack and family life meant to most sapients in the *Great Family*.

Vvv, the city, where traditions come to die. Social commenters have been lamenting the death of the Pack, the Herd, the Clan, and traditional matronage for decades, based on the increasing percentage of unattached sapients in our colonies and urban centers.

While the latter statistic is accurate, the pundits tend to overlook its underlying complexity. Some of the trend is due to personal preference and the increasing viability of a lone lifestyle. Whether caused by mental deviation or natural variation, some sapients – despite biological needs – just choose not to join a family. Unless their isolation somehow drives them to antisocial acts, where's the problem? If the loners *are* losing out, only they are hurt.

Yes, I know the concern is that unattached rogues are dangerous to society: uncontrolled and unstable. My life is proof that Pack membership is no guarantee of stability or morality... and that sometimes, going it alone is more socially productive.

More problematic are those sapients who really want to belong, but have no family due to circumstance (death or other separation), rejection, or personal difficulties.

I spare little sympathy for those exiled from their family due to their own harmful acts, but some groups can be cruel and exile a member just for violating a taboo or failing financially. You'd think Pack-bond would incline us to forgiveness, but there are types of insanity other than self-isolation: some bad eggs can and will turn a Pack against one member for a relatively minor infraction. Terrans call it 'scapegoating': dumping all the blame on one victim for the good of the group.

There are a handful of other reasons for isolation. A simple lack of opportunities is a surprisingly high entry on that list. Despite being closer together in a city, sapients still sometimes fail to bond with any group. Vislin do our best to encourage social activity and group activities that will lead to Pack formation, but even the best organization can't ensure a connection for everyone.

In the bad old days, adolescents were forced into a Pack with no say in the matter. Funny how that practice was also discovered to lead to dysfunctional behavior. The alienation of a few unlucky isolates is a smaller price to pay than dysfunctional Packs tainted by resentment.

A related problem is inappropriate bonding, where Vislin form bond feelings with groups that do not – or cannot – qualify as Packs. For example, a workaholic might suffer from a misdirected bond to their coworkers. If you can't get what you need at home, it's tempting to try and substitute the associations you *can* form.

The problem there is that you miss out on forming a real Pack. A bad or non-mutual bond can be as strong as a good one and isn't any less exclusive. Sometimes getting fired comes as a blessing for those types, provided they survive the rejection stress.

Increasing travel across wider and wider stretches of space tends to spread sapients apart and reduce their bonding opportunities, particularly when employed in positions that demand such travel. For some duties, unbonded youths are actually preferred, so that their associations can't bias their performance.

For example? Collective representatives. It is actually *hoped* that young Vislin will bond with non-Vislin teams, improving their understanding of other sapient species and guaranteeing their impartiality when handling disputes. You can't match that level of fundamental institutional loyalty with any other sapient species.

Add those variables together, allow for a significant intersectional factor, and you easily meet the level of isolation observed in any major city. I personally didn't understand the beak grinding on the issue. It was predictable, cause and effect. There was no way to go backwards to some ideal past of family harmony… even if such a past ever existed. If we wanted to "fix the problem", then maybe a few new institutions were needed to help all us lonely souls find one another.

In the meantime, we did the best we could. If Tskksk had that aspect of her life well covered, well done for her. If anything, an existing Pack – one a potential mate might join – made her doubly attractive.

I busied myself with such musings on the way to Taburket's, a hotel used mainly by off-world visitors. I had no idea what language or culture the name came from. An isolated Hrotata dialect? A Terran language? Honestly, I didn't know much about the hotel, at all. Most of what I remembered came from their advertising. I'm not their target customer.

The aircar route ran around and past the shuttle port, taking a longer, curving path in order to stay out of liftoff space. Taburket's was on the opposite side, away from the city center.

Broken Record

I wondered what made Pkstzk choose that particular place. There were cheaper rooms to rent, either closer to her workplace or further out of the way, if she was looking for privacy. Maybe her choice had to do with the clientele. A hotel catering to outsiders would be a less likely place to bump into an acquaintance.

Even within the limited category of tourist hotels, there existed other, cheaper options. I had to hope Pkstzk wasn't naïve enough to use a place with a personal connection, like a friend in management or a discount deal through her employer. Actually, her smartest choice would be random, selected by chance from the business listings. It's what I would do. At least, it's what I would do if I could afford to rent any hotel room.

I decided to stop questioning my good fortune and enjoy the amenities. Who knew; Taburket's might have an indoor sun room! The place certainly looked promising when I stepped out of the aircar: a ten-story, blue-grey building with a big, overdone façade, its own garage, a private courtyard garden… all advertisements for the wealthy and comfort-seeking.

I went up to the ornate wooden doors and found them unguarded but locked shut. A card reader was mounted on the frame between the two doors, just below a video intercom panel. I presented my room key and was rewarded with a synthesized bell tone. I pulled open one door by its handle, entering the hotel's lobby.

I saw a Hrotata check-in clerk but no other staff. A male Terran guest was also in the lobby, chatting with someone on his compad. Knowing Terrans, there was probably a second guest *in* his 'pad. Maybe he was talking *to* his A.I. I did my best not to find out. I'm only an eavesdropper when it's done on the job.

I figured that since I already had a key, I could bypass the desk and go up to the room. I walked past the clerk and to the lift, drawing no protest. Next to the desk was a pile of grav lift plates: fancy tech, but cheaper than full-time luggage haulers. Rewired, they could be a lot of fun in the hands of a clever, wild young sapient. I should know.

The lift opened in response to another wave of my keycard. After I stepped in, the system prompted me to insert the card into a reader, then I pushed a single button to start moving. There was no option to select a floor. It was a decent security measure, but nothing I couldn't bypass... the kind of trick that only added another obstacle and some extra exertion to a thief's plans. Still, sometimes, making it inconvenient is enough to reduce crime.

I was released on the eighth floor of the ten-story hotel. I wondered, belatedly, how a guest would access the hotel's public facilities, assuming there were any. The place might save on costs by cutting out things like a gym, sun room, pool, or even a restaurant. I hadn't seen signs for any of those facilities, anyway. I'd have to see what was listed in the room. Maybe everything else cost extra, but became available once you had the right permissions added to your keycard. That made sense.

The card said "Room 818", so I followed the numbers down the hall until I found a door with 818 stenciled onto its surface. It had one more swipe card lock, a third checkpoint guests for guests to pass.

While reassuring for purposes of privacy and security, I had no doubt all those card swipes were being logged, creating a record of activity within the building. Frost it, if someone wanted to track Pkstzk, I'm sure she and I already appeared on video records both at the restaurant and at the hotel. Leaving such evidence was inevitable. Professionally, I often relied on its existence. We just had to avoid giving the constables – or anyone else – reason to look closely at our activities.

The door to the room unlocked at my card swipe, but I had to lever it open myself. Kkk, already getting spoiled, Stchvk? The room inside was spacious, a bedroom bigger than my entire apartment. Plus, two doors in the far right wall promised an adjoining bathroom and a second room, possibly a walk-in valet closet.

I decided to check out the space. Besides needing to use the facilities, old instincts cautioned me to inspect unfamiliar surroundings. At first, I was thinking about bugs... electronic ones, not the crawling kind you'd expect in cheaper hotels. The windows were also wide and the curtains open. I wanted to check if anyone would have a view from outside. Business or pleasure, I wasn't planning on giving the neighbors a show.

Broken Record

I let the door close and crossed the room to close the curtains.

My instincts saved my scales. As I walked, I heard a scratch from inside the further room. Whatever was making that sound, it was even bigger than the local bugs. My hand went to my holster and I released Rtrtr. Heater in hand, I turned toward the far door just as it burst open.

A smaller, dark-scaled Vislin in modern tactical armor jumped out, both claws on a small automatic ballistic weapon. I managed to shoot first, tagging him in his closer hand. Rtrtr's beam turned his flesh into charcoal. His gun jerked aside as he lost his steadying grip. A stream of bullets spat out of the little weapon's barrel, tracking across the floor and throwing puffs of stuffing out of the bed mattress. My attacker screamed behind his visored helmet.

He struggled to straighten out his aim, still firing as if his trigger hand was stuck. At the same time, the bathroom door opened and two more Vislin poured out. They were both taller and tougher-looking than the first attacker, but wore the same armor. The vests and helmets were probably laser-proofed, which meant I couldn't hope for a fatal shot with my little heater. At best, I could cripple them with skillful (or lucky), well-placed shots. My good fortune would probably take longer to arrive than they'd need to blast my poorly protected hide.

The lead assassin had another ballistic weapon, a large-bore shotgun. He leveled it as I dropped to the floor. A hail of pellets scattered over my head, shattering the windows and kicking shrapnel off the wall and furniture. I felt a few stings from flying shards of wood and plastic.

My position was not tactically viable. If I stayed down, one or the other of the shooters would get close, fast, and have a clear line of fire. The third attacker was at least not firing. I wasn't sure if they had a weapon, but they didn't need one; they could just stand back and keep me from going out the door.

I made a snap decision and rushed to my left, toward and then past the first shooter. Between pain and surprise, he was too slow to hit me with his still-barking gun. Plus, he provided me a moment of cover; his confederate hesitated to fire while an ally was in the way.

I kept running and flew through the opened door. It looked like I was right about the room being a walk-in closet. Empty hangers rattled around me as I slammed into the far wall. I whipped around and pulled the door closed, taking a shotgun pellet in my left arm but deflecting several other projectiles with the heavy panel.

Frost, that hurt! I was lucky that my arm wasn't broken, but the pellet had gone through the meat of my forearm. At least I still had my gun and could use it. For that reason alone, it's smarter to carry a one-handed weapon.

I jerked to the side just as several more bullets tore through the door. I lined up Rtrtr to cover the opening, in case they tried to rush in after me

I'd suffered worse injuries before and, believe it or not, been in worse situations, so it wasn't as hard as you might think to manage my frenzy urge. A civilian Vislin would have bolted for the exit after the first shot. I would have, ten years ago. Maybe there was something to the idea that suffering makes the victim stronger.

Still, my position wasn't very good. Mortal danger and pain were eroding my rationality. I fought to think clearly and quickly. My best hope was to slow my attackers enough that the constables could arrive. Someone must have heard all the shooting and made an emergency call, by then. Did these guys want me dead badly enough that they'd risk getting stuck inside the hotel, surrounded by law enforcement? Would they risk my counter-fire to come in and get me faster?

Another volley of fire smashed against the door, reducing it to splintered boards. Then, a whining sound caught my attention. A section of the far closet wall glowed and burst into flame. Great. A laser. They could burn me out or even hit me around a corner with a lucky reflected shot. There was enough shiny metal in the closet to make that possible.

Thinking about cover or a shield, my eyes lit on a feature I'd missed upon entering. One of the grav lift pads was inside the closet, plugged in and charging. The levitation device was a handy courtesy to move bags or furniture around… also, loads of fun for innovative couples.

Broken Record

I bent down and yanked the lift away from its socket, grunting as the movement made my injured arm burn and bleed. At first, I planned to hold up the pad as a shield. Lifting it up, though, I spotted the mechanism for the gravitic disc underneath. Crazy that they used such powerful tech as a domestic push-cart.

A third round of bullets and another laser shot prompted me to think faster. The door was nearly gone at that point, and I could hear the assassins shifting around for a better angle. My life had been saved once already by the building's sturdy construction, but I couldn't count on its protection much longer.

I used a couple of well-placed heater shots to fuse several contacts in the grav lift's circuitry, shortening the path between its battery and the lift disc. Besides increasing the power to the disc, the short circuit bypassed safety features meant to keep the lift moving slowly and near the ground. I wanted a very different range of operation.

My next shot went out the door, aimed at nobody in particular. It only set the bedroom's wallpaper ablaze, but achieved my intended purpose: the attackers paused a moment to make sure they weren't in my line of fire.

Without no further warning, I leapt out of the closet, smashing through the tattered remains of its door. I held the grav lift in front of me, hoping it could serve both its original purpose as a shield and its newly engineered purpose. If it suffered too much damage – or if I did – my idiotically clever plan would fail in a smear of blood.

The shooters paused only a moment, long enough for me to cross the bedroom and approach the broken window. The third assassin, with the laser, fired first, and I felt a section of the grav lift's outer surface heat and melt slightly, singing my claw tips. Infertile eggs forever for him.

Kktkrkz' endless digestion for all of them. Why were they trying to kill me? A question for another time.

As I launched myself out of the open window, a hail of bullets helped me on my way. I took most of a shotgun blast to the back, which hurt but didn't penetrate anything vital. Good armor. My best armor.

The automatic weapon was still having trouble finding me, which was just fine, but a chance shot grazed my lower leg as I flew past. *That* hurt, tearing deep and spraying blood and scales into the air.

After that, the remainder of me, blood and scales and bones, was in the air. Midair. Eight stories up.

I prayed to the entire frosted pantheon that my alterations to the grav lift had been enough. I hoped my slippery memory had given me the right details from my tinkering childhood. If not, both the lift and I were going to suffer the unforgiving effects of unopposed gravity.

I fell five heart-stopping stories before anything happened. When the lift kicked in, I wondered if my slowing descent was just an effect of the fabled time-dilation experienced just before death. I didn't get a replay of my life. Instead, my common sense registered the crackling whine of the overloading grav lift.

It was working! I'd converted the lift into a repulsor landing pad. Not as much fun as a racing sled, but more practical for my current needs. I dropped below terminal velocity, slowed steadily, and actually coasted down the last five meters like a feather. A really heavy, bloody, clumsy feather, but far better than landing like a blood-filled balloon.

A scattering of bullets against the turf of the courtyard reminded me that I wasn't safe yet. I scrambled on all fours, seeking cover behind a fountain on the hotel grounds.

These were *not* smart killers. Good armor, decent weapons, but terrible planning. Even if their initial ambush was successful, they still had the problem of getting out of the hotel. When I escaped, they couldn't do much more than shoot from above... with every second they wasted giving the hotel more time to alert the authorities and lock down the building.

I didn't bother to shoot back. At that distance, there was no point, and I was still safer under partial cover than exposing myself to try for a lucky hit.

Broken Record

I finally heard the howls of constable cruisers. The sound seemed to alert the shooters that their time was up. Stray shots stopped raining down. I waited, crouched behind the fountain, trying to decide whether I'd be safer holding still or leaving the courtyard. I wasn't looking forward to talking to the constables, but I was also leaking from several injuries. None were life-threatening, but I couldn't go far without leaving a blood trail, and the leg wound would slow me down.

This case had gone from the investigation of a cold trail to an active gunfight against multiple opponents. In that light, I was better off talking to official detectives and enlisting them to arrest my would-be murderers. While it was almost inevitable that my connection to Pkstzk would come out, I might be able to keep our dirty past out of focus. Although, if these hunters were connected to that past, to Rsspkz, then I needed to know that, too. A chance at going to prison was better than the certainty of being hunted and killed.

As a screaming, glowing constable 'car landed in the courtyard, I raised my hands and flagged them down. Armed, armored strike-forcers climbed out: a Vislin/Taratumm pair. The stomper lowered a nonlethal sonic cannon my way. I dropped Rtrtr to the ground and stood slowly, staggering as my leg flared.

"I'm the victim!" I shouted. "I'm hurt. There are three of them inside, room 818, black tactical armor and all armed."

The Taratumm bellowed, "Stay where you are," but her Vislin partner spoke into a collar radio, repeating my words to other officers.

More cruisers landed around the hotel. I could see lights from its roof, as well. These jokers weren't going anywhere. I was looking forward to an explanation once they were interrogated... presuming they didn't end up accidentally dead. Frost, what if they got desperate and took hostages?

I was trying to help the constables by thinking ahead, anticipating possible outcomes, but shock was muddying my thoughts. Honestly, if they hadn't accepted my surrender and threatened to shoot, I might have gone over into frenzy. I felt safer in custody, but I wasn't in a good situation yet.

Thinking about that sequence – a frenzied flight, after going through a window – brought on a strange surge of familiarity. When had I ever been in a similar situation before? I'd think I would remember falling eight stories… assuming I survived the fall. I'd been shot at before, sure, even ambushed in a closed room, but the last time that happened I'd shot one attacker, bitten another, took a laser to the shoulder for my bravado, then ran away down a hallway.

In that case, smugglers caught me rifling through their warehouse records. I understood why *they* were willing to kill. Snuffing me would protect their secrets. But what was the point of *this* attack?

My head was getting light and starting to hurt. Otherwise, I would have recognized one likely explanation for the ambush. Deduction would have to wait until later. I swayed where I stood and nearly fell to my knees.

The Taratumm threatened with her sonic and was about to say something, then realized why I had moved. She kept me covered but gestured to her partner, pointing in my direction.

Added to the Vislin constable's messages was a call for an ambulance. About time.

I chanced moving my hands to cup my perforated arm in my good hand. Though I felt naked without Rtrtr, I had enough experience to know not to even *look* in my weapon's direction. Bullets had hit dirt not far away, not long ago, and the constables would be jumpy. Any half-clever perp could claim to be the wounded victim, then bolt away… or start shooting… the moment you let down your guard. I'd learned that lesson the hard way.

After a long wait, the Vislin constable approached me. He warned, "I'm not going to restrain you, but if you try anything, my partner will drop you on your face." He gestured toward the parking garage. "There's an ambulance coming in over there. Can you make it?"

I tested my torn leg. It hurt terribly, but supported my weight. "I suppose, if they can't come to me. Let's go."

Broken Record

To his credit, the constable looked torn between suspicion and sympathy. When I reached the sidewalk surrounding the hotel block, I stumbled and would have fallen, except that he stepped forward and caught my arm. From there, we hobbled together to the garage.

The pair got me to the ambulance, where my good arm was strapped to the rail of a stretcher bed. Then the medical tech (Hrotata, female) got to work wrapping my holed arm, restraining that also. Last, she pressed an absorbent pad into my ripped leg, leaving the leather greave strapped on around it.

"Some shrapnel… back…" I slurred to her, the aftereffects of the fight draining my energy away.

"We'll take care of that at the hospital," she assured me. "Any allergies?"

"Nope, give me anything," I confirmed, hoping she was asking what painkillers I could handle. All of them? Simultaneously? I had managed worse pain before, but I was already tired of dealing with the current suite of agonies.

The paramedic obliged with a quick injection between the scales of my elbow. Before the medication could take effect, my body accepted its suggestion and dropped me to sleep.

What a lousy first date.

Chapter 8 - Patient Investigator

I woke up still attached to the stretcher, but in a hospital room. A tan-striped auburn male Hrotata in nurse's scrubs was checking my vitals, transferring numbers from a readout to his work 'pad. Noticing my eyelids fluttering, he leaned over and shone a light in my eye. I restrained the urge to snap at his hand.

"Welcome back," he said, utterly without sarcasm. "You've had a rough night."

I cleared my throat. I couldn't bear to let the obvious straight line go to waste, but my tongue was so dry and thick I couldn't respond.

"Feeling dehydrated? You left some blood behind at your last stop," the Hrotata continued, "plus the analgesic is probably drying you out. Wait a while to talk, until we get fluids into you. Just rest for now. You're all stitched up. We've got the lead collection from your back bagged and waiting, along with some ventilated armor. The armor helped, but you might want to invest in something thicker, next time."

Great, a comedian. Plus, he was stealing all my jokes. I groaned, and not in appreciation.

"Sorry about the discomfort. You're not due for another dose of the good stuff." He grimaced, which was just visible in my peripheral vision. "*Officially* not due."

I caught his meaning. Technically, torturing a suspect was illegal, but constables could delay administration of painkillers, in the interest of a witness' "lucidity." I hoped I could speak well enough to satisfy them before the agony became unbearable.

Anticipating my concern, the nurse plugged in a drinking hose and inserted the nozzle at the corner of my beak. The flexible tip would open and dispense small amounts of water whenever I bit down hard enough. I sipped a little without choking and he looked pleased.

"Other than that detail, there's a signal box by your right hand. Push the button if you need anything else. You've been spared a catheter, but I have to get someone to release you if you need the bathroom. Surprised you didn't mess yourself when the shooting started... must be a tough lizard?"

His use of the common slur surprised me, but his tone was hardly dismissive. I wondered how much of his patter was his normal persona and how much was an act tailored to each patient. I was a suspect from a gunfight, so I got tough banter and slang. A little old Hrotata matron with a heart condition would probably get a different routine.

Hey, his patient, his show. I was just happy he wasn't rude... or terrified of me.

I tried speaking again and managed: "Where am I?"

"Vaktrri Medical," he answered without further jokes, "Room 1021. Post-surgical recovery."

Vaktrri? I'd been there not too long ago... but why? I didn't remember being admitted recently, and my regular doctor was closer to home... not that I saw him very often, either. Plus, I didn't have the insurance to afford care at Vaktrri, one of Layafflr's upper-tier hospitals.

The exact circumstance eluded me, but I was sure I'd been to Vaktrri Medical for something recent. A case? To see a wounded client? The partial memory, along with the other oddities I'd noticed over the last few days, was aggravating.

Another anomaly: Vaktrri is in an entirely separate neighborhood from Taburket's. In fact, it's half the city away from the shuttle port. It isn't even close to where I live. It *is* close to a major constabulary office, so maybe that was their reasoning in hauling me so far away.

Even if there was a reason, it was still irresponsible to transport me so far. No matter how minor my injuries, I should have been taken to the nearest emergency room. Maybe my injuries were worse than I thought. Vaktrri does have excellent surgeons. Right then I couldn't remember much about the hospitals around the port. Maybe Vaktrri *was* a logical choice for reasons I couldn't guess.

The nurse slipped out of the room while I was lost in thought. I chewed a few more swallows out of the drinking tube and tried to relax. Twinges from my arm, leg, and back kept me awake. Those aches, coupled with the strange events of the previous few days, sent my mind racing. Working on the case might make my head hurt, but it distracted me from my other pains.

What happened? Three well-funded but amateurish Vislin street soldiers jumped out of hiding and tried to kill me.

Why? Was this attack related to the case I was working? Was I missing some past grudge someone would want to kill me over? Had Pkstzk set me up?

Wait, wait, wait. Why was I assuming they were lying in wait for *me*? What an ego. *I* hadn't reserved the room at Taburket's… Pkstzk did. It was far more likely they were waiting for *her*. To kill her? It was possible they only started firing after *I* did. They might have been there to kidnap Pkstzk or maybe just threaten her.

Maybe one of the three killed her mate… or maybe all three were hired by whoever bought Vzktkk's death.

Whatever the reason, there was something deeper involved in Vzktkk's murder. Pkstzk hadn't warned me of potential danger. It was possible she honestly didn't know about any. Did she even know what was going on with her mate? Did she know about the possibility of assassins? If she did, had she avoided warning me so I wouldn't be scared off the case?

Worse chance, maybe Vzktkk died as a consequence of something *Pkstzk* did. The assassins might have been coming after her as the original target, then and now. I might have narrowly avoided being the second casualty of her doom.

I still needed that conversation with her, delays notwithstanding. Plus, I had four additional interviews lined up: a constable detective and perhaps the three attackers… presuming they hadn't died at the hotel. Once again, I fervently hoped no civilians had died, in a crossfire or as hostages. Trapped idiots with guns and without scruples tend to cause collateral casualties.

Broken Record

I also needed to make sure Tskksk was all right. I might have seemed paranoid before, worrying about her, but after the case's new twist, my fears weren't so irrational anymore. I would warn the constables to look in on her. Hopefully they already had her evidence and knew her value as a witness. If not, I could relay her recording and explain its significance.

The waiting started to wear on me. I hoped my nurse was notifying a detective that I was awake, waiting, and in genuine need of medication

More water, more time, and more stray thoughts: one of the thugs who attacked me was packing a laser weapon. Vzktkk was shot with a laser. Was that significant? Given the weapon and Tskksk's recording, could we verify a match? It was probably coincidence; there were plenty of weapon-grade lasers in Layafflr City.

When my potential leads and their interconnections began to run out, my thoughts turned to my own personal mysteries. I was forgetting some events and remembering others without context. I've suffered a lot of injuries over the years, but not that many were blows to the head.

Well, I was in the hospital already. I could ask the doctors to scan and test everything. I'd be in permanent debt and have my biometrics on permanent record, but maybe the costs would be worth it to salvage my health.

The wait itself was painful. The pain was painful. I was almost aggravated enough to signal the nurse and ask him for a time estimate. His peace was preserved by the arrival of a stranger. A large female Hrotata eased into the room, opening the door no wider than necessary to shift inside. She shut it again behind her, while I craned my neck to see my guest more clearly.

She was pale cream almost all over, with darker markings on her nose and around her ears. Her large size was partly length and partly weight. I wasn't the best judge, but she looked a portly for a Hrotata. Any markings on her body were hidden by a formal robe, a heavy grey garment usually worn by important matriarchal leaders but sometimes adopted by other authority figures. This female wanted to make it clear she was In Charge.

She gestured that I should lie back, saying, "Investigator Stchvk? I'm Detective Nrissilli, Layafflr Central Constabulary." She stepped closer to the bed, within my comfortable field of vision. "I'm going to ask you a few questions. Answer to the best of your ability, and we'll be done sooner…"

"…and you can be home before dinner," I mumbled. I started to spit out the drinking tube. She reached forward to help, and I tensed, anticipating the contact that would transfer the Hrotata's narcotic saliva. To my surprise, she was careful not to touch my mouth or scales, but only picked up the tube by its base and lifted it away.

"Right," she answered with a smile, "you've played this game before. I'm familiar with some of your past work. You want to sit up?" she asked, gesturing toward the bed controls.

"Please," I agreed, "save my neck some strain."

She adjusted the bed until I was halfway upright. The elevation let me unbend my crest as well as look at her without turning my head. Unfortunately, the change in position brought blood rushing out of my head and into my body. My wounds stung and itched.

I must have looked uncomfortable. Detective Nrissilli winced sympathetically and said, "Sorry I can't unbind you just yet. We need to make sure you won't run off anywhere, first."

"I do have places to be," I muttered sullenly. "Some rotted eggs interrupted my plans for the night."

"Let's start with that, then." She produced a compad from a sling beneath her robes and tapped it awake. "What happened last night?"

"I was going to a room at Taburket's – Room 818 – to wait for a friend. A female friend, named Pkstzk. We were going to meet at her room and see how the evening went. She reserved the room. Have you checked on her? Is she safe?"

Nrissilli nodded, scrunching up her nose in a Hrotata expression I could never reliably interpret: either irritation or amusement or both. "We're sending a unit to look for her at home. She left work as usual, took a public 'car toward the shuttle port, then nothing. She wasn't at the hotel, if that's your concern. Any thoughts where she might have gone, otherwise?"

We were trading information. It wasn't a fair transaction, but it was nice not to be answering questions into a vacuum. I supposed senior officers were allowed some latitude on interrogations.

"No, I don't even know where she lives. I think she chose the hotel partly to keep it that way." Talking so much was drying my mouth out again, but I didn't want to ask for the drinking tube and chance contact with the Hrotata again.

"You went into the hotel. Any sign something might be wrong? Any fore-warning this could happen? Looks like you were armed: an old-model heater?"

"I always carry that. I have a permit, under file along with my P.I. license."

"I know. You're a throwback that way, too. Not everyone with a weapon and a license feels the need to carry all the time."

"I do. You never know when you might be attacked. Obviously."

"Sure. That's a no, you didn't suspect anything?"

"No. As far as I knew, I was going to an empty room to wait, maybe clean up, nap, see what I could afford from room service."

"All right, then what?"

"I opened the door and went to the window... the curtains were open. I heard one of the shooters moving inside the closet and drew. He came out and I shot him... left hand. Vislin. Darker scales, short, maybe 1.7 meters. He had a small automatic ballistic, squarish, no idea what model. There were two others that came out of the bathroom, also Vislin, both taller and lighter. Didn't get a good look at them. All three had black tactical armor, catalog-order stuff but good enough. I didn't get a chance for a second shot. One had the shotgun. That one missed me the first time when I dropped. Number three had a laser, but I didn't find that out until later. I managed to run into the closet, which they shot up for a while."

I paused for a breath and to moisten my tongue. The detective took advantage of the pause to observe, "I knew that much; I've seen video of the scene."

"Good," I started again. "You'll know everything matches up. My heater didn't hit them again. I found the grav lift inside the closet... rewired it... used it as a shield and then as a cushion after going out the window."

"About that," she interrupted again, "I wondered how the lift was involved. So, you shorted it, yourself, in a couple of seconds? With a heater pistol? Then, trusted that work with your life?"

I clacked my beak in rueful laughter. "I did. Good thing I did the job right."

"As unlikely as that sounds, it does fit the evidence. Your survival was pretty unlikely, too, if everything happened like you say. I can see where your history supports belief, judging from some pretty narrow escapes, but it also suggests some dangerous talents, too."

At first, I tensed up, thinking she was referring to my *youthful* past. Unless the old Pack started talking, though, there shouldn't be any official record linking me to our past crimes.

I had to assume she meant my prior official cases. It was true; there were some dark marks on my record. Most of the felony charges were dropped out of discretionary gratitude for services rendered to the City. I beat the one complaint a city attorney actually decided to pursue. A few of my misdemeanors – breaking and entering, evidence tampering, witness harassment – were enforced and served with fines in order to make a point.

I *was* surprised if the official records mentioned any of my more impressive feats. I always figured the constables who witnessed my talents or took down statements afterward would gloss over my achievements. Maybe I had a fan or two on the force. Then again, they did have to keep verbatim records of my witness statements, and *I* wouldn't have spared any self-praise.

"At the risk of seeming conceited, that's the truth. I had a secret rendezvous. Three unknown thugs tried to kill me. I got away by flying on a jury-rigged lift."

Broken Record

Detective Nrissilli continued taking notes, betraying only a slight smirk. "Let's go back. It sounds like you didn't recognize any of these sapients."

"Correct."

"Was there any reason to think they were there to 'kill you'? You fired first. Did you initiate aggression?"

"They had deadly weapons, pointed and ready to use. I wasn't going to wait and see if they wanted to talk. It's possible they were there to kidnap me... or Pkstzk. She could have been the target. That's why you should find her right away."

She reassured me again, "We're doing everything we can think of on that account. Is there anything else you can add that might help?"

She was offering me a chance to spill everything I knew, for Pkstzk's sake. I gave her a few more drops to see how much she already knew. "Her husband was killed recently. Shot. I was looking into it for her. We were going to talk about my progress on the case."

"So Pkstzk was employing you? As a P.I.? To investigate her husband's death... nothing else? You said she was a 'friend'..."

It had been too long since I danced. I misstepped earlier, and the detective caught me out. It was a shame, since I really enjoyed the rhythm and found I missed it.

"You know how it happens sometimes... a grieving widow, a handsome male offering assistance, bonding over shared danger..."

She fixed me with a stare like *she* was the one in pain. "You're saying the relationship turned non-professional."

"Well, I had hopes. I'm not proud."

"And here I had you scented as purely professional. I guess that changes when romance gets involved... except it doesn't. Not for Vislin. Not in such a short time. Her mate's been dead barely a week. You didn't show up on the case until two days ago. So, try again."

I clacked again, as best I could around my thickening tongue. "I'm... a fast mover. Guess she is, too."

"I don't buy it, Stchvk. Someone tried to kill someone else last night. You're involved, and your 'client' is involved. Odds are good it's related to the death of her mate. I want to know how. I think you're hiding something... and you're usually good about sharing knowledge. I'm not letting you go until I know everything you know."

The setup was too tempting. "We could be here a long time, then. I could starve."

"You can eat *me*, if you keep stalling like this."

Why was I finally meeting such interesting sapients, when I had something to hide? When I was being honest, all I met were stiffs and crooks. I really wanted to help the detective, but a lingering fear of my past prevented me from adding the last piece.

I tried a diversionary tactic: "There *is* something else I can share. I have a recording of all the EM disturbances from the street where Vzktkk was killed, including the time of his death and the entire evening before and after."

"I have that," she replied, "from the compad store owner..." She checked her 'pad, scrolling through her notes. "...Tskksk. She mentioned you. I know this part. She said you were looking into the pet importer/exporter across the street. What was that about?"

Bait taken. I set the hook: "That's where the shooter fired from. I found a pane of glass in the door lintel wiped clean, where the others were dirty. The cashier's counter inside was also wiped down, no dust... I figure they stood on it to line up the shot."

"That would have been nice to know. When were you going to share these important details?"

"After I talked to Pkstzk. Which was supposed to happen tonight. This conversation is actually right on time, although in a less comfortable setting."

Broken Record

"All things considered, I'm not sure which option I would have preferred. Actually, I would have preferred the one where you shared your insights *before* creating a military incident."

I winced, only partially from my own pain. "Anyone else hurt?"

"No civilians, if that's what you mean. Just you. No constables hurt, either. In fact... we never engaged the shooters."

"What?" It was my turn to be incredulous. "How was that possible? They were trapped inside."

"That's *my* question. We know they were there. Hotel cameras show the gang checking in, going upstairs, going into the room... and then running out when they heard sirens. We know they keyed the elevator... and then nothing. Pffft. Vanished. Any idea how?"

I was stumped. I was also angry. "Now, *I'm* suspicious. If constables were covering every exit, like they should, how *could* armed, armored suspects get past? Tunnels? Maybe you should let Internal Affairs know to look into those officers' credit accounts."

She bristled at the implication, but said only, "I'll take it under advisement. I actually hoped you might have an idea. Short of Ningyo space-fold tech, they shouldn't have had any way out. No other guests saw them run by. No constables even saw them. We had a unit on the roof and yes, at every exit. A scene tech swept for any hidden escape routes or lingering spatial distortions... nothing."

"That's fast work," I said with honest praise. Layafflr City might see too many of these sorts of armed incidents to get excited about one more, but the extra note of weirdness prompted a quick, thorough investigation in this case.

"Thanks. So, no ideas. Anything else on the other case? Connections to this mess?"

"I don't have any real leads, yet. Again, I'm hoping Pkstzk can warm some eggs... sss, provide some help." Kkk, bad choice of metaphor.

"There was one other thing, if Tskksk didn't mention it… I was attacked at the pet store, too."

"She mentioned some abandoned animals. What happened there?"

"Someone left three rktpk and maybe some other animals locked in the building to starve. When I entered – my fault on the lock, by the way, I'll cover the damages if the owner wants to call me – the sole survivor broke out of the back room and tried to take a bite out of me. I shot it dead. You'll find the corpse on the floor. I didn't want to handle it."

"Another crime scene I wish you'd mentioned earlier. It's going to stink something awful by now. Guess who'll be touring that store next?" She gratuitously pointed at her own chest.

"Sorry. I wanted to wait until I confirmed a connection between the building and the murder."

"You *wanted* to have the whole case wrapped up for your client before you fulfilled your obligation to the public," Nrissilli accused. "I get that from every other P.I. poking around in this city. I didn't expect it from you."

She sounded like she had really followed my career, more than I might expect. While the attention might be gratifying in another context, right then she sounded like a conscience. Not my *actual* conscience, which had grown up with me and understood the complexities of my life and work. Some other conscience, freshly assigned to the job, without any such experience.

"Maybe. Maybe, I waited too long. Maybe, I got too concerned with impressing this female. Guilty. But I wasn't deliberately hiding anything. I got Tskksk's recording to you. Honestly, if I knew something more or if I discovered more after meeting with Pkstzk, I would have called it in right away."

I was delivering an impressively mingled blend of truth and deflection. I was honest with Pkstzk when I warned her I wouldn't conceal criminal acts from the authorities. I really wouldn't give her the name of her mate's killer without first advising the constables.

Broken Record

At the same time, I did tend to keep the law at a distance until I was ready for them to be involved. It made certain investigations easier. It was a practical deception, not a deliberate criminal act.

Detective Nrissilli spoke my thought for me: "I mostly believe you. But you're still lying to me. Maybe you're lying to yourself, too. I'm taking a break here so I don't have your suffering on my conscience… but I'm coming back later. I hope you'll have recovered a few memories by then."

I hoped so, too, but not in the way she meant. I kept quiet while the detective left the room.

Shortly afterward, the nurse returned and slipped a syringe into my intravenous line. The stuff made my extremities feel cold and tingly, then steadily less painful. As I started to drift off, I thought about the detective's demands and my possible responses.

I wasn't Pack-bound to Pkstzk. If she was involved in something bad, I'd have no problem turning her in. I was protecting myself as much as her, by keeping her secrets. If those secrets started to jeopardize my safety, I'd give them up.

But I also didn't want to hurt Pkstzk, *if* she was a victim. If I thought my silence was endangering her, I'd choose her safety over my reputation or freedom. I wasn't quite convinced the situation was that dire, yet. I was biased enough toward myself to need a clearer reason before I talked.

If Pkstzk couldn't be found soon, the balance might tilt toward complete disclosure. If I got a hint that Rsspkz, her former mate, my former Pack-mate, was involved, I'd *know* it was time to come clean.

We weren't to that point yet. I didn't owe the detective anything. Unfortunately, if she chose to keep me in custody, I couldn't do anyone any good. Could I offer something more, in good faith, and earn my release? Or should I stay mute and see if she'd believe I was tapped out? If she was uncertain about her suspicions, she might err on the side of trust and let me go.

The only thing I was certain about was that I shouldn't give everything away at once. Frost, explaining the entire story might convince Nrissilli to arrest me right away. Then, where would Pkstzk be? If it wouldn't actually help anyone to speak up, I shouldn't.

Actual ethics isn't about the law. That's especially true in a city like Layafflr, where crime is woven into the laws. I'm sworn to uphold those laws, but I choose to fulfill their real purpose, not the interpretations favored by the gangsters in charge.

Big words, I know. But I'd *been* a gangster, even if just a little one. I recognized their patterns when I saw them. Even if Detective Nrissilli was the best of sapients, the people above her cared more about power and control than justice and the safety of individual citizens. I'd keep my own counsel and avoid their games.

Chapter 9 - Clean Bill

For a night that ended so badly, my morning was full of pleasant surprises.

Unpleasant surprises, too, like being woken up every couple of hours by my nurse. The cheery Hrotata male withdrew blood once, replaced my intravenous fluids once, and checked my bandages three times, once for each wound. On each visit, he also reviewed my vitals. The first visit was hazy, but the subsequent two were clearer.

By the time I was ready to stay awake, my head felt considerably less clouded. That was the first pleasant surprise: I was clear-headed, neither woozy from medications nor overly distracted by pain. Either the pain meds weren't scrambling my brains as much as usual, or else they'd lowered the dosage as my wounds healed.

I had a strange moment when I tried to stretch: both arms and legs ached in protest. This wasn't surprising for my arms, since both of my wrists were tied with medical cuffs to the bed frame. On the left side, this served an actual purpose: keeping me from moving my injured arm. I wasn't formally a prisoner, but the cuff on my right arm said I was in custody until the constables were satisfied.

My legs *weren't* restrained. My right leg had a bandage wrapped around its lower half, securing a pad which covered an embarrassing amount of sealant glue. I was actually lucky the bullet that caught me ripped parallel to the muscle, rather than through a major artery or bone… but the scar would be impressive.

That left the key question: why was my uninjured, unrestrained leg also hurting? For a brief hectad or two after waking, it felt like I had casts on both ankles. After that sensation faded, the ache in my good leg went away, while the pain in my right side migrated to the torn muscle above.

After the symphony of pain had settled down to a few notes, those notes faded to a more muted background noise. I was aware of the pain, but it didn't aggravate me the way it had when the detective was questioning me. It certainly wasn't as severe as I remembered from past bullet wounds.

Good drugs? Or good medical care? Vaktrri Medical was a better facility than I usually visited. It was possible they had materials and/or techniques more advanced than at lesser hospitals.

Frost, that was the soul of inequality, wasn't it? Not only did the poorer neighborhoods get less care, despite needing it more often, the patients even suffered more pain per ailment. If the doctors at Vaktrri could fix me up faster and with less pain, it had to be a function of their available funding.

I waited, half-awake and bored, spiraling around my own thoughts, until the nurse returned with breakfast. I might be a prisoner in my room, but at least they offered room service. The smell of broth poured out of a covered dish as the nurse set a tray next to my bed.

"Are you going to feed me?" I asked him, rattling my bindings for emphasis.

"Sorry to disappoint, but no," he answered lightly. "We've got another drinking tube. I hope they'll cut you loose before we move you up to solids."

The nurse opened the bowl and retrieved another flexible siphon, putting one end into the broth and the other at the corner of my beak, replacing the water tube. I took an experimental sip and found the liquid thicker than expected and also better tasting. Actual meat had been cooked down and then pureed into the broth. For hospital food, the meal was far better than the synthetic, rehydrated swill I drank most mornings.

Since I wasn't going to be conversational for a while, the nurse stepped out to let me eat quietly. Drinking out of a hose aside, I managed to enjoy breakfast. The meal also gave me time to think.

It was possible I would be moved from the hospital into a prison. My involvement with Pkstzk's case might end there, along with any ability to help her. On that path, my concerns would focus more on keeping myself – and her – out of worse trouble.

Broken Record

Alternately, the detective might question me again and then cut me loose. I was savvy enough to realize that this outcome would be a trap. Detective Nrissilli would have me watched closely to see where I went and who I met afterward, in the hopes that I would incriminate myself further... or take risks for her while finding the actual criminals. Either outcome might be worth the risk of letting me go 'free'.

I could get lucky. The third, least probable outcome was if the detective decided that I was not only not guilty, but that I could be an asset. In that scenario, the constables might share their information in return for mine and trade my assistance for my freedom. It had happened before, but not often. Usually, the best returns I could hope for were dropped charges and a warning to say out of constabulary business.

In this case, the third option actually wasn't much better than the second. I'd still be dancing across a minefield, trying to pursue whoever killed Vzktkk, whoever tried to kill me, and possibly someone who meant to kill Pkstzk. If those weren't the same party, or if one or both parties were linked to Pack Vzrrk, I might not be able to dance nimbly enough to dodge the explosions. I definitely wasn't in prime dancing form, what with my recently perforated leg.

I expected my next visitor to be either the nurse or Detective Nrissilli. Instead, an unexpected third party stopped in: a male Vislin in beige doctor's robes. His scales clashed with the light fabric, most of them a black so dark it reflected blue from the indoor lighting.

He carried an official compad and wore an ident badge, so I assumed he was, in fact, a doctor. That wasn't a given. I had pretended to be a doctor at least once before to sneak into a hospital room. An assassin could easily do the same to get access and catch me defenseless.

My paranoia was reduced by his demeanor: he did absolutely nothing to put me at my ease. An assassin would have either shot me outright or tried to lull me into feeling safe, in either case making sure I didn't call for help. This doctor gave me plenty of time to inspect him, suspect him, and worry. I could have called the chief of constables in the time he took dawdling around.

He checked over his compad, looked at me without catching my eyes, then looked back down at his screen again. Then he crossed to my vitals monitor and compared its display with his 'pad's. Like the nurse, he made a few notes with a claw-tip. The entire time, he neither spoke to me nor acknowledged my presence. It was like being dark matter studied by an astronomer; I was apparently invisible but somehow produced measurable effects in his universe.

It wasn't until he removed the feeding tube from my beak and I muttered, "Thanks," that he indicated any awareness of a patient inside the bandages.

"Stchvk?" he mused aloud, glancing from his compad to me and back.

"It's true. I do exist," I quipped back.

He either missed the joke or ignored it. "I'm your doctor, Ssvktk. I'll need to check your injuries. We'll start with your leg, see how the sealant is holding."

He put the compad down somewhere behind my field of view and came around the opposite side holding a tray and a pair of scissors. He continued his monologue: "I'm going to lift your leg slightly and cut off the bandages. There may be some pain from both actions."

I finally put it all together: his muted demeanor, his averted gaze, his careful warning… Doctor Ssvktk was afraid. Even with my arms tethered, he was afraid of me. What had the constables told him? That I was a suspect involved in a public firefight? Or had they just left it at "dangerous suspect" and let him fill in the details?

I suspected that this section of Vaktrri Medical didn't see many patients in custody. Otherwise, the doctor might have come in with a security escort.

I was tempted to abuse my position and terrorize the doctor. That urge passed quickly as I recognized that he was *my* doctor and – for what it was worth – my healing was in his hands. I stayed quiet and still as he lifted my leg, which protested only slightly in response. He cut away the bandages, which clung slightly and pulled at the wound, then inspected the seam on its underside.

"Chchch?" He clicked, which I assumed was doctor-speak for either "That's bad," or "That's odd."

Broken Record

It turned out to be the latter. As he wrapped my leg in new gauze, the doctor informed me, "Either the injury was less severe than we thought, or you heal quickly. It's already knitting… our surgeon can't take credit for that much improvement."

From past hard experience, I knew that I wasn't a "quick healer". I was willing to believe that the gunshot wound had looked worse – and felt worse – than it actually was. Cleaning up the blood, removing the loose and impacted scales, and sealing up the tear would improve its appearance considerably. Still, it had hurt quite a lot at the time, and if past experience was any indicator, it still ought to sting badly.

I assumed that pain medications were suppressing that sting. But maybe they had less work to do than usual?

The doctor moved on: "Let's take a look at your arm now. I will need to unbind your arm. Please remain still. Any sudden motions could damage your injury further and will be exceedingly painful."

I had had enough. I blinked theatrically and informed him, "Look, Doc, I appreciate the play-by-play, but I'm not dangerous. I ended up in the right place at a bad time and some actual criminals put some holes in my hide. Just do what you need to, and I promise you, I won't do anything 'sudden'… or stupid."

I didn't add: you can untie me, and I won't go anywhere, I promise. I was tempted, but that's exactly what a criminal who was planning to escape would say.

Doctor Ssvktk didn't respond directly to my statement, but he did stop pre-narrating his actions. He used scissors to gnaw through my left wrist restraint, then to snip the bandages on that arm.

This time, I could see the injury, myself. I knew the bullet had gone through my forearm, not far from the wrist. I was fortunate it missed the bones to either side. Even so, I expected a nasty, puckered wound, stuck together with some difficulty or packed to keep the bleeding down.

Instead, I saw neat straight incisions on both sides of my arm. It looked like the bullet opened the flesh with minimal effort and politely closed the doors on the way back out. That wound had to be the tidiest gunshot wound I'd ever seen.

Nathan Large with Laine Megan Lundquist

The doctor gave his little click and started in: "This is very good…"

I interrupted, "It's surreal, is what it is. Is Vaktrri experimenting with some next generation medical tech? If so, I'm not complaining, even if I didn't sign any research contract. Or were my attackers using some experimental 'low damage' ammunition?"

I tried not to sound angry. The weirdness probably wasn't my doctor's fault. I really wasn't complaining, either. Being less hurt was a good thing. I just wished I could explain it.

I couldn't blame Doctor Ssvktk for giving me a pained look. He shook his head and stepped back, setting down the tray with its discarded bandages and retrieving his compad. He took a picture of my arm and tapped the screen a few more times, likely transmitting the image to a colleague. Possibly, he was querying the surgeon who saw my wounds originally.

"No, while Vaktrri Medical is the state of the art for ChttKttp, no otherwise special techniques were used in your surgery," he finally and flatly stated. "It is possible that armor piercing rounds were used, and you had the good fortune to be struck only in non-vital areas."

I stared at the doctor in disbelief, long enough to make him uncomfortable again. He looked away and then shuffled off to put down his compad again.

He returned with a new tray and said, "Last, I'll look at your back." At least he spared me any further instructions.

I rolled over obligingly, balancing myself on my good arm where it remained tethered to the bed rail. My abused tail stretched automatically, flicking against the mattress. I hadn't realized how cramped it was until painful tingles started running from its base to tip. A hospital bed was a poor substitute for a proper nest, no matter how ergonomically it was designed… and no bed is comfortable when you're strapped in place.

The doctor didn't flinch when my tail moved. I took that as a sign that he was relaxing. He pulled at one of the patches on my back and dropped the bandage onto his tray. He probed around the area with a claw-tip, I assumed to check for any remaining embedded shrapnel.

Broken Record

"I'm going to attribute this result to your armor and distance," he offered right away, rather than clicking and pausing first. "The shot didn't penetrate deeply, but even so, you ought to show more impact trauma. Bruising."

"It sure kicked hard enough," I responded, nudging our rapport toward camaraderie. "Practically threw me out a window."

He did click, once, in reply to that statement. He worked quietly and quickly afterward, removing and replacing pads. I counted them to entertain myself: eighteen. Eighteen separate pock marks from my shoulders down to my tail base. I supposed I was fortunate my tail kept any shot from going up my backside, but I was also glad my low angle kept any projectiles from smacking into my skull.

So, three armed attackers had done their best to murder me in a locked – though admittedly spacious – hotel room, and I came out with nothing worse than twenty-one minor scars? Between medical glue and self-absorbing sutures, I'd be almost intact in a few days.

Pretty good deal, all told. Very good. Too good. If I were more religious, I'd owe a Goddess or two an offering for such amazing luck. Maybe I had been blessed for my virtues? Let's laugh a moment at that thought. K-k-k-k.

The doctor cleaned up as I considered more secular reasons for my good fortunes. Had they been *trying* to wound but not kill me? I reviewed the attack in my memory, which was functioning amazingly well for recent events despite its problems with more distant recall.

No, they had definitely been trying to kill me. Maybe they were a little slower on the trigger than seasoned professionals, but that could be explained by a) surprise at seeing the wrong Vislin in their trap, and/or b) not actually being seasoned professionals, despite their expensive gear. Other than their hesitation, they certainly spread enough lead across the suite to make a convincing case for murderous intent.

My evasive skills weren't the reason for my survival, either. I have a pretty quick dodge, honed by necessity and natural talent, but I'm no trained martial artist or soldier. If I managed to run and twist enough to minimize injury, that wasn't by any skilled reflex… just luck, instinct, and a little experience.

I supposed, lacking any new information, I'd have to reluctantly ascribe my minimal injury to sheer stupid chance. I guess every so often, even a hard-luck case gets an undeserved favor.

Another bit of luck: the doctor didn't bother to re-bind my free, injured arm. I wondered if that was deliberate, but I was alert enough not to mention it. No need to remind him of forgotten duties.

He nodded to me as he started toward the door, only belatedly remembering to throw in some basic courtesies. "Medically, I believe you can be released today, citizen Stchvk. You should require only further rest with minimal strenuous activity for the next half-cycle, before being evaluated again."

He continued, reciting the rest of his dialogue from a familiar routine: "Notify your physician if you notice any swelling, discoloration or discharge from any wound site, if you experience increasing pain, numbness, or warmth, or if you have fever or weakness lasting more than one day."

Last, he went off-script to note: "Of course, your discharge depends on the constable overseeing your medical coverage. You may be moved to a holding facility at her or his discretion. In either case, I likely will not be needed again. Thank you and good day."

He was out the door before I could respond. Busy sapient, other patients to see, still afraid for his life, you know, the usual. I settled down, this time on my side, and prepared myself mentally for another long wait.

I missed out on the anticipated boredom. Less than a decad after Doctor Ssvktk stepped out, the door opened again, and Detective Nrissilli returned.

I straightened and tried to settle my left arm back into place. "Detective, welcome back," I greeted her. My ruse clearly didn't work, as her eyes went to my freed arm. Instead, I lifted it and waved slowly. "It appears I'm in good hands."

"So I hear," she confirmed with a smile. "The doctor says you don't need to stay here long, although you might want a crutch for that leg."

"What's next, then?" I asked, getting right to the point.

"I think that's up to you," she countered. "We're still where we left off."

I clacked at her in irritation. "Except today, I'm not in as much pain."

She had the grace to look embarrassed, even lifting a paw and tilting her head down before stopping short of grooming an ear.

"You know that's standard procedure. I'm doing my job according to protocol. Otherwise, I might do something unethical, like letting you go and seeing if you lead us to Pkstzk... or having you shot up with hypnotics until you tell us where she is."

"She's still missing?" I sat up a little, betraying my concern.

"Officially, she's not 'missing'. But she hasn't been located, either. As a person of interest in an attempted murder – possibly the intended victim, possibly the instigator – she's being sought by the authorities. I'm confident we'll track her down soon, assuming she's still alive. Sorry."

I waved off the attempt at sympathy. "I agree with your fatalism. I'd like to join the search myself, but I suspect there may be difficulties there. I assume my attackers haven't been located, either?"

The detective looked irritated. "No, and I was hoping you might have remembered something else... because otherwise, they've vanished. You're fortunate other guests and the clerk remembered them entering, because otherwise, I might doubt your story. Now, I'm not disputing the facts of the firefight up there..."

She held up both paws to forestall my nonexistent protest. "...because there's plenty of broken glass, holes, and a fried grav lift to verify your story, not to mention your wounds, which I doubt were self-inflicted. But how do I explain three armed and armored Vislin getting in and out of a hotel without leaving any sign on video?"

She paused, actually waiting to see if I could offer an explanation.

Actually, there *was* something nagging at me... "Wait, no video? I thought you said you saw them going in, on the recordings from the lobby cameras."

Nathan Large with Laine Megan Lundquist

Detective Nrissilli stared back at me and answered smoothly, "Did I? I must have been assuming we had that. It turned out we didn't. After visiting you, I talked to the officer who reviewed the video… no images of them."

Was she lying? Was she lying back then? Was she actually sloppy enough to claim evidence she didn't have, by mistake? My instincts said she meant what she said earlier, which meant she was either lying later… or testing me? It wasn't uncommon for a detective to deliberately misstate facts in a case, seeing if a suspect or witness would let the error pass, get caught in a lie, or reveal their actual uncertainty about a detail. I had used the technique myself in the past.

But what possible value did it hold to alter that particular detail? What suspicions about me were related to the hotel video? Did she think I somehow removed or altered the recordings or had someone else do it? Did she think having – or not having – those videos would be a problem for me?

I didn't get much time to consider the possibilities. Most of those questions occurred to me later in the day, after our conversation. At the time, Detective Nrissilli pressed on, changing the subject in a way that was suspicious in itself.

"To be honest, there's little evidence indicating you committed any crime: no bodies, whether or not you fired in self-defense. At worst, some property damage. We've already searched your compad: you were clearly working the Vzktkk case, but I didn't see any earlier calls between yourself and his mate.

"Actually, we didn't find *any* calls between the two of you. Very clean work, even for a P.I. We know you two met at her place of employment, had a drink, and she gave you the hotel key there. A check of your recent travel shows that you were out of town at the time of Vzktkk's death."

I did my best to keep my feelings out of my response: "All accurate, and thank you for noticing. Very thorough work, yourself. You are correct: there is no evidence I did anything illegal, because I haven't. Improper, maybe. Imprudent, definitely. But I'll swear to you, if it will help: I'm just the hired hunter here, trying to find a killer. Maybe I found three. I'll be the first to admit this case got bigger than I expected and I walked into the middle of it."

Broken Record

She stretched taller and looked down her nose at me. "I still think there's more between you and your 'client' than you're telling. Why hasn't she called you yet… why didn't she call you before, at least once? What would you or she be afraid of that required phone silence? If it was the fact of your hire, then why meet with you in public?"

I had an answer for that question, at least: "She came to my office while I was out of town and left me a note to meet her. She figured coming to her workplace would give us an excuse to talk without drawing attention."

True that far, but then I reversed away from the truth: "I don't know why she was being so careful. She said she didn't want anyone knowing she was hiring private help. Maybe she thought I would be more effective if the killer didn't see me coming. Maybe she thought she was protecting me from whoever shot her mate."

"That didn't work so well," the detective offered, deadpan.

"I assume she didn't know they would track her to a reservation at a dock-side hotel," I suggested. "But she booked the room under her own name, so she wasn't being totally cautious."

"I'm still not convinced," Detective Nrissilli warned, "but I will admit that I don't have anything – yet – to hold you on. Given your injuries, I'm going to trust your good sense and let you go home to recuperate. Consider yourself *off* Pkstzk's case. Un-hired. If she makes contact, you let me know. My number is on your compad, which you can pick up when you check out here. We have to hold your heater as evidence until the hotel incident is resolved. You can have your armor back, although I'm not sure it's worthwhile to repair at this point… maybe bury it with honors?"

Her tone was light but her words heavy. I understood the warning. She wouldn't expect me to honor her order to drop Pkstzk's case, but I was no longer protected there as a working P.I. If the constables enforced jurisdiction, I was fully liable for any damage or infractions caused while pursuing the case.

I was already guilty of one known break-in and entry. If I persisted, I would lose any friendly witnesses regarding the shootout at Taburket's. Plus, if I was found later at any scene related to the case – like Taburket's, the restaurant, or the murder site in Isstravil – I could be arrested on sight for evidence tampering or trespassing.

The same threats applied if I had any contact with Pkstzk before the constables found her and didn't call the detective immediately. That oversight would be considered "interference with an investigation" or "obstruction of justice".

Not to mention, holding my weapon, Rtrtr, hostage to my good behavior… that was just cruel. Besides leaving me unarmed, keeping my heater in lockup was only punishing a good weapon for its owner's misfortunes. The detective probably didn't realize how much I loved my sidearm, but she understood that I was less likely to start any more trouble without it. Yes, it actually was evidence, but that excuse was a secondary concern.

My body must have betrayed my frustrations. Detective Nrissilli squinted at me and added: "Do we have an understanding? Your release on good behavior?"

"Sure. Fine. I'm not happy, but I get your meaning. I'll be good for a day or two, anyway, just to make sure these wounds don't unseal. I hope you'll have everyone rounded up by that time."

"I'm hoping to have your three, plus Pkstzk, in custody by the time you're discharged," the detective shot back. "And you're not entirely loosed from my claws: Stay in town and out of trouble. You may still get a ride downtown if I hear something I don't like."

"Heard. So, can you cut me loose here?" I indicated my bound wrist. With all the turning and twisting, the restraint tie was constricting enough to make my fingers feel cold.

The detective obliged, digging out a pair of scissors and cutting off the bindings the same way the doctor had. I flexed my good arm and hand gratefully, moving the blood back where it wanted to go.

"Stay in bed, for now," Detective Nrissilli warned. "Besides your good health, there's still a guard outside. Don't make him nervous."

"No problem," I confirmed. "I'm still not sure how well I can stand up. I'll wait on the nurse to help out there. Ttt, one more thing: Would you mind if I call Tskksk, to make sure she's all right?"

Broken Record

She twitched an ear in agreement. "We have a patrol checking in on her. She opened her store on time this morning, no signs of any trouble. She doesn't answer her 'pad very well, though."

"I noticed that." I relaxed slightly, relieved that at least one possible victim of this case had avoided trouble. "Thanks. I don't expect any threats toward her, considering you already spoke with her and others in the neighborhood about Vzktkk's murder. I haven't mentioned the new evidence to anyone else… and I'll keep it that way."

"Good," the detective replied. "Although I don't know yet what value that evidence holds. If someone does come after her, that would tell me it's important."

I didn't like the sound of that. I countered, "But even if that was the case, now that we have the recording, there's no reason to bother her."

"Sometimes, criminals don't need good reasons. Murder may have a motive, but that doesn't mean the motive isn't irrational." Her lecture was strange, coming from a constable detective to a private detective who, she knew, had dealt with more than one murder case. Then again, she was far ahead of me in years and experience. She had been dealing with death for a long time.

She was right, too. Just knowing that Tskksk provided evidence that might implicate them, the killer might target her for retribution. I hated the thought. It gave me additional incentive to ignore the detective's warnings and find the culprit that much faster.

"Well, let's not give them any reasons, either way," I declared.

"The recording won't be public knowledge until we have the killer on trial," she confirmed. "And then, only if it's relevant. Get some rest, would you? You're winning here, don't push it." On that note, she left the room, locking the door behind her.

I didn't feel like a winner. Fortunate, yes. But the game was still being played. And by the empty shells of my mother's unlaid eggs, I wasn't about to get off the field just yet.

Chapter 10 - Abrupt Discharge

In a relative sense, matters progressed quickly after Detective Nrissilli's visit. That is to say, things went faster than you might expect for a multiple gunshot victim waiting in custody. From *my* perspective, time dragged on with agonizing slowness.

I sat idle until lunch time. With no video screen, compad, or other entertainment, I was alone with my thoughts for several hours. Given that those thoughts were focused on a single subject with no new inputs, I wasted the time looping without any new results.

Crime detection does not involve sudden revelation after extended contemplation. You have to go out and collect facts – far more data than you strictly need – before a pattern becomes apparent. Sometimes, you have to actively provoke your prey into motion, not just follow its trail.

I needed to get back *onto* that trail. The tracks led back to Pkstzk. To keep moving forward, I needed to find her. I was still concerned about her safety and her good opinion, but these motivations were rapidly losing ground to a close third: a growing need for answers.

What had her mate, Vzktkk, been doing on an unremarkable side street in a seemingly random middle-class neighborhood? Why was someone waiting there, inside a defunct pet store, for him to pass? Why *had* they shot Vzktkk? Why had someone locked starving animals inside said pet store, apparently primed to attack anyone investigating the place? Who called whom, right before and right after the shooting? All of these puzzles led back to the key question: Who killed Vzktkk?

With my attack, the case gained some new questions: Why were there three well-armed Vislin waiting in Pkstzk's hotel room? Had they been waiting for me or for her? Why did they try to kill me? Why had they done such a poor job of it? Where had they gone afterward? And why was there so little evidence of their exit... or even their entry?

Just to round out the riddle-game: Who *were* those guys? Were they connected to Vzktkk's murder, and if so, how?

My claws itched for my compad, so that I could at least list my questions. I was probably still missing a handful of important concerns. There might be relevant evidence in Tskksk's EM recording from the night of Vzktkk's murder. I wanted to talk to her and bounce research ideas.

Pkstzk's behavior, when we met, had been questionable. I wondered if her co-workers knew anything I should know. She certainly knew a lot I should know. I wanted to bounce a few theories off *her* to see what made sense.

Bouncing off of either female would normally sound like a great idea. Sadly, I wouldn't be up to such strenuous activity for a while. Thinking about my injuries reminded me that, legally, I wasn't supposed to be following up on the case at all. I was going to ignore that order, of course, but I'd have to be subtle in my approach.

Not that I didn't usually try to be subtle; nobody wants to be caught breaking and entering, pickpocketing, borrowing evidence, conning a witness... you get the idea. But I'd have to cut down on the personal visits and physical antagonism.

Shadow and claw all the way, then. I started my deceptions by playing "good patient" as much as possible.

When the nurse arrived with lunch, he was thrilled to find that I'd earned my hands' freedom. He upgraded my diet to solids: fried ground meat patties topped with salted belly-fat strips rendered and crisped in the oven: a childhood favorite. I also got another serving of broth, this time served in a cup. I thanked my visitor for the meal and let him know I would give him a tip, if the constables hadn't confiscated my credit strip. He assured me that he'd tack a service charge onto my hospital bill.

Kidding aside, it was a solid meal, better than any I'd eaten since returning home, better than most I'd eaten before my recent expense-paid vacation.

Nathan Large with Laine Megan Lundquist

Given my appetite and the emptiness of my holiday memories, I might consider the hospital food more *enjoyable* than anything I'd eaten while abroad. After life on short rations the last couple of days, the grease rumbled a little in my lower gut, but the discomfort was worthwhile.

I tried to make the meal last, but eventually I had to lick up the last oily scrap and return to contemplating the already contemplated. Given the freedom of my hospital room, I considered testing my limbs, maybe pacing a bit.

I decided not to tempt either the medical staff or my constable guard by causing trouble. I also needed to save my strength for whenever I *had* to strain my damaged muscles. For example, when I inevitably needed the toilet.

Could I nap, instead? I had only slept through part of a night, under sedation. That didn't count much for rest. I was woken regularly during the early morning hours. Combine that fatigue with the soporific effects of my painkillers, and I was, in fact, feeling drowsy.

True sleep continued to evade me. Even though I couldn't do anything more to resolve Pkstzk's case, those troubles still intruded when I tried to rest. I settled for physical inactivity and closed my eyes while my mind continued to churn.

I realized, eventually, that I could still work the case without Pkstzk's input. I could work it backward, starting with Vzktkk's personal business and acquaintances. At the least, I might get some idea what he was doing on that street in Isstravil... something Pkstzk might not even know.

I could even subcontract personal meetings to a third party acting on my behalf. I knew a few reliable fellow investigators who could handle the assignment. The problem there was that I couldn't *pay* them for their services; a cut of the nothing Pkstzk was paying me was still nothing. She might be able to pay something – I'd never had a chance to ask – but relaying that credit would require contacting her. Did I trust a third party to manage that contact, too? Would Pkstzk trust a request for payment coming from anyone but me? There were a few shared secrets I could use to reassure her an intermediary actually came from me, but most of those secrets were tied into our mutual association with Pack Vzrrk... and I didn't trust *anyone* with that information.

Broken Record

I wasn't owed any favors. Could I persuade anyone to work on credit? Offer unspecified favors to be repaid later? Did I know anyone who actually wanted my personal favors? The answer to all these questions, much to my chagrin, was no.

I briefly considered sharing the details of Vzktkk's murder case with Tskksk, to beg for her help tracking down possible suspects. That line of thought should tell you how fuzzy-headed I was. Getting a civilian – a potential witness, no less – involved in a case was a terrible idea. Even worse, if Tskksk succeeded and the case did connect to Pack Vzrrk, like I feared, she'd have a claw to my and Pkstzk's soft bellies. Tskksk didn't seem like the sort for blackmail, but that knowledge could be as much a danger to her as an asset.

Rrr… did I have anyone I could blackmail into helping? I did have a neighbor who tampered with his water meter to keep its readings low. He'd be useless for investigative work, though. I should save that gambit for the next time I needed free plumbing.

That was it, almost no resources at all. If I were shadier, or the case less so, I would have more potential assistance. Being a good guy in a bad situation limited my options sharply.

I *did* have a small amount of credit in the bank, still. Was it worth spending everything I owned on a single hire, for a single assignment, if it meant complete poverty afterward?

It might be, for Pkstzk. If she was innocent of any wrongdoing, I ought to be willing to sacrifice for her. I'd have to see who would work cheap but still thorough. At least, with me providing most (if not all) of the background research on the case, they would only be managing the person-to-person interface. That service shouldn't cost as much as the complete P.I. package.

I spent the remaining decads of my "naptime" reviewing potential candidates for the job. Mostly, this involved thinking of names and trying to remember what they'd done to or for me, what I'd done to or for them, and what scandals I could remember if any.

I amused myself by comparing my assessment of each competitor with their likely assessment of me. In most cases, I came out unfairly lower in their eyes than they did in mine. I wondered how many sins other P.I.s kept successfully hidden. How would their skeleton collections rank against mine?

I was dangerously close to self-pity when the door finally opened again. I was also dangerously close to a digestive accident. I hoped whoever was coming in would oblige by helping me to the bathroom.

A female Taratumm in constabulary armor entered the room. Not my first choice for personal assistance. In fact, I'd had nightmares that started the same way.

While I was trying to decide between one embarrassment and another, she spoke up: "Stchvk, you are released from custody. You may stay or leave as you prefer, depending upon your doctor's recommendations. I will be leaving shortly, myself. If you have any concerns about your personal safety, please contact Constabulary Precinct Kef to request further protection."

I nodded to acknowledge her statement and she let herself out, duties completed. Once she closed the door, I carefully turned and lowered myself to the floor. My offended leg pulled and protested, but supported my weight just fine. I didn't feel any tearing as I stepped cautiously across the hard, cold floor. Another good sign. I made it to the toilet without incident and settled down for another long stretch of contemplation.

So… nobody would stop me from leaving the hospital, but nobody would stop an assassin from coming *into* the room, either. I wasn't expecting anyone to shoot at me there, but then again, I hadn't expected it at the hotel.

I wondered what I'd have to say to warrant an official protective detail. Certainly, I needed more solid evidence than I already had. Given that I was officially barred from *pursuing* said case and its evidence, the offer of protection seemed like a meaningless gesture. I supposed I'd know there was a problem when it started shooting at me again. Of course, it might be a little late for the constables to help at that point.

I wouldn't even have my sidearm for self-defense. The constables seemed confident I had nothing to be afraid of, leaving me unarmed and unguarded. I hoped they were right, though there was a strong possibility that I would deliberately prove them wrong.

Broken Record

I briefly considered buying a new heater. Kkk, while I was at it, why not shop for a fully automated self-defense drone, with mini-grenade launchers and a fluoride gas laser? It seemed like whenever I had a little credit saved up, I quickly found ways to spend it away.

It could take a cycle or more until my Rtrtr was released from evidence, depending on how long it took to find my attackers. I wished, uncharitably, that all three assassins would be shot by constables. That outcome would spare us all a long trial and spare me a protracted separation from my weapon. Alternately, less violently, the egg-suckers could all turn themselves in, confess, and simplify matters that way. Kkk, the death-by-constable scenario was far more likely.

I wouldn't normally wish a painful death even on attempted murderers, even when the murder they attempted was mine. But this attack wasn't personal, whether it was aimed at me or Pkstzk. These were hired guns, practically mercenaries. They were the worst sort of evil. It didn't matter whether they were family enforcers for a Pack with an interest in Pkstzk's death – possibly to end her inquiries into Vzktkk's death – or anonymously hired assassins. I live in a city full of crime, most of it petty and profit-oriented, but professional murderers are at the top of my hate list.

I'd pull the trigger on them myself, if it came to that. If I had a trigger to pull. I supposed I could settle for throwing them out an eighth-story window: justice at its most poetic. To be honest, though, I hoped I'd never see any of those egg-kickers or their like again. Revenge fantasies aside, it was better to avoid mercenary killers entirely rather than hunt them down yourself. Let the constables find and punish them. I'd accept whatever method of execution was approved. Or a life sentence, if necessary.

I supposed it was a badge of honor that everyone else who'd ever tried to kill me was either dead or in prison. I hadn't made that many personal enemies, to begin with. The impersonal enemies rarely bothered to try and murder a nuisance P.I.. Like a constable detective, a private snoop is an inevitable consequence of crime. There's no point attacking an investigator. It's wiser to avoid me entirely.

If a culprit wants to stop an investigation, they have to deal with my employer, instead. Just offing old Stchvk would only save my employer the credit they owed me... which they could then use to hire a new P.I. Even if the idea was to scare off *any* investigator from taking a case, you'd have to kill two or three P.I.s before the risk overrode our desire for profit. I suppose if a case piled up enough P.I. bodies, it might price our hazard pay above the employer's budget... but scaring us away was tough.

Sapients in my line of work get used to a certain risk of attempted murder, so simple threats aren't effective. Plus, there's truth to the old saying: the harder they're trying to kill you, the closer you are to the nest.

The greatest danger came from panicked criminals caught off-guard; fear can make them forget the pointlessness of violence. By that point, their death or capture is virtually assured. Either their guilt is certain and they're just desperate to escape, or else the assault creates that certainty. So, while getting shot at wasn't a rarity for me, being pursued beyond a single shootout *was* rare. I didn't expect to be hunted down this time, either... but surprises do happen.

It was at about that point, as I thought about armed killers coming to find me and finish the job, that I realized I could just stand up and walk out of the room. I could even request my discharge if I so chose, although I suspected leaving would be against doctor's orders. First thing, though, I should finish up in the toilet and make sure I could walk well enough to walk out.

Once I left the stall, I took a few experimental steps around the room. The movement still hurt, but no more than before. With a compression band on my leg and maybe a cane or crutch for support, I could probably hike downstairs and reach a transport stop. Doing so, right away, would probably cause some internal damage and worse scarring, but that cost might be worthwhile if it spared my sanity and improved my safety. I didn't have the luxury or patience to sit still and conduct business by remote.

By leaving, I was giving up a couple of other perks: regular pain relief and guaranteed, edible meals. Those two sacrifices, alone, should tell you how much I hated the idea of further downtime.

Besides mere freedom, there was another important need driving me out the door: time. The longer I waited to pursue my case, the better the killer could hide.

Broken Record

Given the week that had already passed between Vzktkk's death and my initial investigation, a day or two might not seem like much... but if the hotel attack was related, that meant that the case was still hot. *Someone* was concerned about what I and Pkstzk might learn.

I was willing to put up with additional pain and hunger if it meant a better chance at some answers. I limped over to the door and found it unlocked, as promised. Opening the door showed me a hallway somewhere on the tenth floor of Vaktrri. There was a nurses' station about a hundred feet away. My mealtime friend and sleep-time tormentor wasn't visible, but I saw a Taratumm staffer at the desk. He looked up as I hobbled down the hall.

"Are you all right, sir?" the nurse asked.

"Amazing. A credit to the doctors here," I told him in a strained voice that contradicted my words. I was trying *not* to be sarcastic, which was nearly as difficult as hiding the winces and gasps.

"Can I... help you?" he persisted. His expression suggested that I needed all sorts of help, but he was only interested in the kinds he could directly provide.

"I'd like to collect my belongings. I want to be discharged as soon as possible." I phrased this request politely, as a preference rather than a demand, but my tone hinted that I would make life difficult for him if he opposed me.

He tried to placate me: "I'll notify your nurse and doctor." He didn't make any move toward a 'pad or other comm device, though.

I continued, in case he was waiting for acknowledgment: "Please do, and soon. I need to check on a friend's safety."

My added excuse was a mistake. He challenged me: "If you have immediate concerns, couldn't those be addressed by the constables that were in your room earlier? I can have the officer who just left paged..."

I did my best to humor the officious stomper. "They told me she's fine, but they won't spare an officer to protect her full-time. Could you please help me here? I'd like to do this the right way, rather than storming out and undoing my surgeon's good work."

Nathan Large with Laine Megan Lundquist

The desk nurse looked down at a wide display set into his station's surface. "All right, I see you are cleared for release at your discretion… although the doctor did recommend you stay an additional day for observation. I'll ask that your belongings be brought here from secure storage and notify your nurse. Please wait in your room until we're ready to authorize your discharge."

I realized this response was probably the best I would get. Fine. Let him have his little moment of authority. I wondered how many patients gave him trouble by asking to leave early. Maybe, not many. If I had the time, I'd have milked a stay at Vaktrri for every day my insurance would cover. The damage was already done in terms of my billable deductible. Every pill or meal after that copay was free, paid by the City's coffers. Normally, my policy *wouldn't* cover admission at Vaktrri, but since the constables brought me there officially, I couldn't be blamed or up-charged. Anyone else already paying the high private premiums to qualify for Vaktrri Medical care probably wouldn't waste their hard-earned comfort, either.

Then again, there might be a few workaholics, claustrophobics, and other anxious sorts who refused to stay in the hospital a hectad longer than necessary. I supposed I fit that category. I *was* leaving so I could get back to work. Plus, there were some anxieties involved. But I wasn't making a fuss, just asserting my freedom to leave and manage my healing on my own recognizance. I hoped this medical bureaucrat wouldn't delay my exit any longer than honestly necessary.

Having done my best, I turned and slide-stepped back to my room. It was after I opened the door to go back in that I finally registered one final anomaly. Why hadn't I noticed it before? Maybe my thinking was sharpening with increased circulation, upright posture, and a declining amount of medication in my system.

The weird thing was: no intravenous line.

Almost every other time I was admitted to a hospital, the first thing they did was start an IV. Whether transfusing blood, antibiotics, or just rehydrating saline, IVs were standard practice for paramedics and other medical responders. I was pretty sure they installed a line back in the ambulance. Why, then, had I woken up without one? I didn't even have a bandage, a wound, or a sore spot from an intravenous needle. Surely, after my wounds and surgery, I needed some trans-fusion of fluids? I was fairly sure antibiotics were called for after major injuries, even the relatively minor major injuries I sustained.

I didn't *feel* dehydrated… or infected, for that matter. It was possible I was thoroughly pumped with whatever I needed before I woke up. Maybe Vaktrri Medical had become so advanced that they could manage without older tech-niques like a tube in your arm. Maybe the doctor was bright enough to recognize that I didn't need an IV and respected enough to override standard orders.

But maybe the omission was due to oversight. Maybe it was neglect; when the constables ordered "no painkillers", someone detached the IV, then forgot to bring it back later. In that case, I was fortunate I hadn't suffered from its absence.

Whatever the reason, I hadn't had to dance with an IV stand when going to the bathroom or exiting my room, for which I was grateful. I just hoped I wouldn't pay for that minor liberty with a dehydration headache or anemia, later.

I sat back on my bed, trying to wait patiently. I'd give them… some reason-able amount of time. Without a clock, view-screen, or compad in my room, I had no way to measure time exactly. I expected that I'd be anxious and bored after maybe half an hour, so that would do as a deadline.

I never reached that level of discomfort. I hadn't even gotten comfortable yet, when the door opened and my Hrotata nurse arrived.

He looked me over with rhetorical exaggeration, taking equally theatrical notes on his service compad. I watched him and avoided spoiling his act. I did tilt my head from side to side like an audience rapt with attention to a performer.

Finally, he looked up from his records and told me, "I wish I could find a good reason to keep you. All I've got is a warning that your arm and leg wounds could reopen if you strain them too much. You'd be safer here, especially with me checking your vitals, but there's nothing potentially fatal about you resting up at home… quietly. That is, provided you get there in a well-cushioned vehicle. Do you have anyone there to change your dressings?"

Nathan Large with Laine Megan Lundquist

"Actually, I'm sort of hoping to use these bandages for sympathy, to see if I can persuade a certain female to take care of me. That was the friend I mentioned before. You know, I guard her back, she rebandages mine…" I offered an eye-roll and click to sell the friendly joke.

He looked serious. "I hope you really do have a friend. If you leave those pads on to fester, you'll be back here with a blood infection… if you're lucky. You're a native, right? You know how the microbes are here. You don't stay clean, you pay the price."

I knew what he meant. "Spore" wasn't just a clever name for the planet. Our lush world was home to a profusion of monocellular detritus: actual spores, pollens, bacteria, and a few unique parasitic microbe types. No few of those organisms would relish a foothold in my exposed flesh. Most would be suppressed by a decent antibiotic – and I planned to fill that prescription along with the best painkiller they'd allow me – but letting my dressings sit and get foul would give the crawlies too much advantage for any antibiotic to overcome.

If it came to that, I'd drag myself to the neighborhood emergency clinic for maintenance. It'd cost a bit, but not as much as hiring an in-home nurse. It definitely wouldn't cost as much as sitting idle in a hospital room, if you counted values beyond credit.

I summarized these thoughts to the nurse by answering, "I understand. Yes, I have someone to help me. I'll follow the discharge instructions. No offense to your excellent work. If it wasn't urgent…"

He squinted at me as he interjected, "…you'd stick around and wait for the next constable visit. No, I understand. I overheard a little about your business. Well, good luck. I hope we won't be seeing you again soon… hmm, I mean, in the hospital. Don't end up dead, either."

He managed to recover without stammering. I respected that. His discomfort showed that he cared, despite his hints at my less-than-noble motives. He could think whatever he wanted, provided he hurried up my discharge.

"All right, here's the form," he obliged, showing me his compad screen. The illuminated document thereupon ran to several pages of text. I made a show of reading it like any other legal release form, which was to say I skimmed the headers and ignored the rest. I was accepting all risk, the hospital wasn't to blame for any harm I caused to myself, and so forth. I was a little late to be risk averse. I scrolled to the bottom of the document and signed the screen with a claw tip.

There was a second signature required, releasing information to my insurer for payment and accepting any allowable charges. Seeing that document hurt more than my injuries. The deductible would eat half of my remaining credit, by itself. I could claim it as civil damages if they caught and convicted my shooters, but I'd gladly forfeit that claim if the culprits died first. Frost, I'd *pay* that much to ensure they were dead… Sss, hypocrite. Pay *who*? A contract killer?

After that formality, we were done. The nurse, whom I finally found out was named Thrisstil, wished me well and confirmed that my belongings were being delivered upstairs. I could wait by the elevators if I wanted, although he recommended taking advantage of my hospital bed just a few decads longer.

I obliged him that much. No point in compounding the strain on my leg. I sat patiently while the circuits of medical bureaucracy cycled. I tried to be grateful that all my records were networked and integrated, with no paperwork to shuffle. I was only waiting on the system's organic components to do their part.

Eventually, the nurse returned with a plastic crate. Inside were my compad and my tattered armor. Since I wasn't excited about going outside in my patient robes, I chose to risk the armor. The back plate was tattered, of course, and the left greave shredded, but the anterior pieces were only scuffed, mostly from my landing. There was enough material intact for basic propriety, even if I would look like… well, someone who had been shot. I chose to think of the look as 'wounded soldier' rather than 'murder target'.

Thrisstil stepped out to let me get dressed. Once I was done, I woke my compad. A handful of messages were waiting for me, among them the note with Detective Nrissilli's contact info. There was also a formal issuance from law enforcement regarding my detention, another about my release, and a third spelling out my status: restricted from travel out of Layafflr City until further notice and forbidden from any activity pursuant to investigating the murder of Vzktkk.

To my surprise, there was also a short video message from Tskksk. She apologized for missing my earlier calls and reassured me that she was just extremely busy, not avoiding me or in any trouble. That was nice to know, although since her call was eleven hours old, its reassurances were slightly out of date.

Last was a message from my landlord reminding me that rent was due. Great. One more expense to deplete my remaining credits. It seemed inevitable that I would return to poverty, one way or another. My only choice was the route by which I arrived.

I typed back a response to the detective to acknowledge receipt and mentioned that I'd heard from Tskksk, finally. I also reminded Nrissilli of her permission to contact the tech store owner, an option I intended to exercise. I *didn't* notify the detective of my intention to call Pkstzk, as well.

I figured that since our relationship – as employee and employer – was already exposed, I could get away with a live call. Hopefully, Pkstzk would answer. Still, I wanted to wait until I was safely away from the hospital and any prying ears before calling. For all I knew, nurse Thrisstil was reporting back to Nrissilli. The big, matronly detective might have persuaded the young, impressionable male to track my activities. She had more to flash at him than just her badge.

I walked out of the room and down the hall, then waddled past the unstaffed floor station. My pace was slow due to caution more than pain. The wounds and my endurance were holding well. Eventually, though, I'd need to get off my feet, not to mention pick up and take my medications. Assuming the hospital submitted the authorizations properly, I should be able to claim my antibiotics and analgesics at any networked pharmacy.

I made it to the elevator, down to the lobby, and out the doors before I believed that I was free. For some reason, the whole time, I was expecting someone to rush up and order me back to my room, perhaps even tie me down again.

This paranoia struck me as odd. Granted, paranoia is my default state, but usually I reserve my fears for bigger hazards: death, injury, unexpected expenses, public humiliation, and the like. Spending extra time in the hospital wasn't exactly a frightening prospect.

Broken Record

The fear, I realized, came from my urgency. I was beyond wanting to protect Pkstzk and myself. I needed answers. Too many unexplainable circumstances were piling up. My various mysteries might not all be connected, but solving one case would at least clear away its particular oddities. Then, I could get to work solving whatever was producing the other anomalies, like my memory difficulties and erratic sleep patterns.

I found a public aircar station, logically, on the grounds of the medical center. The surge of familiarity I experienced when approaching the kiosk was becoming a familiar experience. An adjacent public comm booth evoked another dim memory. I *must* have visited Vaktrri at some point in the past, but my brain was frosted and wouldn't give up the details.

I rented a 'car, barely feeling the sting of one more expense. From the aircar station, I stopped at a pharmacy and picked up my waiting pills. I took the recommended dosages immediately, assuming I had already waited sufficiently long since the hospital gave me anything. I kept the aircar waiting while I shopped, then dragged myself back inside when I was done. The hold cost more, but I had no alternative if I wanted to spare myself an unnecessary walk to the next kiosk.

Finally, it was time to go home. I was tempted to visit Tskksk in Isstravil or go looking for Pkstzk, but I knew my condition was too poor – physically, financially, and legally – to take such risks. At the least, I shouldn't venture out without a plan. I could still place calls from home. Calling anyone connected to Vzktkk's case was still against constables' orders, but it would take them longer to notice that offense than if I made contact in person.

Since the aircar ride from uptown to my neighborhood was a lengthy one, I decided to use the time unwisely. I searched for Pkstzk's number. Maybe it was the drugs kicking in, or maybe just my short patience, but I hardly considered the risk involved in calling my confederate immediately after getting my compad back. I hadn't even scanned it for monitoring devices or software.

Then again, if the law was going to such lengths of surveillance, it wouldn't scruple at bugging my apartment, tapping the call remotely, or indulging any of a hundred other eavesdropping tricks. I was good at avoiding physical security measures, but I was no adept at virtual stealth.

Nathan Large with Laine Megan Lundquist

There was no answer to my call, anyway. Pkstzk's continued unavailability kept me out of further trouble. I left a message letting her know what had happened: I got to the hotel; some armed Vislin tried to kill me; I escaped, then was arrested and taken to the hospital; I was out of the hospital in surprisingly good shape; and now, I was resting up, worrying about her safety, and hoping she could please call and reassure me she was alive. Also, if she didn't mind stopping by and filling me in on all the background details of the case I was no longer officially working, that would be great, thanks and goodbye.

It was an exhausting voice message. I felt fatigued as the aircar covered the last few miles to my home. When it signaled arrival and opened its door, I could barely haul myself out and stagger through my building's entrance. As I pulled myself up the stairs, one at a time, I wondered how long I would sleep this time. Half a day? An entire day? Or would the pain wake me periodically?

I reached my door before I even thought to pull out my card key. I checked the slit pocket in my armor where I usually kept the key along with my P.I. license and ident. My other cards were there, but the key was missing.

I was certain I hadn't dropped it, even with all the jostling the previous night. Someone must have removed it. But why? To search my apartment? There wouldn't be anything interesting in there. Anyone who knew me would know I didn't have any valuables to steal, other than my compad and heater, and those would be on my person if I was out. Besides, if they took my key card while it was in constabulary custody, they could have taken the other valuables already.

If the idea was to wait for me inside the apartment, then the door would be unlocked and *that* would be suspicious. On a sudden hunch, I checked the *other* slit pocket on the armor's opposite side. There was the keycard. Someone took it out and replaced it on the wrong side? Possibly, an innocent mistake while the detective went through my possessions. Possibly, a telling mistake for someone who borrowed the card and put it back later, *wanting* me to come home without noticing anything.

I tested my door: locked. That didn't mean there wasn't another hit squad waiting inside, watching for me to unlock and open the door. I could oblige them. Or, I could just stand in the hall. Or, I could go somewhere else… but where? How foolish would I look, getting spooked over nothing? Besides, I was *really* tired. The possibility of danger perked me up some, but there was no certainty that I could get to the local aircar station without dropping unconscious on the sidewalk. I might be able to crash at a neighbor's apartment – one of the few neighbors I trusted – but avoidance was just postponing the inevitable. I didn't have enough reason to call the constables.

Inside, then. If I was still armed, I would have drawn Rtrtr before turning the latch. As it was, I rotated the lever slowly, standing close to the door as I slid it open a crack. My idea was to look and listen through that gap, ready to jump back at the first sign of presence or motion.

Instead, my warning came from the door itself.

I have entered and exited my own door thousands of times. I have a certain familiarity with its range of motion and its sticking points. I encountered resistance at an atypical point as I pushed the door open. That oddity plus my heightened nerves were enough to send me stumbling backwards.

My reaction turned out to be exactly correct. A concussion wave of force and flame hurled my apartment door against its frame and buckled it outward. Only my caution and the barrier itself spared me from a crippling impact. As it was, the blast was merely agonizing. The explosion threw me across the hall, aggravating the wounds on my back when it slammed into the opposite wall.

After I landed, my torn leg gave out and I toppled to the floor. My face and hands stung from the heat of the flash, but didn't feel worse than first-degree burns. I couldn't hear anything after the initial roar, which meant I'd been deafened, but at least my eardrums weren't perforated. Believe me, a Vislin knows when their sensitive ears have been traumatized. A burst eardrum would have knocked me unconscious.

I'd also been spared shrapnel wounds from the shattered door. The few shards of hardwood that flew past were fairly large; smaller pieces bounced off my armor. I wasn't having generally good luck, but my recently acquired talent for avoiding serious injury seemed to be holding.

Nathan Large with Laine Megan Lundquist

The non-serious injuries were still enough to keep me flat on the floor, gasping. If I hadn't been so stunned, I might have been frenzying down the stairs. I hurt more than the pain medications could manage.

A flickering light from inside my apartment caught my attention. It was burning. That was bad. Among other unpleasant things, a fire meant that I couldn't keep lying in the hallway. Fire would hurt a lot. Smoke was bad, too.

A more recent or expensive building would have fire suppression systems, ending any serious blaze within seconds. My stack of shacks had only fire reducing materials in the walls and sprinklers in the halls. My apartment might be engulfed but at least the neighbors would be spared. They still might inhale the smoke, though. I needed to sound an alarm. Actually, the explosion should have alerted everyone to the danger. I needed to get out of the way before they stampeded over me.

Evacuate. That was the word I wanted. My abused brain was having problems with basic functions… like standing up. I lifted myself to hands and knees three times and collapsed twice, before staying halfway upright.

It turned out the effort was moot. By that time, my upstairs neighbors, a small, young Vislin Pack, had emerged and spotted me. I was privileged to see their expressions as they looked from my battered body to my shattered door. I'm sure they weren't surprised to confirm my apartment as the source of the explosion. I hadn't often taken business home like this, but they knew I was a P.I. To most citizens, that translated to "trouble-seeking idiot".

What they couldn't reconcile was the fact that not only was I hurt, I was already bandaged. I looked like I'd come home prepared to be blown up. Considering that the damage to my armor was on the back, but my burns were on the front, *I* would have been confused at a first glance.

Credit to their character, the youths didn't pause long to think. One, a slight male in slick synthetic armor, stooped to pick me up by the unbandaged arm. His beak moved. He might have said something to me. Maybe he was talking to a Pack-mate. I couldn't hear at all and couldn't see well, either. I *could* smell smoke and see haze beginning to obscure the air. I did my best to help as my rescuers hauled me toward the stairs, one on my arm and another hoisting me by the waist.

We hurried downstairs as fast as the group could manage and spilled out onto the street. Still thinking smart, the Pack crossed the street, my old carcass in tow. It was unlikely the fire would spread or that anything else would explode in our building, but better to be safe. Not knowing the reason for the sabotage, the citizenry might be leery about additional bombs.

What *was* the reason for this attack? This time, I was certain I was the target. But why? As I slumped down against the building wall where my rescuers settled me, I tried to summon enough awareness to decipher this new danger.

Why try to kill *me?* Usually, when someone tried to kill me, I was getting close to something sensitive. I had no idea what I might be close to. What did I know that was worth killing over? What might I eventually learn if I kept prying? I didn't even know what my case was *about*, aside from murder.

Was the attack due to my association with Pkstzk? With Pack Vzrrk? Was I a target because I'd stumbled onto and/or foiled the ambush intended for Pkstzk at Taburket's? Or was the bombing entirely unrelated to my current case? Was it somehow related to a *previous* case? Maybe the case I couldn't remember? An angry arsonist was worse than a memory gap, but only by a matter of degree.

Whether it was the new trauma, the old wounds, my situational narcolepsy, or some combination of all three, my thoughts ended there. I finally passed out, relieved of duty once more.

Chapter 11 - Sudden Movement

I returned to awareness through layers of emotion. First came aggravation, due to the protests from my abused body. Second was relief that I was waking up at all. Third was confusion and discomfort from finding myself lying on pavement, staring up at young Vislin faces and the tops of buildings. The fourth and last emotional layer was a mixture of gratitude for my rescue and appreciation that at least one of my saviors was rather nice to look at.

She was named… Vstktrr? Vstkrt? Something like that.

She was also part of a Pack who'd never bothered to give me their name, despite living in the same building, only two floors above. I hadn't tried hard to get to know them, either. Like I said earlier, we usually only meet our neighbors during times of crisis.

Blended into the emotional mix was guilt: regret that I was the cause of their troubles that day. Granted, I was also the main sufferer of those troubles, but none of us would be sleeping at home that night. Plus, their apartment and belongings would have smoke damage. They'd be smelling the stench for cycles to come.

I wondered how much *I* had left. My real items of value were mostly outside of the apartment: my compad, which was on me in its carry-case, and my heater, which was in a constabulary evidence locker. I regretted the loss of my hand-carved wooden desk, particularly since it was *my* hand that carved it, along with the accompanying chair. And my coffee table. And my living-room chair. Most of my furniture, actually.

I wanted to cry, then wondered if that would look pathetic in front of Vstkrt. Maybe she liked vulnerable types? The moment passed in a haze of conflicting priorities.

Broken Record

I thought then of my other item of value: my drugs. I looked around as best I could from my prone position.

These were my kind of kids. They figured out what I was looking for right away.

"We picked up your medicines on the way out," one of the males told me. "You looked like you needed them... even before that explosion."

Ttt, I could hear again! I tried my voice and found it also functional. "You read that right. Thank you..."

"Rptrkch," he supplied, "Pack Tksshs. We live above you."

"I've seen you around," I acknowledged, "Thank you, Rptrkch... Pack Tksshs. I appreciate you rescuing me *and* my meds. Could I have one of the blue ones, please?"

The female ratcheted open the correct bottle and handed me a large blue pill. She looked at the label with unashamed interest while another of the males helped me up enough to swallow. The fourth of their number, a third male, handed me a sports bottle full of electrolyte solution.

"Good stuff," Vstkrt said, praising the painkiller directly. "I guess whatever's under those bandages is serious."

"More serious than what's outside of them, thanks to Kktkrkz' quick claws," I agreed with rare, genuine gratitude. I swore by my family's totem-goddess frequently, but usually for ironic effect.

The male who was holding me up was an upright youth. He nodded and echoed, "Thanks to Her." I didn't know if he meant we shared totems or he was just paying respect to mine. Either way, such pious sentiments were unusual in the City, particularly in our neighborhood.

Vstkrt stuck to her area of interest. "That was your apartment that blew up, wasn't it? But you came home *from* the hospital. Someone trying to kill you, detective?"

Nathan Large with Laine Megan Lundquist

Why was it always the females? Supposedly, Vislin weren't that different in temperament across genders, but I always got more trouble from females. Maybe the answer was in the questioner; I treated them differently, myself. The fact that I also provoked Hrotata and Taratumm females disproportionately might or might not be related.

I braced my back against the building where I had slumped earlier, still holding onto the sport bottle. My expression of genuine pain helped hide my discomfort at her question, although it reinforced her reasons for asking it. I took another swig of the briny athletic drink before handing the container back. It gave me a moment to think about my answer.

I decided to start with honesty. "It seems so. Twice now in two days. First time, some commandos shot at me. I guess when that didn't work, they delivered a homecoming present."

The stares I got in return were worth the confession. Kkk, if I couldn't be young and attractive, I could be old and experienced. In reality, detective work is mostly boring. Some of my competitors are scrawny, pale clerks. The dashing, buff, martially-trained P.I. is a rare creature outside of entertainment.

Still, there are moments *I* would like to be more athletic, not to mention dashing. Besides being more fun, those traits would make my job easier. I'd settled for being canny and resilient. I could at least flaunt my scars.

I had plenty to flaunt right then. I could feel the skin tightening on my face and hands. I'd be fortunate if I only lost a few scales. The burns actually didn't hurt too badly, just a dull tingle like too much sun exposure.

Rptrkch was the first to react. He asked, "Should we be concerned... I mean, more than just about the bomb in our building?"

"I doubt it. Especially if they think they succeeded. I should disappear for a time. The constables are already searching for the guys who shot me... hopefully they're the same ones who did this or else know who did it."

I added the last bit to reassure the youths that I wasn't working alone. I was going through official channels and everything, like a good citizen. Kkk, I'm a chilled fraud sometimes.

"Well… good," the male with the drink bottle said. "None of us is getting back inside tonight. The fire crew should be here soon, right? I'll need to get my ident if we're renting a room."

Vstkrt clacked at him. "If they don't cover our emergency shelter, I'll file a complaint myself. We're victims of a criminal act. That qualifies for assistance, as does the fire."

Rptrkch groaned. "Our insurance is going to explode, too. We're already paying back half of what we save by living here on the theft premiums alone. Now we've got a fire claim…"

Vstkrt cut him off: "Seriously? You're budgeting *now*? Priorities go in this order: immediate crises, potential threats, *then* money."

While I make it sound like they were arguing, the feeling was more like a series of in-jokes, though strained by the stress of the situation. I was seeing a Pack in its formative years, when the members weren't quite integrated into a comfortable whole, both enjoying and straining against their tightening bonds.

For my Pack Vzrrk, that formative period also involved the occasional bombing, although in a different way. We were usually the ones *setting* the bombs, not for murder but for arson or just a night's entertainment.

This was a very different kind of Pack and very different kids. I felt terrible mixing their world with mine. Still, they'd have an interesting story to tell their families and friends, later.

We all recognized that the emergency responders were being slow to respond. Ours was a low-priority neighborhood. We'd never be completely ignored, but the fire department and medical crews never seemed to respond to the fringes with the same urgency as when calls came from further inside the City. After a bomb report, first responders would be even less enthusiastic.

I took advantage of the delay to catch my breath, then used it to make a request, speaking to the Pack as a whole: "Ttt, Tksshs, could I ask a favor? I haven't talked to the client on my current case since I got shot. Given this mess, I'd like to make sure she's all right. If I'm here when the authorities arrive, I'll be held for treatment and questioning. They can collect me from her place just as easily as here. Could I possibly ask you to bring a 'car around so that I can fly there?"

Rptrkch looked uncertain, while Vstkrt seemed to consider my request. The third male, the one I could see, looked agreeable, like he bought what I was selling. And I *was* selling. Completely lying. I had no idea where to find Pkstzk. Even if I did, I wouldn't go straight to her home. I didn't want to be questioned by the constables, period. I *did* want a place to crash, just not a client's home. Some anonymous hole would be best.

I actually had one particular lodging in mind: one I'd already researched, one related to my current case and close to the someone I wanted to check on. That private rental building in Isstravil might not have a reservation for me, but I could potentially overrule that problem.

Finally, Vstkrt clicked her agreement. "If we said no, you'd probably try to go anyway and hurt yourself worse. Still, leave us the address? That way, if something happens to you on the way, we can let the constables know where to look for your body."

Such a cheerful youth. I had to agree with her, though. "Kzk Tsstkt, in Isstravil. I don't remember the building number, but it's next to a computer store."

Rptrkch trotted off right away, likely bound for the aircar station a few blocks down. These really were good kids. I regretted that I hadn't talked to them before, under better circumstances. I regretted, again, causing them trouble. Last, I regretted abusing their trust to pursue my own goals. At least I wouldn't be endangering them further by sticking around. For all I knew, a military strike team was on its way to level the block, just to make sure I was dead.

That idea was silly, but then, the entire situation was becoming absurd. While I waited for Rptrkch to return with the aircar, my mind went back to the questions I was considering before I blacked out. Why target *me*? Who did it help to have me dead? What was I getting close to that needed to be kept hidden?

My decision to fly off to Isstravil had more to it than just a desire for intellectual closure. Checking on Tskksk was actually fourth down on my list of reasons, just below my need to avoid more official questions. At the top of the list was a growing, ignoble, but honest anger. I was furious at whoever blew up my home, whoever was targeting me and Pkstzk, and whoever was hiding from justice by these acts.

I had never been threatened like that before. I mean, I had been threatened, but it was usually more direct and specific. Someone would call, say "drop the case or die", and maybe explain which case they meant. Sometimes I would get a gun or claw waved in my face. But this… this *hunting*… this was new.

I was going to Isstravil because that seemed like a place my opposition would *not* want me to go. I'd be in deep trouble with the constables for going there, but if I worked quietly enough they might not notice me until I found a lead. I intended to pry harder into the clues I already had. If I moved into one of the rental units in the area Vzktkk was visiting, I could talk to the neighbors while I recuperated and see if one of them recognized his image. I could research Tskk-sk's evidence without pulling her away from her business. I could even search the pet import store again, if the constables didn't have it under guard.

Even if none of that research was productive, I might still provoke the killers by being in the neighborhood. Let them *think* I was getting closer. That plan wasn't the smartest, safest idea, especially with me unarmed and hobbled, but like I said: I was more angry than rational. Plus, if I *didn't* pursue the case further, I'd chew off my claws from frustration. Idle safety wasn't a healthy choice.

Maybe it's just as well I've never mated and reproduced. I don't have the best traits for self-preservation. My continued survival sometimes seems like a statistical quirk rather than a product of personal merit. Even my Pack-mates in jail are better off than I am, some days. At least they're eating regularly, sleeping normally, and not being blown up.

I continued to wait, preparing my mind and body for the effort of moving again. I remained prone on the concrete and willed my bloodstream to cycle pain blocking molecules to their designated nerve receptors. The effort seemed to work. While the burns on my front and the bruises on my back were new contributors to my overall agony, I didn't feel more tortured on the whole.

Nathan Large with Laine Megan Lundquist

During and immediately after the explosion hurt horribly, just like being shot burned and stung, but once I recovered from the initial trauma, it seemed like my mind established an upper threshold of pain. My new hurts only filled up that pool, rather than overflowing it.

Once again, from prior experience, I knew that the reverse was usually the case. Every new injury added to the whole, and there *was* no upper limit, at least not until shock knocked me unconscious or frenzy overrode the torment. Or a new, more painful injury could become the focus of attention, if it exceeded the current peak. The idea that I had suddenly developed a cap on my ability to sense pain was absurd.

Maybe it *was* the drugs. Rather than just lowering the overall sensation of pain, this prescription somehow held the mix at a manageable level. While I'd prefer total obliviousness, there were medical advantages to such an effect. I could remain more aware and avoid worsening my injuries.

Well, good on Vaktrri Medical, again. It might have been nice if they told me they were prescribing me something other than the standard narcotics, but I'd accept the gift nonetheless.

By the time Rptrkch returned in the rented aircar, I surprised everyone by standing up. Once I understood that my pain was limited, I wasn't sparing myself. As long as I didn't actually fold up and fall, I would be all right.

Not once did I believe that I might be recovering from my injuries faster than normal. Like at the hospital, I expected neither my natural fortitude nor medical science to spare me a normal recovery time. Instead, I ascribed my seemingly miraculous functionality to the wounds having been less serious than originally thought and the drugs being better than usual.

Call it luck or call it reflex, but I had avoided a broken back, serious burns, or shrapnel impalement from the booby trap. Maybe the same fortune spared me earlier. The idea that something *else* was manipulating my luck hadn't yet arrived, even after a series of ridiculously minimal wounds.

No, at the time I just hoped that I could keep going long enough on luck, chemicals and pure force of will to learn something useful before I was forced to collapse and recover.

Broken Record

I pulled myself into the aircar seat with a little help from my new friends. I waited until the lid closed before giving my destination's full address. Not that I didn't trust my young Pack of neighbors, but what they didn't know they couldn't reveal… to the constables or to my hunters.

The aircar soared away. I took advantage of the travel time to catch some actual sleep. No further questions or hypotheses troubled me during the flight.

An automated chime woke me in Isstravil. I spilled out of the 'car, blinking and stretching, only belatedly realizing how bad an idea it was to straighten my back. My body reminded me about each of its various insults. I took another blue pill, swallowing it dry.

Trying not to look even more conspicuous, I checked the building where I was deposited. It was the right address. The unassuming apartment block was older than my own building but in better repair. Given good maintenance and its preferable location, the rent was likely half again what I normally paid. I was about to find out.

I walked around to the front entrance and tapped the comm request button on the entry pad. After a few hectads, an answering chime acknowledged my signal and connected an audio line. I heard a rough voice, probably Taratumm by the accent, answer, "Your business?"

"Looking for a short-term residence. Do you have a unit available?" I kept my replies short, simple, and quick, hoping my interrogator would assume whichever interpretation was most desirable.

"We do. You have credit and ident?" the voice rasped, worse even than a Taratumm speaking the K'khztk dialect.

"Of course. My last place was *too* cheap; I just barely survived a fire there." I figured the speaker could see me, so I provided a thin cover story for my obvious injuries. "I've decided to look for something better while I wait on the insurance case." There you are: a reason to seek lodging on short notice *and* a promise of future income, meaning assured rent payments. I may not be a paragon of honesty, but at least I have a talent for keeping my stories simple.

"All right. I will show you what we have, but minimum is three cycles, all paid up front."

There went my entire credit account. At least I'd have a comfortable home while I starved to death. Yes, there's food assistance in Layafflr City, just like any civilized Great Family city. But you have to register for it, which means showing up in person and providing an address, both of which worked against my current purposes. Hiding from the constables would mean going hungry. I'd have to bend my personal ethics and beg, borrow, or steal a little credit, at least until the case was finished and its dangers eliminated.

The entry pad chimed again, three times, which I correctly interpreted as a signal that it was unlocked. I opened the door and stepped into a lobby of convincing faux stone. The carvings were too regular to be anything but mass produced pressings, but the overall effect wasn't bad. The smell was even pleasant: moisture and limestone and warm grasses. Somewhere inside the ventilation system was a scent synthesizer, a bit of comfort for tenants coming home. I wished that I was actually moving in, long-term.

A side door opened up and an elderly, hunched Taratumm emerged. He – or she – was at that age where it became difficult to distinguish gender. Usually female Taratumm are noticeably more massive, but some females lose weight as they get older and some males put it on. I decided I didn't need to know and mentally defaulted to female.

'Her' voice was just as grinding in person as it had been over the circuit. She welcomed me: "Let us see the ident."

I tried not to wince, either at her demand or at my aches, as I withdrew my ident card and presented it for inspection. She produced a compad and waved the card over its reader. The 'pad's screen lit up with an image of my face, younger and less battered. She compared the scan with my current appearance and grunted, apparently satisfied. The 'pad would also inform her that I was self-employed, give her my former address, and produce a background file listing any public offenses. There was plenty on that list – even omitting my publicly *unknown* offenses – to give a landlord pause.

Broken Record

She didn't seem put off, though. That was good. If I had the right idea about this place, a few misdemeanor convictions shouldn't disqualify me from residency. Frost, she might not care if I had a murder charge and prison time, so long as my credit cleared.

"Follow me. I will show you the open unit," she directed, shuffling toward elevator doors tucked into the backside of the lobby.

I obeyed. After she pressed the call button, the doors opened, and I squeezed into the too-small car next to her. She didn't bother with small talk, which was a blessing. At close range, she smelled like seaweed and cheese. I could only imagine how much her breath might reek.

The elevator opened onto the third floor landing. I exited as best as my limp would allow, jumping at the reprieve from elderly-Taratumm odor. The landing was a basic small foyer with four doors: one for the stairwell, one for a utility closet, and two for hallways leading to the individual apartments.

Grandmother Friendly turned to the left and I followed. She opened the hallway door with a small code-stick key, rather than a card, then continued into the hall. We went past three doors, ending up in front of apartment 309. She was just reaching down to unlock that door when my compad signaled an incoming call.

Pkstzk. I recognized the number as soon as I looked at the screen. Great for her to call; lousy timing to talk.

I waved my 'pad toward the foyer and apologized to the landlady: "Friend checking up on me after the accident. I'd better let her know I'm all right."

"Make it quick. I need to get back downstairs," she grudged.

I retreated while tapping the 'pad to accept the call. Pkstzk's face appeared along with her voice. Her appearance was welcome, even if her words weren't.

"Why are you calling me?" she demanded, sounding more annoyed than afraid. "I understand the situation has gotten more complex, but that's even more reason to avoid unnecessary contact."

- 216 -

I cut off whatever she was going to say next. "You don't even know the half of it." I dropped my voice to a near-whisper. "After I called you, my apartment exploded." Even being quiet, I couldn't be sure I wouldn't be overheard, so I didn't say *someone tried to blow me up*.

She looked absolutely furious, but when she spoke, her voice dripped with concern. "Why… why would that happen? Who would want to hurt you? Where are you now?"

"Finding a new home. The old one is a mess. Look, I can be overheard here. Real fast: the constables know I'm working on your mate's case. They officially warned me off. If anyone asks, that's why I called: to let you know I'm quitting. But I'm not. I'm working on an idea now. I still need to know what you know, but I'll have to work out a way we can meet without being noticed. I'll let you know when I'm settled."

She protested, "Tell me what you know… what you can. I might know who was waiting for me at Taburket's, and why, but I don't want to bias your thoughts."

I was spared a response by the landlady's bellow: "Hey, Lucky! Are you coming? I do not have long… I could die while you keep me waiting."

I looked back her direction, exaggerating the gesture for Pkstzk's benefit. "Like I said, not now. I'll call again soon, I promise."

I could practically hear Pkstzk's beak grinding from frustration. After a hect-ad, she spat out, "Fine. But don't keep *me* waiting long. I want to know what you know about Vzktkk."

Not: *Who killed Vzktkk?* Not: *Who tried to kill me… or you?* Her phrasing troubled me. At the time, I interpreted my emotion as disappointment at her callousness. I covered my dismay by closing the call.

"Sorry!" I called down the hall as I headed back.

The landlady's bulk was propped against the wall of Apartment 309 when I entered. It wasn't a bad space, actually. The area wasn't much more than in my former apartment, but it was laid out better, with less space wasted in the main room and more allotted to a separate nest-room. The kitchen appliances were

Broken Record

more recent, and I suspected the bathroom was less decrepit, as well. The walls showed signs of age, but this was a mixed curse: while decayed, they also held more character than the cheap extrusion cement of the tenements. Actual plaster friezes in floral patterns joined the walls to the floor and ceiling, and colored stain formed pleasant blobs of natural color in-between.

I nodded, needing little effort to look pleased at what I saw. I was basically arranging long-term hotel lodgings, so I could do much worse. If I wasn't limited by my geographical needs, I *would* have chosen worse, to save my credit.

I made a show of looking into the bathroom and walking the apartment's perimeter, surveying the view from the one small window, turning the taps and generally pretending to check for flaws. In the meantime, my host didn't move, other than to shift slightly in place, rasping her age-roughened scales against the wall.

"Well?" she finally burped.

"It looks good," I admitted. "A little small, but all right for short notice."

"Small?" she scoffed, "I saw the address where you were living. This is a palace by comparison."

Frosted old-time local. She had regional knowledge I could only dream of acquiring, if I managed to live that long. So, she knew my neighborhood. That was a possible hazard for my anonymity, not to mention my bargaining position. At least I hadn't planned to negotiate much.

I waggled my crest a little, feigning embarrassment. "True. But since the insurance will be paying, I had hoped to find someplace nicer."

"And if you abuse that benefit, they will drop your payments," she warned, with the cynical wisdom of someone experienced in petty fraud.

"I suppose so," I sighed. "What are you asking, since we're at that point?"

"Nine hundred a cycle. Half that for a cleaning deposit; you get it back if you do the cleaning yourself. Three cycles up front, six cycles minimum lease." Her recital suggested she could quote me the entire lease contract from memory.

I kept up the first few dance steps just so she wouldn't think anything was strange. Kkk, anything else besides my appearance and story, at least.

"Nine hundred? Thirty-one-fifty all together? That's tough; that's most of my savings. Could you leave me a couple hundred for the week and I'll catch it up later?"

She was just lowering her head in negation of my offer when my compad chimed again. This time the caller was Tskksk. I glanced down then up again, looking as apologetic as I could.

"Another friend? Good to have friends," she grunted. "Go ahead, but the price is fixed. Say yes or say no when you are done there."

She heaved herself upright and started toward the door. "Lock it behind you. I will be in the office. If you agree, bring your credit chip and I will trade you for the key."

I missed the initial call, but called Tskksk back as the landlady's steps retreated back toward the elevator.

Tskksk started talking first, as her image appeared. "I caught the caller again!"

"Chchch, what? What's that?" I couldn't decipher her statement at first.

"The one from the recording? The calls right before and after your client's mate's death? I set my security program to notify me if any signals matched that one."

I was once again torn between the urges to propose mate-ship or employment. Instead I said, "You can do that? And you got a match? When?"

"Just now. A decad or so back. Well, it's half a match. The incoming half. Whoever called the person who was here in Isstravil just called someone else – someone different – but near the same location."

I still wasn't getting the message clearly. "Slow down for the elderly. You mean someone in this neighborhood just got a call from the same person who called the possible shooter?" My blood started to warm from fear. I wondered if I should be concerned for my safety. Had the unknown enemy tracked me to Isstravil?

"Slow down, yourself. *This* neighborhood? You're nearby? How close?" Tskksk asked, sounding pleasantly surprised.

"At an apartment building down the street. It's a long story, but I need some-place new to live and figured I'd move closer to work. Are you at work? I'll head that direction once I'm done here. Rrr, just so you know, this is all unofficial now. That constable detective you talked to, Nrissilli, wants me off the murder case. So, we're just talking out of personal concern… checking on each other's well-being."

She didn't respond for a long couple of hectads. Finally, her head cocked to the side and one eye scanned my image, probably taking in my singed scales and dilated pupillary slits.

"*Are* you all right?" she asked slowly, "Should I be concerned?"

"No, I'm not, and yes, you should," I answered with plain honesty. "But hopefully not much of either. Keep your involvement with me and this case private from anyone you can't completely trust." I didn't tell her to "tell no one". If she did have bonded Pack, she'd want to let them know about any possible danger, even a remote one.

"I'll tell you more in person," I finished weakly. "I understand if you'd rath-er have that meeting somewhere other than your place of business."

"No," she waved me off, "I feel safer here than anywhere else. I can block surveillance and throw down the security gates if I have to."

"Not what I meant, but thanks," I replied. "All right, keep scanning the waves and we'll compare notes soon." I hung up before she could say anything else foolish.

Young, resourceful, and braver than she was cautious. That combination was familiar, but she lacked my early disregard for the welfare of other sapients. No, she was going to get herself hurt trying to help someone – namely, me – rather than trying to rip someone off.

Nathan Large with Laine Megan Lundquist

Lately, I was meeting a lot of surprisingly noble characters. Even the crusty old landlady seemed to be gruff for show but decent underneath. The bartender at Kzztkrt Tk, Vulletine, who cared so much about Pkstzk, his coworker. The cheery nurse and skittish but competent doctor at Vaktrri Medical. My neighbors in the Pack upstairs. Even Detective Nrissilli wasn't so bad, despite our inevitable professional conflict.

This rare surplus of worthies contrasted sharply with the anonymous villains who tried to shoot and then detonate me, whoever had shot Vzktkk, and whoever might still be stalking me and Pkstzk.

I didn't know much about Vzktkk yet, whether he fell into the 'good' or 'bad' category or was a normal, slightly selfish average like most of us. Pkstzk clearly fell into the 'average' category along with me. We wanted justice but weren't going to limit ourselves to purely moral lines of action.

While I mused, I left the apartment, locked the door as instructed, and then took the elevator down. I returned to the rental office and signed paperwork with some further perfunctory griping about the price. Then I presented my credit chip, which rested on the landlady's 'pad while it scanned my biodata. She handed me the stick key to my new home, purchased at the cost of every worldly asset I had left, minus the armor on my back and the compad in my carrier.

I still had my life, too. I supposed that trade was a fair deal. I wouldn't actually be getting any insurance payments, but I planned to extract satisfaction from the scales of my prey. Once the case started to reveal its secrets, I looked forward to ruining the lives of some criminals as much as they had ruined mine. Vzktkk's killer, my attackers, and anyone else connected to them… they would suffer. Legally, of course. I might be able to collect damages, but that was unlikely. Really, my only likely profit would be Pkstzk's gratitude. Plus, I still needed to know if the case had any connections to Pack Vzrrk. I needed to rebury those secrets… otherwise my life could still get worse.

I left the office, not bothering to explain to my new landlady why I wasn't going straight upstairs to collapse. If she asked, I would have said I needed to buy a nesting pad. Actually, I was just walking a few doors down to Tskksk's shop. A nap would have been wiser, but I had many reasons to delay my rest

Broken Record

We had a lead, a real lead. Somewhere nearby was a potential link to Vzkt-kk's killer. Tskksk and I could triangulate the newer call's location, especially if the same caller – or the original recipient – appeared again. If my hunch was right, the local contact was within one of the buildings nearby, possibly the same building I was now calling home.

As it turned out, that hunch was exactly right. Some of my other assumptions were dangerously wrong.

Chapter 12 - Threshold Lurker

Given my injuries, I shouldn't have walked even the short distance to Tskk-sk's storefront. My leg continued to tug and ache. I was past due to change the bandage. My discharge orders said I was supposed to be lying down with the leg elevated. Seeing as how I didn't own a bed, obeying would be difficult. I would be paying for that disobedience later.

Ignoring a critical lead would have been even more difficult and painful. Urgency helped me push aside my discomfort. I might need another pill after the excitement passed, though I was already exceeding the recommended dose.

I kept my pace measured, resisting the urge to lope the last few steps As I entered her store, I spotted Tskksk in her usual place at the back, hovering over a work table tiled with active 'pads.

She looked up as I crossed the threshold Her wide eyes grew wider at my battered appearance.

"Detective… you look terrible!"

"Thanks. Sorry, I can't return the compliment," I managed, saving the rest of my breath for recovery.

Tskksk clacked irritation and found a folding stool from somewhere in the back room. "Here, sit down," she insisted. "I'd suggest you lie down but there's nowhere suitable in here."

Lie down? Won't you join me? I was too tired to catch the easy setup. It was just as well. I was also too sore to enjoy anything physical, in the off chance that a pitch was successful. Kkk, right, I also looked awful, so my chances were low.

I accepted the offered seat with mumbled gratitude. Tskksk started to run off to get me water but stopped when I croaked, "The call. Any progress?"

Broken Record

She winced. "No, not really. I have the timing of each call, the distance from here to the local caller in each case, and the frequencies for all three comms. If any of them connects again I'll have comparison data. I'm still waiting on the original local caller to show up again, though I've only been monitoring since this morning, when I got the security program recompiled."

"Sorry, I'm not following, and not just because of the drugs," I admitted. "Recompiled?"

"I rebuilt the code... changed the program so that it watches for certain patterns and alerts me if they show up. That took some time. I'm sorry I ignored my calls while I worked."

"It turned out all right, though I was concerned. I'm flattered you kept working on the case without being asked."

She turned a questioning eye on me. "It's a puzzle, right? I wouldn't work with tech if I didn't like solving puzzles. I figured I could be useful. The constables use the same tools, they're just limited to when and where they can use them. I'm a private citizen living near the crime scene, so I can do something they can't."

"Something *I* couldn't do, either," I added. "Really, you're pretty impressive. If this approach works, you might be able to hire out as a consultant. I'd hire you... if I wasn't dead broke." I wasn't sure what prompted the admission. I'd praised her because I wanted to and because she deserved it. If I was trying to seduce her with flattery, my last comment wasn't exactly persuasive.

Her crest twitched... embarrassed about being noticed?

She swung the focus away from herself by interrogating me instead. "You're not getting paid up front? It looks like you should ask your client for hazard pay, between that rktpk and whatever tore you up this time. You smell like smoke, this time... was there a fire?"

I could have diverted her questions, but I took the opening to impress upon her the dangers of getting involved: "A bomb. In my office. I came down here to find a new place to live. As a bonus, the move lets me search this neighborhood more closely. I might draw out Vzktkk's shooter, by the way. This could be the last time I come here in person, until everyone involved is caught."

Nathan Large with Laine Megan Lundquist

I indicated the bandages on my arm and leg, "These... are from *three* killers that came after me two nights ago. I think they were aiming for Vzktkk's mate, my client. Either way, someone's working hard to remove anyone connected to this case."

"Which means they might come after me." Her voice was steady, but her body language gave away her fear. Her legs spread, claws splayed, as if getting ready for retreat. Her crest went down and her shoulders tightened.

I couldn't be very reassuring. "It's possible, but only if you find something critical, and then only if they know about it. Although, I'm still wondering what *I* might know that could be important. We – I and Detective Nrissilli – agreed to keep your name out of any reports, just in case. Even your evidence isn't logged yet, not until we have everyone in custody and are ready for trial."

"But you don't have any suspects yet," she reminded me. "There isn't anyone, is there?"

"A few possibilities," I exaggerated.

"Call them," she suggested. "Or have them call you. Either way, I'll be able to compare the signals. I was considering going through the comm listings for the buildings around here and calling each one myself, to see if one matched to the earlier recipient, but I figured that would be too time-consuming..."

"...and dangerous," I concluded for her. "A brute force approach has its uses, and I applaud the general idea, but I agree that it's an impractical plan. Also, illegal, particularly for the constables."

She looked irritated. "So, I just have to wait and hope the killer eventually makes or receives a call. While I'm searching, I'm in trouble... but *not* searching means it will take longer to find this egg-biter."

I savored her vulgarity and the righteous loathing which spawned it. I could really work with her, and not just as a potential mate.

She was right: the morality was murky. Ethically and legally, I couldn't ask her to do anything more, but I really needed her to keep working. If she might reveal a murderer, it was wrong for her *not* to try.

Broken Record

I settled for a semi-moral compromise. I told her, "Do what you decide is best. If you learn something more, call me. I'm not allowed to call you, but I don't have to refuse a call, especially if you might be in danger."

She confirmed, "I get you. Anything else you can leave me before you have to disappear next door?"

"I'd like to leave you a weapon, but the constables took mine as evidence. You have any protection?"

"A stunner. I hate to keep it out, though. I don't want to tempt a robber to use it on me."

"Carry it on you. It might look strange, but if anyone asks, just complain about the bolder thieves these days. If it's already on your hip, they'll have to tangle with you to take it away."

"That's not much comfort. I'm a shopkeeper, not a fighter."

I waved off her disclaimer, "You're Vislin. We're all dangerous, at some level. Just don't let them know you've evolved past feral violence. *I'm* actually a cuddly mammal underneath, despite looking like a pit brawler. I just have good survival instincts."

The conversation had taken a strange turn. I fought to bring it back to business. "What was the time on that last matching call, exactly?" I pulled out my compad, intending to take a few notes before I left.

"It started at five hours and seven decads," she relayed after checking her records. She added, "and fifteen hectads… running until five and eleven decads, thirty-three hectads." Her precise measurements were typical of someone for whom minuscule units of time were professionally relevant. She might use diagnostic programs that distinguished events in the micrads.

I punched in her numbers, tickled by a sense of recognition about the time window. Well, she *did* say the call came in very recently, while I was at the apartment building. Just before she called. When I was…

Nathan Large with Laine Megan Lundquist

Feeling shaky in a way that had nothing to do with physical injury or drugs, I switched programs on my compad and brought up my comm record. My last two calls were listed first: Tskksk's, at five-and-fifteen... and the previous one, starting at five-and-seven-and-fifteen. Ending, of course, at five-and-eleven-and-thirty-three.

Pkstzk. She spoke to me at precisely the specified times. Therefore, she also spoke to someone in this neighborhood, right before her mate died... not far away. Then, she spoke to that same recipient again, shortly afterward. I didn't like the picture my mind was painting. I searched for alternatives, but couldn't ignore the obvious.

"I think I know who the caller is," I forced through a clenched beak.

"Chchch? Who?" Tskksk asked, innocent of my distress.

I looked at her, hoping I didn't look too pathetic. "My client. Which means either your recordings are trivial... or they're telling a very bad story."

She put it together fast. "She was the one on the line before and after her mate was killed? So maybe he was calling her? No, wait..." She turned back to the compad holding her security recording. "First call, second call, both short but a little long for a simple 'call me back' message. Plus, the modulation doesn't look like a long ring time on either. Whoever called her wasn't left waiting for an answer."

"You can tell who initiated the calls?" I asked.

She clacked assent. "If that's her, your client was called *from* here both times. That's why I labeled her side the 'receiver'."

"So, not her checking up on Vzktkk," I concluded grimly, "and not him calling home, not afterward. The Ancestors don't use compads."

"Who would have been calling her?" Tskksk voiced the question for me.

It was like I was talking to myself, but better, since part of me suddenly understood computing technology and wasn't hurt or drugged. Plus, this other self was a lot prettier.

Broken Record

I paused, but managed to stay professional. I ventured, "The shooter? If I finally admit that maybe, my client had her mate killed." The admission churned my empty stomach.

"Or a friend in the area, telling her Vzktkk had been shot... or that he didn't show up for an appointment?" Tskksk offered. Nice of her to provide an alternate theory.

"Right. Everything depends on *who* was making the calls from here. But now we know that someone around here knows my client. It *might* mean that our mystery caller knew Vzktkk, if only indirectly. And the calls might or might not be connected to the murder, but the evidence is suggestive. Add in the fact that she didn't mention these calls to me..."

"Maybe she didn't think they were relevant," Tskksk suggested, still propping up my ego. "She might not have matched the timing with her mate's time of death. It could be a coincidence."

But it might not. I should have considered Pkstzk a suspect from the beginning. Did I not want to admit the possibility? Was I really blind to her potential for betrayal? For murder?

Worse, had I been fooled by a classic ruse: a client hiring a detective to investigate her own crime in order to make her look innocent? Was that why she hired me, specifically? Because I would work free, be sympathetic, and potentially provide her with cover? Or did she want me to sniff out any incriminating details she might have missed?

Another hypothesis: Pkstzk could be involved in some other way without being directly responsible for Vzktkk's death. Indirect complicity was as plausible as her putting a hit on her mate. The pair might have been involved together in criminal business. Maybe a deal went bad. Being mated to a bad egg who over-reached and got everyone in trouble would fit her historical pattern.

My new theory fit almost *too* well. I suspected it precisely as a projection of our shared past onto the present. Yet, wasn't my own behavior mirroring past habits? Wasn't I once again the outsider worshiping Pkstzk, blind to her flaws and thinking her blameless when she followed another male into folly?

I might be wrong on all counts. Pkstzk might be innocent. I eventually stopped my misbehavior; she could have done the same. I couldn't assume she was guilty on the basis of past faults and a couple of points of coincidental – if suggestive – evidence.

For the moment, I could only be angry at myself for my lack of objectivity and skepticism. I could be angry at Pkstzk later, if I found a good, proven reason.

Tskksk stayed quiet while I contemplated, though she did force a glass of water into my hand. I obliged by taking a few sips, but my stomach was still unsteady.

Finally, I reassured her: "Several possible explanations exist. That said, we have a connection here between someone at the crime scene and a person linked to the victim. That coincidence can't be dismissed. You mentioned triangulation… could you compare signals to tell if the local speaker was standing at a particular location?"

She thought about it a moment, then answered: "Yes and no. I can calculate distance from the recording point, here. I could draw a circle and see what falls within the given range. There's no way to derive directionality, though. I can't really 'triangulate' unless I have a second, simultaneous recording of the same signal from a different location."

"I'll bear that in mind in case I find someone else nearby using the same security program." We both knew that was unlikely.

"What I have should still help," she said, turning back to her information and using a third compad to bring up a local map. "Relative strength… assuming a standard compad transmitter… divide by… got it. The source was about nine hundred fifty meters away, give or take ten." She sketched a circle on the screen showing the map, indicating the estimated distance from her store.

When I started to get up to look, she waved me back down and brought the map over.

"Sorry I hadn't done this earlier. Everything takes time and attention. On days like these, I get liberal on the A.I. issue," she quipped, adding, "It would be nice to have someone else do the work for me in a fraction of the time."

Broken Record

"That's how the demons get you," I joked back.

The Great Family is officially opposed to the expansion of true sentient A.I. beyond the Terran sphere of influence, but in reality, our Family is probably the Collective culture least offended by artificial minds. Declining resistance to A.I. among Great Family citizens is a common theme in humorous entertainment, which suggests that our official resistance is a hollow shell, a mask worn for the reassurance of other, more conservative Collective cultures. The Family had lost the chance to develop artificial intelligence on its own, but if the balance of sentiment eventually shifts, we might someday import and improve upon the Terran 'Brin' model.

Until then, we have to manage non-routine research using our own biological intelligences. In this case, drawing a logical conclusion became easier once Tskk-sk translated the digital data into analog maps.

The dashed circle created by Tskksk's sketch clipped through buildings on the same block, north and south. It included two spots on the back street – one far to the south and one to the north – and two spots on the facing street. The more southerly of those spots was a familiar landmark: the pet store. If I traced the line down and allowed a little extra distance, it crossed comfortably inside the building itself. Our search area could easily include the front room of the pet store, where someone stood while aiming a laser to punch through Vzktkk's skull.

We looked up together, needing few words.

Tskksk tilted her head in mimicry of a caller addressing their compad and acted out the scene: "He's here… it's done, he's dead."

"Could be," I agreed, "but there are other possible locations and interpretations. It looks bad, but this much wouldn't stand up in court… not by itself, and for good reason."

"I know that," she complained, finally sounding tired of my reticence, "but coincidental or not, the coincidences are getting decreasingly likely."

"I know." Something finally crossed my mind. "Nrissilli. The authorities. You need to contact them and pass on this analysis, without mentioning me."

"But how would I have known it was your client, if you didn't tell me she called you?"

"You can't. You'll have to leave Pkstzk's name out... not covering for her, just keeping me out of the story. Hopefully, the constables can bridge the gap themselves."

She agreed, "I understand. But I can still mention that the radius fits the pet store's location... which you'd already told me about. And that I picked up another call today matching that original recipient. I wish we could tell them it was her, though."

"Detective Nrissilli seems sharp. She'll figure it out eventually. Even if not, I intend to look into my client further. I'll have to meet with her, eventually, somewhere private. In the meantime, keep listening."

"Will do, detective." She stopped short of saluting, but I caught the obedience in her voice. Kktkrkz's insane laughter, the last thing I wanted was to recruit her as an apprentice. Colleague, partner, sure, maybe. But not a student. Not a subordinate.

I made sure to look as pathetic as possible as I rose and walked out. Pay attention, kid. These bandages are what a P.I. usually earns. Keep quiet, be smart, and don't think this job carries any glamour. I'm using you, sure, because I have to, but I never want to use you up or sacrifice you for my goals.

I was already legally damned by talking business with Tskksk. I'd encouraged her to continue looking into the case. I didn't need to be literally damned by getting her hurt.

I excused myself from the compad store, not knowing which direction to turn next. Back to the new apartment to sprawl on the bare floor and attempt rest? Over to Pkstzk's restaurant to try catching her there? Back to my old apartment to see what I could salvage... presuming it wasn't under surveillance? Straight to the public assistance office to sign up for food and housing support?

I still had a window of time before the charges went through for the new apartment rental, where I could make a few purchases. I could overdraft my credit slightly *without* bouncing the rent payment and forfeiting the contract deposit. If I wanted to pay for any significant travel, it would have to happen soon.

Maybe I should just fly to the nearest constable station and turn myself in for credit fraud, obstruction of justice, and disobeying an officer. Frost, I might want to confess all my past crimes while I was at it. My concealment might not last much longer.

If I did have to confront Pkstzk, she would certainly use our sordid history as a threat to keep me quiet about her misdeeds. Little would she suspect that I'd already advised Tskksk to talk to the constables. I couldn't be blackmailed, but Pkstzk could ruin me on the way down.

If Pkstzk *was* guilty and *did* try to fight back, I had a slim chance: deny everything, accuse her of fabricating stories out of spite, and hope she didn't have enough evidence to make her accusations stick. Just calling me a thief or a confidence trickster didn't prove anything, unless she remembered precisely what I had stolen and when.

Her old mate in prison could help her with those details, but why would he betray me now if he hadn't before? Who knew, he might be still Pack-loyal to me. In purely pragmatic terms, it wouldn't save Pkstzk to ruin me, even if Rsspkz was inclined to help her at all. Plus, talking about our past exploits could still harm Rsspkz. Another conviction would doom his chances of parole before dying of old age.

I realized I could address several goals at once, without spending credits to travel. I was waiting for Pkstzk's call anyway, so why not go 'home' until then? I could loiter in my new building's lobby and see if any of my new neighbors passed through. If my hunch about the apartments proved valid, I might stumble upon a resident who knew something useful.

Undercover isn't easy, but if you need to watch a particular place without looking like a snoop, moving in can work.

That strategy was as valid for Vzktkk's killer as it was for me. My new building seemed like the perfect home base for a stalker. The older apartment complexes nearby would require more background scrutiny and a longer lease, if not a higher rent. The other buildings with short-term tenancy were reserved for businesses or their clients. There was no hotel close by. Therefore, I was following one path my hypothetical killer might have taken.

There were plenty of alternative scenarios. Perhaps Vzktkk had a pre-existing travel pattern that regularly brought him through this neighborhood. Then, the killer only needed to lie in wait at the pet store on one, single night, in order to zap him dead. Still, the precise lineup of the shot argued against the single-night scenario. It also assumed the killer knew Vzktkk's route ahead of time, without observation.

Alternately, an assassin might have waited in their chosen hunting blind for several nights, until Vzktkk finally walked that precise route needed to line up his skull with their cross-hairs. More plausible... but then it was surprising that no one saw a stranger enter or leave the pet store on at least one of those nights.

Two other scenarios were more likely. One, the killer staked out the area far in advance, observing Vzktkk before executing any plan. Two, the killer arranged Vzktkk's presence, luring him to the right spot. But how was it arranged? Who was talking to who?

Who were the players, for that matter? What was the game? It certainly seemed like someone was working hard, setting bombs and hiring mercenaries. Such activity suggested that there was something worth covering up, maybe something bigger than a single murder.

The big secret could be some business Vzktkk was involved with. Possibly, something involving Pkstzk, if not the both of them. If so, I'd have bet that any meetings related to that secret business were conducted in Isstravil, near my apartment building if not necessarily within it.

What secret business? What plot? My imagination offered up uncountable possibilities. I counted a few, anyway.

One: Vzktkk and Pkstzk were planning to defraud his business or rob her workplace, until she decided to cut him out of the plan.

Broken Record

Two: The two had been threatened in order to ensure their compliance in a criminal scheme, then Vzktkk was shot as an example, either for his defiance or Pkstzk's.

Three: Vzktkk was cheating on Pkstzk and she had him punished.

Four: Some assassin, on the orders of Pkstzk's old mate, Rsspkz, killed Vzktkk out of jealousy.

Each theory would make a solid plot for a detective thriller. I could make money off such tales, if I was any good as a writer. My fantasies were also as speculative as they were entertaining. Each fit the facts in evidence, but introduced more unknowns than they explained anything known.

As a starting point, I needed to know who called Pkstzk, from Isstravil, on the night of the murder. I needed to know where Vzktkk was coming from and where he was going. And were any of these targets the same?

I would have liked some physical evidence linked to the killer, but he or she was too careful for easy identification. The constables would have swept the pet store already. They had better forensic tools than I could hope for. If *they* hadn't identified the culprit yet, there probably wasn't any genetic detritus or other telltale clue left behind. My body oil swab was rendered moot.

Instead of rushing around, for one afternoon, I would sit down, relax, and watch the passersby. I was also letting the passersby see me. I might not discern much from reactions to my presence – I doubted anyone would walk by with guilt lowering their crest – but I might provoke action if a guilty party felt threatened. At the least, obvious loitering was one more thing I could do that the constables couldn't.

The building lobby didn't have any chairs I could rest in. That discourtesy was deliberate, to discourage the sort of lingering I had in mind. However, there were open steps leading up to the side stairwell. I settled in as comfortably as the molded stone steps would permit.

It would have been nice to have something productive to do with my idle time, but I was out of ideas. My remaining leads were either Pkstzk – with whom

I was reluctant to speak until I had a clearer head – or work associates of Vzktkk who might know more about his business in Isstravil. I'd get better answers in person than by comm. To pursue the case properly, I needed greater freedom of movement than I could afford. Until that changed, I had to hope that a nearer witness would give me something substantial.

No one entered the lobby during the first half-hour, while I sat playing puzzle games on my compad. I started to wonder if I would have to wait until the evening.

Then, my first prey arrived. A well-dressed Hrotata couple descended from the upper stairs. The glossy dark female wore a purple dress gown cinched at throat and waist, with an archaic collar arching over her head. The male, whose fur was a calico mottle of red, white, and black, did his best to compliment her coloration with his charcoal-colored formal robes. Both wore bootlets on their back feet, an affectation rarer on ChttKttp than on civilized worlds like Hrotata Prime. The pair looked like high rollers out for a night at the casino or possibly, theater patrons.

Their padded footsteps gave me just barely enough warning to stand aside before they reached me at the bottom step. As they passed, I took the opportunity to impose upon their attention.

"Excuse me, Mistress, Master?" I addressed them, trying not to sound too pathetic. My battered appearance was bad enough. I looked like a war veteran begging for change.

They treated me like a beggar, too. The female didn't even look in my direction, and the male only glanced briefly then turned away fast. They walked around me like I was furniture.

I chose to be polite but firm. "Excuse me… I'm moving in here today. I was supposed to meet my Pack-mates, but they're not answering. Could you *please* tell me if you've seen them today?"

The female tried to leave with a mumbled dismissal, but the male tugged at her forehand, saying, "Hold on. I'll take care of this."

Broken Record

He took a protective step forward, putting himself between me and his partner. He said, "I haven't seen any strange Vislin today, other than yourself. Do your Pack-mates live here?"

I clacked confirmation. "We're all moving in here. There's a female, Pkstzk... about my height, lighter scales, a little heavier... and her mate, Vzktkk, taller, checkered pattern, but closer to my build. She might have been wearing a waitress' uniform?"

The male indicated uncertainty. I jumped on his hesitation to bring up my compad and show him pictures of Pkstzk and Vzktkk: public ident photos, a little outdated but still recognizable.

The male looked, with an expression that shifted from irritation to amusement. "I've seen the male here before. I didn't think he lived here... just a visitor. The female isn't familiar. You say she's his mate? Is there another female in your Pack? There's one upstairs, but she lives by herself."

His commentary brought his companion back, to peer over his shoulder at my compad screen. She interjected, "You don't mean Shtvtsk in 401?"

The male's nose bobbed up several times, sniffing a recovered memory. "Yes, that's the one. This male was at her door... a week ago?"

The female Hrotata gave a nasty laugh as she turned away. "Dear one, you're so adorably naïve. That priestess sees a great many parishioners in her temple."

He caught her meaning right away and cringed in embarrassment. It took me an extra second to translate from Hrotata idiom. A 'priestess' with lots of visitors... Hrotata clergy sometimes include sex as part of their ministrations.

Now, Vislin don't have a cultural heritage of prostitution... certainly not the way mammals do. A female Vislin offering sex for payment would be considered mentally ill by most. However, there are psychological aspects of mating that *are* worth a certain cost. A particularly lonely, Pack-less Vislin – male *or* female – might desire the attention of a temporary mate not for physical pleasure, but for company and for reinforcement of their self-worth.

I myself wouldn't pay for sex, but if I had the credit, I might be tempted to hire a companion for an evening out or for a few days' vacation. Then again, my particular madness tends more toward physical interest and less toward emotional difficulty. Being alone wasn't as bad as being constantly tempted by bodies I couldn't have and shouldn't want.

Working off those insights, it wasn't hard to play my chosen part. I protested, "I'm sure you misunderstood. Vzktkk wouldn't be coming here for *that*. He and Pkstzk are happily mated. Maybe he and Shtvtsk worked together before, or they're clutch siblings?"

The male eyed me suspiciously. "Wouldn't you know? I thought Pack-mates knew everything about one another."

I did my best to feign embarrassment. "We're… newly bonded. Just moving in together. I don't know, maybe Vzktkk wanted to add this female to our Pack."

The female took advantage of my perceived emotional weakness to taunt me. "I'm *sure* you'd all be *thrilled* to have such a popular priestess among your number. You can't over-estimate the value of regular spiritual counseling."

"401, you said?" I directed my question back to the male, deflecting the conversation. Changing the topic would be expected to avoid further teasing, but it also served my underlying purpose: to back out without further uncomfortable questions.

The male confirmed: "First door off the stairs."

His mate huffed and added, "Perhaps your Pack-mates are already there, worshiping together."

I couldn't resist the urge to pay the society matron back. "Kkk, no wonder they're not answering my calls. I'd better go knock. I wouldn't want to be left out."

Flipping my crest at her, I turned around and started to climb the stairs. My limping gait probably made the action more ludicrous than I intended. Even so, I left them startled at my shift from blush to bravado.

Broken Record

Hrotata think of their Vislin and Taratumm siblings as prudish by their own orgiastic standards. For one of us to indicate a hearty interest in carnal pleasure could provoke either shocked confusion or pleasant surprise, depending on the sort of Hrotata who witnessed the revelation.

I might have blown my cover by indulging my humor, but it's always fun to disrupt expectations. Besides, the pair had given me plenty of direction already.

So, Vzktkk was visiting an escort? If it was a dead Hrotata or Terran I was investigating, there'd be an obvious explanation: jealous wife kills cheating husband. That might still be the story, although the Vislin version would involve one mate irritated about the other wasting their shared credits on personal entertainment and jeopardizing their mate-bond. You know, practical considerations rather than petty emotional ones.

Kkk, frost that. The reaction would still be emotional, just for different reasons. Resentment due to a lack of communication. Shame from being supplanted. A blow to the ego, that you weren't good enough. Basically, all the same reasons *except* sexual disgust.

As I hauled myself up the stairs, I recognized that other explanations could fit. This Shtvtsk could be part of some criminal enterprise involving Vzktkk. The two might have had a disagreement, resulting in Vzktkk's death. Frost, maybe he was her procurer. Maybe the two of them were blackmailing her clients.

But then, what was the connection back to Pkstzk? Maybe all three of them – Shtvtsk, Vzktkk, and Pkstzk – were complicit in something dirty. Or maybe they were friends together, all innocent victims of a fourth party. I had added one to the number of players in the drama, but that didn't mean I had the entire cast or even a sense of the plot.

I was still getting closer, faster than I expected. My instincts about the building had been right. Amazingly right: a laser's focus compared to my usual scattershot.

Rather than proud, my lucky guess made me slightly suspicious, instead. The case *could* have wandered off in any of a thousand directions. I thought I would need Pkstzk's information before I could make any sense of Vzktkk's death.

Nathan Large with Laine Megan Lundquist

Instead, I was hopping from stone to stone on a helpful footpath across an ocean of possibilities. I was *never* so lucky. Usually, I have to dig and push and provoke far more to get anywhere on a case. Sometimes, I fail despite every effort. Shocking, I know.

Most of the time, my successes come from a combination of physical evidence, experienced logic, and painstaking observation of known suspects. In *this* case, I had nearly no evidence or suspects to begin, yet leads were practically multiplying at my touch.

The push-back was also strangely rapid: the ambush at Taburket's and the bombing at my apartment. Usually, criminals wait until I'm ready to name names, before they will risk a physical confrontation.

I was beginning to feel like a playing piece in someone else's game, with only the illusion of making my own moves. That impression might be more than metaphor. I already suspected Pkstzk of manipulating me. She might not be the director in this production, though. She might just be a means to get me involved... a game piece, herself.

I looked forward to collecting more insight into this strange case. I reached the fourth floor and found Apartment 401 right next to the stairwell, as described.

Knocking on the door, I prepared my approach. No doubt, this Shtvtsk would be attractive, if the suggestion about her profession was true. I'd have to be on my guard. At the same time, my best tactic to get inside and ask some questions, without raising suspicion, would be to inquire about her services. If I was actually required to make a payment to prove my interest, I'd overdraft myself into bankruptcy. At that point, I might as well take full advantage of my purchase... a sacrifice I'd suffer for the sake of justice.

As it turned out, my preparations were unnecessary. No one answered my knock or three signals on the door bell. I risked listening at the door, but heard no movement inside.

Looking at the door again, I withdrew my own room key. The code stick used a basic magnetic scan, low-tech even for Layafflr City, probably original to the building's construction. I could recode it with an electrical current... the wall sockets in the hallway might do. If I wasn't interrupted for a few minutes, I could enter Shtvtsk's apartment without her permission.

Manipulated or not, I was tired of wandering blind. If something relevant could be found in that apartment, I wasn't going to be delayed. In fact, if Shtvtsk *was* involved in Vzktkk's death, her absence was an unexpected benefit. If all went well, I'd have time to search her apartment for information.

Then again, maybe the opportunity wasn't so unexpected. It fit my sudden run of good fortune. If it wasn't for the bullet wounds in my body, the loss of my home, and my empty bank account, I might start to think my luck was changing.

Chapter 13 - Empty Nest

It took almost a full decad and a couple of painful shocks before I managed to reformat my magnetic door key. Then, using the blank and my compad battery, I realigned the key's code until it matched closely enough to fool the lock to Apartment 401. I came close to draining my 'pad's charge. I'd have to keep its use minimal until I could plug it in again.

Still, the complicated approach was better than shorting out Shtvtsk's lock or kicking the door down. If tricking the lock didn't work, I might have been tempted. Having few investigative options was making the leads I *could* pursue more urgent. I wanted to know Shtvtsk's connection to Vzktkk. I wanted that knowledge in a manner more carnal than intellectual.

Even feeling that urgency, I managed to slide the door slowly and quietly. I listened for movement, breath, or anything else that might indicate an occupant. There shouldn't be anyone asleep inside, given my knocking, but I couldn't assume Shtvtsk wasn't a heavy sleeper.

The apartment remained quiet up to the limit of my patience, the five hectads I spared to listen. I opened the door wider and stepped inside. It was a nice, comfortable space: a little bigger than my apartment downstairs, but not by much. The impression of extra room was enhanced by large houseplants and strategically placed mirrors.

The main living space felt like the reception area of a business. Maybe it was. Prospective clients might wait there before being escorted elsewhere. "Elsewhere" didn't necessarily mean the nest room. The full faux mate experience probably included homemade meals in the dining area and grooming in the bathroom. Some of her clients might prefer to go out – to a restaurant, to the theater, maybe to a sporting event – rather than spend the day "at home".

Broken Record

Those would be the clients *not* worried about insulting an existing mate. Being seen in public with a new female acquaintance isn't scandalous, no more than hanging out with a male friend, but if you go out often enough with the same person, especially to social events, questions arise. You certainly will be noticed treating a stranger like Pack, if they're neither Pack nor mate.

If the gossip had Shtvtsk labeled right, that closeness was what her clients wanted: the emotional support of being accepted and spending time with someone. Was Vzktkk one of those clients? I hoped to find out. Quickly.

I made a discreet dash for the nesting room. I assumed the lady's boudoir was the most likely resting place for any clues. Maybe I'd find a written note, as rare as those were becoming. Maybe there was a piece of armor in Vzktkk's size, discarded or hung up.

It was over a week since Vzktkk's death, so the chances of finding any personal belongings were slim. Unfortunately, the key evidence I wanted – an address book – was probably on Shtvtsk's personal compad, which would be on her person.

Or not. I froze in the entryway to the apartment's nest room, stunned by my luck. A compad. On a low table, right next to a *very* comfortable looking padded nest. I barely noticed the rumpled linen sheets and the smell of musk and perfume. I was just that amazed.

The paralysis wore off fast. I darted for the 'pad, not wanting to waste time puzzling over my rare opportunity. Still, confusion lingered. As I booted up the unit and considered the password screen, I was still wondering why any Vislin – much less one with an alleged business requiring careful privacy – would leave their 'pad behind.

A stomper might leave a 'pad at home, sure, but they're not as fond of personal electronics. They prefer to meet up in person whenever possible. I'm not criticizing. I find their social traditions and ideals pretty admirable. Taratumm sociability might be one of the few redeeming qualities of the noisy lumps of muscle.

Nathan Large with Laine Megan Lundquist

I'm just saying, they don't keep their compads as close to the heart as Vislin do.

I tried a few default passwords just to see how far my luck would stretch. Not that far. Shtvtsk was savvy enough to set up proper security. I knew a few different options to bypass the password lock. I could just steal the whole compad, but theft was messy and would lead to complications. For one thing, Shtvtsk would know the unit was missing and know someone had broken in. If she *was* connected to Vzktkk's death, she'd be wary and come looking for likely culprits... me... or send someone else looking. Living in the same building as my quarry, I would be easily spotted, watched, and caught. Or shot.

Frost, I might already have been seen. Though that was somewhat my intent in moving to Isstravil, I didn't want to create trouble *too* soon or on terms I couldn't manage. As long as Shtvtsk thought I was only poking around, she might not overreact. If she *was* linked to the mercs who shot at me – and possibly blew up my apartment – then setting her off too soon could be deadly.

I could try and borrow the unit just long enough to break the security. Tskksk might help with that, if her curiosity and willingness to help overrode professional ethics. *I* was curious if she could confirm this 'pad as the source of the calls to Pkstzk on the night of Vzktkk's murder. The problem with "borrowing" was similar to outright theft: I'd have to remove the whole 'pad, risking Shtvtsk's return before I could get it back in place.

I could try to hack the compad myself. I dismissed that option quickly. For one reason, I doubted my skills were up to the task. Even if I managed to puzzle out the right approach, I probably didn't have enough time to finish before Shtvtsk came back.

Finally, I decided on a hybrid solution. Voiding the compad's warranty, I unsealed the back panel with a claw tip, then popped it off, exposing the component structure. I might not be an electronics genius, but I knew enough to find a memory matrix. Most components of a compad are integrated for size and simplicity, but the memory is always removable.

Broken Record

Repeating the opening process with my own 'pad, I removed a blank memory bead. Then, I pulled all the beads out of Shtvtsk's matrix and replaced them with the single blank.

When Shtvtsk booted the 'pad, it would report a blank, reformatted memory. I was counting on her to be insufficiently savvy to spot the dramatically reduced memory capacity, instead ascribing the problem to a hardware error or virus. My subterfuge would be spotted immediately if Shtvtsk popped the cover, but most users are loathe to do so... precisely to avoid warranty issues.

If I was *really* blessed, Shtvtsk would take her malfunctioning 'pad to the nearest local service location... Tskksk's little shop. That's where the removed beads would be, after we finished copying their contents. Tskksk could easily swap back the original beads, seal up the 'pad, and make up a story about some hardware fault... or something.

That scenario assumed I could convince Tskksk to not only help with the data transfer but also lie to a customer. I was also assuming a lot about Shtvtsk's likely response. She might be cleverer than I assumed. Or she might take the 'pad somewhere else. When she found out all her original memory was stolen, she'd go looking for the culprit.

Ideally, by then, I'd have the case solved. I could either apologize for the mistake or gloat at her through prison bars.

The whole swap, including time to reseal both 'pads, took me less than a decad. I likely had more evidence than I could have hoped for, but I still wanted to sweep the rest of the apartment. I gave the nesting room a cursory search, but with less desperate intensity.

I found nothing else out of the ordinary. Nothing screamed "male" or "foreign". As much as I might have wanted to linger over the bedsheets, I had no legitimate reason to hang around.

Instead, I stepped out and checked the dining area. Nothing on the counters; nothing in the cold box; nothing in the drawers. Well, nothing about the *case*. There were plenty of modern electronic conveniences, plenty of food in the box, and some respectable knives in the drawers. Shtvtsk wasn't hurting for kitchen supplies… or much else, for that matter. By contrast to her luxury, my old apartment looked like the aftermath of a robbery… even before the explosion.

The old place looked much worse afterward, I was sure. Clean nothing is better than burnt everything. Shtvtsk's apartment was fairly clean, I noticed. Other than the rumpled nest and a couple of stains in the kitchen, the rest was almost pristine. The bathroom was polished and the living area tidy.

Other than admiring the housekeeping, my remaining search of the apartment didn't produce any results. Checking the living room drawers turned up a couple of take-out menus and some business cards, but nothing really personal. There was a small locked security box in the front room, under a chair, but I decided not to test my luck trying to pick the lock. If I had to guess, I'd say it contained anonymous credit chips from customers or tokens of affection, possibly valuable.

If my check of the compad memory turned up nothing, I might return for that box, but I suspected I had everything I needed about Shtvtsk already… if there was anything to see

I had just decided to finish up and slip out when a familiar chime caught my hearing: an incoming call. I checked my 'pad, but the call wasn't for me. It was Shtvtsk's 'pad pinging from the nest room.

I briefly considered picking up the call. Unfortunately, with the address book extracted along with the 'pad's memory, I wouldn't know *who* was calling until I answered. I couldn't risk being exposed. Particularly if the caller *was* Pkstzk, I'd give away too much. I could try answering while turning the camera away and staying silent… but that would still be an anomaly, one the caller might mention to Shtvtsk.

While I considered my course of action, the opportunity passed. The chiming stopped. It was just as well; my best idea was to do nothing, anyway. The event wasn't without value, though. I marked the time on my own 'pad. Hopefully, Tskksk could do something with the information… maybe we could confirm Shtvtsk's 'pad as the source of the earlier calls to Pkstzk.

Broken Record

A moment later, I was peering through the gap of the apartment door, watching and listening for witnesses. The hallway looked clear. Locking the door behind me, I slipped out into the hall and scrambled back to the stairwell. Once I reached the third floor, I was safe. No one would have any reason to suspect I was doing anything other than going to my own apartment.

There *was* one last problem. My key was still coded for Apartment 401, not 309. I'd need to clear and recode it again before I could enter. Fortunately, there was another power outlet on the third floor, but I'd need another uninterrupted decad to fix the coding… not to mention a recharge on my compad battery.

It appeared I'd have to walk to Tskksk's shop a second time that day. I needed to go there anyway to copy the stolen memory beads, but it might have been wiser to do that the next day. Two visits so close together would be suspicious, if anyone was watching. Repeated visits also upped the probability that I'd run into Detective Nrissilli or another constable, if they were checking in on Tskksk as promised.

But sooner was better for other reasons, like getting her data transferred before Shtvtsk noticed the absence. I could check if her recent call set off any matches. And I could recharge my 'pad and fix my key. Seeing Tskksk again was just one of the many benefits that outweighed the risks.

I dry swallowed one more pain pill. The meds were working admirably and without noticeable side effects, other than an understandable fuzziness of thought. I begged the chemical to keep me going just a little longer. I promised my body a long rest afterward, even if it was on a bare floor. I could make it that far. Besides, I had to unravel this case before I could actually relax.

Afterward, I'd still be broke, injured, and dealing with whatever neurochemical damage I'd developed, but at least I could stop worrying about being arrested or murdered. Maybe I'd even end up ahead, with a new friend… or two or three. I was fine as long as I could still work. Murder wasn't the only way to end a life. Imprisonment and/or losing my license were almost as frightening as death.

Chapter 14 - Hard Decisions

When I reached the compad shop, I was aching and panting, but still holding myself upright. Seeing the "Closed" sign almost dropped me to my haunches, though. Had Tskksk closed up early? It was almost evening, but it wasn't quite dusk. I hadn't bothered to check the shop's hours, though. It could be her normal closing time for the day.

The security door wasn't down, at least. I prayed she was still inside. I rapped on the door and waited a few hectads.

Fortunately, that was all the time it took for Tskksk to come loping to the door. She waved at me through the window as she disarmed an alarm and retracted the door bolts. Her greeting was more enthusiastic than I expected or deserved.

"Stchvk! Great timing! I got something!" She bounced on her hind-claws as she backed up to let me enter.

I hated to spoil her surprise, but couldn't resist showing off. "You got a hit on the other compad: the one that called out locally."

She stared back at me, eyes narrowing. "How did you… did you find out who it was already? Was that where you were?"

"Could be," I answered without meaning to tease. I elaborated, "I talked to some people in the neighborhood. They pointed me to a likely friend of Vzktkk's in the area. While I was at her apartment, she got a call."

"But she didn't answer," Tskksk prompted, playing along rather than getting irritated at my lousy narration.

I flicked my crest. "No, she didn't have a chance. She wasn't home. I was there alone."

Broken Record

Tskksk looked up and down the street through the windows, a conspirator in mime. "Sounds morally questionable. I'd better close the door."

She did so, her crest also flicking in amusement. She whirled on me right afterward, holding out her hand.

"What?" I asked, pretending innocence. "The door was unlocked. I went in to make sure she was all right. Are you implying I might have done something criminal?"

She flexed her claws, palm still up and waiting. Finally, I reached into my compad bag and pulled out the handful of memory beads. She looked disappointed as I offered the components.

"You didn't get the whole 'pad?" Then she brightened with realization. "Ttt, you swapped out the memory! That works. Most of the important information will be in there anyway."

"Most?" I asked. "I thought *all* the files would be on there."

"Ttt, they will. Contacts, call records, messages... But the actual call signal and frequencies the 'pad uses are firmware, built into the comm components. We'll learn almost everything from the saved files, but they won't give perfect confirmation."

I tried not to sound too hurt about my implied ignorance. "Well, this isn't for evidence. If the owner is involved in Vzktkk's death, the constables will have to make their case on other grounds."

"Involved? You said this came from a *friend* of the deceased. You mean this person might be a witness? Or a betrayer?"

I paused, wondering how much more detail I should provide. Could I trust Tskksk, ally though she might be, with the specifics of a *personal* case? More importantly, should I lead her deeper into an dangerous situation?

I decided that, for all my concern, she was already tangled in this mess. Denying her more information actually put her at more risk. I wasn't going to give away more than necessary, but she needed details to proceed effectively.

I explained as much as I could while I plugged in my compad to recharge.

"Friend might not be the right term. Business associate? Special friend? Co-conspirator? I don't know which term is more appropriate. The neighbors suggested Vzktkk was seeing this female, named Shtvtsk, for paid companionship. From what I saw, that certainly seemed to be her profession, or at least one of them."

"So, the victim was cheating on his mate? I can understand why she might be upset... wait, but wasn't his mate the one calling this Shtvtsk? That doesn't work..."

I agreed. "I can think of some explanations, none of them good... but none of them very plausible, either. I didn't tell you before, but since you'll get the name soon enough anyway: Vzktkk's mate, my client, is named Pkstzk."

She interrupted to boast: "I knew that already. Vzktkk's obituary mentions her."

"And you read the obituary after my last visit," I finished for her.

"Yes. You were saying?"

"What you *won't* find in the public record is that Pkstzk and I are old acquaintances, ourselves. I'd appreciate if you didn't share that with Detective Nrissilli, by the way... or any other constable. Let's just say I know Pkstzk, her past and her personality. She might rip a wayward mate bloody herself, but hiring someone else to kill him? Not likely. Contacting the her competition to conspire also seems out of character. Then again... maybe Pkstzk called to threaten Shtvtsk and demand she stop seeing Vzktkk."

"Or to gloat? Maybe the first call was, 'I know he was with you tonight', and the second was 'Now see what you did'," Tskksk offered.

"Again, that assumes Pkstzk was involved. I don't think so. No benefit to her to have Vzktkk dead. She'd sooner use shame to control him than pay to have him shot. Gain over loss."

Tskksk winced, "She sounds lovely. If I can ask, *how* did you know this Pkstzk? Coworker? Brood-sibling?"

Broken Record

"It's complicated."

Tskksk flicked her claws, releasing that particular prey. "Fine. I can tell when I've hit a firewall. You realize I may find out while browsing through these?" She rolled the memory beads around on a table-top for emphasis.

"If it becomes relevant, you'll know," I allowed, "but it's enough to say I've seen Pkstzk get *very* possessive. *If* she was going to blast anyone, it would be the other female. Her mate is *hers*... at least while she still wants him."

Tskksk paused and offered tentatively, "Well, is it possible that she *didn't* want her mate anymore? I admit it sounds really cold, put that way."

Her question made me think harder. "I wouldn't have said so, at first... but it's not an impossible theory. Not a dissolution of the mate-ship, but something else. It's possible she wasn't *ever* interested in him. I've been thinking about her as a grieving ex-mate, but there's enough about this case that suggests some other plot stalking under cover."

"Chchch?" Tskksk asked, without voicing her question further.

I raked the air with a hindclaw, killing the subject. "Later. When we know something more solid. For now, yes, I would be very grateful if you could extract everything from those memory beads and give me a copy, plus the originals in case I get a chance to return them. Doubly grateful if you avoid prying deeper into the contents of those records. If you get a visit from a neighbor named Shtvtsk, before I'm able to retrieve the beads..."

"Swap them back in under pretense of 'repairs'," Tskksk finished.

"Like you read my mind," I joked. She clacked back, still in good humor.

I felt obligated to remind her of serious matters. "Don't forget, I've had two attempts on my life since I started this case. One was definitely aimed at me; no reason to think that it wasn't related to my investigation. Once whoever-it-is tracks me to this area, you could be at risk.

"Don't take any chances, don't mention the case, and keep your security up."

She acknowledged my warnings with due sobriety. "I understand. Normally, I'd curse you for bringing me trouble… but I could have warned you away the first time. I'm aware and accept the risks. Besides, now I really want to know how this mystery turns out. If I'm threatened, though, I still reserve the right to panic and run."

"Fair enough. I'm the only one here who sold their right to self-preservation."

"Is that what clients pay you for?"

"Exactly. Investigation is one percent intelligence, ninety-nine percent recklessness."

"I'll stick to electronics repair, then."

"Good idea."

We finally exhausted our wits and settled into a satisfied post-banter silence. I excused myself from the store, retrieving my compad from its charging plug. Without prompting, Tskksk locked up behind me, pulling down her security door and turning off the lights in the front showroom.

As I left, I glanced toward the pet store across the street. Technically, there had been *three* attempts on my life since I started the case. I couldn't decide, though, if the rktpk attack should be considered random or connected in some way to Vzktkk's murder. There were still too many loosely connected incidents to be sure about causation.

I was counting on Tskksk's work to cast some light on the case. Otherwise, I was low on leads again, not to mention overdrafted on credit and short on time. Eventually, my would-be killers would make another attempt. I needed to identify them (or their employer) before then. At worst, I should anticipate and have constables waiting for their next visit.

I wasn't avoiding the constabulary forever, after all. I'd eventually have to get their help, either to protect myself or to wrap up the case. All hopes of keeping my involvement private burned away when a bomb went off at my apartment.

Broken Record

When I discovered Pkstzk's connection to Isstravil, the revelation further reduced my chances of obscurity. More than just a client, she was part of the case.

I still retained some hope of hiding my past. Ideally, Pack Vzrrk had no relevance to Vzktkk's murder. If the constables could close his case without further investigation, they might be satisfied without the deeper detail.

It wasn't the first time I'd counted on constabulary neglect to preserve my freedom. Like I noted before, successful investigators are allowed wide legal latitude in exchange for the returns they produce. A P.I. only ends up on the receiving end of prosecution if they create more problems for the law than they solve... if they become an embarrassment.

Being noticed publicly – particularly when flouting the law – is the worst possible sin, followed by implicating a constable in a crime. Basically, never make the law have to defend itself. It will fight and it will fight hard. I was fortunate I'd never had to face that conflict. If I ever pull a case involving official corruption, I'll have to tread carefully.

I think for the most part, the constables who know about me consider me a lucky loser: a sapient who solves cases by persistence and trickery, coupled with a repeated failure to die, rather than any particular genius.

I say "loser" because I never seem to parlay my successes into a better class of clientele... whose fees would provide a nicer office, wardrobe, and home. The constables notice such outward signs of success... or their absence.

The truth was, my detractors are mostly right. Given the types of cases that come to me – and the few cases I have turned down – I generally have to get my claws dirty to win and don't earn much *for* winning. I could advertise better, but my innate fear of discovery tends to sabotage such plans.

I'd only argue about the "lucky" part. Sure, I was still alive, but my aches and pains sometimes made me regret that. I wasn't lucky in a lot of ways: love, Pack, money, looks...

The shred of pride left after I finished abusing myself argued that I *had* solved most of my cases, not by luck or brute force, but through logic, insight, and cunning. I *am* persistent, yes. My "tricks" are hard-earned and useful skills, abilities that could frosted well pay me back for the difficulty of learning them.

Plus, I'd added talents to my repertoire since my misspent youth. I've learned how to hack a conversation, just as much as a compad or a magnetic key. Find the right cues, tap the right nerves, and some locked people open up. It's no more noble than picking a lock, but it's more legal. Granted, getting caught breaking in gets you in almost as much trouble.

Enough rambling. As I returned to my new apartment in Isstravil, I brainstormed. How were Pkstzk, Vzktkk, Shtvtsk, and the mercenaries at Taburket's related? Were any of them related to my apartment bomber? Were any of these parties connected to Pack Vzrrk? What was Pkstzk's game? *Was* there even a game, or was Pkstzk unaware of any role Shtvtsk played in her mate's death? *Was* Shtvtsk involved in killing Vzktkk or having him killed? There were many possibilities, some more likely than others, but none completely disposable.

In parallel, I was thinking about how to extricate myself from the case once it was resolved. I wanted to keep my profile in the official reports as minimal as possible. It was beginning to look like my only means of doing so was cooperation with – and the good graces of – Detective Nrissilli.

I thought I'd earned some trust from the Detective, or at least sympathy. She did release me from custody. Then again, it was possible the Hrotata let me go just to see where I ran. Or else, she was staking me out as a sacrifice to see what predators emerged.

I wasn't faulting her in either case. I would have left custody willingly, even knowing her motives were underhanded. We were just playing our roles. The Detective didn't know my true background, ability, or plans. I didn't know hers, and it didn't matter anyway. For this round, we had to play the game by standard rules.

Dusk was creeping around the edges of the skyline as I arrived home. It wasn't an enthusiastic homecoming. I still didn't have a nest; a bare floor waited for my aching, fatigued body. Even before resting, I needed to reprogram my door key just so I could get inside.

Broken Record

I entered the familiar foyer, reminded that I had spent more time there than anywhere else that day. The hall's utilitarian appearance summarized my day pretty well: doing what one must, without luxuries.

Speaking of comfort, I realized my pain meds were wearing off. The drug was probably waning for several decads already, but I was noticing it more as my thoughts turned toward rest. I checked the bottle rattling in my armor pocket: about a dozen days' worth. It was supposed to be a fifteen-day prescription, but I'd been leaning heavily on the pills after the explosion.

I allowed myself one more dose for the night, dry-swallowing with some difficulty. Couldn't they at least afford a water fountain in this cave? As I straightened up, steeling myself for three flights of stairs, I heard a beak click calling for attention.

Turning around, I saw a tall, graceful, female Vislin standing at the base of the stairwell. She must have entered from the side doors, or else she came out of the landlady's office. She walked so quietly that I hadn't noticed her approach until she was already in the foyer. That alone was quite a feat, even given my distraction.

Her stealth and physical presence weren't the only exciting qualities about her. She wore a simple armor sheath of soft white leather plated with titanium panels over belly, thighs, and inner arms. It complimented her pale cream scales, a perfection unmarred by variations in hue. Her eyes were deep, clear, and focused pleasantly on me in an expression of interest. She performed a simple nonverbal greeting, adding a tail flick that indicated genuine pleasure to be in my presence. And her voice... when she finally spoke, she coupled the precise, clear diction of a scholar with the modulations of a Great Pack leader.

"Stchvk? I must assume it is you. Even if you've suffered some wear since your public images were recorded, your pattern of scars is distinctive."

I didn't recognize her. Believe me, if I had met this female before, I would remember her. I would remember her daily and while asleep at night. Just knowing that she knew my name and showed such curiosity about me was scrambling my mental functions.

Nathan Large with Laine Megan Lundquist

Do you know, Humans call their "lower", more basic mental functions their "lizard brain"? It's funny, because Vislin actually suffer comparatively less interference from our basic biological urges: arousal, hunger, aggression, and fear. That's not counting frenzy, of course, or the demand to protect Pack and offspring. But day-to-day, we tell fewer stories of Vislin thinking with their hormones, compared to mammals.

Well, right then, I was belying that pride of species. My urge to stare silently was fighting against the urge to say something equally fascinating in return. I really, really wanted to impress this female. The partisans for silence argued that, no matter how clever I thought I was, whatever came out of my beak right then would be idiotic gibberish. In response, the speaking faction countered that quiet could be mistaken for stupidity. Finally, the two sides signed a treaty and compromised on mysterious simplicity.

"I am Stchvk," I confirmed, "Who are you?"

"I'm surprised you don't recognize your neighbor. You've had plenty of time to look at my personal effects."

She spoke without anger, but I froze as I understood her words. *Shtvtsk.*

I should have recognized her from the images in her apartment, yet even the best recording wouldn't have prepared me for the sight of her in person. The few glimpses I saw were of a younger female, surrounded by other Vislin and the occasional Hrotata or Taratumm. She was either buried in the press of a party or else soberly staring into the imager. She certainly hadn't been wearing *that* armor in any of the images.

How did she know I broke in to her apartment? The reasonable guess was a confederate in the building. The landlady? Frost, the Hrotata couple that told me about her might have tipped her off to my interest, being equal opportunity gossips. Kktkrkz devour all chatty rodents. Then again, she might have hidden cameras in her apartment to watch for intruders… or to record clients.

I hadn't thought to check for such secondary security measures. My haste in searching the apartment was no excuse. I'd hit more private targets before and always thought to thwart or destroy recordings. I just hadn't expected such things in a small apartment.

- 255 -

Broken Record

Maybe she'd reveal her tricks. I struggled to haul my psyche out of its erotic mire. I summoned my personal charm to see if I could out-charisma a master. I'd start with a soft approach rather than hard-bitten accusation. I hated the thought of spoiling her lovely air of attraction, whether it was genuine or just an act.

I started out slow: "I'm sorry? Your personal effects? I'm not sure I understand."

"Let's not play games, Stchvk. I assume you're uncomfortable standing here and will only become more fatigued the longer we clash beaks. You know who I am, and I have a general idea who you are… and why you're here. Discussing our business together here, in public view, is likely to become embarrassing. So why not come upstairs with me, and we'll talk? More privately. More professionally. More… comfortably."

Professionally was right. I was sparring well outside my class, and we both knew it. The only question was, was I fool enough to follow her onto her home territory, giving up one more advantage? All I had on my side was a little more knowledge, including the bargaining chip of her compad memory. She had many obvious assets, including a very inviting apartment and the implied promise of other comforts.

My resistance was already low, as she correctly assumed. The only tether keeping me from complete surrender was the reminder that this female *might* be Vzktkk's murderer. I hadn't seen a laser weapon in her apartment, but I hadn't been looking for one, either. Her invitation could be a trap. A really pleasant looking, well-designed trap.

But it *might* be a legitimate invitation. Not just for pleasant companionship, either. She could be a witness wanting to come clean about her role in Vzktkk's death. She might have information about Vzktkk or Pkstzk to share. Frost, she might have taken my break-in as a sign that her anonymity was lost and chose to make her confession to me rather than the constables. I could be doing a civic service.

Maybe it was the nature of the invitation that made me nervous. It just seemed too good to believe. It was everything I wanted: a seductive, available female, a lead on this aggravating case, and, worth mentioning, a soft nest for my aching corpse.

Maybe it was a death trap. At that point, I was willing to take the risk. Better to lie in a comfortable grave than suffer on a hard floor, alone, wondering what I had missed.

I mustered my most confident crest display and answered her: "All right, lead on. Then again, I could lead... I already have a key."

Chapter 15 - Trade Negotiations

Preparing myself for confrontation with Shtvtsk was confusing. What kind of confrontation was I expecting, exactly? Seduction? Other bribery? Threats? Foul play? A hidden laser? Knife in the back? Drugged drink? A really nasty argument?

I kept my nerves under control largely by ignoring any anticipation. I tried to assume that we were going upstairs for a quiet chat, maybe including some details to help my investigation. That outcome *was* still one of the possibilities.

But if she was simply an informant, why did Shtvtsk know my name? I remembered that I hadn't given my name to the uptight Hrotata couple, so she couldn't have heard it from them. The landlady, of course, had all my public data, so that route remained a possibility. The last and most likely source of intel was Pkstzk. I already knew that she and Shtvtsk were in contact.

So, the question became: how did the two females know each other? The timing of their calls around Vzktkk's death was suspicious at the least, chilling at the worst. Had they been in contact even before that fatal night? Were they already associates, with Vzktkk's visits social or related to business *other* than Shtvtsk's apparent profession?

And even if Shtvtsk and Pkstzk were on speaking terms, before, during, and after Vzktkk's death, why wouldn't Pkstzk mention her to me as a lead? Granted, Pkstzk and I hadn't had much opportunity to talk. Maybe Shtvtsk's name was going to come up that night at Taburket's, if our meeting hadn't been interrupted.

Sss, enough speculation. I was going to learn something, even if it meant I had to plunge directly into the water without checking it first. Should I hope it to be deep, warm, and pleasant… or cold, shallow, and shocking?

I preceded Shtvtsk as offered, giving her plenty of access to my unguarded back. Not that I expected any attack in the stairwell, but a trivial show of trust might count for something. I even unlocked her door with my still-modified key, showing her that I had nothing to hide. In truth, I was hiding plenty. Confirming that I broke into her apartment was a confession intended to forestall deeper suspicions.

As we walked into the apartment, Shtvtsk spoke behind me: "Please, sit down. I'll be with you in a moment. I just need to check my messages."

Frost. I had to wonder: did she just realize that her compad was here, in her apartment, unguarded, at the same time I had access? Would she discover its malfunction and connect it to me? Or had she already been home, found the 'pad blanked, and figured it out herself? Was her comment meant to taunt me?

I gave away nothing. I chose a padded, leather-wrapped lounge chair and settled myself carefully into the soft cushions. Shtvtsk drifted past me into the nesting room, the low light glowing off her pale scales and silvery armor plates.

I tried to watch without staring. There was something fascinating about her, something almost unnatural, that had nothing to do with appearance or behavior. Not that she didn't have plenty to appreciate physically, but she was also fascinating personally. She radiated strength, confidence, and danger; attractive qualities in almost every species.

Yet, I had known females with each of those qualities before, sometimes all at once. And yes, I was attracted and excited by most of them, but not like this.

Pkstzk had the lure of the forbidden, the taste of youthful nostalgia, and a certain reckless enthusiasm. Granted, that energy seemed to have drained out of her, over the years. But Pkstzk also never seemed *competent*, always relying upon others to execute her wild plans and support her needs.

Tskksk had fresh, young energy, plus a competent and devious intelligence. She also had some shapely curves, if not exactly muscular and imposing. But Tskksk seemed as safe and orderly as a starship, no threat at all.

Broken Record

Shtvtsk was another kind of creature. She maintained a business – I was assuming – which hovered on the edge of legality and challenged one of the supports of Vislin culture. Prostitution might be legal and even encouraged by the Hrotata side of the Great Family, but again, the Vislin and Taratumm view of such activity is unsympathetic. A Vislin escort might be prosecuted on the thinnest excuse, such as an accusation that they deliberately encouraged a client to violate their mate-ship contract.

Shtvtsk was the kind of Vislin who could make such a profession pay. I could see why males would prefer her over an actual mate and pay her to pretend she was theirs for a while. A lonely, unmated male would certainly be drawn to her, even if he had only an average libido. Again, it wasn't just sex. It was the feeling that, if such an impressive creature was interested in you, you must be an impressive being, yourself.

I was certainly feeling more important, just sitting in her waiting room and waiting on Shtvtsk to return. Whether or not she came back cursing, I was still part of her life. She wanted to talk to me. We might even have a meaningful conversation. The worst outcome I could imagine was being dismissed as unworthy of further attention.

That realization was what cleared my head, as Shtvtsk returned to the room. Yes, I have been attracted to many females in my life, mostly unwisely, certainly excessively. But never before had I failed to see – and often, appreciate – their flaws along with their assets. I never treated them like goddesses. My brain and other organs were trying to *worship* Shtvtsk.

It wasn't chemical, though, at least not like Hrotata toxin. The world wasn't dissolving into a soft-edged happy haze. No, the unreal aspect was concentrated on her and my reactions to her. You remember how I frequently mention my "unique reactions" to Vislin females? The chief advantage of experiencing attraction so regularly is that I'm more aware of its presence, its nuances, and its limitations. A novice wouldn't have had a chance against Shtvtsk. I flattered myself that I had recognized that something was amiss.

Not that I didn't melt further into the chair when she fixed me with a steady yellow stare and addressed me in pleasant tones. "Nothing of importance," she said, implying that *I* was more important than any other person who might have called.

No messages? Her compad shouldn't even have booted its comm program. She was covering her reactions well… and possibly waiting to see mine.

I thought I managed to hide my surprise well enough. "That's a shame," I answered, "I'd expect you to have frequent callers."

Instead of teasing back, she frowned, settling herself onto the couch to my immediate left, just barely within reach. "I'm not sure what you mean by that. Are you implying something, Stchvk?"

Her regular and familiar use of my name was another clue. Not "Detective". Not "Citizen". Not "Master". Nothing formal. She assumed both superiority and informality right away.

I persisted with my own approach. "Just that an attractive creature like you should have plenty of company: a mate, a Pack, or interested bidders for either position. Plus, you're clearly not hurting for credit, so I'd expect business calls, either for work or to offer services. And from your images…" I waved a claw toward the displays in the waiting room. "…you clearly have friends."

Her scales flickered momentarily darker, a warning. Yet she leaned closer to me as she intoned, "You seem very interested in my 'business', Stchvk. Should I take that as a compliment… or a threat?"

"Both. Let's not waste too much time here. You know I've been asking about you, and that I took the opportunity to look around your home. I'm assuming you have some idea *why* I'm interested. You also know what your neighbors think, or at least, what they assume about your livelihood."

Her crest rose at that: interested. "My neighbors get the basic idea right, but have strange thoughts about the particulars. I would say I am a companion, an escort, maybe even a therapist for those in need. They just have the wrong idea about which needs those are."

"I figured that part out. And I'm not judging. But that isn't my real interest."

Broken Record

"No? Not originally, perhaps. But are you interested now?" She was close enough to smell, probably close enough to transmit pheromones. If she got any closer, she could check for herself how interested I was. I wondered if she was wearing any psychoactive love potion, something subtler than outright musk.

"I admit that I am," I agreed with admirable calm, "but I doubt I could afford your services. I haven't been paid well lately." Like with Tskksk, it hurt to mention my poverty, especially in the context of mate-interest. I imagine it's like a mammal admitting to impotence or infertility. Just don't bother, move on, this one's useless.

Shtvtsk didn't reel back in disgust, though. She didn't even pause to reconsider. "I don't always work for credit. Barter often provides more value than money could."

I warred between offering to trade information outright, versus playing a longer game. I had already as much as received a promise of "services" in return for… something. So, what did she want? What did she think I could do for her? Answer her questions? If she gave me what I needed, I'd have happily traded secrets back, maybe more than I should. She didn't need to offer herself, personally, in trade for information.

I have to admit, though, I like verbal games. Sometimes, I suspect I've stayed an investigator so long just for the puzzles and the conversational sparring. An erotic frisson was added spice to my preferred meat.

I answered, "Barter? What kinds of trades do you accept? What are *you* shopping for?"

"Sometimes, I just need a skilled friend. Pack is wonderful… and I do have one, by the way… but you don't always find the talents you need among your loved ones. A mate? I have one for every day of the year, Stchvk. I wear the one that suits the occasion. The right client is like the right accessory; fashionable and functional. If you fit my need, then you don't pay *me*, I buy *you*."

Her words were cynical, better suited for a bitter rant or defiant boast. Yet she delivered her cold assessment with warm, enticing charm. She made her mercenary ways sound like sensible, even admirable behavior. Frost, I caught myself *wanting* to hang in her closet… and on her shoulders, when she chose to take me out.

But if she was that desirable, that successful, shouldn't she be settled in a penthouse in the city center? Nesting in a private hunting lodge, kept as mistress to a planetary politician? Why, if she was so obviously valuable and willing to trade on that value, had she not traded up to something better than a one-nest apartment in Isstravil?

I wanted to deflate her, but also I wanted to sympathize. Obviously, her fortunes were as poor as mine. Maybe she had a similar ethical limitation keeping her from claiming everything her talents could earn. Neither skepticism nor pity would endear her to me, though.

Instead, I ignored her boasts. "All right. I'm flattered at your implication that I'm worth trading for. I didn't misunderstand that, did I?"

Her crest fell. "No. That was the idea. I mean, you're not ideal. I did notice your intrusion, not to mention your investigation. Even before today, it looks like you were recently caught where you shouldn't be." Her gaze took in my body, lingering on my wrappings. I still couldn't help wishing she'd linger elsewhere, but appreciating even that attention.

"I'm working with limited time and resources," I countered. "If I had more leisure, I'd work more subtly and with less injury."

"That sounds like an excuse," she chided. "The best in their field don't let such pressures interfere with their performance. I can get equally good results in a decad as in a day."

"I'm sure you can, but then again, you rarely have anyone directly opposing your work."

She flared again, lifting her head higher to look down into my eyes. Checking my expression for more clues?

"You know that's not true. Although, I suppose *my* opposition is less likely to resort to violence."

Broken Record

We were finally getting to something substantial. Part of me wanted to break past innuendo and cut directly to the bones of our situation. *How did you know Vzktkk? How do you know Pkstzk? Did you kill Vzktkk? Do you know who did?*

I might eventually get around to raking her with such nakedly sharp questions. But I'd seen enough witnesses freeze when ambushed to know better. Shtvtsk obviously had an approach planned, with some proposal or scenario in mind. If I kept playing along, she might still give away what I wanted to know.

I pushed as carefully as I could. "I guess you do have opponents: social, maybe personal. Maybe that opposition gets violent on occasion. Has that happened much?"

"You can see me as well as I see you," she retorted, lounging back on her couch to make the point more elaborately. "Do I look like I've been assaulted?"

"You don't look like you *lost* a fight, no," I agreed, giving her displayed body the expected inspection.

"That's because I never do the fighting myself, in person," Shtvtsk confided. She settled back into the couch, her legs and tail toward me. "If I have a problem, I usually find a friend who can solve it."

"So, I should be a friend, rather than a problem."

My summation struck home. She stiffened, and her crest dipped involuntarily. She recovered, relaxing back into a pose without betraying any aggression.

"We should all strive so," she lectured. "No one should create trouble. Everyone should please one another. Don't you agree?"

"Absolutely. But my career is predicated on the fact that sapients create trouble for one another. And I have to be a problem for *those* sapients. If I have any disdain for your work, it probably comes from the fact that you work to make your clients happy... whereas I frequently make my clients unhappy, even when I do everything right."

"Vvv, but surely *someone* is happy when you succeed? The constables? A victim? Society in general? Anyone?"

Her tone implied the answer we both knew. All too often, nobody was pleased when an investigation found the culprit of a crime. Sometimes, sapients preferred not to know, if the answers were painful. Society itself was sometimes the criminal, either through direct corruption or indirect causation. Shtvtsk seemed sympathetic... although her tone suggested that I might profit more from failing, once in a while.

That insinuation stiffened something inside me... and no, not that. I can bend a lot of principles, but I sensed we were heading toward a bigger bend than I could accept. Even the thought brought me sorrow. I would eventually disappoint this gorgeous, amazing, provisionally-willing goddess.

I tried to warn her: "I am. *I'm* happy. When I solve a case. Otherwise, this job wouldn't be worth doing. I don't want to insult you... I certainly don't want to discourage you from what you're doing right now... but my real pleasure is finding what's being hidden. I hope you get some pleasure, yourself, out of solving your client's problems?"

If she was offended, she hid it well. Obviously, she knew that showing genuine anger would ruin the spell she was trying to cast. Instead, she tacked to a new approach. I could admire her craft and persistence even while recognizing the maneuver. Being savvy didn't immunize me against enjoying her work... or doubting my analysis. I still wanted to be on her side and in her favor. I hated treating her like a suspect.

"I do. I didn't mean to sound so dismissive of my clients. Call it pride, both personal and professional.

"Stchvk, you don't think badly of me, do you? I sensed we had some understanding of one another. We're both hard workers, struggling to earn what we deserve for our talents. We're both under-appreciated by society. I just manage my business differently: a different domain, different currency. We could work together, as partners, rather than separately. We don't have to be at odds."

There it was, the center of our conversation. I still didn't know anything substantial about the case – just a loose weave of suspicions – but I knew why Shtvtsk had approached me. She wanted me on her side, whether she was a culprit, a victim, or an innocent bystander. She spoke with calm, confidence, and conspiratorial fellowship, but she needed my cooperation.

In fact, I was impressed all over again to watch how smoothly she shifted stance. Since naked appeals to my personal pride and lusts hadn't worked, she was working on my professional pride, instead. She had me pegged as defined by my work, ruled by achievement above ambition or physical desire.

She wasn't wrong. I want a lot of things, but when priorities clash, the job always wins. The real job: finding the truth and doing the right thing, not just meeting a client's demands. The main reason I'm not more successful is that, in Layafflr City, "success" occasionally means you let a villain get away... or you convict the innocent, instead. On those terms, I prefer to fail.

Having that desire manipulated was annoying. Implying that I would pursue my case any differently, with or without her favor, was insulting. She might not have meant to impugn my integrity, but she was lowering my opinion of hers.

If only this female's goals and mine were in alignment! I could stop resisting her charms. That synchrony was what made Tskksk a much better interest than other females. While I might not ache after her body as much, I didn't get repelled by any emotional incompatibility.

My silence encouraged Shtvtsk. She turned around on the couch, leaning toward me across its length, flipping from reversed supine to a facing prone crouch. Her crest rose slowly, her beak parting, claws pressing into the leather surface. She could really fake interested arousal well.

I knew what I had to do. There was only one way this encounter was going to be resolved. Shtvtsk had made it abundantly clear: she wasn't giving up any real information until she was sure I was hooked. She was going to keep probing my controls until she found a way to make me another obedient friend. To get what I needed out of her, I had to end this farce.

I looked deep into her bright, yellow eyes, leaned forward, and said what I had to say:

"You're right. I think we *could* work together. What did you have in mind?"

Chapter 16 - Interrupted Intercourse

Shtvtsk looked pleased at my agreement, but didn't show any evidence of increased trust. Instead, she pivoted to sit upright, maintaining eye contact.

"I'm glad to hear you're open to partnership, Stchvk. I know what you want from *me*. We can work on arrangements as we go, but first we should offer a few good-faith tokens. I feel like I've contributed first: I haven't blamed you for intruding on my privacy. And I let you know, right away, that I knew."

"How *did* you know, by the way?" I interrupted.

Her crest fluttered as she laughed. "Kkk, kkk, already asking for more? I'll tell you, if you explain how you got a copy of my key."

That trick wasn't too much of a trade secret. "I made my own copy. These magnetic scan locks are easy to fool. In fact, it's almost like they want to be tricked: the reader itself exerts force on the key, highlighting the regions where it expects differences in polarity."

I stopped before I got too technical. Shtvtsk seemed like the type to get bored easily by tech talk.

She only shrugged athletically and replied, "I see. At least I don't have to sue the landlady, although I should probably speak with her about upgrading my lock. I thought you might have slipped my key out of my pouch... but I think I would have noticed you."

"You don't know... I could have quiet, nimble claws."

"I'll have to see if that's true," she trilled. "But it seems your mind is trickier than your hands. Part of the standard private investigator package? Or a personal talent?"

Broken Record

It was my turn to hold out on her. "That sounds like a new question. For now, let's say I have many talents. Which ones, and how I learned them, can be the topics of future discussions. But it's your turn now. How did you know I'd been in here?"

She finally showed some irritation. "A micro-camera hidden in the room. I always make sure to make a record of any visitors, in case of disputes about services rendered. *Not* in the nest, by the way. I'm lawfully recording business transactions, not creating entertainment."

I raised a hind-claw in defense. "I understand that. So, are we being recorded right now?"

"We are. But it's entirely modular and local. I could turn it off, if I choose. I'll also delete the record if we decide anything gets too private to risk. But until I know I'm safe, the record is a little extra insurance."

She managed to be both reassuring and threatening at once. A good trick. So was the recorder. I really should have anticipated something like that An escort with video documentation generally got paid more reliably… or could start demanding even higher payments.

Or he. As rare as mate substitutes are among Vislin, it's a gender equal profession for the same reasons. I'd never *met* a male escort, but then again, I wasn't a potential client.

Shtvtsk, herself, increased my experience with female escorts to two. The other one was an extortion mark for Pack Vzrrk. We weren't threatening to expose her; we just offered insurance so that her clients wouldn't get robbed while they slept. Unexplained thefts on their property tend to ruin any business.

"I see. It's your turn. What else do you want to know? Keep in mind, what you ask is just as revealing as what you answer."

"Don't try and teach *me*, detective. We both read people as a professional skill. I need to know what they like and dislike; you need to know what they're hiding. I believe I've already plumbed more of your secrets than you realize… maybe more than you know about me."

"Chchch? Maybe I should see if that's true. I'm curious what I've given away."

"You'll stay curious. I can't be teased into revealing my techniques." She ventured to reach toward me, tapping a foreclaw against my left shoulder guard. When I didn't flinch away, she ran the sharp tip down the leather plate, leaving a shallow scratch.

I did shift my gaze to watch her hand. She was right to assume my lack of reaction implied a desire for more physical contact. Holding still also conveyed a certain degree of trust. The question was whether she realized that my stasis was the result of deliberate restraint, rather than indecision or desire.

She *could* have tried to tear out my throat, right then. She could have hooked my armor and dragged me close for a bite. She could have thrown me to the ground, pinned me, and searched my pockets for weapons, keys, or her missing compad memory. There were lots of risks, though all those scenarios seemed unlikely. She had no reason to assault me... that I knew of. Even so, I was tempted to pull away. I suppressed the reaction to prevent her from realizing I entertained such thoughts.

You might think this is a lot of complicated processing for one hectad's action. True, I probably overstate the depth of my thoughts. But some of what I'm describing is an elaborate, verbalized version of a much faster set of instincts. We were trading nonverbal cues faster than either of us could explicitly recognize and interpret. Like martial artists, we were reacting on trained reflex more than actually planning out our attacks and counters.

All of that is true, plus I probably interpret my actions more kindly in hindsight. I'm sure my actual reasons were dumber than the explanations I came up with afterward.

So, she touched me, I didn't jump, and our relationship entered a deeper level. Good job, instincts.

For similar reasons, I feigned irritation and demanded, "That's fine. Unlike most of your clients, I didn't come up here to talk about myself. I'm pleased you're so interested in me and my job skills, but I'm more interested in the reason our paths crossed today."

Broken Record

Her beak gaped open, a child's petty demand. "Vvv, Stchvk. Don't get tedious on me now. I'd like to keep this exchange as pleasant as possible, for as long as possible. If you start setting terms, then I have to draw lines as well, and lines just divide us. Remember, you agreed to work with me."

I stuck with my stern approach. "I did, but I can't 'work' without knowing what you're offering or what you want in return. I'm not saying spell everything out, but at this rate, we'll be past our prime before we ever get serious."

"Fine," she huffed, drawing herself up even straighter. Her hand fell away from my shoulder and her beak continued to flex, exaggerated petulance.

The Chill. Next tool in the manipulation kit. Give a little attention, then pull it away. Make them apologize and offer something to get back in your good graces.

She didn't freeze up for long. Turning to glance back at me across one shoulder, Shtvtsk relaxed and offered: "You're looking for information about Vzktkk's death, aren't you?"

"A question and an answer, all in one. I like that," I praised, rubbing a claw down the arm of my chair. "And in reward, I'll confirm: I'm working his *murder*, yes. Mind sharing what you know? I already heard that you and he knew one another."

She blinked, but that was her only sign of hesitation. "We did. I appreciate that you don't assume *how* we knew one another. I'm sure your informants did."

She paused, working out what to say next. I suspected she was deciding how much to tell me, and how much of that information would be true. She had me hanging on her words. She probably knew that, as well.

Finally, she hissed and said, "Kkk, they were right. Vzktkk was seeing me... professionally. He was leaving from a visit when he died. The constables haven't connected us yet. We were both discreet outside of this building. His mate didn't know he was my client.

"I knew both of them, if you didn't find that out already. Socially. Pkstzk and I used to work together, three years ago, as house-cleaners. She introduced

- 270 -

me to Vzktkk, after they started courting. I noticed when things between them became difficult, after they'd been mated a year. I offered my help; he accepted."

"Your help being..."

"Professional companionship. Look, Stchvk, I'm not ashamed of what I do. Let's be clear about that. I've just found that being too explicit ruins the experience for many clients. It spoils the illusion."

"Whereas, I'm not fond of illusions."

"No. No, you aren't," she mused in return. "You want all the grime and spatter of reality. I wonder if I'm more appealing to you than an actual mate. Of course, to many of my clients, I *am* more appealing than any real mate, but as a fiction, not as my real self. Am I right, Stchvk? Are you more interested in Shtvtsk the escort than Shtvtsk the female next door?"

"We've come back to me as the topic," I cautioned. "But I'll admit you're right: I like you better when you're being honest. As to whether I'd prefer an actual mate, that I can't answer. It's not like I've had an offer to compare. Most females want a mate with a better life expectancy."

"I assume you mean your obvious job hazards," she trilled, her gaze running over my wounds. "Not some chronic disease."

I rolled my eyes. "No, it's a disease. I occasionally break out in bullets."

"Vvv, sarcasm. You spared me that until now. If you thought I might find it unattractive, you were right. Don't deflect or deflate. Let me tease, Stchvk. Let me play. It's my privilege. More, it's my professional talent. If you pick at my phrasing, it spoils the effect."

"I thought you just said I liked it better without role-playing."

I couldn't help it. I can't resist the temptation to provoke. It's a tendency that gets me in trouble with potential friends, as much as it proves useful with certain suspects.

Broken Record

I could see the edges of her self-control starting to fray: the tightness around her knuckles, the sharper clamp of her beak at the end of words. I didn't *want* to get her angry, but it seemed the more I annoyed her, the harder she had to work to keep up the pretense of seduction.

I admit it; I'm a terrible client. I wouldn't shut up and let the sorceress weave her spell. Too bad.

With thinning glamour, she rallied: "Let's not get tangled in particulars. I can give you whatever you want. It's up to you to decide what that is and whether you want to accept."

When I didn't respond to that bare offer, she continued: "I gave Vzktkk exactly what he wanted. I reminded him how successful, noble, and generally worthwhile he was. Between what he told me about Pkstzk and what I'd seen of her at work, I could reassure him that any problems in the relationship were completely her fault.

"*That* wasn't a fiction. Their problems really *were* her fault. I doubt you want a full recounting of her flaws, but the chief one was: she was an awful mate. She neglected him. Used him. Took his credit plus kept her own, spending it all with no accounting for where the funds were going. She was away from home more evenings than she was there. It sounded like *she* was the one seeing someone else, rather than him."

I wondered if Shtvtsk knew what she was doing, incriminating Pkstzk. When *I* knew Pkstzk, she was a doting, loyal, supportive mate to my old Pack-mate, Rsspkz. Sure, she was happy to spend every credit Pack Vzrrk collected from our various enterprises, but she spent them *with* Rsspkz. I saw no reason she wouldn't be as devoted to a second mate... unless she was still mated to the first. If she wasn't giving Vzktkk her love, it might mean she was still loyal to her original, imprisoned mate.

Worse, she still might be supporting Rsspkz in one or more ways. Credits can be funneled in and out of prisons, even in a secure, law-abiding city. In Layafflr, the jails have holes only small enough to keep the prisoners from slipping out.

Nathan Large with Laine Megan Lundquist

Frost, Pkstzk could be visiting Rsspkz, in person. She said their mate-ship was canceled when Rsspkz went to prison, but she could have lied. Conjugal visits would explain both her absences and her cool behavior toward Vzktkk.

Shtvtsk was giving me a lot to worry about. She was providing a perspective on Pkstzk that I wouldn't have obtained, otherwise. The value of that information immediately made me doubt its validity.

Shtvtsk could be pointing me toward Pkstzk to divert suspicion away from herself or away from some third party not yet identified. She could be setting up Pkstzk as a suspect out of revenge, spite, or lingering loyalty to her deceased client. She could be biased against Pkstzk from her conversations with Vzktkk. She could even be impugning Pkstzk without any intent to implicate her as a murderer. Sometimes, suspects lie without meaning to.

"So Vzktkk's mate was ignoring him," I summarized, "and you provided what she couldn't. I get that. That's why he was in Isstravil. The problem is, someone *knew* he would be here. You either weren't as discreet as you thought, or else you're a likely suspect: either to shoot him yourself or to advise the killer about Vzktkk's whereabouts."

"Why would I kill Vzktkk?" she countered. "I liked him. More than that, I worked for him. I had no reason to wish him ill."

"No reason that anyone knows about," I persisted. "I could come up with several possible reasons why an escort might have a client killed. Failure to pay. Violent, abusive behavior. Ending the relationship. Getting a better deal from someone who wanted Vzktkk dead and offered to pay for your help."

"You really don't think well of me," Shtvtsk replied, all apparent seriousness. "For someone who doesn't like illusions, you spin a lot of stories. None of those scenarios has any support in fact. Vzktkk paid me well, in credit *and* in trade. *He's* the reason I could leave that housecleaning job without any lingering difficulties… just like he was for Pkstzk. The cleaning company we worked for isn't wholly owned by its public stockholders, if you understand my meaning. It's a difficult employer to leave. Vzktkk made it more trouble for the management to harass me than to let me go peacefully.

Broken Record

"He was nothing but a gentleman. In fact, if he wasn't so honorable, him-self, he would have left Pkstzk several cycles ago. There was no chance he'd end our arrangement. He needed me. I won't claim I would have fought for his life, but I wouldn't want to end it, no matter what I was offered... not that there was anyone offering."

"Hearing more about Vzktkk, I'm even more sorry about his death," I commented. I managed to make the potentially sarcastic comment sound heartfelt.

Shtvtsk gave me a questioning glare but didn't probe further. She remained quiet, creating a silence that stretched uncomfortably until I gave in and spoke.

"So... do you know who *would* want Vzktkk dead?"

She deflated at the question. "The classic detective line. Motive. I can only help you a little there. Vzktkk was getting paranoid the last few times we met: about Pkstzk, about being followed by unnamed persons, about being investigat-ed at work... He thought he was in danger. It turns out he was right. But noth-ing he said to me suggested a threat on his life... just someone looking into his affairs: business and pleasure. I don't suppose that snoop was you? Your turn: how did you get involved with Vzktkk's case?"

I watched her closely. If she had any specific suspicions, she hid them well. I thought about evading her question or lying outright in response, but recog-nized that my most productive response was the truth. I wanted to hear what she thought about...

"Pkstzk," I answered. "Vzktkk's mate asked me to find his killer."

She nodded, as if expecting that answer, but added, "No wonder you're starved for credit, if you're doing charity work. That rktpk doesn't have much left to spend and wouldn't spend much for Vzktkk, so I imagine you're working cheap, if not free. Let me guess: she wants you to get the constables off her tail. It's the only reason I can see her caring about his death. That, or if there's an insurance payment suspended pending the investigation."

Her bitterness didn't seem forced. Maybe Shtvtsk did care about Vzktkk. She certainly had formed a low opinion of his inadequate mate.

Nathan Large with Laine Megan Lundquist

I tried to remain neutral. "I shouldn't comment on my clients, though I realize the hypocrisy in that position. But I *am* keeping a healthy skepticism about Pkstzk's motives, yes. As to what she's paying me... I have practical reasons to keep that confidential, beyond ethics."

"We *are* beyond ethics here, Stchvk," Shtvtsk chittered, quietly. "But I can assume from your reluctance that you know you're getting underpaid. Maybe she's even offered what I offer. I assure you, *my* offer is much more honest. Even if she follows through, I'd be more enjoyable."

She paused as if waiting for my protest, but then continued, "I wouldn't be surprised if Pkstzk was involved in killing Vzktkk. You might have reasons for a different opinion. But I have reasons to think she was checking up on him."

I avoided pointing out how, a decad earlier, Shtvtsk had boasted that Pkstzk knew nothing about her and Vzktkk's liaisons. Instead, I offered a silent vacuum to draw out her thoughts.

She obliged, adding, "I was receiving calls from her this cycle, more frequently than ever before. We maintained social contact after leaving the housekeeping job, but usually only talked a few times a year. In the last week, I talked to her three times, and she seemed very interested in my activities, acquaintances, whereabouts..."

I could see the path she was leading down. I gave her credit: her dialogue was one of the most subtle and thorough indirect accusations I'd ever heard. She never outright said Pkstzk had Vzktkk killed, but suggested it was possible. She hinted at clues and signs. She outlined a scene with Vzktkk as the noble victim and Pkstzk the corrupt villain.

The worst part was that I could believe the scenario she was building. It held just enough correspondence with what I knew – provided I discounted a few personal assumptions about Pkstzk – to take seriously.

The main thing that discouraged me from buying the package was how hard Shtvtsk was selling it. Her insistence sounded like deflection. The fact that she hinted around her point rather than outright arguing it only made me suspect a setup more.

Broken Record

Was Shtvtsk implicating Pkstzk just to hurt an enemy? Or was she building cover for a different murderer? Who? Herself? Someone else of her acquaintance? Another client? She could be selling more services than mate surrogacy.

I did my best to hide my thoughts, as I asked, "And when did you talk to her last?"

Her eyes narrowed. Freeze and crack. Shtvtsk was putting pieces together. I'd fouled enough encounters to know when a suspect was about to shut down.

Abruptly, I felt a wave of vertigo. It felt like the floor had vibrated, slightly. At first, I thought I was suffering from fatigue, anxiety, drug aftereffects, or some combination thereof. I thought: *not now. Not when I need a clear head.*

The shaking intensified. I could tell from Shtvtsk's reaction that she felt it, as well.

"What was that?" I wondered aloud. I started to rise, but was hampered by stabbing pains across my tortured back.

Shtvtsk looked unconcerned. "An earthquake? It wouldn't be the first time the forecasters missed a prediction. Or maybe an aircar went down."

I continued to lever myself upright. Shtvtsk put out a hand, either to help me up or nudge me back down. I didn't find out which. As she moved, I had a sudden thought: *Tskksk. FROST.*

I straightened with agonizing speed. My pain could wait. If Tskksk was in trouble, it was my fault. If she wasn't, I still couldn't take the chance to ignore that possibility. I shrugged away from Shtvtsk, forcing myself to move. It was possible I was already too late, that Tskksk was already incinerated. The thought only drove me harder. If the worst had befallen, I could at least observe the scene and maybe catch the culprits nearby.

My pain didn't want to wait. Whether it was the sudden movement or the drugs wearing off, my leg flared like it had been shot anew. My arm joined in, wailing its own protest. I staggered as Shtvtsk reached out, supporting me under my good arm.

"What's wrong?" she asked. I was hurting so badly, I couldn't analyze her reaction for genuine concern.

I pulled away from her, another unconsidered move. I headed toward the door, calling back, "The people who tried to kill me. They might be back."

Her response as I opened the door nearly made me stop and turn around: "Why go out to meet them, then? Stay here, where they won't look... where it's safe. Why would you need to go out there? Unless there's someone else you're afraid for? Who are you running to save, Stchvk?"

Even in my haste and distraction, I heard enough of her parting words to file away for later digestion. Why would she think I was going to rescue someone? Was she just making a general assumption about my altruistic nature? Or did she have someone specific in mind... someone she shouldn't know about?

Chapter 17 - Out of Business

I half-hobbled, half-fell down the stairs. Halfway down, I realized I could have taken the elevator. Shtvtsk's copied key would grant me access. But by then, it was already too late to bother. Changing direction would waste more time.

I admit, I was beating myself up on purpose, self-flagellating for assumed harm to Tskksk. If I crippled myself in the effort to rescue her, it was less than I deserved, especially if she died.

Flashbacks to my old Pack-mate, Fzpktk, crept in: she had been shot by constables in the aftermath of a job gone bad, the one that put Rsspkz in prison. I hadn't caused that death, but I hadn't stopped it, either. I hadn't participated in the fatal operation, but I let them take the job without protest. I owned some part of the blame for two deaths there: Fzpktk and the victim she shot first.

My guilt was even greater in Tskksk's case. I knew I was putting her at risk. I persisted, even so, discounting the hazard and ranking it below my own needs

My worst fears were confirmed as I stumbled out of the apartment building's front door. Flickering light poured down the street from the electronics store. Smoke funneled upward to cloud the narrow strip of sky above. I could hear the crackle of flames and the bursts of smaller secondary explosions.

I could only hope Tskksk wasn't in the building when the blast went off. I suspected, though I hadn't confirmed, that she lived upstairs in the same building as her shop. Maybe she was out visiting, drinking... anything. She had already lost her business and her livelihood. I only prayed she hadn't lost her life.

As I fought my body, begging it to move faster down the street, I really did pray. I offered a desperate sapient's honest prayers: to the Ancestors, to my totem, Kktkrkz, and to any gods or goddesses who cared to listen. I asked them to protect Tskksk, the way I hadn't.

Nathan Large with Laine Megan Lundquist

I was nearly there. I could see the storefront, shattered and vomiting fire. This explosion hadn't been a concussive blast, like the one used at my apartment. It was incendiary, deliberately destructive, not just murderous. Either the culprit wanted to make sure Tskksk was wiped out financially, in case they missed wiping her out personally... or just as likely, they were destroying evidence.

A few other sapients stood on the street near me. I thought I recognized a small Herd of Taratumm from my earlier canvas of the neighborhood. They hadn't told me much. I hoped that if *did* know something related to my case, they were stewing in guilt.

Probably not. Most of the residents, including the handful emerging to check on the explosion, were clueless about the criminal activities around them. Besides being workaday sorts who barely noticed the world outside of their home and workplace, Isstravil's inhabitants were more likely to ignore trouble, as if denying problems would make them disappear.

At least my neighborhood... my old neighborhood... acknowledged its evils, even if the residents couldn't or wouldn't do anything about them. Or *were* the evils, themselves.

Along with the strangers, I noticed that Shtvtsk had followed me downstairs and outside. Funny thing to do if she was worried about assassins. She'd probably claim to be concerned for my safety. Totally noble, no ulterior motive.

I didn't spare her enough attention to discern her thoughts I pushed myself as close to the burning storefront as I could bear, the raging heat prickling at my face and wounds.

As far as I could tell, there was no safe approach. The back of the building seemed less damaged than the front, but I'd have to go around the block to check for a rear door. The thought of that walk was almost more than I could stand.

I almost *couldn't* stand. My leg wanted to rest, if not separate itself from the rest of my body. It was justified if it wanted to revoke its support.

My thoughts were wobbling just as much. My brain was an electrochemical chaos. I was having trouble focusing on a single line of thought, much less a plan of action. I thought of the stolen memory beads, mourning the loss of my only substantial lead, then immediately afterward chided myself for thinking that way when Tskksk was probably dead.

Where were the fire crews? For that matter, why wasn't the fire suppressant system in Tskksk's building reducing the fire, if not putting it out already? How had the fire gotten so powerful, so fast? There were methods of packing a lot of accelerant into a small package, but that still didn't explain why I wasn't seeing foam, powder, or at minimum, water sprays cutting into the inferno. Frost, *my* building had decent fire control, and I was sure the builders cut so many corners it was practically a sphere.

Was it possible to sabotage a fire suppressant system? Short of cutting the water supply or sabotaging the sensors, I couldn't think of a way to prevent countermeasures. Had the arsonist been that thorough? I couldn't imagine Tskksk would miss such extensive remodeling inside her shop, awake or asleep. The thought encouraged my hope that she was elsewhere.

But then, if the intruder could break in and stay inside so long, why blow up the building? Why not steal everything – memory beads, compads, paperwork, whatever – and avoid a spectacle? Why not kill Tskksk more quietly?

This attack was a message: maybe a warning to me, certainly a pointed threat to Tskksk. Who knew, maybe it was aimed at Shtvtsk, separately or inclusively.

I wanted to rush in and see what could be saved, but my last vestiges of good sense teamed up with my sensory nerves and kept me from any potentially fatal acts. Instead, I waited, and watched. I flattered myself that I was being a better observer than the gawkers. I was paying attention to the little things.

Those little things kept battering against my scattered mind. Why? Why blow it up? Why wasn't the fire going out? What did Shtvtsk know about this? Why Tskksk? What did they know, and how? Why destroy *this* evidence and not the pet store? Would I find the pet store empty and scrubbed clean? Even if so, why go subtle there and explosive here?

If Pkstzk was at the root of this trouble, how would she know where I was or who I was talking to? The question answered itself, if she already knew to watch

Isstravil for my presence. She could have a confederate in the neighborhood, possibly a resident. Paranoia is only a problem if you give it too much freedom. Sometimes, though, it gives accurate warnings.

Having Shtvtsk standing close behind me was only adding to my paranoia. Her disparagement toward Pkstzk could be cover for an alliance with the other female. Or, she could be the local agent for another mastermind... of what?

What, Stchvk? What convoluted scheme were these two females supposedly hatching, and why does that plot hypothetically include the remainder of Pack Vzrrk? Maybe Shtvtsk was actually Tklth, after extensive plastic surgery and mental reconditioning. In the absence of evidence or judgment, it was just as plausible a theory as any other.

I stood there staring, shaking, wanting to run somewhere... forward, backward, sideways... it didn't matter. I'd never been so miserable before in my life.

That's saying something. On really bad days, I've seen my own protruding viscera. Physical pain, even the pain of impending death, is nothing compared to the horror of failure, grand failure so vast that it causes deaths, lets killers run free, and leaves you baffled and snapping at empty air.

I heard Shtvtsk step forward, claws clicking against the heated pavement. I willed her not to touch me, not to even speak. Hurt as I was, I might lash out at her, verbally or physically. In my pain and confusion, I was the basic, undecorated Stchvk: protector, hunter, fighter, survivor. She did *not* want to become a threat.

Shtvtsk started to say: "Stchvk, you should..." I didn't get to hear her advice. Instead, a more welcome voice overrode her.

"Stchvk!" I heard. A young female shouted from somewhere behind us, down the block, at the intersection past the apartment building. The sound was distant, but very loud, and it sounded like...

"Tskksk!" I called back, turning to see her sprinting up the sidewalk toward me. "Thank the gods!"

Broken Record

Her crest rose high as she crossed the last few meters, stopping a meter short of me. "Thank my grumbling gut. I was out for dinner when I heard the place had gone up. It had to be…"

Then she stopped, noticing Shtvtsk close behind me, paying attention to our conversation. Other bystanders had turned to listen upon hearing her shout, but Tskksk realized that this strange female was 'with' me.

"Hello," she began again, weakly. "You look familiar. Are you one of my customers?"

Clever girl. Don't assume, don't imply, don't give anything away. My relief at Tskksk's safety was doubled by a feeling of undeserved pride. I could pick the good ones. Maybe someday, one of them would pick me back.

Shtvtsk narrowed her eyes as she answered: "No, just a neighbor." She made a formal bow of greeting. "I'm glad to see you weren't harmed, Tskksk."

Her formality was made strange by the flickering firelight behind us, the remnants of Tskksk's property going to ash. The heat and light from the blaze washed over us. In fact, once Tskksk was there, we didn't have a reason to stand so close anymore.

Another concern: "Tskksk. Is there anyone else in your building?"

She waved negation. "No, I own the whole thing. Owned. Frost!" She blinked rapidly, shifting from foot to foot in distress. The reality of her loss was starting to sink in. I struggled past my own agony and agitation, preparing to support her when the emotional crisis crested.

"Good," I answered. "I know this is difficult, but we should probably move back. It isn't safe this close, and the fire responders should be here soon. We don't want to be in the way."

Both females stared at me in surprise. They didn't argue with my sudden outbreak of sensible caution, though. They backpedaled down the sidewalk, away from the burning building. I followed, forward and at a reduced pace. I wanted to pass out, but fought back until I was certain the crisis was over.

"The fire teams should *be* here already," Tskksk wondered, echoing my thoughts. "What's keeping them? For that matter, how did it get this bad already? My suppression system was just inspected. My insurer is going to own that fire protection company… and my security provider, too."

"Either they're all incompetent… or whoever caused this fire was more competent," I suggested, watching Shtvtsk's reaction.

Shtvtsk didn't even blink. She asked, "Do you think this was deliberate? Not an accident?"

Of course, I thought it was deliberate. I'd said as much when I fled her apartment. She was acting for Tskksk's benefit. Why? No reason for that on my account. Was she playing dumb for the other female? Come to think of it, she hadn't introduced herself or explained her proximity to me. I'd see how she liked being on the receiving end of someone else's game.

"Tskksk, this is Shtvtsk. She lives and works on Kzk Tsstkt, too. We were discussing Vzktkk's murder. I think she might have given me some ideas about what happened."

Tskksk looked closer at Shtvtsk, as we paused ten meters further away from her burning store. She kept up the charade like a pro: "Ttt, great. You know, I wished I could have been more helpful, when you came around earlier… and now I really wish I could help you catch these nest-foulers. If you think it's related, that is. Would they really come after me just for talking to you? Is Shtvtsk in danger, too?"

Her mock concern was a thing of beauty. Yes, I realize that I'm praising the qualities in Tskksk that I criticized in Shtvtsk. I'm a self-aware hypocrite.

But to be fair, Tskksk's performance was that of a talented amateur achieving beyond her training, while Shtvtsk was a seasoned pro barely giving it her best. I expected less of the former and more of the latter. Plus, Tskksk was obfuscating *for* me, rather than against me. Like I said, self-aware hypocrite.

The contrast between the two females was further highlighted as we stood together: Shtvtsk, tall, pale, slender and muscled, with bright clear eyes and an aura of confident, calculating hedonism. Tskksk, shorter, mottled, rounder and softer, younger and more innocent despite her attempts at clever subterfuge.

Shtvtsk didn't venture a response to Tskksk's provocation. She only looked at me closely, searching my reactions for a clue. I watched her, in turn.

I nudged a little more. "Possibly, but I think there's a difference. I talked to Shtvtsk, here, just like I talked to a hundred others in Isstravil. Nobody else was targeted. I think they went after you to destroy your evidence."

I confused both Tskksk and Shtvtsk. Tskksk was probably wondering why I'd given away our secret. Shtvtsk was hopefully wondering what evidence I meant. Did she guess I might mean *her* evidence?

Shtvtsk broke first. "Evidence? You mean you know something about Vzk-tkk's murder? Why didn't you mention that before?"

I couldn't tell if her offense was real or manufactured. I was starting not to care. But complacency was as dangerous as pain, if it led to inattention. I fought to control my reactions and my phrasing.

"Don't be upset," I chided her, as calmly as I could. "We just hadn't gotten to that part of the conversation. To be honest, I wanted to see if your observations matched Tskksk's, before I biased your memory with what I knew."

Her expression could have started another fire. She stared lasers into my eyes, barely managing her own agitation.

"I see. That's fair, I suppose. But you'll understand if I feel misled. I thought *I* was your best lead, perhaps your only one. But I see now that you had multiple *leads*. I'm sure you had the best of reasons for deceiving me."

I wanted to laugh. Her entendres were too absurd given our surroundings. Her attempt to sound like a jilted lover was more farce than fury.

The urge to laugh piled up against my restraint, a hysterical pressure. I fought hard to keep my beak still and my crest low. As much as I hate to taint a suspect, as much as the circumstances forbid humor, as much as I wanted to curl up next to Shtvtsk and play house… it was funny to see her implode. She was realizing just how little her hard work had accomplished with me.

Not nothing. She had gotten some information out of me. And to be fair, I hadn't gotten that much out of her… but I knew she was involved. I knew she was thick with Pkstzk. I could build on that foundation.

I got the feeling Shtvtsk knew much more than she would ever reveal voluntarily. She certainly wanted me under control, preferably pointed away from her and toward some target. I knew where I wanted to look, instead… and as soon as I could act, I would be moving in the right direction, for a change.

It was a frosted shame to lose those memory beads, not to mention Tskksk's whole store. Still, she didn't sound too worried; she might come out of the situation all right. I might manage, myself. Even without the hard evidence, I might pull out a win, after all.

As Shtvtsk and I stared each other down, Tskksk hissed in discomfort, drawing our attention. The younger female actually stepped backward at the intensity in Shtvtsk's eyes.

She looked embarrassed at interrupting, but explained herself: "I can keep an eye on things from here, if you need to get back to your conversation. It's not like we can do anything to put out the fire, by ourselves."

She wasn't being sarcastic. There literally wasn't any way we could deal with the fire. We were miles from any open water. A few buckets filled from taps weren't going to make a dent in that conflagration. Portable extinguishers would be equally impotent. Unless someone had an industrial wrench handy, we weren't going to be tapping into the water mains. The fire responders usually used chemical suppressants, anyway.

If the fire crews would just get there… and there they were. As I strained to listen, I was rewarded by the screech of sirens. All hail the rescuers, finally arrived.

Hearing the approaching vehicles, the crowd started to disperse. Some, only there to make sure the blaze wasn't going to spread to their homes, hurried back inside to barricade themselves against smoke and chemical dust. Others just backed away, continuing to watch but staying out of the way.

Broken Record

The remainder probably wouldn't move even for the authorities, but followed their more responsible neighbors to the opposite side of the street. Sometimes, herd mentality does cause better behavior.

Large aircars dropped into the urban canyon, taking the center of the roadway for themselves, cutting off the spectators from the burning storefront. Even before they landed, firefighters started lobbing powder bombs at the front of the building, pushing the flames back to give themselves a wider safe area for offloading. The fire team, mostly Vislin with a couple of Taratumm, wore full-body environmental suits with air filters, looking like the first explorers on a toxic planet or ancient heat-suited night warriors.

The three of us stood uncomfortably, watching the assault get underway. I started to reply to Tskksk: "They might need you, once the fire is out. I guess we should get back..."

Shtvtsk interrupted to say, "That's all right. I think we were nearly done, anyway, and this commotion exhausted me. You're probably about ready to drop, too, Stchvk. If you can get yourself safely back home, I'll bid you a good night?"

She was leaving a tail-tip close enough for me to nip. I thought about jumping for it, trying to salvage her good graces and maybe even recouping enough credit to get into her nest for the night. Then, I realized that the mental effort would be more painful and tiring than sleeping on my bare floor.

I nodded and gave her a parting bow. "That sounds fair. I can get back, no problem. Have a good night... sorry to drag you out on my tail."

On the surface, our words were polite, neutral, maybe even slightly friendly. But underneath was a growing chill. Shtvtsk might not have tagged me as an enemy yet, but I wasn't the friend she hoped for. That was a shame on several levels. Though, if she was the kind of operator I suspected, I didn't want to be that sort of friend. I'd had *Pack* like her, and I wasn't scrambling to get back into their company. I could live without Shtvtsk's attentions.

That didn't stop me from watching her tail, regretfully, as she walked away.

For all her troubles, Tskksk wasn't distracted enough to miss my interest. She asked, quietly, "*Did* I intrude on something?"

I gestured for her to hold her beak tight a little longer. Shtvtsk was still close enough to overhear, even with the noise of the fire and its circling opponents.

Tskksk turned away and started to walk toward the fire vehicles. I followed her a little way. When I felt that we had enough distance between us and Shtvtsk, I answered Tskksk's question.

"You didn't intrude, but this fire did break up a very interesting conversation. She's definitely involved with the case. She knew both the victim and his mate. I was just getting to the details of that association when we heard the blast... although, I'm not sure she was going to give up anything substantial."

"Kkk, I wonder about that. You look like you wanted something from her."

My visible pain came from more than just injuries. "I'd like to say I was playing along to keep her interested..."

"But so was she," Tskksk finished. "It's fine. I get it. You're working on something important, but distractions happen."

I suddenly wanted her good opinion back, in a very different way than I wanted Shtvtsk's approval. But unlike the glib banter I offered upstairs, I found myself unable to choose the right words to appeal to Tskksk. Such a great manipulator, Stchvk, until it actually matters.

Tskksk's expression softened and she turned to look at me more closely. "You look like a mess, actually. I'd offer you a place to sit down and clean up, but..." She gestured toward the dwindling flames. The gutted storefront poured out more smoke than light, and responders were entering the space that once held tables and compads.

"I was actually thinking of offering you a place, but it's just a place. I don't even have a nest to offer, inappropriately." I winced at my weak attempt at humor. My stress hormones were definitely wearing off. My focus was getting sharper, but my strength was fading fast. I shivered, a reaction Tskksk couldn't miss.

Broken Record

She also interpreted it correctly. "You idiot. You came out here to help and you can barely stand, yourself. All right, time to turn to Pack."

She hissed, resigned to further difficulty. "Sit down, stay here, and I'll make a few calls."

Tskksk pulled out her compad and scrolled through her contacts. She added, while she searched, "I don't suppose you have family or Pack to stay with... otherwise you'd already have called them, yourself."

I dipped my crest and claws in shamed negation. "I've been isolated for years. No sympathy needed. I lost one Pack and haven't been able to replace them."

"Well, I might want to lose mine, but that's just childish spite talking. I love the idiots and they love me, but... you'll see. We're very different sorts, which Pack-bond didn't take into account. Just promise me you won't talk business while we're visiting them?"

"That's an easy promise," I agreed, while slumping against a wall, my tail pinned awkwardly against the concrete. "Right now, I don't want to *think* about this case for a while. Enough time to start chasing leads again tomorrow. If you can get me a nest and a meal, I won't say a single word for hours. Promise. And for me, that's a big concession."

"I can hear that. Now shut up and rest." She tapped the dial button and waited while her compad rang the number.

I had a sudden worrisome thought: "Wait. Will we be putting your Pack at risk? Maybe I shouldn't go anywhere."

She looked at the 'pad, then at me, then muted the call at her end before the other party picked up. "Stop being stupid. I wouldn't ask them if I didn't think they'd accept the risk. And I'm not about to let you stay around here given the circumstances. We're both safer somewhere else. You think you're the only one with noble ideals? Let me worry about your safety for a change, hero."

"Fine, fine," I assented, spreading my claws in surrender. She had me figured out, better than Shtvtsk managed.

As her contact answered, Tskksk exchanged greetings and then explained the situation. She told the other party that she'd had a building fire and couldn't sleep at home that night. It sounded like my explanation to the landlady, even down to the complaints about building safety and the downplaying of any sinister causes. Her audience clacked loudly, irritated, but agreed to make space for her at his home.

When Tskksk indicated that "a friend" was also homeless as a result of the fire, she received some protest in return. "We're not operating a charity," was one warning I heard, along with: "Why help this person? Do you know him well? Why hasn't the Pack met him before?"

Tskksk waved off the interrogation, explaining that I was a new neighbor, a coincidental victim of the same disaster, and that she felt obligated to help me out, considering that the fire started in her store.

This explanation earned her another lecture about her poor building maintenance and the mistake of buying the building in the first place and why couldn't she have just contributed to the farmstead like everyone else...

Farmers. Sss, blight the fields and Kktkrkz trample the rest. We were going to the great green wilderness. No wonder Tskksk lived apart from her Pack. She was a tech-trading city lizard among dirt-crusted country folk. I supposed I'd be getting my claws dirty. Hopefully they could send the wagon around to haul us to the backwoods.

Tskksk managed to end the conversation on an agreeable note. We'd have to take public mass transport to reach the Pack's farmstead, but we were welcome there, both of us, for as long as we needed to recuperate... and if Tskksk wanted, she could stay there like she should have in the first place.

My heart went out to her. My Pack-less life suddenly looked less bleak. Imagine being bonded to someone like that, whose idea of supporting and defending you meant warning you away from all your choices and trying to convince you to follow *their* plan for your life, instead.

My thoughts must have shown as Tskksk hung up her call. She said, "At least, he means well. Fsktcht is the most solid, reliable Vislin I know, just..."

Broken Record

"Righteous," I offered.

"Always right, yes," she confirmed.

"I can't criticize. Literally. I'm almost asleep here. Mind if I doze while you call for transport?"

"Just don't pass out. I think I could lift you, but I'd rather not. I'm almost ready to collapse, myself."

"Do my best. And thanks. You shouldn't be doing any of this for me."

"Shut up, Fsktcht."

As I drifted off, I grumbled a last thought: "You might want to keep an eye on any bystanders. One of them could be the arsonist or a lookout for them. Seeing if you survived. Confirming the damage."

"Kkk, you're still working, even half-awake. All right, I'll take a look. I wish I could go inside and see how bad the losses are."

"No chance. Arson investigation. Insurance. Owner never gets to go in until afterward, then escorted," I slurred, struggling to get the thoughts out. "Besides, you don't want to see. It hurts."

"It already hurts. It won't be any easier later, either," she answered as she wandered away.

Her voice changed tone as she added: "At least I didn't lose everything."

Her humor caught my dwindling attention. "What do you mean?"

She shook her compad pouch, producing a musical rattle like crystalline beads bouncing together. "We've still got your lead. We can spend our time in the country copying and reading the contents."

I managed to crack one eye and stare at her. My crest bounded upward. I got my beak open enough to say, "Be my mate?"

She didn't respond, but her embarrassed pleasure was evident. I lapsed into unconsciousness with that beautiful sight lingering in my memory.

Chapter 18 - Rude Awakening

It wasn't until I woke up again that I connected my sudden fatigue with the string of previous slumps.

I came back confused at first. I smelled smoke and acrid chemicals. The wind whipped around me, carrying the lingering chill of dawn. There were a few sounds of machinery, but otherwise, my surroundings were quiet.

As I roused further, my body reported its complaints. My tail was numb from being pinned against a cold concrete sidewalk. My back ached, both from the shotgun wounds and my uncomfortable sleeping position. When I struggled to sit upright, my perforated arm protested, too.

I rolled gingerly to my knees, sparing my lower legs as much as I could. When I finally got my eyes open, I received a double shock. First, I was still on the street, Kzk Tsstkt in Isstravil. Second, nobody else was on the street with me.

The fire crews had finished and gone. The neighbors who stuck around to watch were long gone, in bed or off to work. There weren't even any constables or investigators lingering to search the site. A plastic and wire barricade closed off the front of Tskksk's gutted storefront, warning away intruders with the threat of trespass charges.

And Tskksk... Tskksk was gone. Why had she gone without waking me?

My first coherent thought was that she must have been called away somewhere urgent. Into the store to retrieve her personal effects, under constable guard? To an aircar depot, if she couldn't get pickup from the street? Maybe to a pharmacy, to get supplies for me? The worst thing I could imagine was that she had been arrested, charged with arson for insurance fraud. That would be brutally unfair: to have someone destroy your business and then get accused of the crime yourself.

Broken Record

I struggled to override my protesting flesh and stand upright, intending to search for Tskksk. As I sat straighter, my compad chimed. I pulled it out and tapped the screen awake. I didn't recognize the caller code. My first assumption was that it was Tskksk, calling to let me know where she'd gone. We'd never called one another, so neither I nor my compad knew her code.

I accepted the call and was relieved to see Tskksk's face. Then, I processed her expression, and my heart sank. She looked miserable: crest flat, eyes dry, scales rippling with fearful patterns. When she spoke, her voice was tentative and quiet.

"Stchvk. I'm so sorry…" She sounded close to despair. What had the constables done to her? I swelled with anger, imagining a righteous rampage into the nearest precinct house.

"Tskksk…" I started, but she spoke again before I could reassure her.

"They found me. They were watching, just like you said. I should have believed you. They took me right off the street… threatened your life if I didn't come quietly."

Shock kept me listening to her rambling words. Finally, I asked, "Who? Who took you?"

"I'm not sure," she answered. "But they're working with whoever killed Vzktkk. I was told to tell you hello from the Pack… I'm not sure what that means. Your Pack?"

I wanted to vomit onto the pavement. Considering I hadn't eaten in over a day, that wouldn't accomplish much. The small blessings of starvation.

Pack Vzrrk. Bring on the Ice Age. How in the glaciated wastes were those egg-swallowing monsters involved with this mess? And what did they want with Tskksk?

She answered my question by holding up a small scrap of vellum, an archaic medium still handy for simple notes. "They gave me instructions to read to you. I have to say it exactly as it's written… and you have to do what I say… or they'll kill me. Stchvk… I think they're serious."

"Of course, they're serious. Just tell me what it says. I'm listening." I tried to reassure her, but felt only devastation. I could only imagine what her kidnappers might want... nothing good.

She read: "Stchvk. We have your friend. She will die if you do not do as told."

Tskksk paused to swallow, still struggling with her terror. She continued: "You will set up Shtvtsk for the murder of Vzktkk. Go to the pet trader's store and search the back room for a panel in the floor. Inside you will find the murder weapon. Plant it in Shtvtsk's apartment with her genetic material on the handle. You will find a way to obtain a suitable sample."

Tskksk twitched, writhing from the same nausea I felt. These demands weren't just criminal; they were twisted and evil.

She finished reading: "Don't worry; no rktpk will attack you this time. Call this number back when you are finished. Do not get caught. Do not tell anyone else what you are doing. The constables will arrive once you are done, tipped off about where to go. Your case will be solved, your friend returned, and everyone will be satisfied. Or you can fail and disappoint everyone."

Tskksk paused to breathe after she was done. Then she inhaled, starting to say something off-script. I heard: "Stchvk, you can't..." before a hand reached in from off-camera and cut the call.

I fought the urge to slam down my compad in frustration. I prayed, internally but with thunderous force, that no harm would befall Tskksk. Despite my injuries, I would pursue her kidnappers relentlessly, doubly so if they became her murderers.

But who were "they"? There was no one left from Pack Vzrrk at liberty, except myself. Even if you counted hangers-on, they were all accounted for, including Pkstzk.

Pkstzk. Shtvtsk had pointed at Vzktkk's mate, suggesting that she was still connected to her former mate, my Pack-mate Rsspkz. Maybe Pkstzk was behind this effort to point the claw back at Shtvtsk. Pkstzk could be the pivot point between all my recent troubles and Pack Vzrrk. She might have hired me intending to use me to implicate Shtvtsk, all along, then shifted to a more direct approach when that plan was interrupted...

Wait. Why, then, did someone try to kill her, me, or both of us? Maybe Pkstzk wasn't responsible for Vzktkk's death or Tskksk's kidnapping or any of it

I tried out a few other hypotheses, using my fear hormones for something useful. Maybe there was another faction involved, one opposing Pkstzk and me by extension. Maybe Rsspkz was reaching out from prison and trying to destroy both us "traitors". Maybe Pkstzk was acting on behalf of Pack Vzrrk, but hired me to this mockery of a case as part of an elaborate revenge scheme... against *me*. When the conspirators couldn't kill me, they created a setup to ruin me, instead.

At least, the effort to frame Shtvtsk told me she *wasn't* Vzktkk's killer. Or was she? Whoever took Tskksk might be trying to make sure the real killer would be identified.

Why was I even assuming Tskksk really *was* kidnapped? She could have been part of the scheme from the very beginning, inventing evidence to point me toward Shtvtsk... no, wait. I'd never mentioned any problems with my old Pack to her, just that I "lost" their association. Even if I assumed she was a great actress, reading off a letter she herself had written, she shouldn't have known to mention the Pack as a threat. I couldn't discard the theory, but it had big holes.

All these spiraling, branching, mutually inconsistent threads wrapped around my brain and squeezed. The resulting headache just added to all my other pains, opposing my efforts to stand up. At that rate, I wasn't rescuing... or incriminating... anyone.

I rummaged through my pockets and found the pill bottle. I supposed I was past due for another dose, but my reliance on the drug was starting to bother me. Even if the stuff wasn't physically addictive, I was psychologically reliant on it. Once again, a few hectads after choking down a tablet, my various aches faded to a manageable thrum of muted protest.

In addition to the strange drug, I had continuing bouts of unconsciousness and my injuries themselves to consider. I felt like I was reaching a critical mass of inexplicability.

I'd had some very eventful, very strange days in my past, but nothing like the last few days. Even if my body held up, my mind was getting exhausted by all the threats, changes, and yes, even my sudden wealth of love interests.

Plus, there were other weird elements: the previous case that I somehow failed, but couldn't quite remember how. Hearing from Pkstzk after so long. The starving rktpk behind a locked door in the pet store. The life-saving grav lift in the closet at Taburket's. My amazing escape and minimal injuries. The missing video of my attackers. My unexpected release from hospital and constabulary custody. Avoiding the bomb at my apartment because my key was in the wrong pocket. Meeting my neighboring Pack for the very first time. The whole business with tracing the compad calls... an investigative tool I'd never heard about before. And last, the byplay between Shtvtsk and Tskksk, followed by Tskksk's immaculate kidnapping.

All of it together was enough to make me suspicious of the world in general, like everyone was in on a joke at my expense. I couldn't keep thinking that way, though. There existed an underlying explanation for everything... or most of it, anyway, with the rest covered by coincidence and my distracted attention. Whether or not I discovered that explanation, it had to exist.

What was I going to do, first? At that moment, just staying upright and moving somewhere safer seemed like enough challenge. I should get indoors. It was nearing dawn. If I hadn't already drawn suspicion by sleeping on the street, continuing to loiter would definitely get me arrested as a vagrant. As a starting point, I stumbled toward my apartment building.

And then, Stchvk? Come on, you have a serious problem and limited resources.

The easy route, believe it or not, was to frame Shtvtsk as instructed. Tskksk's kidnapper was right: I had the skills to pull it off, maybe even to make the setup stick. Plus, with a clear culprit, almost everyone would be happier: I'd get paid,

Broken Record

Pkstzk would be satisfied, Tskksk would be saved… maybe. Only Shtvtsk would suffer. And justice. Justice would get laid out, bleeding.

It wouldn't be her first beating, nor her last, nor her hundred-thousandth, not in Layafflr City. She might already be dead, for all I'd seen. But I hated the thought of joining the horde slashing her apart, whether living or corpse. I'd be killing more than a concept. I'd be killing my image of myself.

Without Pack, without mate, without much achievement to speak of, all I *had* were my solved cases. I needed a little truth and the feeling that I was making some difference in the world. The detective job started as a salve to my guilt about my many crimes with Pack Vzrrk, but grew into something bigger over the years. Even if there wasn't a job title and license attached to what I did, I'd probably still do it, at least until I got arrested.

The problem was, if I refused the "easy way" and avoided framing Shtvtsk, then I had to live with whatever happened to Tskksk. Her death would be another injustice. I could pretend her murder wasn't my fault – that it was the responsibility of whoever held her – but that was a dodge. Once I involved Tskksk, I should have protected her identity, if not also her physical self. Now that she was deeper into my mess, I had a duty to rescue her.

Some rescuer. Besides being half-crippled, I had no weapon. I also had no idea where Tskksk could be, much less who, specifically, she was with. Any ideas about a roaring rampage of revenge were squashed by those heavy realities.

The constables might be able to track her down using clues from the scene of the kidnapping. Surely, there had been at least one witness who saw the sapient who led her away after threatening me, presumably both at gunpoint. Given time and a little luck, I could probably put the pieces together by myself.

I had very little time. I suspected, also, that any efforts to search for Tskksk would agitate her captors. While I paused in the lobby of my building, I started to come to terms with the idea that I couldn't solve this case. Either give in and frame Shtvtsk or stand by my principles and consider Tskksk their sacrifice.

Maybe I could set up Shtvtsk as requested, then turn myself in to the constables after Tskksk was released? I'd be finished, professionally, but if the kidnappers were honest about letting Tskksk go, it would be worth my own sacrifice.

They might not, of course. They might kill her, me, Pkstzk, and any other loose threads who jeopardized a neat conclusion. If they abductors did renege on their offer to release Tskksk, though, I'd have no reason not to enlist the constables and/or go after them on my own. I felt confident I could eventually track down the egg-suckers responsible, previous failures notwithstanding.

I went to the elevator and spent a long, stupid decad trying to convince it to take me to the fourth floor. Eventually, I remembered that my key was still coded for Shtvtsk's apartment on the third floor. The elevator wouldn't allow me access elsewhere.

I sighed heavily. Either I'd have to forgo resting at home, or else I'd have to recode the key for my own door, then swap it back to Shtvtsk's coding... and there was a chance that with all that manipulation, I might just burn out the device entirely.

I stepped back out of the elevator and sat down on the bottom stair, trying to rally my thoughts enough to settle on a definite plan of action.

My head was settled into my hands. I heard the voice before seeing its owner.

"Detective Stchvk? I thought I saw you outside, earlier."

I didn't want to look up. I recognized the thick, forceful, accented tones that battered me in the hospital.

"Detective Nrissilli," I muttered from between my palms. "What an unexpected pleasure."

"Hrrrm. An obvious arson happens a few blocks away from the site of my murder investigation. Witnesses identify a bandaged male Vislin, who matches the description of an attempted murder victim: also my case. He's been seen going in and out of the bombed store, recently. All this happens in the course of just a few days. Are you really going to call my presence unexpected?"

Broken Record

I raised my claws skyward and looked up with a supreme effort. "You got me. I defied your orders. But in my defense, I needed somewhere new to live and it seemed convenient to move closer to my troubles."

"I saw that," Nrissilli confirmed, not unkindly. She was dressed in a more conventional uniform, a one-piece tube shift with short sleeves and belts to carry various tools: a miniature compad, a stun-prod similar to Tskksk's civilian version, adhesive restraints, and a few other devices I couldn't immediately identify.

Compared to her hospital visit, she was more obviously on-the-job as a constable. She also looked exhausted, with red rings around her eyes and patches of ruffled fur she hadn't had time to groom.

I also noticed that she smelled like smoke and chemicals. She had been working the arson.

"I didn't think anyone died in that fire outside... why is a murder detective investigating it personally?" I ventured aloud.

"Attempted murder still counts," she snapped back. "Unless you think the owner set the place aflame herself? There was plenty of evidence that the safety systems were sabotaged."

I might not appreciate Nrissilli's presence, but she gave up information more easily than any of my other current adversaries. I was right that the fire was uncontrolled.

"I don't really know the owner that well," I started, then raised a claw to forestall the detective's protest. "All right, I met her. I talked to her. She gave me some information and ideas about how to pursue my case... details about the neighborhood. She had the call data, but you already have that. I also talked to another dozen sapients all over the area, including another store owner... all *before* you warned me away... and none of them were threatened."

"*But* you talked to Tskksk again, more recently. As in, yesterday. Don't even try denying it, we have witnesses and video. And yes, only she was targeted. Thus far. So, what else did you *discuss* with her that was more important than what you learned from anyone else? Was she involved with the murder? Or was this just about the call recordings?"

I tried to raise my crest and pretend humor: "No. I considered her more important since none of my other informants was an attractive young female. You remember, you gave me permission to warn her, after I was attacked?"

"I said you could warn your client, while quitting the case. We were going to handle any contacts with this Tskksk. You're already up for arrest for interference, defying a direct order to abandon your investigation. I'm wondering if I should add charges of willful endangerment... or accessory to a crime."

I stared her down, crest dipping involuntarily. "I was *not* involved with that explosion. I came outside after it happened, like everyone else living here. When I saw where it was, I wanted to help... but there was nothing I could do."

"You can relax on that count. We know when you showed up. We also know Tskksk wasn't hurt. Neighbors spotted her, too. In fact, they said you were talking with her and *another* attractive, if not young, female, on the street. So much for two more lies. I'm serious now, 'detective' Stchvk. Start giving me something real, or you're coming to the precinct, bandages and all. For starters, *where is Tskksk?*"

Frost. Frostfrostfrostfrost. If I didn't get past this interrogation, I'd lose my last choice out of my few remaining options. If I was arrested, I couldn't frame Shtvtsk. I could either say nothing and wait out Tskksk's death in a cell, or else spill to the constables and then pray they were competent enough to find Tskksk before she died. Either way, I was finished as an investigator. This wasn't one of those situations where the law would look the other way.

How could I satisfy Nrissilli enough to remain free, even if I used that freedom to pervert justice afterward? Even on my best, most clear-minded day, I might be challenged to outwit a seasoned Hrotata investigator. Right then – fatigued, drugged, and wracked by events – I could barely tell *myself* a coherent story, much less weave a tale to fool an expert.

I started to stand, hoping to forestall her with bluster and maybe a little sympathy. Maybe I could plead for a few hours' rest before I laid out the details. My memory was hazy from all the beatings, that kind of thing.

Broken Record

Then, as I got upright and swayed, my shakiness proved my inspiration. I made as if to take a step toward the wall for support, then completely failed to make contact. Stumbling, I put my weight on my wounded leg, which obligingly collapsed, sending me pitching forward.

Fortunately, Nrissilli was kind enough to catch me rather than watch me slam into the floor. She did curse viciously in an older Hrotata dialect, probably her native tongue. Her body language screamed disgust and aggravation as she hauled me upright and helped me settle back onto the steps.

While we were tangled, I made sure to rub up thoroughly against her fur, paying special attention to the groomed patches along the sides of her neck. I wasn't being perverse; I was making sure to get a solid dose of the natural Hrotata neurotoxins.

Their happy druggy secretions were the key to my plan. For the first time, I greeted the tingle of that complex hormone with welcoming pleasure as it seeped through my scales. It wasn't just that the toxin would blunt my pains even further and put me into a more pleasant state of mind. It was that I would soon become far more receptive to the detective's requests.

If anyone was watching us right then, they would have seen a wounded Vislin accidentally fall, coincidentally coming into contact with a Hrotata of significant maturity. If the victim accidentally let something slip afterward, maybe it wouldn't be his fault.

I had to play the reaction carefully, though. Giving away everything, all at once, wouldn't be excused by any competent blackmailer. I needed to betray just enough to alert Nrissilli, just enough to be explainable by the intoxication, without revealing too much.

I looked up, fuzzing as the relaxant effects took hold. "Thank you, mistress. I'm sorry I'm such a nuisance."

Nrissilli looked at me with a mixture of confusion, irritation, and outright disgust. "You're a mess… and I don't just mean physically. What's wrong with you, snoop?"

"I really messed this case up. I mean, really. A lot. I keep losing females. Pkstzk. We haven't talked since early this week. I think I scared her away. Tskksk. Found her, lost her. Shtvtsk, the other pretty one? Probably will lose her, too. They all leave. You can arrest me. Maybe that way I won't lose you, too."

"All right, joker, you didn't get that much of a pat-down," she answered, still obviously pissed off at me.

Then, she started to process what I'd said. "Wait, Shtvtsk? There's a new name. What do you mean, lost? We know Tskksk is missing. Are there others being targeted?"

I lifted my crest, actually enjoying myself on several levels. "Shtvtsk is the female next door... upstairs... beautiful. But doomed, like all my loves. I want to give them gifts, but I have no credit. I have nothing. No home, no credit, no weapon, not even a pet rktpk to snuggle." I clicked my beak in dramatic hysterical laughter. "Put me in a cell. At least there, I can sleep and eat. If not, my tormentors will put me back in the hospital, where I can rest."

Detective Nrissilli stayed silent, letting me rant, her confused expression slowly giving way to hesitant understanding.

"Who are your 'tormentors', Stchvk? Come on, you can trust me," she ventured.

"I don't *know!*" I squawked, the simulated vowels of our cross-species interlingua proving perfect for my tortured cries. "They tried to kill me... to kill Pkstzk... to kill Tskksk..."

"And Shtvtsk," she concluded for me. "She's in danger."

"They're *all* in danger," I confided quietly. I leaned forward, as if attempting to snuggle up against Nrissilli again. She flinched backward, but let me close to within a few centimeters without actually touching.

I added in an undertone, "They told me so. They're going to hurt everyone... everyone I touch. Maybe you *should* lock me up, before I get someone else hurt."

Broken Record

The detective radiated disgust, either real or feigned, and spat at me: "You're drugged, in more ways than one. You're not making any sense. And I have other things to do right now. Go home, get some sleep, and come to the precinct in the morning, cleaned up. If you don't, I *will* have you hauled in. You'd better have some clearer answers for me then. In the meantime, I'm going to do some real investigation of my own... and if I find out you're deeper into this case than you claim, we really will have a reckoning."

I splayed my claws in submissive agreement. "Of course. Of course. Thank you, mistress. I'm only trying to help. I don't want anyone else to get hurt."

I *thought* she got it. I had to trust not only the detective's perception and intuition but also her ability to pick up cues without giving anything away. She certainly seemed outraged, but she also hadn't arrested me. At best, she was giving me credit for competence. She had access to my past cases. She knew I wasn't the helpless mess I seemed, that she accused me of being. She knew that I could run a con. I just hoped she picked up *which* con I was actually playing.

Detective Nrissilli stalked away, muttering about insane Vislin and their overwrought emotional wiring... at least I assumed that's what she was saying, in her quiet and foreign speech. I hoped she was just overplaying her role and not actually upset with me. I'd find out before long.

The lingering Hrotata toxin was making it easier to ignore my pains, not to mention ignore my problems and feel more confident in myself. I stood, once again surprised that my wounds didn't overflow the artificial pain threshold induced by my wonder drug. Between chemical reinforcements, I felt like I might actually succeed.

I knew I was overestimating my chances. I had to get to the pet store, retrieve the laser weapon, stash it at Shtvtsk's, and get out, all without being spotted by Shtvtsk or *blatantly* seen by a constable. I also needed to leave as much evidence intact as possible and delay as long as I could, giving Nrissilli time to look into Tskksk's disappearance.

Even if she couldn't get a lead on Tskksk, at least she would know to check on Shtvtsk. She would know that the upcoming tip about where to find Vzktkk's murderer and the murder weapon would be false. They might have to arrest Sht-vtsk, but a conviction was unlikely.

The remaining hazards were whether my exchange with the detective would be identified as collaboration with a constable – *if* the conversation was even noticed by agents of my shadowy enemy – and whether I could convince that enemy to release Tskksk. I hoped they would, to ensure my continued cooperation with their frame job.

If I couldn't figure out who was behind this mess and how to find them, I and Tskksk (and maybe, Pkstzk) would be facing further threats, even if we escaped the current crisis.

Kktkrkz devour me, I actually felt ready to get to work.

Chapter 19 - Bad Break-in

My progress back to the pet store took on a strangely familiar cast. The familiarity came from more than just retracing my earlier route. It wasn't from the smell of smoke or the feeling of walking into yet another trap.

The familiarity came, in part, from the dwindling gauze of a Hrotata's secretions. It felt like I'd taken steps like these before: barely escaping an intoxicated interview, racing off against time, going to a dangerous place without proper protection, and feeling that my case was coming to its conclusion, all at the same time.

The situation shouldn't have felt so *final*. Even if I succeeded at framing Shtvtsk and freeing Tskksk, there would be more dangers, more questions, and more work to resolve. If I failed on either or both counts, I'd have to fight guilt and grief along with healing my physical injuries.

The original question – who killed Vzktkk? – was still completely unresolved. And wherever Pack Vzrrk figured in, I'd need to identify the players, their partisans, and the degree of ongoing hazard to myself and my reputation.

That calculation assumed I'd have any reputation left afterwards. Everything could go wrong with the constabulary before my actual enemies got a chance to ruin me. I had Detective Nrissilli's temporary forbearance, but she was one officer out of hundreds. It would take only one overzealous underling to notice my activities and force my arrest. Even if I was cleared of actual wrongdoing, I could still have my license revoked for technically legal improprieties. Not to mention, I also was guilty of several illegal acts, just in the past few days.

I didn't *feel* guilty on those counts. If I played strictly by the legal codes, I'd accomplish very little. No disrespect to the stalwart investigators like Nrissilli, but the same problem plagued the constabulary: they either bent the rules or failed to solve crimes. There was plenty of both cheating and failure going on.

The citizenry just hoped that a minimum of cheating resulted in a maximum number of criminals getting caught. That's not just a Layafflr City problem or a Chttkttp problem, that's the case in every city, on every planet, in every society.

Sorry, but the noble, by-the-book cop who still manages to catch every villain is a fantasy character. There are a few noble constables like that – I'd met some – but they often as not file cases as unsolved, after hitting a legal blockade. Sometimes I resolve the problem for them, granting not only plausible deniability but a completely ignorant denial of wrongdoing, while I do what needs to be done.

There are also officers who claim to be pristine, while knowingly allowing unofficial agents – like me – to do their dirty work. Other authorities break the rules, personally, and lie about it, even if their motives are good. And every so often, an officer honestly admits to breaking the law in order to uphold it. That sort rarely lasts long.

There are a thousand shades of ethical grey. Personally, I'd rather see the laws that protect wrongdoers broken, whether that protection is an accidental effect of an otherwise worthy law or a deliberate use of the law as a shield by a cunning or powerful criminal. My approach seems more ethical than strict obedience. But that's me. And maybe my willingness to discard one set of rules is no better than those who toss aside the imperatives not to lie, cheat, abuse, steal, and murder. I know, those same laws protect the innocent as much as the guilty.

I'm an investigator, not a philosopher. I chose my methods long ago, or rather chose them anew, after seeing the hurtful effects of my original behavior. These days, I act however seems best and let outcomes evaluate whether I chose well. At least I don't ignore one set of outcomes in order to justify others.

For example, what I'd done to Tskksk stung hard. If I knew for certain that burning my future would ensure hers, I'd have handed myself over in a moment: to the constables or to the murderer. Murderers?

Again, I had to wonder just how complex a conspiracy I was really dealing with, and what its actual goals were. Was the killer dealing with the aftermath of a plan gone wrong? Had I disrupted something, or was I playing along as expected?

Broken Record

There was no way of knowing, not yet. The points of fact I had assembled thus far failed to outline any solid shapes. In fact, some of the lines I tried to draw crossed over one another. Observations conflicted and contradicted one another. Was Tskksk victim or collaborator? Was Shtvtsk a murderous seductress or a conniving bystander? Was Pkstzk a grieving widow or a mate-killer?

The web extended beyond the three females. What about the housekeeping service Shtvtsk mentioned? She hinted that the company had criminal ties, probably shadow control through some gang. She also said that Vzktkk helped her and Pkstzk get out of their employment with the company, which would have been difficult otherwise. Was their act of defiance the cause of the present violent rampage?

A bigger organization would explain our enemy's access to bombs and mercenaries. Generally, you needed personnel and/or money to manage that level of threat. Pack Vzrrk, for all its willingness to commit violence, never had the membership or resources to mount such a campaign, not back then and certainly not now. Unless Rsspkz had made some friends I knew nothing about, he'd be hard pressed to hire a single mercenary or buy a single explosive. That was assuming he had someone to contact to place the orders. Pkstzk was the most logical point of contact, if Pack Vzrrk were somehow involved...

I stopped there. I'd stepped into that mental mire already. Wading further into the morass of my filthy past wasn't going to help my present needs. I could keep possibilities in mind, pending future information, but right then, I needed to focus on immediate problems.

I made it to the pet store without collapsing. The Hrotata toxin was almost completely gone, but my pain medication was going strong. Good stuff. I'd hate going back to generic analgesics after my prescription ran out. Then again, I'd rather avoid the circumstances that led to me getting the good drugs: severe injuries in questionable circumstances, which got me transported to an upscale hospital on the public bankroll.

If I *had* been blown up at my old apartment, I'd have woken up stitched with gut, lying on a cot, and grudgingly pumped with cheap narcotics. I exaggerate, but the contrast was stark enough.

Nathan Large with Laine Megan Lundquist

Kkk, enjoy it while it lasts, right?

A new crime scene barrier was installed in front of the pet store. I learned to bypass those while I still had egg-teeth.

Then, there was a new lock on the side door: a warded lock demanding a physical key. Picking that mechanism was trickier. It took me a decad and a snapped claw-tip to hit the right tumbler sequence. The constables knew that solid-state, analog locks were slower to override than mag-locks or other digital solutions… but only by a matter of degree.

If you want to know, the best security is multi-part: a deadbolt *and* a magnetic seal, activated by some combination of biometric scan, analog key, and unique chip card with redundant coding. By the time an intruder has managed to find or forge duplicates of all three keys, they've already exceeded the cost of almost anything you might lock inside. They've also wasted enough time that you could have moved your valuables elsewhere while they worked.

To a professional breaker, a warded lock was only a speed-bump: a big, painful bump, but only a nuisance. While I worked, I proved to myself that I could learn from recent experience: I scanned the hallway for cameras. I assumed that the constabulary couldn't afford miniature jobs. If they were planting micro-cameras, I'd never spot those. But I didn't see any lenses or boxes for standard surveillance equipment.

I might have been observed entering from outside. There was nothing I could do about that. However, when I eventually entered, I also thoroughly checked the outer room of the pet store.

There wasn't anything to see. There wasn't anything left in the room to hide a camera behind. Even the wall displays were stripped, cleared of hooks, tags, and other commercial debris. I didn't feel safe, exactly, but it was unlikely the constables or criminals left anything behind, whether surveillance or hazard.

The floor, too, had been swept clean. Someone wiped up all of the dust and litter, not to mention blood and animal corpses. Unless the constables had collected it first, any evidence from Vzktkk's killer was gone, along with any sign of the starved, dead animals imprisoned there.

Broken Record

The clean floor also meant that I wasn't leaving footprints, though I knew I was tracking outdoor grit inside. Forensics would know someone had entered, even if I was careful not to leave genetic debris and tell them *who* came in. My caution presumed anyone would think to check. I had tried to warn Detective Nrissilli about where to look, but she could have missed the point.

I couldn't waste much more time. Besides recorders, my entry might have tripped a silent alarm. I was probably giving the constables too much credit, again, but assuming the worst was still a good policy.

Opening the door to the back room, I couldn't resist a certain apprehension. There was *probably* nothing back there, but I'd thought that before.

This time, there really was nothing in the back room. The rktpk corpses were gone, of course, but so were the stacks of empty food bags, the dirty animal cages, and even the old desk I'd seen before. Presumably, all swept away into an evidence locker,. And what the constables didn't take, the criminals might have.

Somewhere in the room was a false floor panel with a cache beneath. Funny that the constables searched so *thoroughly*, yet missed that secret. Then again, they might have found the space, but with nothing inside. Nothing said the killer couldn't have returned and dropped the murder weapon *after* the room was searched. It was actually a pretty cunning plan: hide the evidence somewhere already investigated. Few detectives would go back and recheck a cleared scene.

But they might, if they thought something was missed the first time. Cunning or not, there was a certain amount of dumb risk associated with reusing a former murder site. Why not destroy the weapon or keep it in a third, completely unknown location?

Obviously, the killer kept the laser for this frame-up. They probably put it back in the pet store so that I could retrieve it from a location I already knew and could access.

How far in advance was this plot devised? Were the players chosen from the beginning... or was my involvement a later complication? Once again, a whole spectrum of possibilities beckoned, ranging from Shtvtsk being the intended target all along, to her being a convenient scapegoat tagged by my investigation.

I lowered myself to the floor as best I could and searched along the faux-wood tiles for a seam, a catch, or some other access. On a hunch, I started near the former location of the missing desk. Sure enough, at the back corner of the room in that area, I spotted a 'knothole' which had no purpose in artificial wood. Inserting a claw tip, I levered the tile upward.

Underneath was a neatly paneled cache box, built out of the same laminate material as the floor tiles. The owner probably stored credit slips, spare keys, or other valuables down there. As security measures went, it wasn't bad. I hadn't thought to look for it earlier... though I had some distractions at the time. As unlikely as theft was from a pet store, even a dedicated burglar might not inspect the floors.

Inside the box was, indeed, a laser pistol. It was small, simple, and neat, a high-powered mass-produced weapon used primarily for personal protection. Getting shot anywhere but a vital organ was painful but survivable. The beam wouldn't penetrate anything sufficiently thick and opaque. That property made laser firearms ideal for use aboard starships, since they were unlikely to damage shielded systems and were completely unable to breach a hull.

For similar reasons, a hand laser was nearly useless against an armored target. They didn't have much stopping power, either, unless you had excellent aim. But in a close situation with a normally-dressed opponent, you could hurt them badly without worrying about accidental death due to blood loss.

The other properties in a laser's favor were plenty of range and hours of 'ammunition'. You could fire one over and over at multiple attackers or hold down the trigger and sweep the beam over them, hoping that you'd hit something vital. And in the hands of a trained user, a simple laser was sufficient to deliver a fatal wound, at great distance, with just one shot. Obviously.

Was it the weapon that killed Vzktkk? It certainly looked like the right type. I had no doubt that forensic tests would produce an impact effect identical to the hole in Vzktkk's skull. Even if it wasn't the exact same gun, it was close enough to be believable. With Shtvtsk's traces on its handle and her relationship to Vzktkk established, finding this weapon in her home would ensure a quick conviction.

Broken Record

I retrieved the pistol gingerly with the tips of my claws. If I had time, I would have brought gloves or at least a cloth to avoid any transfer of my own. As it was, I didn't even have a spare container to carry the frosted thing unseen. The only way I could transport it without handling it was to put it in my own empty holster.

Placing the laser in Rtrtr's former home felt like cheating. I actually recited a little apology to my beloved heater, telling it I wasn't replacing it, just temporarily holding another weapon out of necessity. I wasn't even going to *use* the laser, I promised, just carry it a little way. I hoped Rtrtr would understand. I already felt terrible for leaving it locked up so long, but what could I do?

I wish I was joking. At the least, I was prioritizing a hostage situation involving a real, living victim above my firearm's release. Sacrifices were necessary. But I really missed my gun.

Carrying the laser openly wasn't a bad plan. It would be visible, but only someone who knew what they were looking for would be suspicious. Otherwise, it looked like I was carrying my own, personal weapon. Hidden in plain sight, one of the classic subterfuges.

On that note, I strode openly out of the pet store, pausing only to lock the door again behind me. Not that there were any witnesses standing on the street, but if there were, my confident demeanor would convince them I was going about business as normal. Everything legitimate, no illegal activities going on here, none at all.

My purposeful strut was spoiled only by a the limp in my complaining leg and a hunch in my abused back. I was also feeling a light-headed from all the chemicals and my continuously empty stomach. Vislin can go quite a while without eating... but only after a big meal. My full room service at the hospital was nice, but it wasn't quite a feast I could subsist on for two days running.

I'd treat myself to a nice lunch after the caper was done. Sss, I'd definitely feel like eating after framing someone for murder. The stress of potential arrest would help, too. Nothing stimulates the appetite like anxiety.

But seriously, I needed to eat, and soon. I was tempted to steal a few snacks from Shtvtsk's well-stocked kitchen. Why not? A little petty theft was minor compared to my other planned violation. It would also be for a good cause: my continued health and survival.

If the sarcasm isn't coming through, I wasn't going to steal anything, no matter how starved I felt. I might tweak the law and preach about having good reasons for my offenses, but taking whatever I wanted, for my own needs, was a good place to draw the line. Petty theft was one place where roguish misbehavior crossed into selfishness. I might be going down a bad path, but I didn't need to backslide into past corruption.

Into the apartment building, up the stairs – the elevator would record any key use, and I wanted to avoid being recorded – to the fourth floor, apartment 401.

I was there. I had the weapon. I had the key. Was Shtvtsk home? There was no reason she should be out, in the early morning hours following a tumultuous day. But there was also a chance Tskksk's kidnapper, my controller, had cleared the way for me by luring Shtvtsk away.

I had only one way to find out. I pressed the signal button. Six hectads passed with no response. I signaled again, then tapped on the door. Another twenty hectads and still nothing. She might be inside, dead asleep. Could I get inside and plant the pistol without waking her? Sss, and get some of her genetic material on the weapon, as well?

The best option for the latter challenge was to check her bathroom for shed scales. If she used a scouring powder, her trash can might be full of abraded material I could use. Despite the caller's insinuation, I wasn't going to try and collect any bodily fluids. Suddenly jumping into Shtvtsk's nest after the scene yesterday would raise plenty of alarms, even if she proved willing.

I remembered the waiting room cameras before I opened the door. I'd have to deal with those, as well. That operation meant spending a few decads to search the room, hopefully finding all the hidden devices before I continued.

The destruction or deactivation of those units would be a point in Shtvtsk's favor if she went to trial. She could claim negative evidence: someone clearly broke into her apartment to plant the weapon. That was assuming a judge believed she ever had cameras installed, in the first place.

Broken Record

Unfortunately, I couldn't screw up in her favor, at least, not blatantly. I had to remove any sign of the cameras' existence, so that her claims about them would be unprovable.

It was possible that the kidnappers would hold Tskksk until Shtvtsk was in prison, in which case I had to do my best to make sure she *was* found guilty. Assuming we didn't find Tskksk before the trial was done, I would have to rely upon getting Shtvtsk falsely convicted. She could be released later when the verdict was overturned.

Removing the cameras was also in my own best interest. It remained possible that I could squeak out of arrest and/or ruin once the mess was done, but not if hard evidence proved my involvement in a criminal act. Detective Nrissilli wouldn't jeopardize her career trying to cover for me in the face of such evidence.

So, when I let myself into the apartment, I immediately scanned the room for any lens reflections, visible wires, glowing lights, etc. I also listened carefully for sounds of movement or disturbed slumber. The door to the nesting room was closed, which was both boon and problem. If Shtvtsk was inside, the closed door might muffle my noises enough to keep her dormant. But I couldn't know for certain if she was in there, unless *she* made a loud noise.

I had to assume the worst and proceed with stealth. My aching arm and leg made sneaking doubly difficult. I had to pick my way around the room, lifting objects to inspect for cameras, while limping slightly and favoring one arm.

While moving aside one digital image frame, I got a good look at the displayed image. As I saw before, it looked like Shtvtsk posing with two other Vislin of uncertain gender. They looked like friends or coworkers out for a drink. More employees of the infamous housekeeping service? Other acquaintances? Pack-mates, maybe?

I was struck anew at how little the Shtvtsk in the picture looked like her current vision of grace. Perhaps she metamorphosed into glamour in the intervening years. Surgical reconstruction, exercise, better diet, and lots of practice as an escort could account for some of the transformation.

But the female in the picture was different in multiple dimensions: snout shorter, nostrils wider, eyes greener, crest less perfectly aligned. It was only Shtvtsk by slight similarity, not a clear match. For all that the pictured female resembled the current Shtvtsk, the image could be someone else's. A sibling, perhaps? A parent?

The frame didn't conceal any cameras, so I put it back down and moved on. But the incongruity lingered, ticking at my brain, joining and reinforcing all the other unexplainable details I was accumulating.

I really, really, wanted some answers. I was tired of anomalies. My impatience was becoming a dangerous force all its own. If I didn't collapse with pain or fatigue, or die during the next murder attempt, I might self-destruct from the pressure of all my intellectual aggravation.

I kept looking for cameras, all the while wanting to go back and check the picture again. I couldn't shake the feeling that it was important. It was probably just my data starved brain hoping that something would provide a key to the case. I wanted something solid to precipitate my dissolved life.

Finally, I found one small camera box, nestled in a houseplant, mounted on a small stake. It looked like a deep-set peering eyeball within a furry green face. The camera was entirely self-contained, with battery, recorder, and memory bead all in one package. I wondered, belatedly, if it also had a wireless transmitter. If Shtvtsk were smart and tech-savvy, she would have remote storage somewhere backing up everything her cameras collected.

She did say the systems were discreetly local. If she was lying, there was little I could do right away. I wished, not for the first time, that I was more skilled in the technological arts. I hadn't a prayer of hacking even a local system, much less a globally distributed cloud account. That's where someone like Tskksk was a huge asset.

Sure, after I saved her from being killed, by grossly violating the law and stealing an innocent sapient's freedom, she'd be *thrilled* to associate with me further. It actually wasn't impossible, but *I* wouldn't have wanted to work with me, right then.

Broken Record

I completed a circuit of the room, poking into every corner that could conceivably hide another camera. I found nothing else. Was that one unit, half-hidden, really the extent of Shtvtsk's surveillance? It could be; that one camera would cost a few hundred credits. If Shtvtsk's business was as poor as I suspected – not as affluent as she boasted – she might not be able to afford another camera.

Still, I made one last round just in case I missed something, looking in even less likely spots: beneath a chair, between two bookcases, in a closed drawer. I cringed every time I bumped something hard enough to produce a noise, freezing to listen for any response.

The apartment, including the nesting room, remained utterly quiet. I started to doubt that Shtvtsk was there. I might be wasting valuable time by moving so slowly and thoroughly. After a second pass of the outer room, I decided that I'd done the best I could and started to move toward the bathroom to check for "genetic material".

I passed the troublesome image again. My eyes were unavoidably drawn to it. I finally realized what I was missing, in the combined context of the bathroom trash, the kitchen, Shtvtsk's finances, a cleaning service, and its workers.

I picked up the picture again and looked more closely. That was it. Shtvtsk then didn't look like Shtvtsk now, but she *did* look familiar. She looked like...

The idea was ridiculous, almost impossible, but undeniable the more I studied her face. The Vislin in the picture looked like Ktchvch, my Pack-mate Rsspkz' sister.

I remembered Ktchvch from back then, a youngster I met at Rsspkz' home the few times I visited. Usually, those visits were only brief stops to pick up my Pack-mate before we went out for a day of mischief. Ktchvch was a little female, too young to bother, even if talking to her wouldn't be offensive in her brother's presence. By the time Pack Vzrrk broke up and her brother went to prison, Ktchvch was independent of her brood, with her own Pack and job.

Food service. I remembered she had culinary interests. When I checked up on her, once after I started my investigation business and a second time just a few days ago, her profession was listed as "line cook" for a restaurant. If Ktchvch was Shtvtsk, that information was false... or at least, outdated.

Wait, that was assuming Shtvtsk/Ktchvch didn't have a separate day job. Maybe she cooked by day and escorted by night. Kitchen skills would certainly add to her value as a surrogate mate. My stomach gurgled just thinking about the subject.

All those possibilities assumed my perceptions were correct and I wasn't just seeing illusions. Yet if Shtvtsk *was* Ktchvch, that would explain the connection to Pack Vzrrk. Maybe Rsspkz was striking at a sister he perceived as disloyal. Or maybe someone else was striking at Pack Vzrrk through its outliers. Ktchvch. Pkstzk. Me.

I really wanted to open my compad and search for new connections. Was Rsspkz' other sibling, his brother Zfzptk, *really* out on an asteroid mining team? Had some accident befallen him, even out in open space? At what restaurant was Ktchvch supposedly working?

I had a disturbing thought that perhaps Ktchvch/Shtvtsk worked the back kitchen at Kzztkrt Tk, the same restaurant where Pkstzk waited tables. That fact could be another useful clue Pkstzk was unable to pass along... not to mention something Shtvtsk avoided mentioning.

Maybe I had something fundamentally wrong. Maybe Shtvtsk had a picture of Ktchvch for other reasons... maybe the two females *were* separate but related in some other way, like having worked together once?

There was enough physical resemblance to think they were identical... but maybe there was another explanation for that similarity. Maybe they were cousins? Vislin siblings don't usually maintain close ties after joining Packs. Contact between more extended relatives is even rarer, but not impossible. Influence from the Hrotata and other mammalians has led more Vislin to maintain and even enjoy extended family ties. As big as Layafflr seems, it can be a small, incestuous world at times.

I considered stealing the imager for reference. The picture was one of those solid points that might unlock other secrets. But its absence would create more problems than its possession would definitely solve. So, I left it on the shelf and reluctantly continued into the bathroom.

That part was easy. I found discarded scouring dust in the garbage, just like I'd hoped. Using the corner of a towel, I lifted some dust and tapped it over the handle of the laser pistol. Then I brushed off the excess, without wiping down the weapon too thoroughly. I didn't want to undo my work, but I also didn't want to make it look like obvious planted evidence. Hopefully, just enough scale fragments would cling to the weapon for identification… and hopefully, the forensic techs wouldn't note the suspicious presence of scouring powder.

Next, where to plant the weapon? I couldn't put it out in the open or anywhere else Shtvtsk would discover. Imagine finding a laser pistol randomly placed in your home! Even if you didn't connect the weapon to the recent murder of someone you knew, you'd be horrified by its unexpected presence. Shtvtsk would likely get rid of the laser right away… and probably do a better job of it than the real killer.

A kitchen drawer? Perhaps less noticeable, but a little odd. Not the place a murderess would hide key evidence against herself. The most plausible spot would be in the nesting room, maybe in the material of her nest… but that wasn't an option, for obvious reasons. Leave it in the bathroom? There weren't any real concealment spots in there, short of the toilet tank. I didn't have a plastic bag to seal it in, for that placement to work.

That left the waiting room. Not the best choice, but at least there were a few options for hiding spots. Under a couch? In a side table? Behind a bookcase?

While I tried to decide, I heard the scratch of claws on the door. I froze as I realized the sound hadn't come from the nesting room, but from the front door. Someone was coming in… probably Shtvtsk.

I chose the nearest available hiding spot for the laser: in a drawer I had left open while searching for cameras in the front room. I managed to slide the drawer closed and drop myself into the adjacent armchair as the door opened.

I did my best to compose my expression, trying to look like a love-sick stalker rather than a scheming intruder. Maybe Shtvtsk would accept my presence as a creepy attempt to win back her affections. *I* wouldn't buy that story, but who knew with her? I'd been selling flimsier covers all week, with surprising success. Even if Shtvtsk got suspicious, I could try revealing what I knew about her and Ktchvch (not much, to be honest), and using that as a cover to explain why I broke into her apartment again.

The door finally opened and a female stepped into the room… but it wasn't Shtvtsk. It also wasn't Detective Nrissilli or another constable, which would be my second guess.

Not only was her presence unexpected in the extreme, her appearance boggled my already-abused mind. She was wearing sleek, black tactical armor, not exactly the same as my attackers at Taburket's, but similar enough. She wore no helmet, which was how I knew it was her. She also carried a small plasma pistol, drawn and aimed.

As she entered and looked around, she spotted me and froze. Her weapon followed her gaze, pointed right at my head. She wasn't just unhappy to see me; she looked like she was prepared to permanently end my investigations.

Her confusion echoed mine. We stared at one another for a long moment, like actors in an overwrought drama.

I decided to break the silence. "Pkstzk! Hello! Should I ask what you're doing here… or should I go first?"

Chapter 20 - Acquaintance Forgot

"*You,*" Pkstzk began. "It's always *you.* I'd shoot you, but I'd probably miss. I can guess what *you're* doing here, Stchvk."

I was honestly confused by her rancor. "Rrr, I doubt it's what you think…"

"I don't mean the whore, you idiot," she snapped. "I mean you're up to something, or you think you are. You've spent the last decade crusading around, wasting your life and all the work your Pack put into you, acting like some martyr… while all you've really done is waste time and gratify a few pathetic victims."

I raised my claws, genuinely surrendering. "You could be right, but where is this coming from? You sound like you've been obsessing over me for years, but you just got in touch with me a week ago, for the first time since…"

"Since Pack Vzrrk was ruined. Since *you* ruined them. And now, you're betraying me more directly. I asked you to find my new mate's killer, and here you are, moved into her nest. Did she offer you something better? Or just something easier? Your loyalties are *so* flimsy."

Her accusations were all over the place. I'd like to say this wasn't the Pkstzk I remembered, but it actually was: spiteful and cruel when she didn't get her way. I'd glossed over that aspect of her character in favor of the soft scales she could show when she was pleased. She was always self-obsessed, too. How had I forgotten that?

I protested, "If you'd actually listen, you're far off-trail. In fact, I think we're both being played by the same enemy. But this isn't the place…"

"This *is* the place," she objected. "The whore lives here, you're here, and Vzktkk died just outside here. I managed what you were having so much trouble with. I found out what they were doing… and why she had him killed."

At that, I couldn't help encouraging her. "Really? Because you're right: I couldn't figure it out. Enlighten me. What's the real story... and how did you get it?"

I was being idiotically brave, with a plasma thrower pointed directly at my face. At that point, though, I didn't care. Either she was going to shoot me or she wasn't. If I survived, I at least wanted to hear what she had to say. Sitting still and staying silent wasn't going to spare me, I suspected.

Pkstzk snapped her beak and scratched the floor, but kept her trigger claw still. She bit off the words: "Vzktkk was seeing Shtvtsk, replacing me. She was using him to collect information. When he found out her game, he tried to break it off... but she wouldn't let him. Did she tell you that? Did she offer to bring you in, to introduce you to her real employer? Or were you satisfied with just her attentions?"

My survival depended on keeping calm, but I was angry. I shouldn't have cared about Pkstzk's opinion of me, especially not right then, but her accusations stung a bit too much. My crest flattened before I could reestablish control, and my legs tensed to spring.

Pkstzk caught my reaction and waved her weapon, either warning me against an attack or daring me to try.

Instead of leaping with beak and claw, I lashed out verbally. "You assume a lot about me. I didn't realize how little you'd changed, and *you* don't understand how *I've* changed. I don't automatically fall in with every gang that offers membership... or every female that shows interest. I was *working* Shtvtsk, myself. Or I should say, I was uncovering Ktchvch. You remember? Your mate's sister? Why might *she* be seducing your new mate, I wonder?"

I hoped my revelation would stun Pkstzk and maybe make her reconsider my value. Instead, the accusation only seemed to infuriate her further.

"You're ridiculous. You think I wouldn't recognize Ktchvch? I *worked* with her, once. There's no way they're the same person."

Broken Record

I gestured toward the image on its shelf across the room. "Look. There's a picture there. Even if they're not the same, they know each other somehow. This *is* about Pack Vzrrk, but we need to work together..."

Pkstzk stiffened at my gesture. She wasn't about to move past me to look at the picture. I started to rise, to pick up the frame and show it to her, myself.

"Sit down!" she chattered. She was having a serious breakdown, which I wouldn't have minded so much if she wasn't heavily armed. "Stop lying! Just admit you've been working with her!"

I wasn't sure how to placate her, at that point. Agreeing with her meant admitting I was guilty, which might get me shot. Disagreeing with her just meant further argument and more agitation. Pkstzk had been fed disinformation against me. I'd love to know the source, but that revelation had to wait on my escape from our showdown.

"Pkstzk. You said you were looking into the case. You found some information. Where did it come from? You said I was the only one you could trust, but now you don't trust me... and clearly, you've been talking to someone else."

Her response was a derisive click. She eventually added, "You'd like to know, wouldn't you? Who sold you out. Who decided to tell me the truth, rather than continuing to play with me. They were going to talk to me at Taburket's, you know, before you tried to kill them."

I *what?* The spin was making me dizzy. I supposed that in her world, I blew up my own apartment. Or else Pkstzk's mysterious informants told her that bomb was retribution for my "attack" on them. Sss, I was dangerous all of the sudden.

I'd never had opportunity to defuse a bomb before, but I imagined this situation was similar. Which lead did I disconnect... or reconnect... to keep from getting blasted? Touch the wrong contact point, and you're dead. I mean, I've *set* bombs before, but the skills don't necessarily transfer to disarmament. And don't forget, that was a long time ago. I was also talking about a female, not a bomb. Not that I've never set... sss, never mind.

Nathan Large with Laine Megan Lundquist

I *had* talked down crazy sapients, not long ago. Of course, those disarmaments sometimes went badly… also resulting in me being shot, once or twice

I realized I shouldn't assume Pkstzk was on a timer. Maybe my best strategy was to delay, to keep her talking and see if she would wind down on her own. I might even be saved by the arrival of constabulary officers. Then again, their intrusion could be the trigger that got me killed. Still, stalling seemed like a better idea than intentional or accidental provocation.

"You've got your story, and I've got mine," I answered, pretending to confidence we both knew I lacked. "We're obviously not going to reach agreement here. So, what's your plan, Pkstzk? Were you coming to kill Shtvtsk? She's not here. I shouldn't be here. I broke in. Like I told you, I'm investigating her. What happens if she comes back? Do you kill her? Both of us? You had to have been seen entering. After that explosion outside, there are constables in the neighborhood. Would you like to know why that happened, by the way? Why a store down the street from this apartment, near the spot where Vzktkk was killed, was bombed?"

"More of your cover-up?" she snarled, still keeping the plasma thrower trained between my eyes.

"Hardly. The owner was an informant. She gave me some clues about what actually happened here. For example, she was the one who picked up the connection between you and Shtvtsk: your phone calls before and after Vzktkk's death."

Pkstzk's features tightened, as did her grip on the weapon. "She was taunting me. She *knew* he was dying, even as I begged her to tell me if he was here. He said he was still helping her with the legal mess…"

"… with her old employer," I finished for her. "But it wasn't a legal issue, was it? It was more like a gang matter. Extortion and negotiation. Diplomacy and bluster. Just like we're dealing with now. Who controls who. Maybe Shtvtsk was in on it, but why? What did it earn her?"

"It was her way out," Pkstzk concluded with mad conviction. "She wanted out, Vzktkk helped her, but he couldn't stop the threats. She probably offered him her love in return for his help. I should have seen it sooner. But they never *really* let her go. Vzktkk became their enemy. When he became a big enough problem, they told her she could earn her release... *if* she sold him out."

"Who are *they?*" I pressed. "Who told you any of this? Please, Pkstzk. If you give me something to work with, we can figure out this mess, see who's lying about what..."

"You'd like that," she spat. "Tell you what I know, so that you can twist it to make your story more believable. Just like Vzktkk. He used me to get to her, used her to fight his enemies... and then she used him, lied to him. You're all the same! At least Rsspkz is an honest criminal! I'd rather be an honest murderer than... like all you liars!"

Pkstzk was working herself up again. Her rational mind was already a smoking wreck, scattered all over the place. I wasn't sure how to avoid the same fate. Appealing to her reason just seemed to further convince her that I was manipulating her. She was using her fury as a shield against argument. *Someone* clearly wound her up and inoculated her against reason. When I found out who, I was going to enjoy disassembling them... their organization, I mean.

Them. They. What kind of weird shadow war were we involved in here? And which side was Pack Vzrrk on? I had the sense that the "Pack's" role was purely historical, a phantom used to manipulate Pkstzk, me, and maybe Ktchvch. But that assumption could be wrong. Rsspkz could still be out there, pulling strings...

...except deception wasn't his method. *I* was the con man, the trickster of the Pack. Rsspkz was the confident, charismatic, but ultimately straight-forward actor. That simplicity was why he got pulled into a bad job; he didn't think deeply enough to recognize the dangers in accepting the contract. He didn't see how he and the rest of the Pack were being used, or how they would be discarded as scapegoats after the job was done. Someone got the mess they wanted and Pack Vzrrk took the punishment. That client never even had to pay for the job.

Who, exactly, hired Pack Vzrrk was an old, cold case, one I'd given up solving long ago. But my frustration from back then fed my frustration in the present. Shadow players. Puppet masters. The real villains of Layafflr City, as opposed to the workaday criminals who generally stole less and paid more for their crimes. I hated that I usually tracked and caught the little predators but couldn't touch the big monsters up the food chain.

I seethed, and Pkstzk seethed, and we were both being agitated by the same enemy... but aimed at each other.

I exploded first. I screeched, "I am *not* your enemy! I have always been on your side, Pkstzk, even when you were my Pack-mate's mate. Yes, you've been misused, but not by me. I'm just me, Stchvk, the clever youngling who liked to play with locks and forge credit signatures. I solve puzzles. So, now I solve them for less pay and better reasons. The Pack betrayed me, not the other way around. They left you behind, too. And now someone's trying to use us again. Frost, Pkstzk! You've known me longer... why are you trusting some gangsters who arm and armor you and send you out to do their work?"

We were unified in our emotional arousal. I felt the tingle of frenzy starting to tense my larger muscles, increased blood flow feeding them oxygen and fuel. I fought to keep my scales from rippling and giving away my urges. My aggravation was genuine, but showing it would force Pkstzk's instincts to label me a threat.

She *did* clench and coruscate visibly. Her crest went flat. She was struggling, fighting an inner battle between my pleas and her prior convictions. It would come down to trust: me versus her newer friends.

I lost. Her slitted eyes focused on me again and she snapped, "I *trust* the one who gives me what I want. Truth. Knowledge. Attention. Yes, weapons. You gave me nothing. You ran and hid from me, back then and again now. You're a lying, betraying coward, Stchvk. You're getting ready to run, even now. Do it. Frenzy. Try to get past me. Then I'll know what you are... and I can kill you like you deserve."

What was I supposed to do? Protest further? Flee like she wanted? I realized then that *any* reaction would have the same result: Bang. Dead. I could stay very, very still and hope she'd be content to hold me there until Shtvtsk – or the constables – arrived, but then, I'd only die a little later.

Broken Record

Frost it all. I was tired of the frosted game. I was sick of trying to deal with the insane to solve the problems created by other crazies. I was tired of talking and getting nowhere. I was even tired of being threatened. I was either getting away or I was getting shot, but I wasn't going to keep sitting there, waiting, tensed up, miserable and powerless.

You've heard of someone dodging a bullet, right? Not just metaphorically, but literally, too. Move aside fast enough and get out of the way of the projectile. It doesn't work like some observers assume. Even for a physical bullet, there isn't enough time between the click of the trigger and the arrival of the projectile. Between nerve transmission and muscle tension... forget it. Take my word, no reflexes are that fast. A plasma burst travels even faster than a bullet... once triggered.

You *can* dodge between the shooter's decision to fire and their actual triggering movement. As soon as you're sure they're about to fire, start moving. If you guess the right direction and timing, you can be elsewhere when the bullet... or plasma ball... arrives where you used to be.

The problem is that by moving, you're making it more likely that the shooter *will* fire, if only in reaction. Even if they weren't going to attack before, they suddenly become committed. That concern isn't as much of a problem if you (or they) have friends nearby who will shoot (or restrain) them after the first shot.

In the case discussed here, only Pkstzk and I were present. It didn't much matter if I misjudged her intent: eventually, she was going to fire. I decided to choose my reaction preemptively. My only real chance was to disarm her.

Moving forward to tackle her wasn't going to work. Between my seated position and my bad leg, she'd drop me before I got close. Dodging backward and diving for one of the side rooms wouldn't work for similar reasons. I'd just get incinerated from behind rather than from the front.

I needed a ranged weapon of my own. The only candidate was the laser pistol. It was close at hand, although I'd have to retrieve it from a half-closed table drawer.

That was my plan as I half-leapt, half-fell out of my seat.

Pkstzk fired, as she had to. A gleaming purple sphere of superheated matter flew over my head, spattering against the far wall. Both its passage and its detonation seared my scales with stinging heat. The instant fire it started on the wooden furniture radiated more warmth.

I ignored those discomforts in favor of my survival plan. I managed to slide open the drawer and grasp the laser. Pkstzk's eyes widened as she realized that I was armed. She swung the plasma gun downward to blast me on the floor.

I was fortunate that the laser pistol was the faster weapon. I survived by virtue of that difference and my faster reflexes... my finely-honed survival instincts. Those instincts include a certain degree of certainty about my own relative value. I didn't hesitate to shoot.

I was unfortunate that my aim wasn't as good as my speed. I meant to hit the weapon, or failing that, Pkstzk's arm or shoulder. Like I said, a laser isn't usually a fatal weapon if you hit an extremity or even the outer torso. But if you catch an unarmored target squarely in the head... like I did Pkstzk... you can kill instantly.

The beam caught her just inside her right eye, between orbit and sinus. As she staggered back and fell, I wondered at the similarity to the shot that killed her mate. Same weapon. Same hit area. Same result.

Pkstzk spasmed slightly as she hit the floor, but she was already gone. Smoke rose from the seared hole in her skull, mingling with the fumes from the burning furniture. Her plasma gun clattered as it struck the laminated wooden floor.

I lay where I had fallen, laser still aimed in case she tried to rise and fire again. Her death didn't register for several hectads. The fact that *I* had shot and killed her didn't register, at first. When I realized she was completely still, the situation finally coalesced within my fragmented brain.

The young female I'd grown up with, the idol of my early adult years, the star of my first erotic dreams, was dead. And I'd killed her. The facts of the event, the elements of provocation and self-defense, didn't intrude on my self-incriminations. The full horror of my action poured in, unfiltered, undiluted by reason.

Broken Record

She was right. For the wrong reasons, but ultimately, she was right: I killed my Pack. I ruined everyone around me. I abandoned Rsspkz and Vztrrp and Fzpktk, the last to *her* death. Tskksk would die because of me. And I'd killed Pkstzk.

I released my grip on the laser. It was part of the evil, part of the destruction. It had killed two sapients, one with my assistance. The room was burning... I was part of that, too. I created hells out of homes: this one, Tskksk's store, my apartment...

I'd burned down the Pack's old safehouse, too, to destroy evidence. Did I not mention that? Arson was one of my specialties, so I knew how to make sure everything burned. No wonder Pkstzk suspected me of the other two attacks. I *could* do it, even if I hadn't personally set the explosives.

I was done. I would never escape. I ought to just stay there, to burn alive in the apartment... but no, the safeties were already kicking in. Water rained down, extinguishing the flames.

I could still wait for the constables and turn myself in. That encounter, the final destruction of Stchvk, frightened me, also. I thought I could deal with incrimination and humiliation. I'd often rehearsed the moment in my mind. Yet when it came to the moment of truth, I was terrified.

I'd been arrested before, many times, but every other time I was either innocent or felt myself justified. Most of the time, I was certain I'd get out of the charges. Almost always, I had. But this was murder. Obvious, unconcealable murder. Using a weapon that already killed another sapient in cold blood. I would never escape my guilt.

That realization, coupled with the reality of Pkstzk's death and my culpability in it, then joined forces with thoughts of the unknown – maybe unknowable – enemy that guided us all into this confrontation. My confidence was ruined. Not only couldn't I fight back before, I'd never be able to fight afterward. I was done.

Some sapients, in such a crisis, collapse into catatonia. Some take their own lives. Vislin generally don't do either, particularly not in a life-or-death struggle.

Nathan Large with Laine Megan Lundquist

I was already halfway to frenzy while Pkstzk and I were arguing. The aftermath of our battle was more than enough to send me over that edge. I leapt to my feet, disregarding the agony from my tormented leg, and ran through the exit.

Down the stairs, out of the building, and into the street, I ran. I had no destination; I was fleeing the area, leaving the neighborhood, and running away from the evil that always seemed to hover around me. I was running from myself. I would never be able to run far enough. Whether it was the city, its population, or me personally, there would always be darkness and horror and death. What I did... who I *was*... would never let me escape that evil, until I died.

As a response after murdering someone, my reaction was terrible. I was visibly fleeing, very obviously leaving some kind of awful scene. I might have been screaming; I don't remember. Even if not, the haste of my travel and my general demeanor would alert any observer that here was a Vislin frenzying away from... something. Something bad. Something the constables needed to look into.

They would. They would see the carnage, take a statement or two, and then follow me to wherever I eventually collapsed.

Hearing this, you may wonder how I was so clear-headed. I wasn't. You're getting this all after the fact, after I had some time to reflect and analyze.

But, as I fled, I did achieve a certain level of clarity. My inner demons, chanting about evil and guilt and shadowy oppressors, said a few sensible things. Someone *had* been manipulating my reality and that of everyone involved in this case. I never had a chance to solve the case, much less to realize that the case wasn't the true mystery to solve.

And the frenzy... the frenzy, itself, was familiar.

At some time, not too long ago, I had frenzied just like that, overwhelmed by the pressure of terrible thoughts. I had the exact same feeling of swarming dread, of unseen tormentors gathered to harm me in every way possible. Too many troubles, in too short a time... in a ridiculously short period of time. Ridiculously many troubles. Ridiculous troubles. Absurd. Artificial. Pain like torture: pain inflicted deliberately and judiciously for some reason I couldn't conceive. Why was someone trying to hurt me?

Broken Record

I was far outside of Isstravil by the time I reached this thought. I wasn't paying much attention to my surroundings, but I had no idea where I was, either way.

I thought: *Who is torturing me?* Then everything went dark.

I didn't pass out from exhaustion, not exactly. I didn't calm down, either. I just stopped. The moment I had that thought – "torture" – all of my other thoughts... stopped.

All my thoughts. Vision, hearing, even the sense of my body disappeared. The frenzy disappeared. My pains went away.

My last coherent, emotionless thought was: *I'm dead. This is what death is. Nothingness.*

Well, frost. Took it long enough.

Chapter 21 - Skipped Track

"He's coming up… he cracked it. I *told* you this one would pass."

"It took him six days."

"Subjective time! Even if I grant that standard, you can't count the imposed time lapses."

"Fair enough, but what about all the wandering around? He even had somatic cues to work with. *Someone* didn't titrate their dosages properly."

"I did so. *You* try to balance multiple hormonal systems in an atypical Vislin while he's dealing with mortal threat, mating urges, *and* Pack loyalties… while covering up a fractured rib and ankles! I can paralyze his extremities, but you can't immobilize a ribcage while someone's breathing!"

The voices were probably talking about me, given the throbbing ache in my flank and the numb heaviness of my limbs. Given my recent adventures, waking up in the hospital – my most likely location – was preferable to not waking up at all. Then again, from what I remembered, I should be suffering from more injuries than just a rib fracture.

What *did* I remember? A confrontation with Pkstzk. Murder… her mate's, her attempt on my life, and her death. Something else… a falsely accused Taratumm. A confrontation with… a Hrotata? Krrutoki. Going out a second-story window in frenzied terror. Wait, no, there were stairs…

The events of the last few days blurred together with the events of the *other* last few days, until I woke up enough to separate the narratives.

My current pains were consistent with the storyline where I jumped out a window. That alignment would normally suggest that my more recent set of memories happened later, but then why didn't that storyline mention the injuries

Broken Record

I sustained in the first sequence? In the case involving Krrutoki, I remembered moving fast, with no prior leg injury. But I didn't remember any reference to the greasy little Hrotata in the timeline with Pkstzk, so his case *couldn't* have happened first.

The discrepancies, taken together, suggested that Pkstzk's case, and possibly, everything leading up to it, were false memories. If that case was a dream, it had been a *hell* of a detailed dream. Long, too.

Still, that theory would explain the sense of missing time and the occasional intrusion of phantom pains. I must have been feeling my broken rib and injured ankles through the curtain of sleep.

Wait a second. The voices talking about "covering up" my pains spoke after I started to wake. Those weren't dreamed. I stopped floating and snapped myself fully alert. My eyes popped open and took in what I hoped were my real surroundings.

What I saw was mostly ceiling: pale grey concrete. Around the periphery were bright overhead lights, glinting off silvery steel appliances hanging from the ceiling and suspended from my bed. I was definitely in a bed; something soft was supporting my spine. Something not-so-soft was cradling my neck and shoulders. When I started to turn my head, I encountered cold, spiky resistance.

"Hey, he's moving! Don't move yet, all right?" The voice I heard had the soft liquidity and accent of a male Hrotata, but was too pleasant to belong to Krrutoki. I heard padded footsteps approaching, then fuzzy paws brushed against my cheek and neck.

Turning my eyes that direction, as far as they could go, got me an image of red-brown arms working on some kind of circlet attached to my temples. I felt a stinging pain in that area and tried to jerk away, but the restraints kept my head in place.

"Fros...," I mumbled, slurring the curse. My mouth was dry and my jaw slow to respond.

"Sorry, sorry. Just hold still while I get the leads out. No real damage done, it just tweaks the nerves when you disengage them too fast." The speaker was doing his best to be reassuring, despite his disturbing words.

I managed to calm down and obey, if only because struggling was unpleasant. There were a few more stabs and prickles as my attendant worked, then the click of a latch being released.

I felt pressure disappear from my neck and skull, a pressure I hadn't realized was present until it was gone. Tentatively turning my neck, I found that I had gained a few centimeters' range of motion.

I could finally see the Hrotata, a red-brown male of uncertain age. He had a long muzzle and elongated eyes, traits uncommon among his species in Layafflr City. He smiled at my scrutiny, flicking his tail into view and watching my eyes track its tip.

"Almost lucid," he announced to someone across the room. I turned my head the opposite direction, but whoever he was talking to was outside my limited visual arc. I was pretty sure the other speaker was Vislin, but I hadn't been listening closely enough to pick out any other clues.

"I... I'm lucid," I protested. "Let me up."

In response, my bed started to shift, lifting my upper half slowly upward. My view of the room shifted correspondingly, letting me see the rest of the ceiling, then the far wall. The white-finished metal walls supported my guess: it looked like a hospital. I was wearing a simple gown, which covered enough for modesty's sake, but was pretty embarrassing even so.

The hospital wasn't Vaktrri Medical, or my local clinic, or even, I suspected, the hospital nearest to Isstravil. It might have been a prison clinic, but I thought not, given its cleanliness and modern-looking equipment. For that matter, the sheer volume and variety of equipment surrounding me argued against any simple medical facility.

I couldn't start to identify the devices installed around the rectangular space. The various instruments seemed to be centered on my body, in a bed at the center of everything. The 'circlet' I was wearing was connected to a monitor system, with wires stretching both upward and outward.

Above me was some kind of funnel-shaped apparatus with a cylindrical barrel angled toward the spot where my head previously rested. It actually looked like the business end of a plasma thrower, a comparison that made me tense and queasy.

Other monitoring devices were attached to my wrists, chest, and neck, with bundled wires draping over the sides of my bed and running outward to the walls. These sensors presumably joined the readouts from my head, displayed on terminal screens near the Hrotata. As I became agitated, something blipped on his monitor. He reacted by lecturing me.

"Don't panic," he suggested. "You're safe here. Trying to move too much at first will hurt, not to mention give you more vertigo." His delivery sounded like he was giving a rehearsed speech, like an experienced medical technician. Medical? Or laboratory tech? The space looked less like a hospital room and more like a research lab, the more I saw of it.

I ignored his recommendation and tried to sit up further. I discovered that my legs wouldn't move. They were further restrained in heavy bindings over top of mesh casts. Why was I so immobilized? Was I really a patient, or a prisoner?

"SSS!" I complained. "Why am I locked into this bed? Where am I, for that matter?"

My struggles made my side hurt worse. It was a sharp pain, a real pain, not a blurred ache like I'd been experiencing for… days? Subjective days?

I looked at my arms. Other than several adhesive pads attached to my wrists, they looked unmarked, aside from the usual few missing scales. No bullet wound. My back also didn't hurt all over. My legs, though… if I wasn't being restrained in some bizarre way, it looked like my lower legs were both broken, and recently.

That injury fit with the fall from Krrutoki's apartment. I vaguely remembered twisting both ankles. So, that was the real, or at least the recent, timeline. Either I'd healed up my perforated arm without any scarring or else that injury never happened.

Nathan Large with Laine Megan Lundquist

I put the pieces together for myself before the techs decided on an explanation. I had been dreaming. More than that, I'd been dreaming a very detailed, very directed story, a fiction with greater credibility and precision than any nightmare.

I thought about virtual reality at first, but what I'd experienced was more detailed than the best VR simulation. I'd tried a few immersive entertainments in the past, when my curiosity and finances coincided. While impressive, those projections would never fool a viewer into thinking they were reality. There were still too many discrepancies, too many departures from true perception, to be overlooked.

Next, I considered all the equipment surrounding me. Plausibly, those were the right appliances to directly manipulate a nervous system. Maybe these were geniuses who had cracked perfect VR: imaging beamed straight to the brain and coded well enough to bypass any discriminatory systems. But then, why were they testing it on *me*? And why concoct that particular scenario?

My dream hadn't been enjoyable, much less entertaining. I was still shuddering from the thought of it, although no longer feeling the side effects – or even the aftereffects – of frenzy.

The more I thought about it, the angrier I became. Whether deliberate or accidental, if these jokers had put me through all that trauma, then I owed them equivalent pain in return.

The facility couldn't be official. Surely, my planet couldn't have become so corrupt that citizens – even criminal suspects or convicts – could be kidnapped and subjected to non-consensual, agonizing experiments. Even as a punishment for an actual crime, what I had just experienced would be considered unusually cruel.

My worst fears, instincts, and hatreds had been drawn out and laid bare for me to suffer. It was the emotional equivalent of flaying, of vivisection.

"LET ME UP!" I screeched. "I want my armor, I want my gun, I want my freedom, and I want a frosted good explanation, in whatever order is fastest!"

Broken Record

The Vislin technician finally came around to my view, walking quickly from behind my bed to my left front.

It was a male, patch-scaled and slight. He curled his claws in supplication as he spoke soothingly. "Please try to relax and trust us. Believe me that our intent was never to cause you harm. In fact, getting up will indeed hurt you. If we explain too much, too soon, or too poorly, our errors could hurt you as well. We are waiting for our superior, who will answer all your questions and do so in the best possible way."

His voice sounded vaguely familiar, but I couldn't place it. Was it someone I knew from reality or from the dream? His measured tones did their job well, convincing me to settle down and give them a chance to explain. One chance. It had *better* be a good explanation.

The Vislin tech moved further across the room, checking a wall-mounted computer screen. He toggled a comm program and spoke aloud: "Could Doctor Ruktpah please hurry to the simulation lab, a bit faster? Our guest is fully awake and becoming agitated."

A female voice of indeterminate species answered him: "Understood. I will advise Ruktpah to avoid delays."

"Yes, thank you," the Vislin answered.

"*Thank you, mistress,*" the Hrotata tech teased his colleague. He had backed away to the monitoring station to my right rear, settling there on his haunches. He rose and moved to a separate device. I noticed that a tube led from that box to my legs, somewhere underneath the restraints and wrappings. It was clear plastic, probably hollow and carrying fluid. What kind of fluid?

"Are you giving me drugs?" I demanded. The Hrotata looked up with a trace of guilt on his furry features.

"Well, yes, analgesics to manage your pain. And a hypnotic, while you were being induced..."

"Could you wait for Ruktpah, please?" asked the Vislin, interrupting his colleague in irritated tones.

"He's going to get the idea soon enough," the Hrotata protested. "No reason to act all mysterious and secretive now. In fact, research suggests that denying information just boosts the resistance index…"

"Don't cite Vkzprt to me, egg-breath," the Vislin screeched back. The argument didn't sound too serious, like the banter of co-workers rather than a violent dispute. He added, "I was reading her research before you ever saw your first psychograph."

I stayed quiet. Even in my agitated, disoriented, drugged state, I realized that letting them ramble could tell me more than interrupting to demand answers. They sounded less like evil scientists and more like graduate students. Granted, they were treating me more like a lab animal than a valued participant, but at least I wasn't a captive hero tied to the Torture Machine.

Yes, I watch some very bad entertainments, on occasion.

"I'm just saying, we're more likely to screw up his reactions by stalling than by saying something the wrong way. He's a resilient psyche; you've seen the 'graphs. We're not going to do any long-term damage by choosing the wrong trigger word. Worst case, Ruktpah can correct the misstep."

A resilient psyche, was I? I supposed he was right, for all that I felt my psyche badly bludgeoned and as fragmented as my legs. I was already assembling a rational storyline out of my various experiences. Now that I was no longer having portions of my past blocked off… probably by their frosted drugs and machines… I was putting together a coherent explanation for what happened.

I remembered: I was investigating a Hrotata, Krrutoki, who somehow drove a Taratumm, Grust of Herd Torbur, into a violent frenzy in public, pushing the stomper into attacking the mate of Krrutoki's unattainable love interest. I may be a perverse, romantically overdriven dupe, but Krrutoki was the twisted extreme of that mania. His manipulation got Grust arrested and put on trial for attempted murder. Herd Torbur hired me to exonerate their hapless member, which put me… eventually… onto Krrutoki's trail.

My confrontation with Krrutoki resulted in the revelation that he was psychically gifted, able to induce extreme emotional states in victims. That talent was how he pushed Grust into frenzy, without drugs or direct provocation. It seemed that his projective empathy was limited to the feelings he himself was experiencing at the time: lust and jealousy shifted to Grust, violent rage imposed upon the Taratumm who attacked me in a bar after I annoyed Krrutoki, and finally, panicked terror transferred onto me, when I confronted Krrutoki in his home.

It was an unproductive revelation at the time, since as soon as I knew what was happening, I was already running away, leaping out of Krrutoki's open window to crash to the street below. Krrutoki's reflected fear of me became my fear of him.

Ttt, *that* memory finally explained the familiar feeling during the simulation, when I went out of the window at Taburket's. It also explained my broken ankles, and maybe the busted rib.

I was dealing with psionics. That factor might explain why the simulation was so complete, so detailed, and so convincing. I wasn't sure about that explanation, though. Suspiciously little information on psychic ability circulates in the public sphere – likely deliberately so – but I was fairly certain nobody could project so much information, for so long, into another sapient's mind. It would be a major public hazard if any sapient could generate such powerful illusions. You could completely paralyze or control someone with that kind of mirage.

The machines were another clue. Combine advanced VR with psionics... and what? Could you pull off the spell I'd experienced, with just those two integrated components? And if you could, why keep it secret? Why use it this way? Why use it on *me*?

The Vislin tech answered his counterpart as I mused: "*You* aren't cleared for those decisions, nor am I. Even if you're right, our wiser course is to remain silent and allow the senior professional to work. That way, we avoid censure... not to mention, worse consequences should you be wrong."

"I'd listen to Kzshtst, myself," came a third, rumbling voice. Definitely Taratumm. I knew that even before its owner entered the room, stepping from a doorway in the room's far left corner.

Nathan Large with Laine Megan Lundquist

While the name I'd heard, Ruktpah, roughly fit the Taratumm naming pattern, it was ambiguous enough that I'd assumed Vislin or Hrotata. Surely, the senior researcher, the superior in a research laboratory... a psychic research laboratory?... wouldn't be a dull stomper.

The new arrival neatly disemboweled my prejudices. He was a massive male Taratumm, thick of limb and crest, but clearly not thick of mind. He wore a neatly tailored suit of synthetic armor, the kind of garment that suggested wealth, taste, *and* the good sense to leave protective functions intact while not flaunting their defensive nature. The armor's color, a silvery lavender, even complimented the wearer's natural coloration: a bluish grey, like fireplace ash.

"Doctor Ruktpah?" I presumed. "Glad you finally made it. Your colleagues here were having trouble dealing with me."

The Taratumm superior plodded to the foot of my bed and stared down at me, not threatening or hostile, just considering. I couldn't tell if he was trying to be intimidating or just came by it naturally. His expression seemed to be neutral: maybe a bit unhappy, but certainly not angry.

Finally, he spoke, adjusting his volume to something comfortable for my proximity: "Private detective Stchvk. Glad to finally meet you, in person and awake. I understand you have had a difficult few days... some of which I need to apologize for."

"Which days?" I asked sarcastically. "The fake ones where I nearly went out of my mind... or the real ones where I tracked down a psychic criminal without any help?"

He blinked, faster than I'd ever seen any part of a Taratumm move. Then he raised his head and bobbed slightly in place, the Taratumm equivalent of a Vislin crest flip. I'd amused him, somehow. What was so funny? I wasn't joking.

He wasn't laughing, either, and answered me soberly. "All of them, then, I suppose. Although I won't apologize for Krrutoki's existence, nor your foolhardy confrontation with him. Your injuries are largely your own fault."

Broken Record

I began to protest, but he raised a forehand to forestall me. "Your actual injuries, less so your fictional ones. I see that you've put together much about your situation. But allow me to place your partially assembled puzzle in its proper frame... and insert the missing pieces."

He called back toward the Vislin: "Kzshtst, could you get me a chair? This conversation may last longer than my knees."

Without protest, the chastened Vislin tech left the room. By the time Ruktpah finished speaking his next few sentences, Kzshtst returned with a suitably oversized, padded stool, which Ruktpah settled onto with unexpected grace. While all this was happening, the Hrotata tech remained quiet at his station, continuing to read out whatever vital data I was projecting.

"So, Stchvk. Investigator. You've spent years solving puzzles, seeking out hidden truths, and helping sapients... some of them paying clients, some not. We have your public record, of course. I examined it myself when you were noticed working for Pack Torbur. We were looking into the same case from our angle – the psychic angle – once the public trial started, but you got to the real story before we did."

"Did I? It *was* Krrutoki, in the Thunder Bar, with the psychic powers?"

"It was. The constables picked him up, thinking he'd thrown you out of his window. He tried to flee Layafflr City, but one of our agents was embedded with the arresting squad. Consequently, he couldn't hide and he couldn't scare them off. We might have missed him without your intervention. Thank you, I suppose."

"See? Even my bad ideas are secretly good."

"That's what we've been seeing. You see, we wanted to know if your success there was dumb luck or a sign of real talent. Some investigators wouldn't even have considered the psychic angle. You only gave it slight credence, but still managed to find the right culprit, using purely mundane and even low-budget methods. Professional constabulary investigators didn't crack this case, with all their training and tools, but you did. Because you considered all the possibilities."

"And you were so impressed, you decided to kidnap and torture me."

Doctor Ruktpah rolled his eyes and paused, finally showing some signs of annoyance. I have that effect.

"If your verbal skills weren't part of your talent, I'd be more offended by that," he rumbled, "but please don't mistake me for a suspect you need to provoke. I'd like to convince you that I'm an ally. My praise is genuinely meant, not a tactic of manipulation. I'm just explaining the circumstances that led us to this point."

"If you're psychic, then you know why I'm on the offensive... and you wouldn't need words to manipulate me."

"You see, that's a common misconception. Psionic talent is diverse. Not all are gifted in the same way, and we specialize further by training. I myself cannot read your mind, not without augmentation, nor do I particularly indulge in projective empathy."

His matter-of-fact discussion threw me off balance. Maybe it was meant to. For all his protests, the big-brained stomper was pretty good at turning a conversation. He was good enough to quiet me down and get me to actually listen, if only by the promise of substantial revelations.

When I didn't snipe back, he settled into his seat and his narrative. "We needed to know how much you knew: if you had psychic ability, yourself, or knew a gifted informant who reinforced your suspicions. A cursory inspection proved that neither was the case."

I admit, I was a bit disappointed to fail the psychic test. Then again, my investigative skills would be less impressive if I had help from hidden mental powers. Whatever I'd accomplished, I managed with my basic five senses and deductive skill.

"We brought you back here, performed the necessary medical treatments to fix your injuries, and kept you out of the claws of the constabulary... you are welcome for that, incidentally. Perhaps you can weigh that deliverance against the discomfort you experienced during our inspections."

Broken Record

As my expression darkened, he corrected himself: "All right, the pain you endured during our interrogation. But I assure you, the process was carefully managed and quite necessary. When we couldn't find any obvious reasons for your success, we set up a scenario that would evaluate your professional and natural skills... not just as an investigator, but as a sapient capable of noticing and managing psionic situations."

He forestalled further protests by continuing quickly. "If you proved incapable, you would suffer from no memory of our simulation. You would be deposited back into a standard hospital, healed in mind and body, with a cover story explaining how you got from Krrutoki's apartment to there. And yes, it would be a better cover story than we used to block out that experience the first time. We needed you unaware, with *no* memory of prior events to make you suspicious about the simulation itself."

Because I *would* have been, sooner," I pointed out. "And I *was* suspicious about a lot of things in that scenario. The beach-front vacation. The memory lapses. The sudden fatigue and unconsciousness. The fact that I still had credit in my account."

"Yes, you were. And that was part of the test," Ruktpah confirmed. "How much discrepancy would your mind accept, before you started to rebel against reality itself? How far could we rewrite the narrative until you became frustrated, no longer able to accommodate the weight of anomaly?

"You actually had me worried; your imagination is extraordinarily resilient, able to fit together the most bizarre coincidences and illogical factors into coherent theory. I suppose that ability is a consequence of criminal investigation: there always has to be an explanation, no matter how strange or convoluted."

I signaled silent agreement. He wasn't wrong there. But I still wondered: why push me so hard? What did they want out of me?

Ruktpah must have sensed my conflict, either psychically or through old-fashioned social cues. He oozed compassion as he continued: "But you did notice. Your perceptivity is also quite high, either as a natural asset to your chosen profession, a consequence of its practice, or both. You pick up on oddities and coincidences. They mount and conjoin and are rarely discarded. That is not a common skill. Most sapients overlook the discontinuities around them, either to conserve attention or preserve their peace of mind… or because the details rarely matter to their needs."

"So, I'm fixated on minutiae and prone to fantasy," I deadpanned. "I could have told you that. Why run a mock-up like this? To confirm my traits for yourselves?"

"Exactly so," Ruktpah answered, still unflappable. "People *say* a great deal about themselves, good or ill, but their true reactions in a real situation are the only certain test of character. Our evaluation program tells us precisely how a subject will react under certain stresses, not to mention how their thought processes work."

I suddenly felt very naked and a bit violated. They had watched not only my behavior but also my thoughts during my most vulnerable moments. Everything I sought to keep secret about myself, about Pack Vzrrk, about my past cases, was laid bare. Not to mention, all my tendencies, deviancies, and secret drives were watched by these voyeurs.

"Subject? *Subject?* Doc, if my legs weren't broken and restrained, I'd be tempted to claw out your guts right now."

"Then you haven't been listening… or rather, you have been listening selectively. Did you notice the part where I mentioned we deal with psychic criminal acts? *You* were there when a rogue actor, untrained, sent you frenzying out of a window. You can imagine how much more difficult it would be to detect, resist, and disable a more experienced psychic criminal.

"We can't hire or trust just anyone. Genuine assets are rare. If you possessed a lesser mind, we'd have deposited you back at home, ignorant and possibly a little richer for your trouble. I'll mention again, in case you missed it: you wouldn't remember any of this, not the simulation, not the arrest, not the fall itself. You would never know you'd suffered any pain. We can manage that much, at least. A simple chemical amnestic suffices, complimented by an augmented scan to make sure no stray memories remain to interfere with the erasure."

Broken Record

"That's a lot of power. Who controls all this?" I demanded.

"Exactly what I mean: you go straight to the point. The simple answer is: the Great Family. From the top. We're unofficial, both due to the nature of our operations and the potential for panic among the populace. But we do report to the greater interplanetary government. If you accept our offer, you can look at the organizational charts yourself."

"Wait, if I accept?" I asked, in still-angry confusion. "Who said I'd want to join or even help you, after this treatment?"

"Actually, *you* said. Before we started the evaluation. You asked if we were hiring, or words to that effect. You can review the recording, if you like, but I'm sure you could dismiss it as a fabrication if you really resist the idea now. It seems the amnestic cleared out that conversation, along with the hour or so beforehand."

It sounded like something I'd say… at least, before knowing what the job interview would be like. I said as much: "I doubt you explained the details of the hiring process."

"And I can counter that, in fact, we did. We didn't go into great detail about the method used for evaluation, but you were informed that we'd need to confirm your mental abilities and potential liabilities."

"I'm sure murdering my childhood love was somewhere in the fine print."

Ruktpah shifted uncomfortably. I'd struck something painful. He grunted, "That outcome was not intended. Your near-suicidal episode was certainly not intended. For that, you have my deepest apologies."

"Mine too," the Hrotata technician chimed in, sounding properly contrite. "That was terrible. We should have ended the program way before that. I'm the one who told them you were hitting bottom."

I stared at Ruktpah a long moment. "You *apologize?* It wasn't *intended?* Let me tell you, Doctor, your program has a serious flaw if it produces unintended effects like that."

He shot back, defensively, "The program is guided by a combination of scripted events and probabilistic reactions to your thoughts and actions. It follows the lead you establish, conforming events to maintain maximum credibility while still nudging circumstances toward choice points which will evaluate your decision processes, value judgments, and selected actions. So, in a manner of speaking, *you* led *our* program into that particular dark alley. Your refusal to back off, your willingness to see the worst in both your enemies and allies, and your persistent avoidance of authority... not that any of these are *flaws*, in our eyes...," he tailed off, holding up a hand to forestall my reaction again.

He added, "I'm not blaming you, just pointing out that, given the initial starting conditions, our evaluation parameters, and your particular mental makeup... bad things happened. Perhaps they might happen so in the real world. I'd like to think that reality is considerably less malleable, more beneficent, and more mundane than in our mock-up... but you and I both know that the world out there is often full of conspiracies, stupidity, malice, and even utter surreality, at times. My job is a case in point."

"What, malice and stupidity?" I couldn't help seizing on the opening, though my accusation lacked any real venom.

He actually seemed amused by my remark. "Sometimes, but only in the targets we track and capture. We *are* the conspiracy... though there have been historic occurrences of psionic cabals. Far more often, rogues are either ignorant or malicious or both, using their abilities to cause harm because they don't know any better. And you've seen the surreal part. Too many otherwise unexplainable events have a hidden psionic cause: emotional manipulation, illusions, telepathic espionage..."

"Now I'm tempted to explain away all my failed cases as the work of secret psychics," I quipped.

"Only one that I know of," Ruktpah shot back. "No, I'm kidding, likely none. Psionics are rare. Very rare. Maybe a dozen or so that we know of on Spore. Now thirteen, until Krrutoki is evaluated and assigned."

"Assigned? You mean, to a prison?" I asked.

Broken Record

Despite my earlier fury, Ruktpah's torrent of information was having the promised effect: I was listening. I was getting answers. I hoped they were true answers, but if they could rewrite my memories, why bother to lie? For that matter, if they could bend my emotions, why bother with a recruiting speech?

"Perhaps. But for all the harm he's done, he's not irredeemable. An immature, emotionally unstable fool, certainly. But young. Surely *you* wouldn't argue that it's impossible to grow beyond the errors of your youth?"

Being reminded of my exposed past was a low strike, and I stiffened in reaction, preparing a curse in reply. But he was essentially correct. Krrutoki seemed like a pathetic, selfish, deranged creep, but those were all qualities that could be repaired. His rehabilitation was doubly likely with psionic wardens and therapists involved.

I hissed but stayed quiet otherwise. Ruktpah correctly took this for agreement and continued, encouraged.

"So yes, we have Krrutoki in custody. You'll be happy to know, also, that he made an acceptable, suitably edited confession attesting to his guilt in the case of Grust of Herd Torbur. Grust has been exonerated and released. If you like, we can even update the official report to mention your role. Fascinating designer drugs were found in Krrutoki's apartment, by the way, supporting your original suspicions."

It felt like a severe ethical compromise, but what else could be done? At least the innocent stomper was freed and the genuinely guilty party named. Covering up the actual method of the crime was a secondary concern.

I still grumped, "As long as I don't have to lie directly about what happened."

"That's up to you, but consider: you'd have no way to prove your claims. For the reasons I've stated, we have to conceal some degree of information about psionics from the general public, at least until official studies and legislation catch up. Can you imagine the prosecutor's case, trying to prove that a Hrotata psychically drove a Taratumm into frenzy? What would the court accept as evidence? And even if the state somehow succeeded in making its case, what would be the public response?"

I could complete his thought: the public would be half disbelieving, half hysterical. As my own reactions proved, the idea of mental control was terrifying, particularly when you didn't know who could do it or how it worked.

Ruktpah made sympathetic noises while I worked out the implications myself. At length, he spoke again: "Another point to consider: you passed our evaluation. Despite the catastrophic ending, your performance showed that you have overcome your spotted past. You are not immune to its existence, but its effects upon your present behavior seem largely positive. In fact, it may be because of your past difficulties, not in spite of them, that you function so well in the present."

"I knew that, too," I countered, "but I'm not so sure about the functional part. Maybe if I felt more mentally stable or could earn more credit, I'd agree more. And as far as the existence of my past, that's always a risk. I'm not sure whether to run from it – leave Layafflr City or even the planet – or stay here, close by and ready to stamp out that fire whenever it relights."

"Well, we can help on all those counts, as it turns out. We have very good ideas how to help you regain your equilibrium… if you allow such therapy, of course. We can also help keep your past hidden and its actors absent, to some extent."

"Pkstzk," I interrupted. "Where is she, actually?"

"Alive," he answered. He amended, "But in prison. Embezzlement from her employer. Very recently, in fact, only two cycles ago. We were surprised your knowledge was that out of date."

"I don't keep up on most of the old gang. Maybe I should. What about Rsspkz?"

"In prison, still, along with Vztrrp. We did our research to make sure everything would conform with your expectations about those individuals."

"And Tklth?"

"No idea. You know as much about her as anyone else. She's vanished into the great wilds of deep space."

Broken Record

I finally relaxed a little, having accepted Ruktpah's general goodwill, if not his methods. I considered what I was being offered. More knowledge was a good thing. Being able to make a difference would be nice, also. If I could put my talents to good use, I didn't mind working within an organization, even a secret government organization. But I definitely didn't like the feeling of impersonal power that I was getting. I'd be getting involved with some dangerous people, with a lot of dangerous powers and tools and some questionable ideas about how to use them.

The alternative was *not* getting involved: going back to my old life, ignorant as ever, with the same threats still active. I thought, also, that this particular conspiracy *needed* someone like me, someone who would criticize and act as a conscience. Kkk, I flatter myself... but I *never* would have played with someone's mind like they did mine, even for technically noble reasons. Some things, you just don't do, even for good purposes.

Like framing someone for murder, even to save a life. Despite my revulsion about having 'killed' Pkstzk, I was proud of myself for struggling against the plot to frame Shtvtsk. I was proud, also, of escaping the virtual snares and seductions laid during my evaluation. I hadn't compromised, hadn't inflicted undeserved harm, and hadn't despaired, at least until the end.

I was temporarily proud of having survived the various traps laid against me, but then realized I was meant to survive. Nothing in the scenario would really have killed me, since that outcome would necessarily end the test. Hence, I was wounded, for believability, but never really endangered or completely crippled.

In fact, I was spared the worst consequences of every error. No outcome would completely stop me from proceeding until they had all their data. Reality wasn't so forgiving.

Still, in simulation just as in reality, what was important was that I kept trying, kept looking for escapes, and kept coming up with ideas. I managed that much, at least.

I also kept my integrity. If that was an asset in my favor, then these psychos had to accept my criticism along with my competence.

"Before you get too full of yourself, bear in mind that you have a few negatives we'd need to work on," Ruktpah interrupted. I realized that he'd interrupted my thoughts, with no other transition from his earlier remarks to the latter one. I squinted at him and snapped my beak nastily. Not reading my thoughts, indeed. The old leaf-licker wasn't fooling me.

He continued on, ignoring my reaction: "Your distractibility is a consequence of your perceptiveness. This couples with your libido to slow down your progress toward resolution. There's a reason I dismissed our female psychometric technician before you woke up. Though, to make my point, I almost considered having her deliver the debriefing. You might have paid better attention."

The cute one with spots, at the interview. I remembered her happily, then became annoyed with Ruktpah for having read me so accurately. I definitely would have been looking at her, if she were still there. Ruktpah might have secured my goodwill more easily with her present, and that just proved his point again. Frost my gonads. No, don't, but you get the idea.

"You'll also have to curtail your tendency to boast and to recruit bystanders," Ruktpah persisted, "with witnesses and with constables. If you're working for us, you won't be able to tell anyone... except us... about your cases."

Again, I saw his point. That was the point of Tskksk's involvement: both her original assistance and her subsequent kidnapping. They wanted to see my reaction when a bystander, a witness, was pulled into a dangerous situation. I imagined hostage situations might be more common and more difficult with a psychic criminal; they could enthrall innocents more easily.

Thinking of Tskksk, I was first relieved that she wasn't actually in any danger... then depressed that she had never existed at all. I had started to bond with a fictional character. Vvv, it happened sometimes, but rarely with such intensity. I wondered if Tskksk were at least based on a real person... maybe that cute female tech? Frost, the way my day was going, she was probably acted by the Hrotata.

What was I thinking about, again? Sss, that's right, psychic criminals and the need to keep civilians uninvolved.

Broken Record

Ruktpah continued to anticipate my line of thought. "Bystanders are a problem with empaths or projective telepaths," he cautioned. "If you thought Shtvtsk was a powerful seductress, imagine her augmented with the ability to induce lust. You couldn't dissuade Pkstzk from her anger. Now, imagine if that manipulation were amplified, with a random bystander... or a beloved acquaintance... aimed toward you as a weapon."

He scored again. I could imagine those horrors with particular clarity, thanks to my recent encounters in the virtual world. I could *almost* forgive the programmers for making me experience those events, realizing how appropriate they were to the real situations I might eventually face.

"*Was* there any psychic influence, in the simulation?"

"Yes and no," Ruktpah answered. "Your emotions weren't directly altered in any way. Shtvtsk was created as an amalgam of the traits you find most attractive, your 'ideal female'. As such, it's particularly notable that you resisted her allure in favor of doing your chosen duty."

At this rate, my ego was going to get rubbed raw. My id was certainly chafed.

"Pkstzk's indoctrination could have been accomplished through mundane means as well," Ruktpah continued, "but the program made certain she would never accept your arguments. You were expected to forestall her, perhaps disarm her manually, or escape. We really didn't expect you to go for the laser."

"Why not?" I demanded. "Given the situation, that was my best option."

"Really? She missed because she was programmed to miss," Ruktpah argued back. "I doubt that, in reality, you would have survived that encounter."

"I sure wouldn't have survived it trying to grab her gun," I griped back. "How many of your programmers have actually tangled in a close-quarters gunfight? I'm guessing not many. Wait, how many 'mundane' field agents do you have? How many have to do their job without benefit of psionic ability?"

"On Spore? None, yet," Ruktpah admitted. "You'd be our first. You can see why, considering how difficult it was to find you... and how difficult it is to evaluate and then persuade a candidate."

"Sss, frost, do you ever need my help," I concluded. "No wonder your simulation went sideways. I'm programmed to deal with *real* situations, having dealt with them. When you put that experience up against a script that includes certain inaccurate variables…"

"Garbage in, garbage out," Ruktpah completed for me. "Careful, though: your good evaluation is predicated on your performance in that program. Question its validity too strongly, and we have nothing to base our estimates on."

"You have what everyone else gets. Your judgment, the evidence of my actions, and a little trust. Kktkrkz sit on my head, I've got a lot of work to do here."

"So, I take it you're agreeable," he replied.

"Provisionally. Let's take it in steps. I'll see what I learn, make sure I like what I see, and decide if this is actually something I can do. You have a lot of data on me, but I'm a little short on details about your operation."

"You talk like someone in a strong position, rather than the only non-psychic in a building full of them, with his ankles broken and casted, and his psychometric diagram being displayed on a screen nearby," Ruktpah cautioned.

"Everyone's psychic? Even him?" I asked, pointing to the Hrotata.

"Yes," the tech answered for himself, "I can make even dour matrons lift their tails."

Ruktpah grimaced at the vulgarity, but confirmed, "Thrussetl, like Krrutoki, is a projective empath. He is also under working probation for that sort of behavior… which we caught before he descended to criminal acts."

The mammal only winced in response, turning back to his displays.

"And they call me a pervert," I muttered loudly enough for him to catch.

Ruktpah rolled his eyes but did not comment further.

"But yes, I do have some leverage," I resumed. "You clearly need my help, otherwise why do all this work? Regardless of your 'evaluation', I can identify, track, and maybe even apprehend rogues like yours, without radiating psycho-neutrons or whatever they might pick up on. I won't raise the same alarms. And I have practical experience, particularly here on Chttkttp."

"I noticed that," Ruktpah mentioned. "In fact, there's an interesting track line over your thoughts of this planet, particularly this city. Did you see it, Thrussetl?"

"Of course," the Hrotata tech answered. "A self-associative line like that is hard to miss. Usually you see a line that strong for a mother. Or a mate. Or in Vislin, a Pack-mate."

"I get it, I get it," I waved them down. "I'm in love with this horrible, filthy city."

"Not love," Ruktpah insisted. "Try to imagine leaving it for a long period, perhaps permanently."

I obliged his thought experiment and found what they were talking about. It *hurt* to consider leaving. Seriously thinking about leaving Layafflr City behind and never returning felt like pondering which limb to give up. I hadn't ever thought of moving away, not even when things got bad. I joked about it, sure, but never seriously.

My expression told them enough, even without empathy to read my feelings. Ruktpah's eyes creased in sympathy.

"That factor explains a great deal about your progress toward maturity and your resilience to adversity, despite some significant emotional complications," he quietly diagnosed. "I'm no therapist, not precisely, but it's not unbelievable that your bond to your Pack has been transposed to a much bigger Pack, one that is more difficult to serve but less likely to demand specific services."

"So, what, I'm Pack-bonded to the city?"

"Might as well be," Ruktpah confirmed, "and that's not a bad thing. Vislin within our organization sometimes show the same affiliation to their coworkers or to other psychics, in general. They're also some of our best agents, utterly impossible to compromise. Frankly, anything that tries to turn you against this city or its citizens has a difficult obstacle to overcome. That includes psionic manipulation... Pack-bonds are psionically resistant."

I wanted to laugh. Me, Stchvk, scoundrel of the ages, mated to law and order. It was the kind of joke that you realized was true, even as you tried to laugh it away.

That revelation was what decided me. These might be a bunch of secretive, privileged, inhumane bastards, but they knew their business. I'd learn a lot from them, and not just about psionics itself. If I thought I was a good judge of sapients before, I'd be unstoppable with such professional training...

First things first, Stchvk. Get out of bed. Take the tour. Meet the psycho co-workers.

"All right, all right," I said aloud. "I'm in. What do we do next?"

Ruktpah rose slowly, stiffly, resting his bulk for a moment before coming fully upright. "*You* rest and heal. Even with regeneration, you'll need a few days before you can stand comfortably. From there, we'll give you the outline of operations. You'll probably be disappointed in terms of workload. We don't have any investigations currently active. In all likelihood, you'll get some training courses, then go back home to wait until you're needed. After that, it depends on what comes up."

It figured. After all that trouble, I wasn't even getting hired full-time.

The mention of home did brighten my mood. My home. It was just fine. My beautiful hand-carved desk was still there, unburned. My good armor was in the closet, not shot full of holes. My heater... was somewhere.

"Hey! Where's my heater?" I asked as Ruktpah straightened up to leave.

"Around here somewhere," he answered. "You'll get it back when you're cleared to leave. No point before then. The kinds of threats you might face around here, you wouldn't get a chance to shoot. They might make you shoot yourself."

I assumed he was kidding... maybe.

Broken Record

"And what about pay?" I called as he turned away. "I'm no good if I starve to death while waiting for work."

"You'll get a modest monthly stipend," Ruktpah replied over his shoulder, "enough to live on, but not so much as to raise suspicions. Get used to the idea of pretending to have clientele... or maybe drum up some more regular business, yourself. Being choosy is fine, but you've got a streak of laziness that could be improved."

Great. A boss who could read your mind and personally tailor his critiques. If the fringe benefits weren't so appealing, this might be the worst job I'd ever heard of.

Stchvk, private psychic detective. At least the title sounded... stupid, actually.

I'd keep it as it was: "Stchvk, Investigations."

It saved the cost of reprinting my business cards.